AN
ARCHER'S
REDEMPTION

OF CROWNS & QUILLS
BOOK 4

3Aussies Press

Contents

Before you begin . . .

To say thank you for joining me on this journey, I would like to give you a gift, a free copy of *Winning His Vote*, the first book in my Nashville Spicy series.

Click here to tell me where to send it.

Riz

Baz

Pez

Alm

Kitchton

Bo

Lynn

Sil

Arto

Fersh

Fleet Town

Cobb

Amnel

Saltstone

Anfar

Melucia

Pantrel

Cret

Crees

Traders' Gate

Orn

Drea

Evn

Freeport

Tuvlai

Uvo

Rea Utu

Vel

Dramatis Personae: The Melucian Empire

Atikus Dani: Mage in Saltstone, adopted father to Declan and Keelan Rea

Ayden Byrne: Ranger Cadet and eldest son of Lord Ronan Byrne

Captain Ewan Whitman: Captain and Commander of Melucian Rangers

Ceryl Burner: Merchants' Guildmaster

Commander Geros: Second in command of Melucian Rangers

Declan Rea: Ranger Cadet and brother of Keelan Rea

Dev Albius: Captain-Commander of the Melucian Guard

Fergus: Mage in Saltstone

Keelan Rea: Guardsman in Saltstone, Melucia and brother of Declan Rea

Lieutenant Kolgan: Ranger Officer stationed in mountains near border

Sil Wesser: Guardsman in Saltstone

Tiana Hurd: Healer in Saltstone

Titus Vre: Master of Arms

Velius Quin: Arch Mage,

Dramatis Personae: The Kingdom of Spires

Alfred Vester: King of the Spires

Barnabus Dask: Crown Treasurer in the Court of King Alfred

Captain Marv Proctor: Head of the King's Guard

Danai Thorn: High Chancellor in the Court of King Alfred

Danym Wilfred: Son of High Sheriff Sebastiano Wilfred, Kingdom of Spires

Destin Carver: Minister of Trade in the Court of King Alfred

Ethan Marks: Lord General of His Majesty's Armed Forces, Kingdom of Spires

Irina Santander: Queen of the Kingdom of Spires One Thousand Years Ago

Isabel Vester: Queen of the Kingdom of Spires

Jessia Vester: Crown Princess of the Kingdom of Spires

Justin Vester: Prince of the Kingdom of Spires

Kendall Vester: Prince of the Kingdom of Spires

Kinsley Parna: Duke and Warden of the East based in Huntcliff, Kingdom of Spires

Sebastiano Wilfred: High Sheriff in the Court of the Kingdom of Spires

Stephan Bril: Minister of War in the Court of the Kingdom of Spires

Willa Parto: Minister of Justice in the Court of King Alfred

Zumi Barcas: Minister of Foreign Affairs in the Court of King Alfred

PART 1

CHAPTER 1

DANAI

I stared at the gilded crown in my hand.

My heart grieved for the one who'd worn it mere hours before.

I had spent a lifetime—no, ten lifetimes—searching for clues that might lead to Irina's return. The obsidian monolith left by her spell had offered more conjecture than instruction, but a thousand years after her death, I'd succeeded in restoring my beautiful queen to the world of the living.

And now she was gone.

Again.

Magical power tickled my fingers as it thrummed within the cold metal. The seven diamonds across the crown's base pulsed with an eerie crimson light. I shuddered, thinking of how each orb was filled with the captured soul of a Gifted who had been sacrificed for the greater cause of Irina's return, the crimson hue of each diamond mirroring the lifeblood spilled to acquire its power.

My breath frosted before me.

It was cold, but not *that* cold.

I swiveled, scanning the peaks and the nearby forest, but found nothing amiss. I rubbed warmth into my chilled arms.

"Danai . . ."

I stumbled down the mountainside as a silky voice whispered in my mind.

"Danai, my dear, you found my crown."

I shuddered.

My dear?

Irina had never called me anything other than my name.

"My Queen?"

"I am here. My Vessel was weak and died when the tower fell, but my spirit is now free."

My eyes darted around, desperately seeking any evidence of Irina's presence. The only thing I found was the deepening chill in the air—and deep within my bones.

"I don't understand. The circle that contained—"

"—was destroyed when the tower fell. Nothing binds me now, but my power is limited without a Vessel. I can

only influence, but never rule . . . until I find a mortal form."

A mortal form? Her spirit needs to inhabit another? Of course, like she did Isabel.

I blinked moisture into my frozen eyes as realization drained the last color from my face. "You want to consume *me*? Take my body for your own?"

"No, my love, I want to share power as we always have."

I swallowed hard.

My love?

I leaned against a tree, struggling to focus. I *had* loved her. From the day we first met a thousand years ago, my heart was hers. Then her parents died. No, they were slain. Killed by our brother and sister Mages. She'd been so broken by grief. I wrapped her in my embrace, supported her vision for a stronger, more prosperous Kingdom, and helped her gain her footing as she ascended to the throne. Even when her heart had turned to vengeance, I remained by her side, steadfast and loyal.

And yet, despite all our time together, I never had the chance—or bravery—to tell her how I felt.

What if I had? Would she have loved me in return? Would she have fallen into my arms and returned my embrace?

I regretted never trying, never learning what could be.

Yet I also feared she might have laughed and discarded my emotions as weakness. She mocked others for their frail minds and weak hearts. While I *knew* my love was a power in itself, I also understood that her heart had darkened by the time I might have opened up to her.

There was no space left for passion or kindness. No room for love.

And yet . . . she now called me *my love*?

After all that had happened.

After I betrayed her and helped free the people of Saltstone even as her troops battered down their gates.

The woman I knew . . . the woman I loved . . . she no longer lived.

Her eyes bore none of the compassion of her youth. They bore nothing but hatred and pain.

They bore rage as she turned against Melucia.

They held merciless wrath as she felled civilians as the Mages had once felled her family.

My eyes brimmed with tears. Yet I hesitated.

I loved her still. My heart longed for her touch. To have her live within me, to be part of me . . . we could forever be together.

And still.

Her presence was overwhelming in life. In death, it *compelled* allegiance.

Unquestioning loyalty.

"Isabel was a weak, feckless fool. You are more worthy than any alive. We would wield power this world hasn't seen since the Sundering. Think of it, Danai!"

I felt a pressure against my chest, as though someone pushed against me, trying to burrow within. I called my Light and pushed back.

"What *are* you—"

"Why do you resist me, my love?" Her voice found a sharpened edge. *"I long to be one. Isn't that what you've always wanted?"*

The pressure intensified, and sweat beaded my brow despite the frigid mountain air.

"Irina, stop, please," I pleaded. "We can find another way, another Vessel."

I held my breath as Irina's voice stilled.

The tension against my chest eased as moments passed in silence. Without her voice, a void of nothingness enveloped my world, and my heart, long ago given to her keeping, shattered at the gulf I knew now spanned between us.

"Irina?" I whispered. "Are you still there?"

What was a palm pressed against my chest before became an angry fist pounding against me. Before I could react or defend, Irina's spirit found purchase within. Her presence knifed through my mental shield, seeking any weakness.

"Never use my name again, Betrayer. Call me Vengeance, for that is all you will ever know from me. Your life is mine, your soul is mine, now your mind and body will be mine. Yield, and I may yet allow some sliver of Danai to survive."

Tendrils of power wormed their way inside the crevices of my mind, seeking a path to seize control. White-hot bolts raced from my head down my spine and throughout my body.

I dropped the crown.

My hands flew to my temples.

I staggered but shook off the shock and thrust the might of my magical reserves at her invading essence.

Fear's tentacles recoiled as Irina's angry screech echoed in my head.

"Resist me all you like. Your pitiful power is no match for my will. I will consume your mind and force you to watch as the world burns."

A shaft of the rising sun glinted off the crown now pillowed in the snow. I snatched it up and slipped it onto my head. A wave of power swelled within my chest and drove me to my knees, but it bolstered my Light with immeasurable strength. I never knew the crown gave more than the seven Gifts, but now I understood it also magnified the innate power of the one who bore its weight.

My lips curled as I called out to my former pupil.

"No! You shall not have me like you did Isabel. I have not survived a thousand years only to lose myself to a *failed* sorceress. I loved you, Irina, but you will not have me now!" I clenched my eyes shut and began muttering a spell, each word stabbing into her invading tendrils. They writhed before me, flailing and thrashing.

When I completed my incantation, the spirit of Irina flinched as though burned, then fled my body and materialized as a spiritual vapor before me.

Hatred burned within her eyes.

"This is not over, Betrayer. The circle was broken, and I am free. When you are weakest, you will become my Vessel, and this world will burn. I will see to that!"

"Irina!" I cried out, but her spirit turned and dissolved into the wind.

I tore the crown from my brow and hurled it to the frozen ground, its malicious intent and un-yielding strength ebbing the moment it was cast aside. Tears formed as I watched the apparition of my lost love fade, leaving me truly alone on the mountain peak, staring blankly at the wintery sky.

CHAPTER 2

DANAI

"Irina, how have we come to this?" I muttered to myself as I wiped a tear from my eye, the first to fall in more years than I could count.

Our confrontation had left me shaken.

She'd turned on me so quickly. She'd born such anger and hatred.

She'd spewed her venom—*toward me.*

And yet, there was a part of me that would always love her. I knew it in the marrow of my bones. I could not see her face, hear her voice, recall the scent she so often wore, without longing to hold her in my arms. Irina consumed my thoughts for centuries, and no anger or bitterness could burn away such deep-rooted yearning.

That caused her words to sting ever more.

How could she think I'd turn against her? Me, a betrayer? I could never . . .

But did I?

I had spent years nursing her back to emotional health following the murder of her parents. I was her strength, her rock, and her shield. I saw the vulnerable girl she used to be in my mind, her rich, ebony hair flowing beyond her shoulders. I saw the quirk of her mouth when she was amused and the way her eyes widened when she laughed. I saw the tilt of her head when she sought answers to some riddle, and the twitch of her lips when she grew annoyed.

I don't know if I recognized the feelings that drove me back then, but a thousand years of reflecting helped me realize how much I had fallen in love with her. Every night, for centuries, I dreamed of her return—her return *to me*.

Mine was no quest. I had no delusions of grandeur or desires for power. I held no aims higher than to reclaim a woman's touch, to see her eyes brighten when they fell upon me. My only desire was a life filled with her laughter and the joy of her companionship.

She'd become embittered following her parents' deaths—as anyone might—but I still saw the young girl, the young woman, the one I loved, hidden beneath her gaze. She was there. I could bring her back, will her into daylight.

If only I had the chance, one moment, to show her the depth of my love . . .

I thought it would be easy.

But returning her to the world of life proved to be the work of many lifetimes.

The words created by her spell couldn't be that hard to interpret, I thought; but the answer to their riddle eluded me. For centuries, they remained obscured, though etched in stone.

So, I invented the Children to help unravel the spell's mysteries.

How had that handful of magical geniuses devolved into a group of mask-wearing idiots?

And yet, those fanatics had proved their usefulness and succeeded in bringing their goddess back to the world of the living.

I never imagined she would come back with *only* vengeance in her heart. Even when she led the Kingdom's armies east the first time, her goal was conquest, not death and destruction.

I didn't recognize the spirit that called herself Irina.

She certainly wasn't *my* Irina.

Was she ever mine?

Did she ever know the depth of my love?

I pressed my palms to my temples and screamed in frustration, then everything tumbled into place in my mind.

Of course she did. Of course she knew.

She's the most brilliant woman I've ever known.

She fed me crumbs—a gentle touch, a warm embrace, a flirtatious glance—all to keep my hope ablaze. She knew I loved her and used it to turn me into her instrument.

And I did everything she wanted.

Anger welled inside me.

How could I have been so stupid? So blind? So willfully ignorant?

I bent and retrieved the crown, then hardened my heart.

Never again. I see you now. You are the Betrayer.

I brushed the crown's band and saw that no snow had stuck to its pulsing crimson diamonds. As much as I learned of magic in my many centuries of life, I was still amazed at the mysteries it held. Unsure of what surprises the crown might still hold, I packed it away in my rough-spun sack, slung the pack over my shoulder, and began working my way down the steep slope of the mountain. My Gift of Travel could whisk me away with barely a thought, but I needed to think through what to do next before I Traveled anywhere.

I never dreamed that Irina's spirit might roam free in the world.

She frightened me in a way no one ever had.

So now what?

I could return to the Kingdom, but what welcome would await?

I had fled the field before the Battle of Saltstone had even begun. While the common soldiers wouldn't know or care, I was sure Bril or Marks would clap me in irons and charge me with desertion. That assumed they survived, which was unlikely based on the massacre I witnessed.

What about going home?

An odd longing bloomed in my chest.

I could Travel to Fontaine, directly to the Palace if I wished.

If Jess sat on the throne, she would likely dismiss me from her service.

That wouldn't be so bad, would it?

I could pursue my own studies, or work with the few remaining Mages in the capital's guild.

But I hadn't seen or heard from Jess since she fled with those two Melucians. She could be dead, or in hiding, or captive somewhere. It would take her weeks to return to the capital. She probably wasn't anywhere near the throne.

So, who would be in charge?

The King and Queen were dead, Justin was dead, Jess was on the run, and Kendall was too young to rule. Bril and Marks were either dead or retreating with whatever was left of their army. The other Ministers were too weak to guide a nation.

What a disaster.

A sudden thought bloomed, and my feet stilled.

In the absence of the monarch, the *High Chancellor* reigns.

Until a new monarch could be installed, *I* was the de facto ruler of the Kingdom of Spires.

Given the disorderly state of the Kingdom's government, a royal selection and coronation could take months—or longer.

Steward Danai Thorn. That sounds better than High Chancellor.

Then doubts crept in.

It has never been a Mage's place to rule.

We advise and guide but never rule.

A voice deep within scolded me for my self-doubt. I counseled dozens of rulers throughout my long life.

Who could have more experience, knowledge, or wisdom?

I savored the sweetness of that thought for a long moment before swallowing it whole.

Yes, I should *lead.*

As images of *my* coronation flooded my mind, I could not halt the vision of Irina striding through the Palace to wrest the crown from my grasp. I knew it was my mind playing tricks, making me doubt, but I could not stop the thrill of her touch.

In that moment, I knew the first thing I had to do.

With a thought, I vanished from the mountainside and appeared before two golden-bronze doors.

CHAPTER 3

DECLAN

I stared out at the island landscape, my feet dangling over the edge of the cliff. Ayden's shoulder pressed into mine. His thumb rubbed the back of my hand as he held it.

His warmth offered comfort and peace.

The last time I sat on that ledge, Órla had been by my side, chiding me for my lack of progress in mastering the many facets of my magic. I smiled at the memory of her barbs, missing her perky voice more than I ever thought possible.

The island shone like a jewel.

Palm trees swayed in the wind.

The ocean crashed sapphire blue against white-gold shores.

Far below our mountain perch, villagers milled about on distant roads, hard at work, enjoying the day.

"The sunrise is incredible, isn't it?" My mother's voice startled me out of my musing.

Ayden's hand squeezed mine as I turned. "This may be the most beautiful place in the world," I replied.

"It really is," Ayden added.

"Come back during storm season and say that." She leaned down and kissed the top of my head, then repeated the gesture with Ayden's fiery locks. I shot him a sideways glance, catching a smile creeping across his lips. "You may find yourself thinking something entirely different when the gods of the sea begin their fights."

"Gods of the sea? When did you get religious?"

The ocean was so lovely. I couldn't picture it angry.

She snorted. "I am the Keeper of Magic. How could I not wonder at what hands guided our paths?"

Ayden lifted a brow but held his tongue when I shook my head. If my mother started walking a philosophical route, we might never get to eat.

As if her mother's instinct had heard my thoughts, Kelså spoke as she turned toward the cavern's entrance. "I made breakfast if you are hungry. I know it is early, but I have seen both of you eat."

"Hey!" I protested as Ayden and I stood. "We're growing boys. We need to maintain—"

"Pshaw. Atikus raised you. That means you *never* stop eating. Come on." She laughed and slapped my arm. Her light tone sobered as she said, "Besides, your journey calls."

"How . . . ?" Ayden and I shared a baffled look. "How did you know we wanted to leave today? I was planning to talk to you this morning about it but hadn't figured out how."

"You will learn that a mother *always* knows, especially when it involves her baby leaving the nest."

I snorted and looked into her twinkling eyes. "Baby?"

She reached up and cupped my cheek. "You will always be my baby boy, and don't you forget it."

Ayden elbowed me. His annoyingly handsome smirk was on full display as he mouthed, "Baby Dec."

I resisted the urge to shove him into one of the stone pillars.

Kelså rolled her eyes, her smile brighter than the sunrise. "I still want to hear more about what happened with Saltstone and Irina. I did not press when you first arrived, but it is important I know everything before you leave."

"Not the best breakfast conversation, but it'll have to do. After you."

As we wound our way through the ancient tunnels, Ayden's hand rubbed my neck. His touch was never far when we were near, and I relished each moment. How anyone could love another so deeply, so completely, was baffling to me. And yet, a single glance from Ayden Byrne could reduce me to a gibbering idiot.

By the lazy arc of the island's sun, we'd spent a few months together on Rea Utu. Battles and wars felt so distant. All that mattered was being together, feeling Ayden close, getting to know my mother and becoming a family.

I had a family now.

The Mages raised me. Atikus was like a father. And Keelan . . .

Kee had always been like part of my soul.

But now, I had a mother who loved me, a mother who wanted me with her, who cared what I thought and felt. I had never known that kind of love. Not from anyone.

And Ayden . . . he was something altogether different.

I could not begin to reckon how long we had known each other. Mainland time and island time moved so differently that the present and past seemed muddled in my mind. However long it had been, each day felt new and fresh, like the beginning of a new eternity with a man who made me want to savor life with every breath.

How could anyone affect me so, wriggle their way beneath my skin and live within my heart and soul?

How could anyone fuel my joy and inhabit my dreams?

I found I no longer cared for answers to those questions.

Ayden did all of those things, and I was a better man for it.

I was better because of him.

Kelså bristled when I first arrived with him by my side—not because I was with a man, but because I had violated the island's sacred rules.

The security of the Well had always been sacrosanct. It always would be.

Still, my heart ached for Kelså to know him. For her to know me, she had to know him, as well. Ayden was part of me now, the better part of all that I was. So I risked her ire and walked him up the Path.

Ayden would never remember the place.

He would lose all recollection of my mother.

There was no reprieve from that sentence.

While I understood and agreed it was for the best, a larger part of me was saddened at what he would lose when we returned to the mainland. Seeing him interact with my mother, seeing her wrap her arms around him so freely, lightened my heart in ways I never hoped possible.

She was my home.

Now he was, too.

The smell of bacon greeted us before we reached the entrance to the kitchen.

My stomach growled.

Piles of food awaited us: eggs, bacon, steaming scones, and a small bowl of assorted fruit.

"Did you make enough for the village? Spirits," Ayden said. I ignored him and grabbed a plate.

Kelså beamed. "I can't have *my baby* going off hungry, can I?"

Ayden laughed and mussed my already ruffled hair.

I ignored them both and filled my plate while Kelså poured piping tea into mugs and set the kettle back on the stove. Long moments passed in silence as we enjoyed our meal, but Kelså couldn't keep her curiosity at bay for long.

"Start from the beginning. You said Grove's Pass was destroyed by the time you returned, but I could tell you saw more than you were willing to discuss."

I took a sip of tea, set my fork against the edge of my plate, then stared into the grain of the table's wood for a long moment. Those were memories I had hoped to never relive, but Kelså needed to know.

The Keeper needed to know what transpired.

"I grew up in the guild in Saltstone, but Grove's Pass had become my home. There were over a thousand rangers who lived, worked, or passed through the town. Most of us lived in the headquarters, a massive complex larger than many small villages. The place always amazed me. Mages helped build much of it, you know?" My voice descended to a whisper. "They were my brothers and sisters, my family. And the people of Grove's Pass . . ."

Kelså set her own fork down and cradled her mug in both hands as she listened, brows creased in worry.

"The innkeeper was like another uncle, one of a hundred I see in my mind. When I first joined the Rangers, I was young and stupid, getting into every kind of trouble you could imagine. I spent more time at his bar than I did in the HQ. He helped a lost boy find some measure of peace and focus. I wouldn't be alive if he hadn't taken me under his wing.

"I could say the same about a dozen of the Rangers." My voice broke. "They were *all* dead when I got there. And the people . . . Who kills children in their mothers' arms? Babies and . . . Who does that?"

Kelså reached across the table and placed her hand on mine. "Show me."

My heart seized at the thought of bringing such memories to life, but I nodded, closed my eyes, and called forth my Light. Ayden's calloused hand gripped mine as images flickered.

A reflection of Grove's Pass solidified above the table.

> *I pick my way through the town's*
> *snow-covered streets. Hands reach up*
> *through the snow. Broken bodies, too*
> *many to count, lay beneath.*

> *Burned-out buildings, charred black, are*
> *all that remain of the Rangers' home.*

The snow blows back.

I see one cadet, then another.

*Men and women—more boys and girls
than men and women—stare up through
unseeing eyes.*

*Wetness tickles my cheek, but I press on-
ward, stepping over one body, then another, until reaching the burned-out tavern.*

*A mound of rubble two stories tall rises
before me. Only a door stands. It mocks
us.*

*Captain Whitman lies interred, forever a
Ranger, forever at his command.*

*He is one of many who will never rise
again.*

My skill with Illusion had grown since my first
time on the island. I could almost smell the death
in my images.

My illusion shifted to Saltstone.

*The proud city's growing fortifications rise
before us, defenses erected prior to the
Kingdom's troops' arrival. People, horses, and carts bustle through the crowded
streets in preparation. Soldiers are everywhere.*

Then we are surrounded.

*The sounds of war boom throughout the
night.*

*Tens of thousands of men, many on horse-
back, watch as stone after stone are hurled
against the invisible barrier of my magi-*

cal shield. The view through Órla's eyes is dizzying, but the inevitable outcome of the scene below is clear.

The city cannot stand.

I could only recall snippets of the battle between Irina and Arch Mage Quin, as I was tumbling down the tower stairs when most of it occurred, but I was in position to remember the blinding light of Irina's fires as she blasted the city's dwellings, killing indiscriminately, exacting a millennium's worth of pent-up rage on innocent people.

There is a grinding of stone against stone as the tower cracks and begins to break apart.

Arch Mage Quin falls, then Isabel's body crumples.

*The Phoenix streaks down and wrenches
Irina's crown from her head.*

Kelså clapped a hand over her mouth and emitted a gasp.

*The Empress's spirit evaporates into the
sky, and the Phoenix sails out over the Silver Mountains, trailing plumes of magical
smoke from her massive chest.*

*Then the Phoenix, many leagues away,
hurtles from the sky into the Kingdom's
army. Brilliant light flares across the land
as magic's guardian sacrifices herself a
second time so innocents might live.*

The images vanished.

Only then did I realize Ayden was sitting back, staring, while Kelså gripped my hand.

She released me and sat back, her eyes brimming with tears.

"We survived, as did most of the civilian people of Saltstone. Our army lost almost everyone, but the Guard remained intact. We've had to recall the

Rangers from the eastern border to begin rebuilding. The new Triad invested in a navy, since most of our fleet consisted of unarmed merchant ships." I rubbed my temples and squeezed my eyes shut, trying to make the images flee my mind. "I don't think the Kingdom fared much better, but we'll be prepared if they try anything again."

"What about Irina? What about her crown?" Kelså asked.

I looked up. "Irina? She died when Isabel was killed, when the tower fell. No one's seen the crown since the Phoenix took it."

Kelså shook her head. "She is *not* dead, Declan. Her spirit was not contained."

Ayden crossed his arms but remained silent. Tension tightened about his eyes.

"How could you know that?"

"The currents never calmed after the battle. I can still sense great turmoil. And in the images, I saw Irina's spirit *flee* Isabel's body. If she had been taken beyond the veil, I would not have seen her spirit. She is still out there."

"Her spirit roams the continent?" Ayden whispered my thought.

I sat back, struggling to grasp the implications of such a thing. "When you taught me about spirit communication, you said spirits could cause great harm if not contained by a circle. You were insistent I learn to draw the circle perfectly with no breaks. When the tower fell, that broke the circle containing Irina, didn't it?"

She nodded.

"Could she inhabit another person, like she did with Isabel?" I asked.

"Perhaps." Kelså stared into the distance. "If she did, she would not want to inhabit just anyone. She would want someone with a strong Gift."

"That could be any number of people, though I suspect that number is much smaller now."

Kelså thought a moment. "She would also want someone with a weak mind so she could control them. That would be a hard combination to find. Most of those with powerful Gifts have a mind to match, making their ability to repel Compulsion far greater. Based on what you have told me—and what you learned from Keelan—she gained most of her power from the crown, which is now missing."

"But if she found the right host, and then found the crown . . ."

"Declan, I wish you could stay here forever, but you *need* to leave." She stood. "You may be the only one strong enough to find and contain Irina."

My eyes widened. "How am I supposed to do that?"

"I . . . I do not know." She stepped around the table and rested her hand on my shoulder. "All I know is that you must try. There is no one else who stands any hope of facing her, especially if she rises to power again."

I stood on the porch of the Keeper's cottage, staring into my mother's eyes.

"Seeing you again was more than my heart hoped for," she said. "Please come back when you can."

I moved onto the first step and wrapped her in a tight embrace. "If I had my choice, I would never leave this place again. I love you, Mother."

Kelså swallowed hard, as if to hold back her tears, then pulled away from my embrace and slapped my chest teasingly.

"Don't you dare make me cry again, Declan Rea."

I smirked and gave her a peck on the cheek.

Ayden chuckled a little too loudly.

"And you, Ayden Byrne." Kelså marched around me and poked him in the chest with a finger. "You take care of my boy, or the Phoenix and I will hunt you down. You hear me?"

Ayden's eyes widened as they shifted from Kelså to me.

"Can she—?"

Kelså and I burst out laughing.

"She's yanking your chain, lordling."

"Oh," he said, returning his gaze to hers but not losing a bit of his childlike trepidation.

Kelså cupped his cheek as she so often did mine. "You are my son now, too. I will think of you often. You boys come home to me, please."

Before Ayden could think of a witty retort, Kelså grabbed him and hugged him close. When she pulled back, his eyes held more than a little moisture.

"Oh, I should've mentioned this before," I said.

"Uh-oh." Ayden found his smirk again.

Kelså spun and planted her fists on her hips. "What is it, Declan Rea? I know that tone."

I lowered my head and muttered, "So . . . I kind of told Keelan."

Kelså's arms crossed, and her already arching brow rose further.

"Yeah. So, I told him about . . . um . . . well . . ." I looked down, trying to avoid her gaze. "I told him about *everything*, but I used magic to bind him to silence and mask the knowledge in his mind. He can't speak about it, even if Compelled."

Her mouth set as she gripped my arm. "What is done cannot be undone. But son, no one else. *Ever.* Do you hear me?"

I nodded.

"I'm serious. Órla gave you—gave both of us—a magnificent gift in letting you keep your memory. More than that, she gave you the ultimate trust. The security and fate of magic itself rests with the secrets you carry. If Irina—or anyone with ill intent—learned of the location of the Well, it could mean disaster beyond imagining."

I nodded. "I know, but Keelan is the most trust-worthy person I know. His whole life, even his Gift, revolves around the truth. Add my binding, and I'm confident he will never betray that trust. Wouldn't you . . . someday . . . ?"

Her eyes flew wide. "Oh, Declan, *of course* I would want to see him, to see the man he's be-come. There's nothing my heart craves more, but my heart can never take precedence over the wel-fare of magic and this world—and neither can yours. That is the burden we both bear."

I hesitated, then asked, "How do I even remember you?"

"What?" Her brow furrowed.

"When I leave this place, how do I remember everything? I know Órla told me things, but could her magic restore what the Keeper's protections took away?"

"All that time with her, and you still do not see, do you?" Kelså smiled. "Órla is beyond us all, beyond any Mage. Only the Well surpasses her in strength and power. If she chose to break a spell cast by mere men, she could do so with barely a thought."

"But . . . if she has that kind of power, why could Irina . . ."

"In the end, Órla had to choose. She sacrificed herself to save the people, but that meant allowing Irina to go free. She can do wondrous things, but being in two places at once is not one of them."

"But couldn't she have stopped her? Before all those people died?"

"Perhaps. Perhaps not. In the end, she gave herself for the good of others. We may never understand more than that."

She stared into my eyes for a long moment, then drew a deep breath and cupped my cheek.

"Enough of that. I *refuse* to say goodbye. I love you. Travel safely and come back soon, all right?"

I wrapped her in another hug. Ayden was quick to join in, wrapping his arms around both of us.

Afterward, with a hand on Ayden's shoulder, I thought of home and . . .

Nothing happened.

"Give me a minute," I said when Ayden shuffled. "I just need to get a place in my mind."

I thought of the Mages' Guild, the place where I grew up.

Still nothing.

"Declan, what is happening? You look like you ate something sour." Kelså's face scrunched in concern.

"I don't know. I don't even feel magic's tingle when I try to Travel. It's like . . . I just can't."

Terrified my magic was gone, I pulled moisture from the air and formed a wobbling ball of water before me. I released a heavy sigh as I let the water splash to the ground.

"My magic still works."

"Have you only Traveled the one time?" Kelså asked.

"Twice. The first time was when I returned to the mainland. I Traveled to Ayden," I said. "The second time was when I Traveled from Grove's Pass to Saltstone, before the siege began."

"Was Órla with you each time?"

I thought a moment, then nodded.

"I do not fully understand the Bond. No one has bonded in millennia. Something about Órla's presence may strengthen your power or respond to your need."

I tried one last time. Nothing worked.

"Maybe you're right. I guess it doesn't matter why; we can't Travel." I shrugged and looked toward Ayden. "Ready for a hike? The gate is on the other side of the village."

Ayden clapped me on the shoulder. "After you, my good sir."

Kelså gave each of us another peck on the cheek. Then, far too quickly, Ayden and I made our way down the mountain path.

CHAPTER 4

DANAI

My eyes roamed along the golden doors, taking in the detailed etching of the Phoenix that dominated their mirror-like surface. No one tended this chamber, yet the doors remained as shiny and perfect as the day they were laid on their hinges. I traced a finger along one of the Phoenix's talons. I couldn't remember touching the engraving before, and despite centuries of work with magic, it brought a boyish grin to my face.

Finally, tired of my rumination, I reached up to the plain metal plate on the wall and spoke the words, "E vesh Irina," *Take my life, Irina.* As the doors swung open, I made a mental note to find a way to change the words required to enter this chamber. Irina was dead to me now—at least, that's what I kept telling myself.

I slipped inside, impatient for the doors to open, and was shocked to find a cloaked figure kneeling in prayer before the altar. As I stepped closer, the outline of a mask, feathers protruding where ears would normally be on an animal, marked the man as one of the Children.

"Child, turn and face me. What are you doing in this sacred place?" I demanded.

The figure didn't move. The incessant muttering of the man's prayer grew louder as I approached. When the prayer ended, the Child rose and turned to face me. The mask was of a snarling bear with what appeared to be an eagle's wings for ears.

Lifeless eyes widened with recognition. The man bowed at the waist.

"Forgive me, High Lord. I did not know you would arrive today."

My impatience grew. "I asked you a question, Child. Who are you, and why have you disturbed this place? None of your Order should even know of its existence."

"Do you not know me, High Lord? I am the Elder of the Children." The man's head cocked to one side in confusion. "I felt our Mother's passing and returned to her stone to mourn. It is a grievous end to our cause."

Is that sadness in his voice? Can Children feel sadness? Or anything, for that matter?

"Irina failed us all," I said with indifference, causing the Elder's eyes to widen at my sacrilege. "I have come to release us from her grip."

I brushed past the Elder and beyond the altar to stand before the onyx monolith that loomed over the chamber. Its lettering glittered in the magical light of braziers standing throughout. I reached into the pack I carried following the siege and removed a coil of thin rope, wrapping one end around the stone and tying it securely. I then walked back around the altar, releasing more rope with each step, until I stood inside the edge of the pool, again facing the monolith. Finally, I reached into my pack and removed the crown.

The Elder gasped and fell to his knees. "High Lord! How? Why do you have her crown?"

"*My* crown," I corrected, then placed the ancient relic on my head.

An intoxicating wave of power coursed through me, and the Gift of Enhanced Strength contained in one of the diamonds answered my call. I gripped the rope, braced my feet against the inner lip of the pool, and pulled with all of my magically enhanced might. By the fourth draw, sweat beaded across my brow, and the pulsing crimson of the diamonds flooded the room with an eerie, bloody glow. On the tenth pull, the monument teetered until it fell with a crash against the altar.

Both shrines to Irina's legacy cracked and shattered.

The golden script burst into flame.

When the last of the fires died, once-majestic words were replaced by charred remnants.

I dropped the rope and wiped my brow, smiling at my handiwork. There would be no second return of the Empress Irina.

"High Lord, what have you done?" the Elder sobbed. "Our Holy Lady is lost to us now."

I pitied the fool.

Even in his hollowed-out state, the man felt the loss of his mistress, the loss of his purpose.

In that moment, a brilliant idea struck.

"Elder, what do you know of the prophecies of the One?"

The man looked up. "Irina was the One foretold, and now she is lost. By *your* hand."

"No." I tilted my head. "You *believe* Irina was the One. She would be standing at the center of the continent, triumphant, had she been the One foretold. Clearly, she was not."

"High Lord?"

"She was a false fork in the prophecy, however compelling we both may have thought her to be."

The Elder blinked, pain and grief pouring through his masked face. But there was something else in his eyes, as well. Curiosity?

"What if the One returned, but *he* wasn't Irina?"

The Elder staggered back, propping himself against the shattered altar. "High Lord, what you say . . . I . . . we would follow the One into the abyss, should she, *or he*, return."

"Good. I will need your support, especially in the months to come, if we are to unify this land and fulfill the prophecy."

The Elder's eyes bugged out of his mask. "You cannot mean—"

"I mean *exactly* what you are thinking. I declare this to you, Elder of the Ancient Order of the Children, Keeper of the Flame: I am Danai Thorn, *the One Returned*, the One prophesied to unite these lands and people. Kneel before me and pledge your fealty."

I called my Light, and the diamonds on the crown flared to brilliance. I hadn't known that would work but figured the dramatic flair was worth a try.

The masked man threw himself to the floor and pressed his forehead to the stone.

"High Lord," the man whispered.

"Enough of that. Address me properly," I commanded, having no idea what title I should use but understanding the need to conform to the people's beloved prophecy.

"Emperor Thorn," the Elder muttered into the stone. "Your Most Serene Excellency."

Hmm. Not what I would've chosen, but it does have a ring to it.

"Rise and remove your mask. The time for skulking is over. The Children will continue to wear the holy robes, but your masks must be cast aside if the people are to accept you as their Priests."

The Elder rose and removed his mask. His hands moved so deliberately that I thought the act might have been painful for him; but what surprised me more was the smooth, unmarred face that stared up once the mask fell away. The Elder appeared to have seen only thirty winters. His skin was pale and smooth from years hidden beneath the bear's snarl.

I nodded once in approval. "Elder, I name you leader of the Temples across my lands and charge you with preparing the way for my return. Spread word of the prophecy's fulfillment, and ensure the people know the One will restore order and might."

The new High Priest bowed low. "It shall be done, Excellency."

I made to leave but looked back and scanned the room again, intending it to be my final farewell to Irina's resting place. A glint of silver from the monolith's rubble caught my eye. I climbed across the broken stone to discover an unbroken silver staff embedded in the heart of the black stone.

Irina's staff?

I reached out and touched the ancient weapon my protégée had crafted a thousand years ago.

How many times had I seen her wield that staff?

How many times had I wondered at its power?

She never told me its purpose, or what Gift might have been Enchanted into its length, but I planned to find out. A grim smile curled my lips as I grasped the metal and it slid from its hiding place.

Without thinking, I turned and pointed the staff at the High Priest.

Calling my Light, magic flowed from my spirit into the cold metal. A thrill of life coursed through the silver staff. Unable to contain the raw energy, the staff bellowed white flame that engulfed the man. Living fire crawled up and down his body, yet he did not burn. His lips parted as if to scream, but the magic rushed in and swelled his chest. When his mouth closed, no trace of the magical flames remained.

The man blinked up at me and quirked a brow, as if something perplexing was taking place.

I took a step forward. "What are you feeling? Speak to me!"

The man opened his mouth to speak, but no sound emerged.

And then it started.

I staggered back a step.

Understanding replaced terror, understanding of the *true* Gift that rested in my hands, the Gift that would place me on the throne at last.

CHAPTER 5

AYDEN

W alking down the Keeper's mountainside Path was surreal. With each stride Declan took, the stones of the Path on which he stepped glowed with cerulean light, then faded to darkness as he moved forward. When we reached the outskirts of the village, children flowed out like the sea's waves rushing toward the shore. Their cries and squeals were almost as loud as crashing waves, too.

The first boy to wrap his spindly arms around Declan begged him to make his tunic flare. Then the second added her voice. Then a third. We laughed and flared our way for hundreds of paces before reaching the town proper.

Adults soon followed, then Larinda, the Mother of the island. Her weathered face beamed as she gripped Declan's face in her palms. He sank into her as one might curl beneath a favorite blanket.

The old woman surprised us both by turning
toward me. "And you must be Ayden." She winked
at Declan, adding, "You've done a'right fer yerself,
boy. This one's tasty."

I turned eight shades of red.

Larinda cackled.

Declan doubled over.

It appeared as though the entire world marked
his passing, welcomed him into their arms, and
lifted him on their shoulders.

The broad smile that parted his lips the moment the first fuzzy-headed boy tried to tackle
him outside of town remained fixed on his face
throughout the hours-long lunch Larinda insisted
we attend. Villagers packed the local inn where
a ridiculously tall, painfully thin man tended bar,
served tables, and wove between rowdy diners
faster than I thought possible.

We ate our fill of fish plucked fresh from the sea
and vegetables grown by rugged hands.

There was no chatter of wars or battles. No one
spoke of evil spirits or long-dead queens.

There was only laughter and an overwhelming
sense of communal love.

At the center of it all was Declan.

As the last of the platters were cleared, and a
final round of ale was poured, Larinda and Declan

leaned toward one another and chatted. My heart warmed watching the pair. No cloak ever woven could have hidden the affection between them. And despite the seriousness painting each of their faces, I knew the reunion filled each of their souls.

For some reason unknown to me, it filled mine with questions.

Before the invasion, when Declan and I were still cadets trying to pass exams and not hate each other too much, I knew who I was. When I realized how hopelessly I'd fallen for him, I knew myself even better. When he professed his own feelings, and my heart threatened to burst free, I knew my path forward.

Now, after spending time with Declan and his mother, the Keeper of the Well of Magic, and seeing him interact with the inhabitants of this island, I was no longer sure I knew anything.

He did not simply have a Gift. He possessed many Gifts. Spirits, he was chosen by magic to guard our world from evil and darkness.

And I thought being a lord's son came with pressure and expectations.

My silly insecurities were nothing next to what everyone demanded of him.

I loved and respected him so much—more than I'd ever experienced with anyone.

It was not the power he wielded or the knowledge he now possessed; it was *his way.*

He drew people to him.

They wanted to be near him, to know him, to love him.

Even without his talking owl, Declan became the center of every room he entered. Now, with a reputation and fame matched by only the Queen herself, he was a blazing sun in a sea of twinkling stars.

Standing by his side was . . . harder than I expected.

I still had no Gift.

I would never have one.

Not that long ago, we shared that failing. It had drawn us together in—I do not know, a shared misery?

Now, I was alone.

Watching Declan and Larinda made me feel even more so.

I knew I was being ridiculous, even when those words were spoken only in my head, but I could not help the feeling as it washed over me, coating me with unease.

Declan caught me staring and smiled.

The moment our eyes locked, warmth traveled up my arms and into my chest. I hadn't meant to smile back. I could not stop myself.

Damned Declan Rea and his mystical spell.

I was entranced.

And I thought he was. I knew he was. He loved me.

But would he always?

When the routine of life returned, and I remained Mute, would the most magical man in the entire world still want me by his side?

Would he tire of my inability to perform even basic magic?

Would he want someone without a golden collar to stand next to him?

We were still young with long lives ahead of us. Would he want me throughout all of those years? Could he want me that long?

Then something dawned on me, something I should have thought about before:

How long would Declan live?

Decades? Centuries? Longer?

He was "of magic," as Kelså said. Would his life be extended, as had those of Atikus and even Kelså herself?

Would my life be little more than a grain of sand in the ocean's depths of his life?

Would he remember me when . . . ?

"Are you all right?"

I nearly leaped out of my chair.

"Sweet Spirits, Dec, you scared the life out of me."

He chuckled. "You looked so serious. Larinda called your name a few times, but you didn't respond. We were beginning to worry."

I ran a hand through my hair, something Declan did when he was nervous, and smiled as though he'd made a joke. "You know me, always deep in thought. I am fine."

Larinda's bony fingers dug into my forearm as her other hand pulled my face down toward her so she could kiss my cheek. "Ayden Byrne, you keep our Declan safe, ya hear?"

"Yes, ma'am," I said, swallowing hard.

"Now." Larinda hooked her arm in Declan's and led us out of the inn. "You two need t' git going. I can feel t' Keeper's disquiet all t' way over here."

The pack of children escorted us out of town.

Escort may have been too kind a word.

They swarmed about us, a swirling, squealing, squalling mass of tiny humanity that never seemed to still. Had I not been so caught up in my own thoughts, I would have loved every moment.

Nowhere in the world had I witnessed such unbridled joy as on the isle of Rea Utu.

By the time we reached the cavern and set eyes on the silver gate, my legs ached and my temples throbbed. I tossed my pack down and slumped onto a cot shoved against one wall.

Declan eyed me but said nothing, setting his pack beside mine and stepping to the table to fill two glasses with wine. "Here, this should knock out your soreness."

"Thanks," I muttered, taking the glass and downing it in one long swallow.

His brows rose as he sipped. "Thirsty?"

I pressed my palms to my eyes. "Dec, I . . . I do not know what . . . I mean . . . dammit."

I stood, covered the distance to the table in three strides, refilled my glass, and downed it again in one draft.

Declan stared and blinked, his glass frozen halfway to his mouth.

"I do not know what to think or feel. You are the Son of Magic or the Bond-Mate or the Heir of Magic—or whatever new title they have concocted that is grander than before." I set my glass down a little too hard. The *clank* echoed through the cave. "What am I now? Your sidekick? Your useless, Mute companion?"

"Ayden—" He reached out for me, but I stepped back.

"You do not need me, Dec. I will only hold you back. I'm . . . nothing next to you."

"Ayden, please don't—"

"See, you can't even deny it. You know it to be true. The moment we get home, you will throw yourself into the world's problems, and I will be tossed—" His lips slammed into mine, silencing whatever idiocy I was about to say next. Firm hands held my head, refusing to let me flee or pull back, forcing me to receive the full weight of his passion.

I only resisted a moment.

Maybe less.

His kiss was ravenous. It felt as though he channeled every moment of desire and longing he had ever felt in his short life into that one act.

My knees buckled.

Then his hands left my head, and he began unclasping my cloak.

"You are my life, Ayden Byrne, now and always. None of this matters without you. None of it."

His breath was hot and wet, and I couldn't drink it in fast enough.

My mind screamed in protest.

Why did I not pull back? Why did my voice falter?

Why could I not resist this man?

Why was I still thinking?

His lips and tongue devoured me, and I felt myself surrender.

In this man's arms, pressed against his chest, this was where I longed to be. It was where I belonged.

We both stood naked, kissing and rubbing and gripping.

The cool cavern felt more like an oven.

And I wanted more.

Declan pulled back from our kisses and rasped, "If anyone ever talked about you like you just did, I would beat the ever-loving shit out of them. Do you hear me? Nobody talks about you like that, not even you."

His words held the conviction of a thousand jurists, and I knew in my bones he meant every word.

How had I won this man? How had the Spirits granted it so?

He dropped to his knees so fast I barely had time to gasp as his tongue teased my already moistened head.

My whole body spasmed as my cock twitched.

"Damn, Dec."

He gripped my balls with one hand, pulling them back out of the way, forcing me to stand even more erect than before. His tongue traveled my length, tickling and teasing, making me squirm and throb. His other hand reached up, and he raked fingers through the fine hairs of my chest. Then he kneaded the muscles, gripping and squeezing.

I threw my head back as his mouth enveloped me, swallowed me down to the base. I felt my head scrape somewhere deep in his throat. As he pulled back, the warmth of the world left me for the briefest moment, then I was inside him again.

And again.

"If you keep doing that—"

"Don't you dare." Declan pulled back and stood, gripping my cock with one hand. "This is mine, you hear me. It doesn't fire until I release the arrow."

A laugh erupted from somewhere deep in my gut. "Going full Ranger on me?"

He squeezed.

"Ah!" I saw stars.

"Hands on the table," he ordered. "You may be a lordling, but I am your superior officer."

"Says who?"

He grabbed my arm, spun me around, and bent me over, forcing my palms flat on the table. Before I could think of some sharp retort, he was spreading my cheeks and spearing his tongue deep into dark places.

Again, I squirmed my way over the damn table.

"Mother of fucking fuckery, Dec. If you get any deeper—"

He spread me wider and shoved himself so far up my ass I thought he might lose his tongue.

I had never felt fire inside me before, but damn, if it didn't blaze within.

His hand reached around as his tongue dove again, and I was sure my control would shatter.

Then he rose, and I felt him press against me.

"Do you want this?" he asked.

"Gods, yes, Dec. Please."

He pressed just the tip inside.

I leaned forward. "Yes!"

He slid in, just a bit more.

"Fuck, Dec, get inside me."

He slid all the way in.

"Ow!"

"You said—"

"Shut up and fuck me."

So he did.

When we were both spent, and the magic of the wine failed to revive us for a repeat performance, I lay with my head on Declan's chest, his fingers stroking my hair. We refused to dress, preferring the coolness of the cavern and warmth of each other's touch to the feel of fabric.

"Where did all that come from earlier?" He kissed my head.

"All what?" I asked drearily.

"That horse shit about you being nothing."

"Oh, that." I nuzzled my cheek against his chest and breathed in his scent, the tang of the sea mixed with his mother's lavender bath oils. "I do not know. I was being ridiculous. There is no need—"

"There is every need." He lifted my chin so he could look into my eyes. "You are everything to me, Ayden. Without you, I would never have made it this far. I would never be able to handle all the stares and questions and . . . shit . . . everything else that comes with being . . . whatever I am. You are the reason I can do most everything. Without you, I am nothing. You hear me?"

I blinked away a pesky tear. I would not let him see me cry. I would not.

It trickled down my cheek.

He wiped it away with a thumb.

Dammit.

"I do not deserve you, Declan Rea."

"Clearly not." He smirked, then kissed my head, then held our foreheads pressed together.

"I love you, lordling, now and always."

His words were a comfort, his touch a salve.

And yet, the roiling of my soul would not relent.

CHAPTER 6

KEELAN

I stared at Atikus as he closed his eyes and created a Telepathic link. He agreed to speak his words aloud so I could listen in on the one-way mental communication, but even with that assurance, I wrung my dusty blue cap as his words tumbled out.

"Jess, it's Atikus . . ." he spoke aloud and mentally at once.

Moments later, Atikus opened his eyes.

His shoulders slumped.

"Telepathy isn't usually so exhausting," he said, pinching the bridge of his nose.

"What made that so hard?"

"Communicating over an entire continent's distance puts a real strain on my magical reserves. I haven't tried using Telepathy with someone that far away in centuries." He blinked a few times, then looked up. "It would have been difficult under the best of situations but so soon after all our travels . . . I'm exhausted."

I shifted from one foot to the other. "Did she say anything? How did she sound?"

Atikus chuckled. "You know it doesn't work that way, son. Telepathy only goes in one direction. She couldn't speak, and I couldn't hear anything on her end. I'm sorry, but you'll just have to ask her yourself when you get to the cave."

I tossed my cap onto the chair beside Atikus and slumped into the cushion, mindless of how I crushed the poor cap.

"Back to that cave," I muttered, trying to banish memories of nearly killing Jess before she fled through the mirror. "Think she's forgiven me yet? I mean . . . I guess I worry . . ."

Atikus lifted a brow and grinned. "Weren't you calling Jess an immature brat before we came home? Why are you so nervous about how she's doing now, about how she will react to seeing you again?"

"Come on, Atikus. I tried to *kill* her. Why wouldn't I be worried?" I ran a hand over my rusty stubble and avoided meeting his gaze. "I mean, what's going to happen when she sees me? When she sees me bringing back her horse or . . . Spirits, you know what I mean."

The Mage's grin grew. "I think I know *exactly* what you mean. When *you* figure it out, come see me and I'll explain what to do about it."

What in the Phoenix did he mean by that? Of course I was worried about how Jess would receive me. She's the Queen now, and I did try to kill her. Sure, I was under Compulsion. It wasn't *really* me. Still, it was my hand holding the knife. If I lived another fifty years, I would never forget the terror in her eyes, eyes that had only just begun to soften when they fell in my direction.

When her eyes fell on me.

A shiver snaked up my spine and down my arms.

Why did the idea of Jess looking at me give me such unease? Was it even unease? It felt so much like when Tiana—

My stomach fell.

Here I was, daydreaming about Jess, wondering if she hated me or might see me as . . . something else . . . and I'd nearly forgotten the woman I was enamored with only a short time ago.

A pang of regret and grief stabbed at my chest.

Tiana was smart and beautiful and funny. Spirits, she had a quick wit and a sharp tongue. I loved that about her.

Loved.

Did I love her?

I couldn't remember ever thinking that word, much less speaking it aloud. I *was* interested. I liked her. I loved the time we spent together.

Was that the same thing as loving her?

I didn't think so, but the whole subject was so far outside my comfort zone that I barely knew where to begin to understand it.

"Just get ready for your trip. Time is passing while you sit here worrying." Atikus wobbled as he stood and braced himself on my shoulder. "I'm going to check on preparations for the ceremony tonight and might stop by to see what the cook's making for dinner. Why don't you come by my chamber later and walk with me to the tower grounds?"

"I still don't understand why you don't want Declan there. He'd want to show his support to you and the guild."

"Because he would outshine all of us, and tonight is for the guild. The one presiding insisted, and we dare not ignore *her* counsel."

"All right. Not sure I understand any of that, especially since you won't tell me who *she* is. I'll go finish packing. See you in a couple hours."

The gray winter sky had dimmed to a moonless night by the time I returned to the Mages' quarters and rapped on the thick door of Atikus's apartment. A moment later, the door creaked open, and the Mage emerged in his long formal robe, two lines of gold glittering on the collar and cuffs.

My eyes widened as I stared into the stripes of his Gift.

The gold *flowed* as if alive.

"Time to get this over with," Atikus said with a tight smile.

"Atikus, I don't remember your stripes *moving* before."

He looked down at his cuff and shrugged. "Theatrics and staging are powerful tools. That's a lesson you would do well to learn, my boy."

"It sure made me look twice. You still sure you want to do this? You're taking on the weight of the entire magical world."

"Look around us. The guild was devastated. Spirits, the whole capital is in ruins. Fewer than three hundred of my brothers and sisters survived—and that's across the entire country, not just here. We aren't just men with Gifts; we are teachers, inventors, historians. While most people will never know the role we play, every life in Melucia is improved by the work of the guild and our members." Atikus sighed as only an old man can. "It will take generations to rebuild our strength. Most who survived are young or highly specialized. I have never wanted the burden of leadership, but sometimes life calls us for a greater purpose. After everything our people have suffered, how can I refuse that call now?"

Pride swelled in my chest as I stared down at my adopted father. He had always been wise, offering kind words and gentle guidance, but until that moment, I had never seen the depth of his commitment to magic and the people of Melucia. His was a life of service. I hoped, one day, I might walk in the shadow of his greatness.

"I guess you're right. I don't think there's anyone else strong enough to lead the guild either, I suppose."

"It isn't about strength, Keelan." Atikus shrugged and stepped out, closing the door behind him.

As we strode away, something in that simple act struck me as poetic, the closing of one door heralding the opening of another.

I always knew my path—to serve in the Guard, to protect others. Now, after losing Tiana in a failed search across the border and our nearly tragic parting with Jess, I wondered—for the first time—if the course I'd set all those years ago was meant for me.

I loved the Guard, but was it my *calling*?

I shook my head at the irony of *me* questioning my place in the world while my perpetually lost brother blazed like a star for others to follow. It appeared someone had switched our roles without bothering to give us a gentlemanly heads-up.

We exited the living quarters and turned toward the tower grounds.

"Why are we doing this at the tower? It doesn't work anymore, does it?"

Atikus nodded. "It is a symbol, an icon representing the might of magic in our world, the place of the guild in the lives of our people. Besides, I think you will find it still has its uses."

With that cryptic pronouncement, we entered the tower square.

In the weeks that followed the siege, hundreds of men and Mages had worked tirelessly clearing rubble and debris from the tower's destruction. Now, an empty courtyard spread before us, leading to the tower's broken base. Every living Mage in the Melucian Empire stood assembled on either side of the central path, forcing us to walk down the center. The path itself was littered with hand-sized cerulean petals of a flower that flared as our feet pressed into them.

Mages on either side bowed deeply and remained in that position until we were well past.

I was startled by the display of reverence, but Atikus marched forward, head held aloft, as though he expected the courtly reception. When we passed Mage Fergus—*Uncle Ferg* to Declan and me—the portly old Mage snuck a wink in my direction before bowing as low as his bulging belly would allow.

The Mages straightened and followed in orderly ranks until we reached the tower's base. I made to step aside, but Atikus gripped my elbow and urged me to continue my escort up the stone steps, where three ancients in billowing robes waited. When we reached the top step, it was Atikus's turn to bow.

The Elders echoed his respect.

The shuffling of feet behind us quieted. I glanced back to find every other Mage assembled in a semi-circle at perfectly spaced intervals. Each Mage's right arm was stretched forward, hand held upward, with a ball of white light hovering above their palm.

The withered Elder in the middle spoke in a voice magnified by magic.

"Brothers and Sisters of Magic, the Arch Mage has fallen. A new Guardian must now take his place. By the Light of the Phoenix, who here bears two or more lines of gold and offers to serve?"

No one stirred.

I peered over my shoulder to find every Mage frozen. The snapping of their robes and whistling of the brisk winter wind was the only sound in the courtyard. When I turned back, Atikus lifted his palm before him, and bright azure flame flared to life.

The elderly Mage bowed and stepped back.

The other two joined him.

The trio began chanting in the Mages' tongue, slow and rhythmic, almost soothing yet incomprehensible to my ears.

Tiny hairs on my arms rose as magical energy swelled from their incantation. I nearly fell backward when the Mages' words swelled, and the shimmering image of a woman appeared before them. A broad smile parted her lips when her dark eyes landed on Atikus.

Then her gaze settled on me, and her expression shifted.

Her smooth brow quirked in confusion, then recognition, and her eyes opened wide. She stared for only a heartbeat, a warm smile parting her lips, before returning her focus to Atikus and speaking in a clear, rich voice.

"I, Keeper of Magic, bring greetings and heartfelt wishes from the Phoenix herself."

An excited murmur rose from the Mages behind us at the woman's invocation of magic's most cherished symbol—and the savior of Saltstone's people. "For two hundred twenty-one years, Velius Quin led this guild with strength, honor, and integrity. His was a life of service and duty. His loss will be felt for generations."

I peered out of the side of one eye to find Atikus's eyes watering at the eulogy of his former leader and longtime friend.

"Now is the time for new beginnings." The woman's voice brightened. "Your beloved city rises from the ashes. Your people's spirit is renewed. So, too, must our guild. Tonight, we choose a new Arch Mage, and in doing so, take our first step into the future."

The Keeper made eye contact with the Mages closest to the steps, causing more than a few to retreat from her penetrating gaze.

"For over twelve hundred years, Arch Mages have been selected from among those bearing two or more bands of gold. To our knowledge, only three alive today carry this distinction: Mage Atikus Dani of Melucia, High Chancellor Danai Thorn of the Kingdom of Spires, and Declan Rea, the Heir of Magic and son of the Isle of Rea Utu." One corner of her mouth quirked as she spoke Declan's name. "High Chancellor Thorn fled the battlefield and has not been seen since. Declan Rea's path leads elsewhere. Mage Dani stands before you."

The Keeper raised one palm, and a ball of flame burst into existence. "Each Mage must now bond his or her vote with magic itself. If you support Mage Dani's ascension, cast your flame upward."

Atikus didn't turn to watch, but I couldn't help myself. My jaw dropped as every Mage around us raised their hands above their heads and released their flames into the night sky. No longer were there hundreds of blazing stars but one massive beacon that shimmered and sparked.

When all were aloft, the Keeper raised her own flame to join the others.

Her flame struck; the mass of magic flared and transformed into a brilliant outline of a Phoenix as tall as the tower itself. Its head reared toward the sky, and it released a cacophonous roar. It belched a stream of magical flame, then dove and disappeared into the vein of raw power that coursed below the tower's base.

The Keeper intoned, "Arch Mage Atikus Dani, turn and face your guild."

When Atikus turned, he must have noticed the dumbstruck expression plastered across my face, as he gave me a quick wink.

The Keeper raised her palm again. Flame leaped from her hand onto Atikus's chest. When it died away, a golden Phoenix emblazoned across his robe shone as brightly as any sun. The gold of the Phoenix flowed like the stripes on his collar and cuffs, and every Mage, including the three ancients who presided, dropped to their knees and bowed their heads.

Atikus, never one for ceremony—and ever quick with a quip—turned and whispered, "Give it to us Mages; we know how to put on a good show."

CHAPTER 7

JESS

I stumbled through the mirror and sprawled across the floor of the dimly lit catacombs. I tried to ease my fall but slipped and cracked my head against the stone. My heart pounded, and I struggled to gather my senses and clear my vision.

Keelan hadn't followed. Neither had Atikus.

I was alone.

As I caught my breath, I realized I was bracing my weight against a large slab of well-polished marble. A quick glance at the golden placard noted it as my great-great-grandfather's sarcophagus. I yanked my hand away and clutched it to my chest while my eyes darted about the room.

A mirror, the twin of the one I had fallen through back in the cave, loomed behind like some specter ready to pounce. When we saw the crypt from the other side, Atikus had suspected the pieces might be portals. My unintentional trip confirmed that theory, but, as I stared at the mirror on the Fontaine end of the journey, I saw only reflective glass.

"Why can I not see Atikus and Keelan in the cave?" I wondered, my words echoing in the lonely chamber.

The crypt felt familiar, but I had never liked the place. Its creepy magical torches cast far too many dancing shadows across the marble prisons of the dead. My father brought me down here when he wanted to impart some deep lesson about the weight of the Crown and our royal lineage. I knew I should revere the sacred ground, but it was hard to get past the idea of walking through rooms full of dead kings and queens who were likely more dust than flesh. To calm me, my father would point out the place where he would one day rest, then where I would follow. That only made my skin crawl more. What child wanted to think about where they would be interred?

I rose and brushed off my shirt and trousers, then took a tentative step. The flickering flames made no sound, released no smoke. In the stillness of the chamber, my thoughts boomed like thunder in my head.

Keelan tried to kill me.

I remembered the crazed look in his eyes as he held me with his blade plunging toward my throat. I knew that man was not the noble Guardsman I had come to know. Someone—*something*—had taken him over, commanded his actions. Still, knowing that truth could not douse the fear coursing through my veins. I tried replaying the moments before I Traveled to the crypt, tried making sense of what had happened.

I'd been sleeping.

Then Keelan loomed over me with wild eyes and a knife.

He had been talking to himself—or wrestling with himself—I could not tell. In the end, Atikus tried to pull the hulking man off of me but had been slammed into a wall for his effort. I hoped the kind old Mage was all right.

I had barely squeezed out of Keelan's grasp before he lunged across the room and pinned me against the shelving, his razor-sharp knifepoint quivering inches away. I could still see the torchlight glinting off his silver blade.

He struggled, fought against whatever, whoever, commanded him to act.

I wondered at the strength it took for him to resist the powerful Compulsion, especially for a man with such a passive Gift.

I was unsure how I ended up flying through the mirror, let alone why it had brought me *here*. I didn't remember breaking from his grasp, but somehow I had hurtled from inescapable death to the safety of a room full of dead royalty.

Had the whole episode not been terrifying, that irony would have made me laugh.

The crypt wasn't large, only a dozen chambers connected by a wide central walkway. Two bronze doors loomed at one end, opening into a room I couldn't remember ever visiting. At the other end, plain gray stone mirrored their golden counterparts. The walls were polished and held only golden plates memorializing ancient monarchs. As I approached the towering doors at the walkway's end, I looked to my right into the last grotto, the one that would soon allow my father his eternal rest.

My steps faltered, and I froze.

I stared into the empty, unlit space.

Its darkness mirrored my thoughts, as images of my father's face rose to the fore.

With all I had been through over the past few weeks, I had yet to grieve, or even focus on my father or brother—*or even my mother*—all of whom were lost to me now. Their faces fluttered before me.

My father's gentle smile.

My mother's glare.

My brother's playful smirk.

The last image stabbed into me more deeply than any blade ever could.

"Oh, Justin. Why did you have to be so stupid? Why did you . . ." A wave of long-pent emotion stole the words.

I hugged myself and stared into the darkness of Father's tomb.

As many times as I relished my personal space, my time without pestering servants or nattering nobles, I had never once felt isolated.

In that tomb, before the resting place of my father, surrounded by the remnants of my distant family, I felt alone.

My younger brother Kendall was all the family I had left, but he was only eleven. He would need me now, need me to be strong, need me to be his rock.

The people of Fontaine would need me—indeed, those of the entire Kingdom.

Then I remembered the looming war.

The entire continent needed me to succeed.

Me. A girl of seventeen. An orphan adrift in a chaotic world refusing to be ruled.

In the silence of the stone chamber, surrounded by the kings and queens of old, I grasped the weight of the Crown, *my Crown*, and I knew I must bear it alone.

Tears broke free, and I slumped to the floor.

A half hour later, I gathered myself, wiped streaks from my face, and stood. I reached for the wooden lever to open the doors, but a tiny voice in my head stilled my hand.

No one here knows I am Queen now. That means they do not know about Father, or Justin, or Mother . . . or the invasion. Will they believe me when I tell them? What if they do not want me as their Queen? Am I ready for this? Where do I even start?

Tears threatened again, but I sniffed them back and stiffened my spine.

I am Queen *now. I cannot act like a scared little rabbit. What would Father do?*

I thought back to the endless hours I'd sat in Council with my father listening to men droning on about taxes or land, farming or Constables, fishing rights or disputed ducal decrees, or a thousand other tedious topics thrust before the King. I tried paying attention, but most of it felt so distant from anything I might need as a teenager. And yet, here I was at seventeen—the Queen.

"Father always said to surround yourself with wise men and listen to their guidance. I might have to amend that to include some wise women, too," I mused. "At least this gives me a place to start so I don't look completely lost. Start with the Council."

I looked down at my rumpled riding clothes and shook my head, then ran a hand through my tangled mess of hair. I sniffed the grime left on my fingers and winced. It had been weeks since I'd bathed, and there was no way I would look—or smell—like a queen until I had a proper bath and a change of clothes.

My steely eyes and upturned chin would have to do.

My father always told me those were more powerful tools than the crown, though I never understood the comment until now.

Without fretting further, I pulled the wooden lever and listened as powerful mechanisms began to creak. A sliver of sunlight grew into a flood as the doors opened.

"What the—" I heard from someone outside.

I couldn't suppress a chuckle as a startled cleric, bent with age, stumbled backward.

"Father, I have risen," I blurted, aware of the implications of my words, considering I stood in the doorway to the tomb of kings looking like a bedraggled corpse recently laid to rest.

The man's eyes widened, and he tripped, landing on his backside. He tried to speak, but his words were more jumbled than his tangled feet, and I was fairly certain the man's eyes would pop out of their sockets if they widened any further.

I bit back a laugh and regained my composure. "Forgive me, Father. I didn't mean . . . Oh, never mind. Escort me to the Palace."

"Of course, Princess . . . Your Highness. Right away, Highness," he stammered as he struggled to his feet.

CHAPTER 8

JESS

As the priest's cart approached the Palace gate, a bored-looking guard in the nearby shack did a double take, then snapped to attention.

"Highness, welcome back. We didn't know you'd returned from your, um . . . journey," the man said, his eyes never leaving some distant point beyond the horizon. I might've been a teenage princess, but the guards knew better than to make eye contact unless it was necessary.

"It is all right, William," I said, placing a hand on his arm. "Would you have the Chancellor's office assemble the Privy Council? I need to speak with them in an hour."

The guard's eyes shot to my hand, his brow rising nearly to his hairline.

I couldn't remember *ever* using any of the guards' names before. I rarely acknowledged their existence, much less was kind or considerate to them. I heard the men often joked about how I'd been raised by the Palace staff but refused to lower myself to learn even their names. My father tried to teach me the value of our people—if I'd only listened sooner.

I will have to work on that if I am to become the Queen I always envisioned as a girl.

"Um, Your Highness—"

"William," I said in a soothing tone. "I know it is an unusual request, but please humor me. I will explain everything to the Council."

I turned back to the dumbfounded cleric before William could reply. "Thank you, Father. I do not think I could have made such a long walk tonight without your steadfast company."

The priest bowed. I could feel his eyes on my back as I lifted my chin and strode into the Palace grounds.

By the time I reached my chamber, the Palace was abuzz with speculation regarding my unorthodox Council summons. One of my maids greeted me at my chamber door. "I had a hot bath prepared as soon as I heard you'd returned, Highness. Will you want your ladies to help you bathe and dress?"

I placed a hand on her shoulder. "Thank you, Tena. I will be fine on my own tonight. Would you ask the kitchen to make refreshments for the Council in the Throne Room? We will be meeting in an hour."

A broad smile burst across the woman's face as she curtsied again and scurried off.

I closed the door and slumped to the floor.

In that moment, safe in my own chambers and alone with my thoughts, the thousand emotions I had kept at bay bubbled to the surface. Losing my father, brother . . . and even my mother. The terror of facing a knife's edge . . . in the hand of a man I trusted. The weight of the crown I now wore . . . or soon would wear.

It was all too much.

How was anyone supposed to face so much?

How was I supposed to bear . . . everything?

My head dropped into my hands, and my chest began to heave.

"Enough," I chided myself, swatting at pesky tears that streaked the grime on my face and rising to my feet. "It is past time I cleaned myself and became the Queen my father taught me to be."

I unlaced my boots and tossed them aside, then wandered to the bath the staff must have drawn the moment they learned I was headed their way.

The water was now tepid, but the lavender oils relaxed my mind as rich soap melted the dusty road from my skin. I could have soaked in that water for hours, had a banging on my door not drawn me out of my relaxation.

"I need a moment," I called.

"Yes, Highness. We will wait outside."

Reluctantly, I toweled off and threw on a simple gown, determined to be seen for my words and actions rather than the Palace's finery. I had to earn respect from the men of the Council, and seeing me as more than a churlish, fashion-obsessed girl was a start.

Or so I told myself.

Two green-and-gold-liveried servants waited outside my chamber. They led me through the Palace halls and opened the double doors to the audience chamber, lowering their heads as I stepped past.

I entered to the side of the thrones and walked toward the Council table where the Ministers were assembled—at least those who remained in the capital while the Kingdom pursued its war in the east. Only four of the eight Privy Councilors stood behind their high-back chairs awaiting my arrival, representing Trade, Foreign Affairs, Justice, and the Crown's Treasury. Notably absent

were High Chancellor Thorn, Minister of War
Bril, High Sheriff Wilfred, and General Marks.

At the far end of the table, a tall, thin man I
didn't recognize stood; his long blue robes lined
with one band of gold rustled as he bowed. The
other men had their backs to the door and startled
at the man's sudden gesture, turning and offering
their own respects.

I approached the table and rested a hand on
the chair at its head, desperate to keep it from
quivering beneath a hornet's nest of nerves that
threatened my stomach and chest.

"Thank you for coming so quickly, gentlemen. A
lot has happened . . . is happening . . . in the east,
and I do not know . . . I am unsure . . . how much
news made it back to the capital." I took a deep
breath and pulled the chair back to sit but found
myself unable to take my seat while everyone else
stood glaring.

Foreign Minister Bacras cleared his throat as he
took his own seat. "Highness, why don't you start
with why *you* called us here. It is most unusual for
. . . well . . ."

"For a Princess to call the Council into session?"
I finished his thought.

Bacras nodded, his lips pursed.

Treasurer Dask crossed his arms and frowned, clearly disgruntled by the presumption in the Princess's summons. He had yet to sit.

I nodded and sucked in another deep breath. These men had never made me nervous before. Why did my heart feel like Dittler's hooves pounding against my chest?

"My father . . . the King . . . he is dead."

Dask dropped into his chair while the others stared open-mouthed at the teenager before them.

No one spoke.

I had no clue what I expected, how I thought they might react. Shouts? Insults? Talking over each other, perhaps a few tears shed for my fallen father?

Astonished silence was not high on my list, but the sound of men breathing . . . trying not to be heard breathing . . . filled the hall.

I looked from one face to the next and fought the urge to bolt from the room.

The men's eyes said it all.

They didn't want *me* on the throne.

In fact, I thought a thread of *fear* ran through their expressions. I decided to take Atikus's advice and play to their paternal instincts.

"No one feels this loss more than I do. It has been weeks since his passing, but it feels like yesterday."

"Weeks?" Dask exclaimed. "How are we just hearing of this? Why was no messenger sent to inform this Council?"

I sat in the High Chancellor's seat at the head of the table and stared into the glossy wood surface.

"After my mother killed the King—"

"Spirits, no!" Minister Carver said before covering his mouth with the ridiculous lace handkerchief he carried everywhere.

The tears I held at bay broke free and trailed down my cheeks. I blinked to clear my vision. My eyes drifted to my hands for what felt like forever, then I looked up.

"Gentlemen, please sit? There is much we need to discuss."

As the final Councilors took their seats, I glanced at the Mage at the table's opposite end. "Sir, please introduce yourself. I do not know you."

The man bowed again. "Your Highne—forgive me—*Your Majesty*, I am Dane Ernest. Since the High Chancellor is in the east with our troops, Minister Bacras thought it would be helpful to have another Mage offer counsel to the Throne."

This was the first time anyone had addressed me by the monarchical title. A surge of nervous energy tickled its way up my spine. *This will take getting used to.*

Then the Mage's mention of the High Chancellor sank in.

I pursed my lips.

Was this another snake like Thorn? Were all Mages? Atikus was a Mage and a good man, but he was Melucian. Did any good men remain within the Kingdom's borders? At least, did any good men in blue robes?

I knew the other men at the table, but should I trust this one? I didn't trust any of my father's Councilors, other than Uncle Ethan, but they were not unfamiliar to me. This Mage was a new variable in an ever-changing landscape.

Before I could speak, Minister Bacras leaned toward me and whispered, "Majesty, he's a good man. Not one of Thorn's, if that's what you're thinking."

"How did you—?" Of course he knew how I felt about Thorn. It was no secret. The entire Palace knew I loathed the little weasel. He barely entered a room before a scowl marred my face. The other Ministers had witnessed my reaction to Thorn's smooth talk at hundreds of Council meetings.

I will have to be more careful about how I let others see my true feelings moving forward . . . about everyone. Did Father struggle to steel himself every moment of every day? Would the Crown always feel so . . . burdensome?

I nodded once to the Mage, and the man took a seat.

A moment of silence hung in the air as the men waited for their Queen to address them. I eyed each man before beginning the speech I rehearsed a dozen times.

"My Lords, the King is dead. Prince Justin is dead. My mother, the *former* Queen, killed them both in an attempt to take the crown for herself. Even now, she leads *our* troops in an unjust war against our Melucian neighbors—all in the name of justice for my kidnapping. We have incontrovertible evidence *she* was behind my kidnapping and attempted murder as well."

I watched shock flood into my advisors anew. To their credit, none spoke.

The massive chamber held its breath.

Each statement sounded more outlandish and devastating than the last, yet the truth was plain when spoken aloud. Their entire world had changed.

"The Children, that ancient cult based in the village of Irina's Seat, were responsible for the Gifted kidnappings that plagued both our nation *and* Melucia. They kidnapped me on my mother's orders and would have sacrificed my life on the altar of their evil schemes if not for the bravery of our soldiers and . . . others." My voice broke. "Prince Justin . . . my brother was lost during my rescue."

I steeled myself before my grief could take control. This was no time to show weakness.

"That is everything I knew before fleeing my mother's men. Your turn, gentlemen."

Still, no one spoke.

They stared at me, as if trying to absorb this news.

In that moment, an odd sensation tickled the back of my neck, and a familiar voice whispered in my head, *"Jess, it's Atikus . . ."*

CHAPTER 9

JESS

"Your Majesty, are you all right?"

I held up a hand to silence Dask as the Councilors exchanged confused glances.

"Jess, it's Atikus." The Mage's baritone thrummed in my head. *"Much has happened since we parted ways. Keelan is headed back to the cave with Dittler and can fill you in on the details. He should arrive in two weeks, possibly a day or two less.*

"The Kingdom army besieged Saltstone. Your mother sent her armies to hunt the citizens of the capital who fled east with orders to slaughter every man, woman, and child. The Phoenix returned and struck down the Kingdom's army. The Phoenix struck your mother down as well. Many died, but we estimate several thousand survived and are fleeing back toward the border. Saltstone is in ruins, but the people survived and now work to rebuild.

"*I can only maintain this link a moment longer, so two important things: First, don't blame your mother. Her consciousness was possessed by the Spirit of Empress Irina. I don't believe she acted of her own free will. And second, please meet Keelan in the cave. Irina's voice is no longer a threat to him—or you. He carries vital information for both our countries and is most eager to see you again.*"

My brows furrowed at the last statement, and I thought I could hear Atikus grinning through the Telepathic link as he spoke. I started to turn back to the Council, each of whom now stared with undisguised concern, but Atikus spoke again.

"*Jess, it was an honor to escort you for a time. You are a strong, brilliant young woman and will make a fine Queen. Believe in yourself and trust your heart. Both the Kingdom and Melucia count on you to be wise and true. When the time is right, we should meet to discuss how we might repair the damage done between our two nations. Until then, Spirits guide you, Your Majesty.*"

When Atikus's voice stilled, I stared across the table at Mage Ernest. "Mage Atikus Dani sends his regards."

The table erupted in a flurry of gasps and questions.

"Gentlemen, please." I waved them to silence, then summarized what Atikus had said, leaving out the part where I was supposed to leave the capital to meet Keelan.

Spirits, how did my tale become so strange?

"Did he mention the fate of Marks, Bril, or Thorn?" Bacras asked.

I shook my head. "No. He said I'd learn more soon but sounded exhausted by the end of the message."

"It is remarkable he was able to send a Telepathic message that far at all. He must hold a powerful Gift," Mage Ernest said more to himself than the others around the table.

"Did you say the spirit of Empress Irina returned and inhabited *your mother*?" Minister Carver asked, incredulity punctuating his tone.

I had to gird myself before answering. "That is what he said. It fits with the ceremony my mother performed in the Children's Temple. Queen Isabel was willing to kill her husband and both of her children. We did not understand their goal at the time, but returning the Empress makes as much sense as anything."

An uneasy silence hung in the air for a long moment before Mage Ernest spoke.

"Majesty, we must turn our attention to the needs of your people. No doubt we lost many fathers and sons in the campaign across the border."

The sincerity in the Mage's voice caught me by surprise.

"Where do we even begin?" I muttered, the shell of my feigned confidence cracking before the daunting task of rebuilding a nation.

Dask leaned forward and placed a hand on mine, violating one of the most cherished courtly protocols by touching the monarch and earning more than a few glances from the others. "Jess . . . Your Majesty . . . your Council has far too many empty seats. Those sitting here cannot hope to repair the damage done without help. We need to rebuild this Council before we try to rebuild the Kingdom."

I looked around the table as Dask's hand retreated. The others were nodding their agreement.

"Fine. But I will not abandon General Marks or Minister Bril. They may yet live."

"Majesty, forgive me, but General Marks and Minister Bril *took part* in the invasion. Is it wise to return them to the Council?" Foreign Minister Bacras asked, his eyebrows furrowed.

I was about to snap at the man and defend Uncle Ethan, but Ernest spoke first. "Minister, many followed the orders of their King and Queen. We may yet learn how they behaved honorably in the face of an impossible situation. Her Majesty is right to spare judgement until all the facts are known, especially for men who have served this Kingdom for decades."

Bacras opened his mouth, as if to argue, but remained silent.

I leaned forward. "Minister of War and General of Armed Forces can wait for now. Thorn *will not* be my High Chancellor, so that is a good place to start. What other roles need filling?"

And so we began.

Names of nobles brought nods, jeers, and jabs as the Kingdom's inner circle began forming a new government. For a few glorious moments, I forgot my fears and threw myself into the task at hand. Hours later, I noticed Minister Bacras staring openly at me, a broad grin spread across his usually placid face.

"Zumi, you look like you ate something odd. Out with it."

The man laughed, a rich sound that felt like a blazing hearth on a winter's day. "I was just enjoying watching Her Majesty work. She has amazed this skeptical old man and might just renew his weary spirit."

I blushed at the compliment, then remembered myself and offered a nod of thanks.

Hours later, I made my way through the private passages within the Palace, headed toward my chamber. The day had been challenging, frightening, exhilarating, and a dozen other emotions I would likely relive in the midst of deep sleep.

All my life, I wanted to be taken seriously, to be seen as a competent, intelligent woman who would rule with wisdom. I couldn't admit it at the time, but the derision—even pity—I'd seen in the Councilors' eyes months earlier had stabbed at my heart.

But not now.

They actually *listened* to me.

I tried to remember the endless lessons of my father, allowing the Ministers to talk themselves to exhaustion before weighing in. He told me many times that educated men needed to make their point long before they would ever hear ours. To act otherwise was fruitless.

I grinned inwardly every time the conversation would lull. I spoke only then. All eyes snapped to the head of the table, as if mine was the most important voice in the room.

And then it sank in.

Mine *was* the most important voice in the room. I was *Queen*.

Events had moved so quickly since I returned that I barely had time to absorb the weight of the Crown I'd inherited. I felt it now. Its burdensome load. Its expectations. The millions of people it represented. Alone in a dim hallway, the immense responsibility that rested on my seventeen-year-old shoulders bore down. I feared I might crumble beneath its weight.

My skin turned clammy, and my heart raced.

I clawed at the choker strangling my neck, gasping, but air wouldn't flow.

Sweat beaded on my brow.

Desperate to gather myself, I slipped into the first room I saw. As I closed the heavy wooden door behind me, I turned and found myself staring at Justin's bed. My mother had barred servants from cleaning her children's rooms to teach us responsibility, and several pairs of riding leathers still lay strewn about, as if he struggled to decide what to pack before leaving on the trip east with the army.

The trip to find *me* after I ran away.

My heart seized. Tears streamed down my cheeks. The scent of my younger brother flooded my senses.

I saw his lopsided grin, his perfectly coiffed hair that screamed for fingers to muss it.

I missed him so much.

"Little brother, what have I done? How am I going to get through all this without you?" I whispered. "So many people are counting on me now. I'm . . . so alone."

I hugged myself, clutching my sides as tears fell.

Long moments passed before I wandered aimlessly around the room. I raised a white linen shirt to my nose, breathing in Justin's scent, then clutched the garment to my heart. My fingers trailed across his desk as I found notes from his studies covered in random scribbles and tidbits he aimed to remember. The script adorning those pages had somehow become precious in his absence.

I reached to open an armoire, but a knock at the door interrupted.

"Jess? Are you in there, Jess?" the voice of my other brother—my *only* brother—floated through the door.

I sniffed and wiped my face with Justin's shirt before realizing what I'd done, then clutched it to my chest once more.

"Yes." I sucked in a calming breath. "Come in."

Kendall pushed the door open, then bolted across the room and wrapped his spindly arms around me. "I missed you, Jessie. I'm glad you're home."

"Me too," was all I could say as I fought another wave of emotion.

A moment later, Kendall looked up and asked, "When do you think Mom, Dad, and Justin will get back? They've been gone a long time."

My voice caught as I realized no one had told the boy anything.

I pulled away from his hug and took his hand, leading him to sit on the bed beside me.

"Kendall," I began, grasping for the words. "I . . . I need to tell you some things. They are going to be really hard, so I need you to be brave, okay?"

Kendall's wide eyes, now tinged with fear, bobbed along with his head.

I struggled with how to tell an eleven-year-old such a grim tale but decided he deserved the truth. I began with my running away with Danym and our harrowing escape through the Spires. To his credit, Kendall listened and maintained a firm grip on his emotions—until I reached the part about the deaths of our father and brother. It broke my barely mended heart as I watched my young brother's grief bloom across his face. I held him and tried to calm his quaking shoulders. His tears were infectious, and we held each other and wept until my maid knocked.

"Hello? Majesty, are you in there?"

How do they always know where I am? I thought as I rose, smoothed my gown, and walked to the door.

"What is it, Sarah?" I called, suppressing the tremor in my voice.

"Cook says a meal is prepared in the family room. Will you and the Prince be dining?"

I stroked Kendall's hair as he shook, then kissed his forehead.

"We will be right out. Thank you, Sarah."

There was a brief pause, then, "Of course, Majesty. Whatever you . . . and the Prince need."

The sympathy in my maid's voice nearly broke my brittle resolve, and I realized how challenging the coming days would be—and not just for those who lost family. The Palace staff worshiped my father, and my brother, Justin, was more beloved than any of us. Beyond that, many fathers and brothers were lost in my mother's foolish campaign. Did Sarah have men in the army? Did my guards or cook or . . .

The staff would hide behind the mask of propriety, but their hearts would bleed for our Kingdom's losses, for *their* losses, as deeply as mine.

As we settled into the private family dining room, I insisted Sarah join us. The idea of a maid sitting with the monarch at the family's table frightened the poor woman to death; we were halfway through the second course before Sarah stopped shaking and began enjoying her meal.

Kendall refused to eat, claiming he wasn't hungry, and begged to be left alone in his room.

For my part, I was glad for their company, such that it was. I could not bear to face the empty chairs around our family's table alone.

CHAPTER 10

ATIKUS

Weeks had passed since I watched Keelan ride into the distance as he headed toward the cave. I longed to hear word of his journey, hoping that Jess would receive him well and the rift between our two nations could begin to heal. I knew it would take time, but the months following the Siege of Saltstone would be critical in ensuring people's faith that peace was possible. Without positive action, fear and animosity would cement into irreparable hatred.

The new Arch Mage's robe, emblazoned with a living, swirling image of the Phoenix on my chest, rustled as I strode toward the audience chamber. I paused to examine busts of prior members of the Triad and artwork depicting Melucia's vast countryside. A thrill tingled up my spine as the weight of destiny settled onto my shoulders. I was now one of a small few who would shape the future of my country.

Since my ascension to Arch Mage, I had barely paused to ponder how my name and actions would be scrawled in history's tomes. Now though, the immensity of my new role consumed my thoughts.

The last statue before reaching the grand oak doors to the audience chamber was of Melucia's first Arch Mage, Elena Greiga. Her majestic gaze scanned high and far, her slender neck leading to a sharp chin and square jaw. The artist somehow captured a depth of compassion and wisdom in her eyes. Surely, this was some work of magic. It stole my breath.

"Is it getting to you?" a deep voice rumbled from behind, snapping me from my daze.

I turned to find Captain-Commander Dev Albius a few feet away, quietly observing.

"And so it begins." I smiled, then turned and strode into the audience chamber where the new Merchants' Guildmaster and the Eye awaited our presence. Albius grunted and followed.

Hours later, the newly minted Triad adjourned our first session.

We barely scratched the surface of the impossible task of rebuilding the capital and repairing the damage to our nation. While Grove's Pass and Saltstone endured the brunt of the Kingdom's attacks, many port cities faced naval blockades. A few lost ports to bombardment. Much of our merchant fleet had also been destroyed, crippling a significant portion of our nation's ability to move goods. The Melucian military, such that it was, had also been devastated, and the Rangers now numbered less than a tenth of their original force. The Captain-Commander replacing the traditional role of the Armsmen's Guildmaster among the Triad was further testament to the sorry state of our armed forces.

Then there were simpler, yet somehow weightier matters—the people of Melucia who had suffered the incalculable loss of fathers, sons, mothers, and daughters. An entire generation of men had been wiped out by Irina's flames and armies.

The returning women, children, and elderly faced lonely gaps that could never be filled, but it felt good to begin to rebuild, even if it was a humble beginning.

I grasped forearms with Albius, and we smiled at our newly shared sense of purpose. Beatrice, our new Merchants' Guildmaster, stepped between us, gripping each of our forearms and pulling them apart. Her next move shocked us further, as she pulled us forward and embraced us awkwardly.

"We've got a lot of work to do, but I'm glad to be doing it with you two. I'll do my best to keep the petty politics of the Merchants at bay so we can move things forward."

I noticed Albius's wide eyes and winked at the Commander. "Dev, I believe she may match you on backbone. You might want to watch yourself."

I chuckled and looked down at Beatrice with affection. She slapped me on the chest. "Don't you get all comfortable, Atikus Dani. It's *my* people who make the food, and I've seen how *you* like to eat. You'd better behave if you know what's good for you."

A rough bark of a laugh slipped from Albius as I feigned offense. "My dear lady, I am shocked you would threaten an old man's hunger."

The embrace broke apart with a sense of relief at our burgeoning camaraderie. I had turned back to my seat to gather my notes when a wave of dizziness caused me to stagger, then collapse onto the cold stone before my chair.

The others raced to my side.

"Atikus, are you all right? What happened?" Beatrice asked with alarm.

I could barely hear her. My head swam, and my eyes turned glassy.

In my mind, a shrill voice echoed. *"You may have won the day, but you will not defeat me. I claim you, Mage Atikus Dani. You are my Vessel now."*

My eyes widened, and I gasped, struggling to breathe.

My hands flew to my head, as if pressure would stop the presence from devouring my self-control. When that did nothing to help, I reached within myself and seized my Light. A brilliant flame exploded through me as I unleashed its raw power.

Irina's spirit screamed an otherworldly wail, and I felt her writhing within my skull.

The pressure began to ease, and I laid my head back to gather myself, but Irina's spirit redoubled her effort.

Searing pain lashed my weary mind.

Tendrils of malice slammed against my brain, probing for weakness.

My mental shield held, but only just. Sweat poured down my face.

"Atikus, can you hear me? Please, open your eyes," Beatrice shouted.

But the battle raged within.

I dared not spare a moment lest my attacker gain advantage.

Wave after wave hammered my protections.

I'd been caught by surprise and was unable to turn the fight. It was only a matter of time before Irina wormed her way inside.

My strength faded. My magic dwindled. Hers only grew.

How is she capable of such power without a connection to the world of life?

Irina's laughter echoed through my consciousness. *"You always were a dense old fool. You are my connection now. I have access to your reserves and your link to the currents. I will never tire, so you may as well relent. Be my Vessel willingly, and I will allow a sliver of your consciousness to survive."*

"NO!" I screamed aloud.

"I was hoping you'd say that."

Irina narrowed her focus into a single nee-dle-sharp point, then rammed her will into my shield with all her strength.

It was all too much.

Her presence flooded through, consuming my individuality and sense of self. The mighty Mage whose mind could forget nothing cowered in the face of Irina's ravenous desires. She dove into the recesses of my memories, searching, clawing—until she found a hidden remnant that shocked her into stillness.

In that moment of respite, I drew into myself and gathered the last vestige of my power. Sensing my end, I held nothing back, hurling all that remained of my waning strength at the spirit.

She did not raise her own defenses, and my magic bore into her, a wave crashing against a rocky shore.

Irina's balance wavered, then her strength faltered. Her spirit was flung from my mind, and I braced myself, walling off my mind with the last of my power.

But Irina's spirit fled.

I fell across the chamber's floor, my shimmering robes spread like spilled blood.

I reached toward the Eye, but my vision clouded as darkness consumed me.

CHAPTER 11

AYDEN

D eclan held me all night as we slept, his fingers twining in my hair and massaging my scalp. I could have lain like that forever, damn the world and its troubles.

The next morning, we returned through the gate to the cavern in the Melucian mountains.

I was still disoriented from Traveling, bracing myself against the Melucian gate, when Declan's whole body stiffened and his eyes grew wide.

"What is it?" I wobbled to where he stood.

"It's Atikus," he said, sudden urgency filling his eyes and voice. "He's in trouble."

I watched in silence as Declan stared into the nothingness of the rough-hewn walls, feeling about as useful as a broken bolt.

"I have to get to Saltstone."

"What happened?"

Declan paced before the gate. "I couldn't tell. He reached out, and I could sense he was in pain or fighting someone, something like that, but he couldn't really speak. He said something about 'her spirit' and 'inside my head.' I think that's what he said."

"That is not ominous at all." Sarcasm dripped from my lips.

Declan nodded, still staring as he sorted through whatever Atikus had told him. Before I could sit and pour some of the ever-present wine, Declan gripped my shoulder and squeezed his eyes shut.

Nothing happened.

His eyes opened, and he flinched.

"Dammit. I still can't Travel."

"Try it without me."

Declan's head cocked to the side, then he stepped back and concentrated.

Still nothing.

"It's not working," he groused. "We'll have to hike down and find horses. There are messenger waystations between here and the capital where we can get fresh horses. If we push—"

"It will still take nearly a month."

Declan fell into a chair and pressed his palms to his temples.

"What am I supposed to do? I have all this power, and I'm stuck here in a cave unable to help."

"Whatever is happening, Atikus will have to face it on his own. He is strong, much stronger than most think." I sat beside him.

"What if my mother could help?"

"Your mother?" My brows furrowed. "The same mother who left you when you were little?"

Declan's eyes widened. A heartbeat later, he shook his head and squeezed them shut again.

"Sorry, I just meant . . . what if the people I met on the island could help?"

"You still haven't told me much about them—or your time there—but sure, if you think they have magic that could get you to Atikus, why not try?"

He stared at me so long I started to squirm in my chair.

"Are you okay, Dec?"

"Fine. I'm fine." He stood and began pacing and muttering to himself. "I should go back through the gate. That makes sense. If she can help . . . Yeah, that's what I need to do."

I watched but said nothing. Discussions of magic and power still made me feel as useless as a dry inkwell. They also underscored just how different we were, how different our paths would become. Spirits, we already walked different paths.

Declan turned and started, as if remembering I sat there with him.

"You should go to Saltstone, help with the rebuilding effort."

And there it was. I could not help him in his magical mission, so he would send me away to work on something a Mute could handle. A bitter taste filled my mouth, and I bit back a sharp retort.

None of this was Declan's fault.

It wasn't fair to lay it at his feet. Still, I could not help but wonder if this was a preview of our lives together: me stuck shoveling shit while he and the Gifted handled more important matters.

I swallowed back the rising bile.

"And you will join me when you can?"

"I will follow you to the ends of the world, Ayden Byrne." He closed the gap between us before I could blink. His lips were warm against mine, and I felt the shroud on my heart lift, if only a little. "I have to go. There's no time to waste."

Before I could hug him or kiss him back . . . or even say goodbye . . . he leaped through the gate and vanished.

For the second time in only a handful of days, I stared into space and wondered at my place in the world, at my place by Declan's side.

Atikus was in trouble.

Irina's spirit roamed the continent.

Declan was needed, now more than ever.

And I sat there, useless, unable to do a damn thing to help him or anyone else.

I filled a glass and sucked it down. The wine revived my body and mind but did little to relieve my sour mood. I doubted there was a magic powerful enough to lessen the sting of what I felt in that moment.

My elbows found the tabletop as my face fell into my palms.

"How long will he keep doing this?" I asked the empty air of the cavern. "How long will Dec want to be with someone who cannot even stand at his back as he fights? Someone who wields no power stronger than a bow or axe? I am no better than a common soldier—and most of them have a fucking Gift."

I refilled my glass.

By the time I finished my fifth glass, I remembered that the magical wine didn't cause drunkenness.

"Great. I cannot even get myself properly smashed. I really am fucking useless."

I hurled the glass into the wall.

It tinkled to the floor, unmarred and mocking my fecklessness.

"Saltstone," I mused. "A month on the road traveling to a city where I will be just as useless as I am sitting in this cave."

I knew Declan's first thought was of rebuilding our home. My father and mother had both survived the battle. Our estate had also survived. I could return and find work with the Guard or other groups helping to repair the Kingdom army's damage.

But I would still only be one pair of hands.

There had to be something better for me to do, some greater purpose. If Declan could save the world, I could at least try to save one tiny corner of it.

But where? What corner needed me? In what corner could I do the most good?

I glanced down at the wine glass still wobbling about on the floor, and something on my boot caught my eye. I reached down and brushed brambles off the leather. The stylized owl pinned to every Ranger's boot shone up at me.

And I knew my path forward.

CHAPTER 12

ATIKUS

I stand on the shore of a massive river of the purest cerulean waters.

Immense power wafts up as mist tingles against my skin.

Currents crash against unseen rocks buried beneath.

Where there should be the briny scent of life, there is naught but crisp, cool air.

The river is mute as its frothy indignation passes without voice.

Curious, I kneel.

Tendrils of translucent mist reach up and entwine my fingers as I hold them above the flow. My eyes widen as the mist creeps up my hand, yet I feel no pain, only the tingle, almost a tickle, of magic's gentle touch.

Emboldened, I extend my hand toward the river's flow and allow the tip of one finger to breach its surface.

T he world flared with brilliant light.

My head swivels as I now stand on a mountain's peak.

The horizon burns with hues of red, orange, and gold atop an endless bed of forest greens. The fresh scent of pine fills the air. Crisp autumn wind pimples my skin.

The vision's transition left me disoriented, yet the sight of such an awe-inspiring sunset still brought a smile to my lips.

A moment passes as I watch the sun's rays surrender to the horizon with evening's first touch. Something dark disturbs the view many leagues to the west.

I squint.

Rank upon rank of heavily armored men ride astride equally armed horses. At the head of the columns, I see a man—no, a woman—wearing a brilliant crown. She clutches a silver staff in her right hand and points forward with her left.

Irina?

Where . . . No, when?

The world flashed with brilliance again, and I struggled to gain my bearings.

I stand in the center of a large city.

Men and women race in all directions as screams of terror flee their lips. I call out, but no one hears my cries. I am nothing more than an invisible witness to history.

My head swims.

Charred rubble from nearby buildings litters the cobbled stones of a thoroughfare. I scan the area to find few structures untouched by fire and destruction. Bodies lie unmoving among the stones.

Bells begin to toll, slowly at first, then urgently.

My gaze rises above the din, and I recognize the gleaming turrets of the Palace of Spires, the heart of the Kingdom in its capital of Fontaine. Smoke rises from watchtowers—not the warm, curling smoke of their hearth, but the angry plumes of unwelcome intruders.

I stumble a few steps, then run toward the Palace.

I round the corner of a stately manor, and the Palace bursts into view.

I skid to a stop as my mind again struggles to process what my eyes witness.

Soldiers in green-and-gold livery lie scattered and broken before ornate iron gates. In their place, men in brown robes, each holding a heavy cudgel, stand vigil. They scan the street before them, ready to strike, but none appear to notice the Mage striding toward them.

I am invisible still.

I reach the first of the fallen Palace Guard and peer down.

The smell of waste and bile assaults my senses.

I stumble back.

A man's throat bears vicious lines, as if rent by massive claws. His arm lies a few paces away.

He's been ripped apart.

I move to the next guard and find similar wounds. Some wild beast has devastated the ranks of the royal elite.

How was this even possible?

I glance up and realize I now stand face-to-face with one of the robed figures. Human eyes glare from behind the mask of death. To my surprise, those eyes hold no anger or enmity, only emptiness. Fear races through my chest, yet the hollow eyes cannot see me.

I take another step toward the gate.

The world flashed again.

When my vision clears, I find myself in the royal audience chamber, paces from the Throne of Spires. Jess stares out, the sunset auburn of her hair trailing across

*one shoulder of her pristine, snowy gown.
A trail of blood trickles from her nose,
and her eyes bear the glassy stare of one
departed.*

*The bulky form of a man in blue lies on the
bottom step of the dais before her.*

"NO!" I scream.

I fall to my knees before Keelan's unmoving form.

*It is impossible to tell how long I hover
over my adopted son's body before the scuffling of boots on marble turns my head.*

*Again, what I see threatens to overwhelm
my mind.*

Five beasts stand in a line before the •
chamber's massive bronze doors: a horse, a
wolf, a bird of prey, a bear, and a mastiff.

Blood drips from fangs and claws.

Each stares directly at me.

They see me.

The world flared again.

I stand on the Eye in the Chamber of the
Triad.

Tendrils of terror lace into my chest with
white-hot rage.

I try to raise a shield, but it is too late—insidious barbs bury deep within my spirit. I feel their hunger, their hatred. I scream in pain as something precious rips from my soul.

Then I hear a voice.

It is a whisper but compelling all the same.

"Atikus, it is Órla. Follow my voice."

PART II

CHAPTER 13

DECLAN

I stood a few dozen paces below the Keeper's cottage and let my eyes roam the landscape.

The day was bright and cloudless, and the tangy ocean breeze tickled my nose. Lush palms dotted the sandy shoals, while squat plants with broad leaves spread lazily across the ground. Gulls called in the distance.

The ocean could be seen from most places on the island, but from halfway up one of its peaks, the undulating carpet of blues and greens and brushstrokes of glittering white stole my breath. I couldn't imagine a more tranquil place in all the world.

And then I heard the scream.

Piercing, anguished, and clearly my mother's cry.

I dropped the pack I had slung over my shoulder and sprinted back into the cave.

"Mother!" I yelled as I raced through the Phoenix-hewn halls.

I found her a few dozen paces inside where we had parted. She sat on the cold ground, her back leaned against the cavern wall. Tears marred her ageless face, and she stared at the wall opposite into nothing.

I squatted, gripped her by the shoulders, and shook her. "Mother, are you all right? What happened?"

She looked up with a hollowness in her gaze. "It is Atikus. His spirit is weak, so faint I can barely sense him."

"Is he alive? How weak?" Then I realized what she'd just said. "Wait, you can *sense* Atikus's spirit?"

What other powers had she never mentioned?

Kelså nodded. "Something has happened. He was attacked. I do not understand how or by whom, but this was not a physical assault. It was magical. He is still alive, but his connection to the currents . . . Atikus has been *severed* from magic."

I ran a hand through my hair and slumped to sit beside her. "But he's the Arch Mage. How could someone—"

"I do not know, but I do not think he was the first to be attacked. I sensed something days ago.

It was unlike anything I have felt before. It made no sense. I do not even know how to describe it—a stabbing? That does not sound right, but it is how it felt, like someone stabbing into the currents."

"When?"

"A day or two ago. I thought little of it at the time because it happened so quickly and then was gone."

She began to stand, bracing herself with one hand against the wall, but I shot to my feet and gripped her by the elbow.

She looked up, her brow knitted with concern. "I know you want to get back to the mainland, but I would appreciate you staying a few more days. Atikus may need help we can only give him at the Well."

"Of course." I nodded. "I'll stay as long as you need me."

We made our way to the cliff's ledge, where the stone circles and magical wine awaited. The latter soothed our frayed nerves and energized our minds while the former focused our conversation.

"If Keelan were here, he would start with, 'What do we know?' He'd make us lay out everything we are certain about, then go from there."

"He is quite the investigator, is he not?" Kelså offered a tight smile.

"The best. At least, that's what they say."

"All right, what do we know?" she parroted.

"First, there was an attack of some sort days before the one on Atikus. Second, Atikus suffered an attack you say felt similar to the first one. Only this one was powerful enough to take his magic from him."

Kelså tilted her head to the side. "His magic was not taken. He was cut off from the flow of magic."

"That's different how?"

She opened her mouth to answer, then paused. "It matters little. He has no access to magic. What else?"

"Atikus is weak now. You said his spirit felt drained, something like that. Oh, you said you could sense his spirit. Can you sense everyone?"

"Hardly." She snorted. "Atikus is . . . unique. I have known him a very long time."

"Could you sense me?" the voice of a small boy asked.

"I could sense you without magic's aid. I am your mother." Her hand reached out and cupped my cheek. "But, yes, I could sense your spirit. You are also uniquely connected to the currents, to magic itself."

I eyed her a moment, hoping for more. When she remained silent, I moved on. "All right, that's all

I can think of. Is there anything else you haven't told me that we need to add to our list?"

"The currents are disturbed."

"How so? More than before?"

She nodded. "They normally feel like a lazy river, peaceful and drifting. Some time ago, they began to move swiftly and thrash about, but only at times. Now, they feel like a river full of rapids, frothing and angry."

"Great. An angry river of magic. That doesn't sound ominous at all."

"Nothing has terrified me so, not since Irina's return, and not for a thousand years before that."

We drank our wine and stared over the mountain's ledge in silence. It felt like we struggled to fit some massive puzzle together but were missing half of the pieces. Seeing the image felt impossible.

Atikus's broad smile and wispy brows filled my mind. The old Mage was one of the kindest men I'd ever known. With his Gift of Memory, he was also more knowledgeable than most any man alive.

"Why attack Atikus?" I asked.

"What?" Kelså's brow rose.

"Atikus. Why him? What makes him special?"

Kelså thought a moment. "He is powerful. His connection to the currents is strong. He has more knowledge than most Mages. He is the Arch Mage. It could be any of those things—or none of them."

"What about his Gift? His memory?"

"What about it? It's a passive ability. He cannot—"

"His mind is the greatest library the world may ever possess. Think about what he has seen, what he has studied, what he *knows*."

"All right. That is a good point. Where are you going with this?" she asked.

"I don't know. Maybe it's just something to add to our list. But it feels important somehow."

We fell into another long silence as I mulled over what I recalled of Atikus and his Gift. I was onto something. I could feel it, but it was just out of reach. How could one so knowledgeable, so long-lived, have his tether to the currents cut like some flimsy ribbon?

When the sun faded over the horizon, we returned to the kitchen for dinner. Unlike breakfast, our evening meal was somber. I helped Kelså prepare a meal of cold cuts, cheese, and bread. Neither of us had uttered a word since coming inside, and fewer words were spoken throughout the meal. Kelså was nearly finished with her last bite when she stopped chewing and gripped my arm.

I looked up, startled. "What? What's wrong now?"

She gulped down the cheese and swallowed a sip of wine. "I do not know why I did not think of this earlier. We need to go back to the Well and speak with an old friend. She may be able to help us puzzle some of this out. Come with me."

Kelså puffed through labored breaths as we entered the chamber of the Well of Magic.

I had been in this cavern many times since returning to my mother, but the place still filled me with awe. Despite the urgency of our task, the little boy inside me couldn't resist bending down to trace a finger and watch as the mist raced to catch up.

As I rose to my feet, Kelså watched, arms crossed with a quirk across her lips. "Done playing yet?"

"Sorry." My cheeks flushed. "I'll never get used to this place."

As we strode across the chamber to the Well, I glanced at the light playing off the crystalline walls and ceiling. A thousand reflections danced throughout the cave.

Kelså stopped at the edge of the Well and breathed deeply as tendrils of wispy power curled to greet her. Fingers of magic tickled her feet, then crawled up her legs until her entire form was bathed in pearlescent mist. The effect was other-worldly—and strikingly beautiful. She turned at my gasp and smiled.

"It tingles," she said. "Come, I need your connection. You will need to approach the Well for this to work."

I closed the distance to stand beside her, and the magic responded, crawling up my lanky body. I shivered, but a giddy grin spread across my face. I looked down at the magic coursing across my hands and played at interrupting its flow with my fingers.

"Connection to what?" I asked.

"*To whom*, not what."

I looked up, perplexed.

Kelså's eyes closed, and she muttered ancient words, barely audible though I stood a pace away. The mist brightened and sped in its flow across our bodies. Another gust rushed from the Well to gather and hover in an undulating mass above the opening, pulsing like a heartbeat, then resolving and taking form.

Kelså continued to chant.

I had only seen the Phoenix herself once, high above the city of Saltstone, but there was no mistake; my mother had called forth the majestic beast. Her shimmering form grew until it towered above and spread across the ceiling. Finally formed, the beast's head snapped downward, and she locked eyes with me.

I staggered back a step. The mist scattered before reforming across my body.

"Órla?" The name croaked from my parched throat.

"Hello, Bond-Mate," her voice boomed through the chamber.

I gaped at the ethereal Phoenix's form.

"Órla! Spirits, Órla, I've missed you so much," I said in a hoarse whisper as tears tickled my cheeks.

"And I have missed you, but I can only maintain this form for a few moments." Her gaze shifted to Kelså. "Keeper, the currents remain disturbed. Irina still haunts the world of the living. While her power is diminished, she may inhabit and subsume others who possess Gifts. She may also sever them from the flow of magic, as the Arch Mage has learned. Atikus is lost to our arts . . . for now."

"How can we help him get his connection back?" I asked.

"You cannot. His Gifts will return in time as his body and mind heal." She paused, and her gaze became a distant stare. "Atikus will heal, but I fear the threat is greater still. I *feel* Irina's presence, her rage. She will stop at nothing in service to her vengeance. No one is safe, especially those with a Gift, while her spirit roams this land."

Kelså braced herself against one of the crystal pillars surrounding the Well. "Where will she go? What will she seek to destroy now?"

"Since her return, her purpose has been single-minded—vengeance. Her defeat at Saltstone enraged her further. Her mind is veiled from my Sight, but I sense a roiling sea within her. When she comes, she will billow and rage as the storm. Her spirit must be banished, or all will be lost."

The mist dimmed and blurred.

Órla's voice whispered in my mind.

"Irina's tomb has been destroyed. She cannot return once banished. Declan, you are the only one capable of banishing her for good. This world will never be safe as long as her spirit wanders freely."

Before I could speak, the Phoenix shattered into a thousand flickers of Light. Pinpricks of brilliance flared like embers but grew icy cold against my skin before they faded into nothing.

In the stillness of the cavern, I stared into the Well, wishing for one more moment with my lost friend.

The river of ancient power beneath our feet flowed but refused to speak.

Sometime later, Kelså and I again sat at the wooden table in her kitchen, each of us cradling a steaming mug. The sweetly bitter scents of honeyed black tea offered some comfort to our frayed nerves following Órla's message.

"Can Irina really destroy the magic of our world? She doesn't even have a body."

Kelså shrugged. "I do not know. She can do damage to individuals, albeit temporarily. If she learned how to permanently separate someone from magic, that could be disastrous."

"What would stop her from devastating the Gift? The Kingdom's bloodline is already thin, and Melucia is weakened following the siege." I looked up and saw fear in my mother's eyes for the first time. The other thing I saw in her eyes chilled my heart even more: doubt.

It was clear Kelså had no idea what to do or how to respond.

She was the Keeper of Magic. If *she* didn't know how to protect our people and their magic from Irina's wrath, who would?

CHAPTER 14

IRINA

I hovered above the Eye and watched the Triad fret over the sagging form of their resident Mage. Atikus had defeated my efforts to excise his soul just as Danai had. I wasn't used to others having more power or strength.

In my first life, I was one of only eleven humans alive with a connection to magic. It wasn't until the others had turned against me that I had accepted my birthright as a Mage and turned my eye toward conquest.

I wasn't used to having my magic rebuffed, not by creatures like Atikus Dani and his pathetic two-power Gift. What was happening to me, to the world, that I would struggle with such a simple task?

Despite my failure, the battle for Atikus's spirit had not exhausted me. I was fairly certain my ethereal form could not feel exhaustion or pain, yet something felt different. It felt as if the shimmering form of my likeness now struggled to hold itself together.

Had the fight weakened me?

I thought back to my battle with Danai and realized that failure, too, had affected my spirit's strength.

Had it diminished me enough for Atikus to have the upper hand in our struggle?

There was so much about life beyond living I did not yet understand. I had never cared about what happened in death—until I *actually* died.

So, what do I know?

A spirit could be contained. The Spell of Return that allowed me to be restored had contained me in that appalling black monolith.

When I was alive, Danai had taught me about the power to interact with spirits and the need to draw a summoning circle lest they be set free to wreak havoc. And here I was, the perfect example of that havoc-wreaking spirit, set free by the breaking of the circle in the Mages' tower.

Even if weakened, I am free.

But . . . could a free spirit expire? Could one be weakened beyond the point of its ability to interact with the living world?

A spike of terror shot through me. What would I become if that happened? Would I be consigned to wander a land and watch a people I could never touch? Would I become some ghostly voyeur who could never again cross the threshold of life? That scared me more than anything.

I needed a host more than I had thought. Within the body of Isabel, I was able to rejuvenate my strength, become brighter and sharper, more in focus. My spirit never diminished or lost coherence. I was alive . . . as alive as death would allow.

Where could I learn even more?

When I inhabited Atikus, I had touched every part of him, including his memories. Surely, there was something in that vast mental library to help me understand myself better.

I focused on the point within my spirit that had brushed against the Mage's mind and was rewarded with a replicate of his every understanding. At first, I saw only a smattering of recollections; but the more I delved, the harder I focused, I realized all of the Mage's memories had transferred to me.

I had not simply inhabited his mind. I had stolen the greater part of its value.

Excitement thrummed through me as I devoured the ancient man's knowledge. Every Gift imaginable—some I never imagined—was cata-

loged neatly, enumerated and defined, allowing
my already immense understand of magic to deep-
en and grow. Gifts of Healing and Warfare, Farming and Horticulture, Travel and . . . every other
Gift known to exist.

It was overwhelming and exhilarating.

So much knowledge.

And then I saw it.

If I could still draw breath, I would have drunk
more deeply of life's kiss than any ever had.

There, lodged in the memories of the man, was
an image of the most beautiful place I had ever
seen. At first, his memory was of a small village
on an island, an idyllic setting that appeared to be
little more than the fond memory of a random stop
in his travels, but there was something *important*
about this place.

I dove deeper, and memory became a vision.

I climbed a mountain.

*The path at my feet flared with an odd
magical glow as I took each step. I felt the
island's ever-present breeze.*

I passed a simple shack, somehow knowing it was unimportant and would not impede my journey, yet understanding that it served some vital purpose. It had . . . a presence.

The mouth of a cavern gaped before me. The dim light cast by torches bearing ever-present magical flame greeted me as I stepped inside. Rough-hewn rock turned smooth and translucent, vibrant with color and light.

The tunnel opened into a massive cavern, and I froze, awestruck.

If my eyes were dazzled by the colors and light of the walkway, my senses were now overwhelmed by the tapestry of shimmering power before me. I looked down and saw a flow—no, a current—in perpetual motion beneath a glasslike surface. As I strode forward, mist swelled up from that river and reached toward my feet, as if yearning for my embrace.

Crystals encasing the walls and ceiling glowed and twinkled with a dizzying kaleidoscope of hues.

As stunning as the cavern was to my eyes, it was the intense sensation of power emanating from across the room that consumed my heart and soul.

I ascended the steps and stilled.

The mist was gentle, even playful before.

Now it raged out of the opening and engulfed me.

The hairs on my arms and neck tingled, and I arched my head backward and laughed at the ecstasy of magic's touch.

Thirsty for more, I stretched out my hand.

The mist swirled between my fingers and parted as I neared its source below. My skin breached the surface of the river, and swells of magic tore into me. It felt like trying to hold a raging beast. Only when I relaxed and allowed the power to flow through me did its anger and fear abate.

In that moment, I knew true power.

This was nothing like the pathetic imitation of mortal power I had sought a millennium before. It was nothing like my quest for vengeance.

It was the power to destroy and the power to create.

It was the will of the gods.

It could make one a god—or goddess.

I grinned at that.

Then another memory slammed into me from the Mage's mind.

A woman with rich, dark skin and deep brown eyes stared up through scrying water. My vision was as clear as if she stood before me. The woman's smile was warm, her eyes sincere. Behind her, crystalline walls shimmered, though only a portion of the cavern's majesty was in view.

The woman's intoxicating voice resounded throughout the chamber. ". . . must help me. Atikus, you and Velius are the only ones alive with knowledge of the Well's location—and of the Spell of Sundering now guiding its flow. For the safety of magic itself, no other can know of this place. The people of Rea Utu have stood vigil for thousands of years and remain to guard our secret, yet even they do not fully understand what it is the Keeper keeps. Only you and Velius."

In that moment, I knew this was where I had lost my power.

Where they'd *stolen* it.

This was where my supposed brothers and sisters had ripped true magic from my grasp and given Gifts to the mundane people across the land.

And this was where I would seize my power once again.

CHAPTER 15

JESS

The days passed in a blur as I spent most of my waking hours meeting with my Council. With most of the men sent to fight in a foreign land, the work of keeping families fed and industry moving rested on women and elderly. My chief responsibility, and my greatest challenge, was balancing the needs of the nation with the simple daily requirements of mothers and children. I could only push my people so far.

The ashes of my father and brother were expected to arrive within a week, and plans were made to honor them both. I overruled tradition and ordered Justin be laid to rest beside our father in the crypt. He would be the first non-monarch interred in that sacred place.

My coronation was another topic burning the tongues of my advisors.

They argued that my throne would not be secure until the crown was firmly seated on my brow. While I agreed with their sentiment and longed to give the people something positive to celebrate, I insisted the ceremony be delayed until I returned from one last mission, the details of which I could not reveal—even to my Council. I told them I had to personally attend an errand vital to Kingdom security. Fearful of who I could trust as my reign began, I dared not share the location—or even the existence—of the cave I had hidden in following my escape from my mother. The place had been a secret for over a thousand years, and I wasn't about to change that.

It might soon be the only place in the world I could be alone.

Two weeks following my return to the Palace, I stood staring at the bronze doors of the Throne Room, a small leather satchel at my side. Mage Ernest, whom I was coming to appreciate for his candor and positive spirit, stood beside my chief guard, blocking my exit.

The guard crossed his burly arms. "This is a terrible idea, Your Majesty. You barely escaped multiple attempts on your life, are finally safe, and now you want to leave the safety of the Palace again?"

"Majesty, I must agree. Surely there is someone else who could handle this errand for you. Any member of Council would go if you asked. I would go in your place. Please reconsider." Mage Ernest's tone was calm, a contrast to the captain's urgency.

I let out a deep sigh and peered up at the men. "Captain, Mage, I understand how this must look and appreciate your concern, but this is a journey *I* must take. There is no one who can speak for the Crown on this matter. I will be fine."

"At least allow a complement of my men to travel with you." The captain's voice held a note of desperation. I knew how hard he had taken it when he learned of the recent deaths of three members of the royal family he had sworn to protect. He did not want to lose another.

I rested a hand on his arm, something I would *never* have done as Princess. "I will be fine. Where I travel, *no one* can follow. You are going to have to trust me, despite how I may have toyed with your trust in the past."

The captain gawked at my admission. I had indeed been a terror to the Royal Guard.

He stared a moment, then relented and stepped aside. Mage Ernest followed suit and bowed as I strode through the gilded doors toward the

Palace's main entrance, where my carriage awaited.

I climbed up and peered out the window at the snow-covered city. We passed through quickly, but people stirred as the sun lit the horizon with a splash of brilliant orange and gold. A few waved and smiled or offered respectful curtsies.

Throughout those first weeks, I tried to keep my arrival quiet, to allow my father's ashes to return before news of my ascension became too widely known, but I learned a vital lesson: A secret known by more than two people would rarely remain a secret. The moment the Council adjourned from our meetings on that first day, half the city was abuzz with news of their new ruler. Wild rumors raced like wildfires, some making ridiculous claims about the King's death, others speculating on insane things the petulant girl who now wore the crown might do next. Few held even a kernel of truth, but each stung all the same.

The warmth I received as the carriage rolled through town was due to the work of Trade Minister Carver. I had always thought he was little more than a smarmy dandy in his frilly shirts and garish coats, but the man knew how to spread word across the inns and shops of the capital. His little mice scurried and spoke to boost their fledgling Queen's reputation. One claimed I had fought crazed assassins in an attempt to save my father and brother while others talked of my valiant efforts to rescue the Kingdom from the iron grip of my now-maligned mother.

I protested the use of falsehood, arguing that my reign should be based on truth and honor.

Carver smiled, as if gentling a child, but explained that I was not well liked or respected as Princess, and some "stretching of the truth" was required to win the people to my side as Queen. After that painful admission, I gave him free rein to carry out his work and determined to focus on the myriad of other issues facing my people.

The carriage rolled to a stop at the steps of the Temple of the One, waking me from my thoughts. I reached for the handle, but the footman beat me to it, snapping to attention as I emerged. The liveried man offered a deep bow.

"How long will Her Majesty be at prayer?"

"You may return to the Palace. I will be a few days," I said. "Thank you, Marcel," I added.

The man's eyes widened as he peered up from his bow. A smile bloomed on his face as I turned and strode into the Temple.

The nave was empty and dark, lit by only a few candles at the far end. A lone priest kneeled before the central altar. At the sound of my steps, the balding man turned to peek over his shoulder. I was only halfway down the central aisle when he leaped to his feet and bolted toward me.

"Your Majesty! Forgive me. I had no idea you were coming this morning," he said through heavy breaths. "What brings you to the Temple so early? How may I serve?"

I waited for the priest to complete his bow and look up before speaking.

"I wish to spend some time in the crypt. I have enjoyed few moments alone since I returned, and I wish to mourn my family in private. Please see that no one disturbs me." I raised a small book. "I will be some time."

"Of course, Majesty." He glanced from the book to the leather satchel in my other hand. He cocked a brow but held his tongue as he turned and led me to the stairs descending into the crypt.

At the top of the stairs, I placed a hand on his shoulder, causing him to startle. "Father, please go about your prayers. I will be fine from here."

The priest bowed, then resumed his position before the altar.

I continued down the stairs, pausing only briefly before the massive doors of the crypt, locking them behind me from inside. The magical flames cast an eerie glow, but this time I didn't care. I marched to the far end of the marble hallway, peered into the mirror resting against one wall, then walked purposefully through the glass and vanished, leaving the flames to ponder the dead without me.

The cave's magical flames mirrored those of the crypt, casting a smokeless glow throughout the rough-walled cavern. I took a few steps beyond the mirror and stopped, a chill running up my spine with the memories of my last visit. I knew Keelan hadn't meant to harm me—that the real Keelan would never hurt anyone without cause—but I couldn't keep the trickle of fear at bay.

Flame light glinted off the silver pitcher resting on one of the round wooden tables, and a smile emerged. How had I forgotten about the mystical drink that waited so patiently for my return? I sat and poured a cup, the first fruity sip washing away my anxiety and fear, leaving only a clear mind and pleasant hint of chocolate.

Finally calm, my gaze traveled around the cavern.

Cots, tables, shelves—just as I remembered it.

Atikus had told me it would take Keelan a week or two to arrive, so I pulled out my book and leaned back for a relaxing read. I had been honest with the priest when I talked about how little time alone I had enjoyed since returning. The quiet of the cave was a welcome respite from my long days shepherding the Palace's efforts.

Even a queen needed a moment's peace.

Hours passed. When I tired of reading, I retrieved a small wooden box filled with blank parchment, a quill, and tin of ink. For once, I had the peace and quiet to think. I turned my mind to the most pressing issues facing my kingdom, starting with key roles I had yet to fill.

A messenger had arrived from the army the day before. I was relieved to learn that General Marks had survived and was leading what remained of my forces home. I scribbled, "Minister of War," then wrote, "Marks?" beside it. I thought a moment and put another note to the side of the name: "Chancellor?" That idea had come to me as I lay awake a few nights earlier, unable to sleep with matters of state spinning in my head. Uncle Ethan had been my family's closest friend and confidant. He might not make a great spymaster, but he could lead my Ministers.

Moreover, I trusted him. He might be the only person in the Kingdom I could say that about. The sad *aloneness* in that thought gave me pause.

I noted several other roles and potential candidates, then decided to think through other items.

The Kingdom faced a dwindling Gift.

Thorn might've been a snake in the grass, but he wasn't wrong about the desperate situation with our magical bloodline. I wrote, "Gift—exchange with Melucia? Island tribes? Eastern states?" I had far more questions than answers when my quill stopped moving. After a moment's pause, another idea struck, and I wrote, "Atikus/Melucia's Guild." The old Mage always wanted to talk about the future, so we would do just that.

For the next several hours, I grappled with rebuilding the Kingdom's military, dealing with the poor educational system in towns outside the capital, the plight of farmers whose crops had been confiscated for the war effort, the endless stream of orphans and widows created by the war, and dozens of other problems I had no idea how to solve. When I set my quill down and leaned back, my mind felt numb.

As I rubbed weary eyes, a horse whinnied beyond the cavern's entrance. Then hooves clomped against the rocky shore. I shot out of my chair and froze, my unwavering glare fixed on the cave's far wall that I knew was a hidden entrance. In the space of a breath, the most beautiful creature I had ever seen poked his head through the magical stone.

"Dittler!" A giddy young girl's squeal flew from my lips as I raced forward. Dittler met me halfway and buried his head into my shoulder. The cheerful clatter of the stallion's hooves made me giggle as he danced with the thrill of our reunion.

"I missed you so much, my baby boy," I said.

Dittler whinnied again and licked my face with a slobbery tongue.

"Your Majesty looks good in drool," a deep, amused voice said from the entrance.

My head snapped up, and Keelan's eyes met mine for the first time in weeks.

I saw only kindness and warmth, no trace of the malevolent evil that had stalked me before. Keelan's face broke into laughter as drool fell from my forehead into my eye, forcing me to swat it away with the back of my hand.

"You realize it is a crime to laugh at the monarch? I could have your head ... or something ... I am sure it would be *very bad* for you," I stammered, trying to walk the line between stern and witty. Dittler startled me with another lick.

Keelan snorted. "A nation of laws. I like it here."

I tossed an empty silver cup in his direction and grinned when he ducked.

He looked up, sarcasm dripping from his tongue as he said, "Regal as ever, Your Majesty."

I chuckled and offered a mock curtsey. "I am so glad you approve, Lieutenant."

The ice now thoroughly shattered by Dittler's slobber, Keelan stepped forward and gripped the horse's reins. His confident face betrayed something I hadn't seen a moment before. He looked down and stroked Dittler's side. "It's good to see you again, Your Majesty . . . I mean, Jess. I . . . I don't even know how to apologize for . . . well . . ."

I was tempted to let him struggle with his apology, simply for the amusement of watching the huge man writhe, but finally saved him. My voice was firm, yet also gentle. "Keelan, stop. It was not you who attacked me, but it *was* you who saved me in the end. I know that. It may take some time to get used to everything, but you bear no blame for what happened. Besides, you forced me to face my destiny, and I am grateful for that."

He cocked his head like a confused pup.

I grinned. "Come and sit. I remember how much you loved this wine, and my cook insists I take cheese, bread, and meat with me everywhere. We can catch up with a small meal."

Keelan ran a hand over his stubble and smiled. "That sounds good. I *am* hungry, and that wine might calm my nerves a bit."

"I make you nervous?" I asked playfully.

"Uh, well, maybe. I don't know," he stammered.

My laughter bounced off the walls of the cave. "I am teasing you. Just sit and tell me, how is Atikus? I miss that funny old man."

The comfort of the cave made it easy to lose track of time, and we talked long past the afternoon and into the night. Keelan omitted few details of his trip back to Saltstone and the weeks he experienced following the Kingdom's failed siege of Saltstone. He hadn't been there when my mother fell but described the events as Declan and Atikus had explained them to him. When he told me about Isabel's order to hunt down the mass of fleeing civilians, tears began to trickle down my cheeks.

"She was horrible," was all I could say.

"Jess, it was Irina, not your mother."

My voice hardened. "My mother *chose* to bring Irina back. She *chose* to sacrifice her husband, son, and daughter on the altar of Irina's ambitions. In the end, it might have backfired when Irina consumed her soul, but it was *my mother's* choices that led to all of this. As much as I may want to forgive her, to love and mourn her as a daughter, as Queen, I cannot forget or forgive the treachery and death that woman thrust upon our two nations."

I peppered him with questions, and he patiently answered each. At the end of his tale, Keelan's stomach rumbled.

I chuckled. "I take it you are hungry again?"

"I'm a big boy. I like to eat." He grinned back. "And I happen to have purchased some salted fish and vegetables from the ferry that brought me across the bay. Would you like some?"

I wrinkled my nose. "Sure. I will try your salted fish, but do not hate me if I go back to my bread and cheese after the first bite. It sounds suspicious, especially coming from a ferry's stores."

While Keelan retrieved the fish from his saddlebags, I walked to the shelving and found plates and cutlery. When I turned, he was standing by the table staring at me. I looked down to see what was out of place.

"I'm sorry," he said as his face colored. "It's just that . . . well . . . the last time I saw you, we were in filthy, dusty riding clothes with tangled hair and dirty faces. I don't think we bathed the whole time we were on the run. And now . . . well, you're . . . beautiful." He looked down as he muttered the last word.

I blushed then grinned at his discomfort.

That's when I took my first long look at the Guardsman in his crisp navy uniform. He had removed his coat and laid it on one of the cots when we first sat to talk, and I hadn't given it much thought.

But now my mind was spinning.

When had he changed into a clean uniform following his journey here? Surely his clothes should stink of the road and the bay, but they didn't.

Why would he change his uniform before entering the cave?

I was puzzling through those questions when Keelan found his courage and took the plates from my hand. I startled and took a step back.

"Sorry," he said with a sheepish grin, then turned and began setting the plates on the table.

As if seeing him for the first time, my eyes traced the outline of his strong jaw. I watched the muscles in his back shift in his tight white shirt. I chided myself for staring and turned back to the shelves, pretending to retrieve something else for our meal before joining him once more.

CHAPTER 16

DECLAN

Kelså took my hand in her own, gripping it firmly, as I stared into the Well. "Declan, tell me what you're thinking."

I squeezed once and pulled my hand away, running my fingers through my unruly mop of curls as I stood. "I . . . I don't even know what to think. If I go back through the gate, I can be in Saltstone in two weeks, maybe a little less if I find fresh horses along the route. Is there any food we can pack for the trip?"

"There may be another way. But—"

"Will it get me there faster? What is it?" I asked, hope creeping into my voice.

"You could ride the currents."

My mouth dropped. "What? *The* currents?"

She nodded.

"I didn't know you *could* ride the currents. They seem so . . . I don't know . . . not good to touch."

"Eloquent, as always." She smiled. "And no, they are not welcoming of human touch, but you are not fully human, Declan. You are the Heir. You are *of* magic. I believe the currents may answer if you call."

I stared. "May? You aren't inspiring confidence here."

She shrugged. "I don't think anyone has ridden the currents before. I'm grasping at ancient knowledge here, trying to gain Atikus valuable time."

"But, what if—"

"I do not know what might happen. The mist welcomes you as it does me. I felt Órla's warmth just as you did. I *think* the currents may also welcome you." She seemed like she was trying to project confidence, but her eyes showed only doubt and fear. "Son, even if you are allowed to ride their flow, magic always demands a price."

"Yeah, I got that. Órla said something like that at the end, before she . . ." I took Kelså's hand again and offered a weak smile. "This isn't just anyone; it's *Atikus* in danger. We have to try everything we can."

Kelså stared up at me for a long moment, then whispered, "I know you're right, but we're talking about a mother letting her son leap into the unknown, into the most powerful force in the world. How am I to accept that?"

"It was your idea." I cocked one brow and offer my best smirk. "Atikus is more than just a distant friend, more than an adopted father. He is now the Arch Mage. More importantly, with his Gift of memory, he is the keeper of countless generations of history. Losing him—and his mental vault—would mean losing the past, losing *perspective*. We have to do everything possible to save him."

Kelså's eyes narrowed, and her brow furrowed, but something tugged at one corner of her mouth.

"What?"

"Sometimes you are so . . . boyish. Then, out of nowhere, you say something wise. You are an enigma, Declan Rea."

My chest contracted beneath the weight of her compliment, however half-baked it might have sounded.

"Mother," I whispered and pressed my forehead to hers. "I *have* to do this. Atikus is a father to Keelan and me. He means the world to the people of Melucia. They've lost so much already. They can't lose him, too."

She pulled back and searched my eyes.

"Here *you* are the one placing yourself in danger, and I am the one hesitating." She released a heavy breath and nodded once, reaching up to wipe away a rebellious tear. "You are right, but I do not have to like it. Neither of us knows what this will do, what price will be demanded, if you can even *survive* the currents. Forgive a mother's fear, even if the Keeper knows this is your path."

I cupped her cheek. "I love you, Mother. Everything will be okay."

She tried to smile, but it refused to reach her eyes.

I leaned down and kissed her cheek. Then, without warning, I turned, took two strides, and leaped feetfirst into the Well.

CHAPTER 17

DECLAN

T he last thought that repeated in my mind as I leaped was, *Stupid idea! Stupid idea! Stupid idea!*

I looked down and watched my boots hurtle toward the open space in the crystalline floor. Then the world transformed into a kaleidoscope. A few feet away, my beautiful mother, robed in elegant white and gold, became little more than a smear of color against the backdrop of hues reflecting against glass.

My golden tunic flared.

I had to squeeze my eyes shut to stop the blazing spots that appeared.

Knives of flame pierced my skin.

The deeper I sank, the stronger the sensation of being burned alive grew.

And yet, oddly, I felt a chill.

I struggled to keep my head wedged in a pocket of air between the river's surface and the cavern's floor as my arms flailed and feet kicked uselessly against the river's pull. The current drew me away from the opening, and I watched through the glassy floor as my mother's image faded from view.

My head submerged, and I felt the pressure of the watery flow carrying me away, yet I didn't struggle to breathe. If anything, sucking in the blueish mist filled my lungs with warmth and exhilaration.

It tasted . . . sweet?

And it felt as if magic *wanted* me to drink it in, to let it live within my body and spirit.

So I did.

I surrendered and lay back, allowing my body to float, buoyed by the currents.

Magic sensed my shift, and the surrounding glow grew brighter. Aches that plagued me from years of hard service with the Rangers vanished, and my body was renewed. I had experienced magic's healing in bottomless pitchers of wine—but while the wine's healing only repaired injury to body and mind, the currents' power restored the soul. In a single moment, I felt reborn, my flesh replaced with perfect, never-worn skin.

I felt my muscles knitting together where scars caused pain.

I became whole and unmarred once more.

Discarding my last shred of caution, I opened my mouth and laughed at the sensations hammering my body and mind. Mist and syrupy thick liquid-that-was-not-liquid rushed to enter. I panicked but soon realized it wouldn't harm me—it couldn't—it was *part* of me, and I was part of it.

This torrent of power was my home.

No, it was more than that.

It was an extension of my spirit and soul.

I belonged here.

And that's when she spoke.

Her voice wasn't muted or muffled; it echoed with sonorous clarity in my mind.

"After carrying me for so long, it is now my time to carry you, Bond-Mate."

"Órla?" I wheeled my head around. "Where are you? I can't see you."

She laughed in my head, and I thought it was the most joyous, purest sound I'd ever heard.

"Have you learned nothing? I am everywhere—in the mist, the currents, the air above, the stone below. Thanks to your heavy breathing, I even flow within you. That's pretty weird, by the way."

I coughed through an unexpected laugh.

Órla giggled.

"I have never been an owl. I am an eternal, limitless spirit of magic. One day you will learn we are not so different, you and I."

Her laughter shifted to a serious tone.

"Declan, I would embrace you every day, but this is not your time. This world needs you. Atikus is in more danger than I thought. He cannot wait for his connection to heal naturally. You must restore him. If Atikus falls, I fear this world will be powerless to resist the rising darkness."

"How do I restore him? I don't know what to do."

"Trust that small boy deep within you, the one who fears and aches.

"He knows the way.

"Trust the boy."

"The boy?" My head spun in confusion.

"The currents will deliver you to Saltstone soon. I fear Atikus may already lie beyond our aid. Do not tarry."

"Órla, what do I do? I still don't understand!" I shouted, but she didn't answer.

The river's light pulsed, and a wave of force swelled beneath me, lifting me above the surface. Without warning, the river surged upward and spat me onto cold, dry stone.

I leaned up on my elbows and stared back. The moment I was expelled from its currents, the surface had calmed, returning to a steady, almost placid flow.

I looked down, expecting to see liquid dripping from my clothes, but was stunned to find myself dry.

Of course you're dry, you idiot; it's a magical *river, not a watery one.*

In contrast to the crystalline beauty of the Well's chamber, the cavern where I now lay was little more than a hole gouged out of the mountain. The only light in the tiny chamber came from the river's flow and the mist reaching up to tease my skin.

Reminding myself of Órla's urging, I rose.

The trek along the winding path back to the Mages' complex was covered in pristine snow. I drew in crisp air and smiled. Despite the desperation in my mission, the thought of seeing my brother and adopted family of Mages—and *especially* Ayden—put a spring in my step.

In no time, I found myself standing at the base of the ruined Mages' tower.

I frowned up at the once-majestic symbol of magic, now barely a half tower surrounded by a rubble of massive, broken stones. I was here when the tower fell and had seen it many times since, but returning home to its decrepit state was still sobering.

"I come out here to think sometimes."

I nearly fell over at the voice that spoke from around the tower's base. A head covered in a blond mess of hair peeked around.

"Sorry, didn't mean to startle you." The boy stepped before me and took a long look, his eyes growing wider by the second. "You're . . . you're . . . Declan!"

Now it was my turn to chuckle as I righted myself. "Glad to see I made an impression last time I was here. And who are you, Mage-Apprentice?"

The boy's eyes widened further, and he stumbled back several steps. Fear, like the dark clouds of a rising storm, spread across his face a moment before he bolted away.

"Wait! Wha . . ."

I watched the boy's oversized blue robe flutter away.

"Not the triumphant return I expected," I muttered.

As I approached the Mages' quarters, other apprentices moved to meet me, excited to greet the man bearing the golden Phoenix on his chest. Yet, as they met my gaze, their expressions morphed from curiosity into obvious fear. Quicker than when the dinner bell rang, the courtyard cleared, leaving me standing at the entrance to the Mages' quarters alone and befuddled.

The door opened, and Mage Fergus bowled into me, knocking me off the steps.

"Watch yourself, young man!" Fergus bellowed without looking up to see who he'd knocked down.

"I would if you'd stop trying to knock me off my feet." I grinned as Fergus looked up.

"My boy!" the Mage exclaimed, gripping my arms with both hands, pulling me into a bear hug. "Welcome home, son."

When Fergus stepped back from his embrace, the Mage's smile fell, and his eyes widened. "Declan, what happened to your eyes?"

"My eyes? What do you mean? Nothing that I know of." I reached to press fingers to my eyes, but there was no pain there.

Fergus scrunched his nose and leaned forward to examine my pupils. "Declan, I think we need to go inside so you can see for yourself."

The old Mage waddled back through the doorway and led me into a sitting room where a large mirror leaned against one wall. A fire in the hearth snapped in greeting and warmth.

I turned toward the mirror and froze.

"I—Ferg—what . . . ?"

The whites of my eyes now blazed with the intensity of the noon sun, and swirled with a light bearing the same swirling azure of the Well's mist. As I leaned toward the mirror, mist curled out of the corners of each eye. I blinked a few times, but the swirling, blazing brilliance remained.

Fergus fell into a large chair by the hearth and poured himself a glass of brown liquor, downing it in one gulp, then refilling the glass.

"How does it feel? I mean *they*—how do they feel? *Your eyes*? How do your eyes feel?" he stammered.

I reached up with a tentative finger and rubbed one eye again, then shrugged. "They don't *feel* any different. I didn't even know they were glowing, or whatever you'd call this."

"Well, I'm pretty sure everyone else will notice. It is rather, um, alarming, especially when you don't know the swirly, glowing magic man is going to glare at you."

I turned, my lower lip jutting out in an exaggerated pout. "Did you just make fun of me? In my time of need?"

"I would *never* do such a thing," Fergus said before breaking out into a wide grin. "But seriously, we will need to figure out what's going on, if there are side effects or other considerations. Before we do, though, let's get you to Atikus. I fear we may not have him much longer."

All humor fell away. "He's that bad?"

"I don't think he's in physical pain, but for one so steeped in magic to have that connection ripped away, well, it would make anyone question their will to live. Seeing you might help—but Declan, he's not the man you knew when you left. You need to brace yourself."

I nodded. "My eyes can wait. Let's go see him now."

A moment later, Fergus rapped on the heavy door of Atikus's chamber.

A muffled voice bellowed, "Go away!"

"Atikus, it's Fergus. Declan just arrived, and we're coming in."

Without waiting for a reply, Fergus pushed the door open and strode into the room.

I froze halfway through the doorway and stared in disbelief.

The stones of the floor were hidden beneath a layer of scattered clothing and books. Tomes of magic appeared to have been tossed about. As I absorbed the scene, I found a lump in a heavily wrinkled blue robe curled on the bed. Atikus's silver hair had thinned, and dark spots of age were spreading across his pasty scalp.

"Atikus," I said in a whisper.

"I said go away."

"Atikus, it's me, Declan."

"I don't care if you're the Spirits-damned Phoenix herself. Get out."

Atikus's voice didn't sound angry. It was hollow, devoid of meaning or life—or more likely the *will* to live.

Fergus gave me an understanding look, then patted my shoulder and stepped out of the room, closing the door behind him.

I stepped forward and sat on the edge of the bed.

"Atikus, please. I came to help."

The lump didn't move. "You're wasting your time. No one can help me. I'm useless now."

"Atikus—"

"Just leave me alone. You're better off without me."

I stared into the man's back.

Seeing my proud, powerful adopted father in this state shocked me more than any of the wonders I'd experienced over the past year. The once-jovial, perpetually positive Mage had been reduced to an immobile, helpless man filled with nothing but self-loathing and self-pity.

My gut turned at the sight.

And yet, beneath sadness, I also found righteous anger.

This man had raised me, gave me hope, taught me to laugh and love. He'd taught me to read and write, to think for myself, and to challenge the thoughts of others. He'd taught me everything that was good and right. What right did he have to shun that love now? How *dare* he give up when the world *needed* him?

When *I* needed him?

In response to my rising rage, my tunic flared, lighting every corner of the chamber with the brilliance of a hundred candles. I stood and stepped back from the bed, then spoke in a measured, commanding voice. "Arch Mage Atikus Dani, get out of that bed before I lift you out."

Atikus's head slowly turned, and he squinted through the tunic's glow. "Fine. I'll get up. Just turn that thing down, will you?"

I couldn't suppress a grin and willed the tunic to dim, but only slightly.

Atikus sat up, his spindly legs dangling off the side of the bed, then rubbed his eyes with both palms. "I'm up. You happy?"

"Look at me," I commanded.

"You sure got bossy since somebody taught you magic," Atikus said before looking up. When he saw my eyes, he froze, his mouth agape. "Sweet Spirits. What in the—"

"We don't know, and it's not important right now. I came to restore your magic. Do you want my help or not?" I wasn't sure if this approach would work, but I sensed the comfort I'd planned to offer was doomed to fail against the rocky shoals of the Mage's languishing misery.

"You are wasting your time. I have been severed. There is nothing to restore."

I reached forward and gripped his arm, shocked at how wraithlike the formerly hale man had become. I focused my intent into the center of Atikus's chest and allowed my magic to flow into the man's spirit.

There was nothing.

My Light flowed through every memory and thought, through every emotion, through every part of the Mage I could search, and still I found no remnant of magic.

I searched for more than an hour.

"See? Nothing," Atikus grumbled, ready to return to his wallowing.

"Hush. I'll be done when I'm done."

Frustrated, I allowed my Light to dim.

My attention had turned to other thoughts when something caught my mental eye. It was a tiny, almost imperceptible dot, something so small and dim I never would've seen it while my own brilliant Light shone. I focused my inner sight and approached the dot, surprised when it didn't grow larger as I came closer.

But something did change when I neared.

It *pulsed*—faintly.

Excitement thrummed in my chest.

I reached out with my magical sense to grasp the dot, hoping beyond hope, but was repulsed by an impenetrable wall that sent a shock wave through my soul. It wasn't a wave of pain but rather a sickness or *wrongness* that oozed through my mind.

I shivered at its touch but was determined to save my mentor.

I redoubled my effort, drawing ever more power from my internal reserve and the tunic. I hammered into the barrier with all my might—only to receive an equally powerful retort.

Bile rose in my throat.

My mind swam.

I staggered and lost my connection to Atikus before tripping backward to land on the floor.

Atikus was down in a flash.

"Are you all right? Declan, can you hear me?" Concern marred the haggard man's face. "I knew this was useless. Please, stop. I can't have you hurt on my account."

"I'm fine." I shook my head to clear my mind, then looked up at Atikus. "But I think you're wrong about being severed. I saw a Light, but it's blocked by . . . something. When I tried to break through, it tossed me back as if I was made of paper."

"That's impossible," Atikus muttered, shocked. "Our Mages searched. None of them could see anything. Are you sure?"

I nodded and grinned, hoping a measure of warmth might thaw him further. "You didn't let the most powerful Mage alive take a look. You know, the one with the mystical, blazing eyes and brilliantly floppy hair?"

I flicked my hair back dramatically.

Despite himself, Atikus laughed. It was small at first but grew into a deep rumble that consumed his entire frame.

Like gazing at the rising sun, I watched as something within Atikus broke free of the malaise that had so gripped his soul.

"You always were *impossible*, never minding a word I said. Why did I think you would just leave me alone when I told you to?"

"No idea. You are a foolish old Mage, you know? That's probably why you thought it would work."

Atikus wiped away his tears and gripped me by the arm. "Declan, I'm sorry—"

I cut him off, wrapping the Mage in a tight embrace and burying my face in his shoulder.

Long moments later, I jerked back, blazing eyes wide. "Not to ruin the mood, but I have an idea. We need to get back to the currents."

Atikus looked up, perplexed. "What currents? You mean *the* currents?"

"Sorry, you call it the *vein*. You know, the vein of magic that runs under the old Mages' tower? That's how I got here so quickly."

Atikus stared in wonder. "You traveled *the currents*?"

I nodded. "I'll tell you about all that later. Right now, we need to get back there and try again. I can draw power from the mist. It might give me enough strength to break through whatever that barrier is blocking your Light."

We helped each other up and started for the door, then I stopped and turned back toward Atikus. "Um, we need to hurry and all, but, well, you stink of wine and who knows what else. I'm guessing you haven't bathed or changed clothes in days."

"I think it has been weeks." Atikus ducked his head.

"Right. At least splash water on your face and change into a fresh robe. We can't let the other Mages see you like this. You *are* still the Arch Mage."

"I am pretty sure no one will notice my robes when they see your eyes. Can we get on with this?"

I shook my head and turned to lead us toward the vein.

CHAPTER 18

KEELAN

J ess stifled a yawn, covering her mouth with the back of her hand. I grinned at her effort to mask her sleepiness but chose to save her embarrassment and yawned myself, stretching my arms to emphasize the point.

"I didn't realize how long we've been sitting here. It must be well past midnight," I said, feigning exhaustion I didn't feel. "We should get some sleep soon. How do you think we should handle the morrow?"

She released an imprisoned yawn. "We should return to Fontaine."

"We?" I asked. "Is that the *royal we*, or actually you and me both?"

She snorted. "I think you and I are past royal formalities such as referring to me as *we*. I have never understood that turn of phrase. There is only one of me, even if I am Queen. Why am I a *we*?"

I grinned. "I believe, Your Most Royal Majesty, the *we* refers to the monarch representing all of the people and the land . . . and whatever else she might claim as her own."

"Look at you playing amateur royal. I am unsure you are correct in your definition, but I am far too tired to argue." She stood. "Besides, I meant that you should return to the Palace with me. The Council will want to hear your account of the siege firsthand. We have received messengers with updates from before the siege, but only one returned after it happened. You will be able to fill in many gaps."

I eyed her. "You've changed."

"Changed? What do you mean?"

"You were so afraid before. Atikus and I did everything we could to get you to talk, but you were locked up tight. And there were times you'd nip at anyone who got too close. I suppose that's to be expected after what you survived, but the woman before me is very different from the girl I knew only a few months ago."

Now it was her turn to eye me. A long moment of silence passed.

I started to fear I'd gone too far when she spoke in a quiet voice. "My father always said the crown changes anyone who wears it. I watched how it changed him over the years. He seemed to always be debating something in his mind." She walked to her cot and sat facing me. "When I was a little girl, he was so carefree, carrying me on his shoulders into the gardens, tossing me into the air before plopping me down on the back of a horse. He loved to ride with me sitting in front of him, his arms wrapped around my sides. I loved it, too. I would snuggle into his chest and watch the world pass by from the safety of his saddle. As I got older, he grew more serious. He . . . lost that playfulness."

"Maybe you lost a bit of that as you got older, too? We all do."

She nodded. "Maybe. I sat in many of his Council meetings and stood by the throne as he heard petitions and negotiated trade or whatever pressed. He loved being King, but the weight of the crown took its toll over time. I guess . . . I am scared it will do that to me, too."

I stepped to my cot, sat, and leaned forward, taking her hands in mine. My eyes found hers. "Jess Vester, you are the strongest woman I know. You've lived through things that would've destroyed most other people, but *you* never gave up.

Of course the crown will change you. How could it not? But you have the power to choose how that change will occur, whether it's positive or negative, whether joy or bitterness grows in your heart, whether or not you hold on to all the special things that make you, well, you."

Jess's eyes fell to our tightly clutched fingers.

"You think I am special?" a child's voice asked.

"Very." I smiled, squeezed her hands, then pulled back. "But you were right about us needing rest. If we're going to return to face the Palace tomorrow, we both need to be at our best."

A moment later, I was wrapped in my blanket, eyes closed, when Jess whispered into the night, "Thank you, Keelan."

"Good night, Your Majesty," I replied through the grin teasing my lips.

By some feat of magic, as the sun rose on the next morning, the torches in the cavern flared to life and brightened. I had forgotten that trick from our last visit to the cave and stared in wonder as the flames danced higher.

"I never knew magic could do so many amazing things," Jess said from her cot. "I mean, Gifts are everywhere, but to make something like this cave, or those torches, or *that wine*, it really is wondrous."

"It's definitely something," I grunted as I rose and rummaged through my pack. "May I fix Her Majesty's breakfast? We have dried meat and cheese or cheese and dried meat."

She smiled and sat up, her head tilted upward. "Our royal pleasure commands cheese and meat, kind sir."

I lifted two wrapped bundles, turned, and offered an exaggerated bow. "As you wish, Your Most Bedheaded Majesty."

"Bedheaded?" Both her hands flew to her hair. "That is not even a word. And don't look at my hair! I need that mirror to just be a mirror before you see me again."

I laughed, a deep rumble that echoed off the rough cavern walls. "No need to fret, Majesty. Your humble servant will busy himself with preparations for our journey while you, well, do whatever it is you royals do in that mirror."

She tossed her pillow into my back and padded toward the mirror. "How dare you mock me! I am Queen!"

When I muttered, "Not *my* queen," under my breath, another pillow slammed into my back, causing me to spill a bit of the magical wine I nearly had to my lips. "Hey!"

She giggled as she brushed the tangles out of her hair. Dittler, who'd remained near the cave's entrance all night, clomped over to the table and nudged my shoulder.

"I know you're hungry, boy. We'll get you some breakfast when we're at the Palace, okay?"

"You two seem to be getting along much better now," Jess said, packing her brush away and smoothing out her dress. "I swear he just sent me an image of you feeding him some kind of fruit. I am fairly certain that image was his way of communicating affection."

"You mean *hunger*. We've reached an agreement of sorts, but I wouldn't call it affection," I said, patting the massive stallion one last time before turning to face Jess.

I froze as my eyes widened.

"What? I did the best I could on short notice."

I shook my head but struggled to speak.

Nothing had changed since we'd spent the last day and evening talking, but it felt like the first time I'd looked at her. *Really* looked at her.

She wore an elegant emerald gown with white lace around the neck and the ends of her sleeves. The green of the fabric shimmered in the torchlight and brought out the auburn tint in her rich brown hair. I'd never paid much attention to that red tint before. In fact, I'd never *noticed* her before. She was a girl I rescued, a girl seven years my junior, not unlike many other victims of crimes I'd helped back home.

But for some reason I couldn't explain, the woman who stood before me in that moment was someone entirely new.

"No, no. You, um, did fine. I mean . . . you look fine . . . good . . . you look good," I stammered, then ran my hand over my stubbly chin. "I'm an idiot. Ignore me."

Her smile brightened the magically lit cavern more than any sunrise I'd ever seen.

She offered a mischievous wink. "We need to work on your complimenting skills, but that will do for now."

She sat and began spreading cheese across what was left of our crusty loaf. Dittler made a sound I thought bordered on a laugh.

"Thanks a lot, *friend*," I said to the horse, patting him one last time before turning to sit.

An hour later, our packs were fastened, skins were filled with wine, and we stood, hesitating, before the mirror.

"What's it like? Going through that thing?"

Jess shrugged. "It is like going through a door. One minute you are in this room, the next you are in another. I did not feel anything unusual, except a little disorientation at returning in the crypt. That part was creepy." She turned and reached up to pat Dittler. "Maybe I should lead him through. He will have the hardest time walking through a portal."

"Okay, but he led Atikus and me into the cave and didn't have any trouble walking through faux solid stone," I said. "For the record, *that* was creepy."

"Okay, baby boy, you need to follow me," she told Dittler as she gripped his reins, then stepped through the mirror, horse in tow.

I watched them vanish, sucked in a nervous breath, and followed.

I emerged in the crypt and bumped into Dittler's flanks with my first step, receiving a snap of tail to my face in return.

"Oof! We're going to have to practice that some. I'll be picking horsehair out of my mouth all day now."

Dittler and Jess shared a chuckle at my expense.

"Woah, this place is . . ." I trailed off as my head swiveled and my eyes took in the crypt's majestic creepiness. That's what I called it in my head, but I didn't dare insult Jess's royal line by voicing that opinion.

"What's in here?" I asked, running my hand across the Phoenix etched in a pair of golden doors that towered to the right of the mirror. I yanked my hand back as magic's glow flared and followed my touch.

Jess shrugged. "I have no idea. My father did not know how to get into that chamber. We guessed it is some ancient king or Mage, but no one knows for sure."

My investigator-brain kicked into overdrive as I examined the door and the metal plate on the wall beside it. "Well, someone knows what's inside."

Jess's head snapped around. "Why do you say that?"

I pointed to the plate, my face only a few hands from its gleaming surface. "Look here. There isn't any dust on this plate. That would've helped us see if it had been disturbed recently. But . . . you can still see parts of a very faint handprint." I pointed and stepped back for Jess. "The oils on a person's hand almost always leave a trace on metal, especially when it's cold like it is down here."

"The priests who maintain this place are down here every day. It is likely one of them decided to try their luck. Those doors have not opened in centuries, probably longer."

Jess stared a moment, then reached up and pressed her palm to the plate. The Phoenix flared, and magical light swirled in its grooves, but the door didn't stir. "Well, it was worth a try. I thought maybe the monarch's touch might open it, but there is likely something else required. A password or magical phrase that has been lost to time."

She turned back toward me. "Are you ready to be scrutinized by the entire royal court? The moment we return, tongues will wag about who you are and what you have done to me."

"Done to you? What do you mean?"

"I left alone but returned with a Melucian. That will be curious enough to start all sorts of rumors, but when you join in Council meetings, some will grow jealous or suspicious—or both."

"You want me to join in Council meetings?"

She nodded. "Some, yes. They need to hear firsthand what you saw when you returned to Saltstone. They must know what your people experienced. They will want to question you, some quite aggressively."

The concern creasing her face touched something in me in a way I didn't understand. I studied her face a moment before responding. "I've spent the past few years being questioned and scrutinized by the toughest old man in Melucia, the Captain-Commander of the Guard. On occasion, I've stood before the Triad on the Eye. There's nothing quite like that experience. I'll be all right, especially with you there."

"Keelan, listen to me. I won't be able to help you. When we walk out of here, I will be Queen. You will have to address me as such, and I will need to treat you as a visiting . . . hmm . . . dignitary? Emissary? What are you?"

"Guest is fine. I don't need a fancy title."

"I see you have never been in a palace or dealt with nobles. *Titles* are everything. Without one, you will be invisible, barely worth their notice." She thought a moment before her eyes lit up. "*Ambassador.* You are Melucia's new ambassador to the Kingdom. That will work."

I barked a laugh and shook my head. "I'm pretty sure the Triad has to make that appointment on behalf of our country."

"It will be fine. This can be temporary until they appoint a permanent one. I am sure Atikus will smooth things out on his side of the mountains." She nodded to herself. "That is settled. Let us go, Ambassador."

Without another word, she gripped Dittler's reins, strode to the end of the crypt, and opened the doors leading up to the Temple.

CHAPTER 19

KEELAN

B y the time Jess and I entered the Palace, the whole of Fontaine was abuzz with news of the Queen's return, though more rumors revolved around the handsome Melucian in the blue uniform who had escorted her through the city's streets. At least, that's what the footman who greeted us said beneath his breath and roguish smile.

"Your Majesty, it is good to see you returned to us safely." Mage Ernest bowed deeply as Jess entered the Throne Room. I strode a couple of paces behind. The Mage straightened and appraised me without a hint of expression. "And Lieutenant Rea, it is a pleasure to meet you. You are quite a famous investigator."

I was surprised anyone this far from home knew who I was. I couldn't think of anything to say in reply, so I offered a curt nod. My Gift remained quiet, indicating no deception or falseness in the man's welcome.

Jess glanced between us, then seemed to remember I was a stranger in the Palace. "Forgive me. Keelan, may I introduce my Court Mage, Dane Ernest. With High Chancellor Thorn missing, Mage Ernest is sitting in to provide the Council a magical perspective."

Before either of us could speak, Jess stepped through the chamber toward the door to the royal residence. "Come along, Keelan. I will have a servant show you to your chamber. Mage, please assemble the Council in two hours. We have matters to discuss."

Without so much as a glance back, she barreled through the door and disappeared. I shrugged at the bemused Mage and followed in the Queen's wake.

When the door closed behind me, Jess was waiting.

"If you let these men start talking, you will never get away. My father taught me that when I was eight, and it might have been the most valuable lesson I ever learned." She smiled up at me, and something in my chest squeezed tight. "Now, we will put you down the hall. I cannot have you near the family chambers, but I would rather have you in our wing and out of arm's reach of nosy nobles."

A maid happened by and curtsied.

"Lydia, please show our guest to the Emerald Chamber. He will need a bath drawn. As you can see—and likely smell—he had quite a journey. He will also need a few outfits appropriate for court. See if the clothier can figure his size; it's somewhere between large and enormous." She chuckled at the maid's stricken expression. "Oh, and have his Guard uniform cleaned."

Lydia curtsied again, sneaking a glance at me. "Right away, Majesty."

"Also, tell the kitchen we would like something light before Council." She turned conspiratorially toward me. "Never meet with Council on a full stomach. You will not be able to stay awake if you do."

Lydia looked to smother a grin and curtsied yet again as Jess turned and disappeared down the grand hallway, leaving me staring speechless at her vanishing form.

Lydia cleared her throat. "Sir, if you'll follow me, please."

When I turned, the woman's eyes were roaming up and down the length of my body, her eyes alight with interest.

"Oh, right. Yes. Um . . . thank you," I sputtered and blushed.

My head had just emerged from steaming water when a tentative knock sounded at the door to my chamber.

"M'lord, may I come in? I have your clothes," Lydia's muffled voice called through the thick wood.

"One moment, please." I rose from the bath, toweled off, then tied the towel around my waist. With my height and the size of the towel, I was barely covered halfway from my knees to my nether, but it would have to do.

"Come in."

The door crept open, and Lydia strode in, her arms loaded with several sets of clothing. Her eyes roamed my bare, muscled, poorly dried chest, then fell southward toward the rest of my nearly naked form.

"Forgive me, m'lord. I didn't mean—"

"It's all right." I blushed nearly as brightly as the maid.

She bobbed a curtsey and bustled to the armoire to hang the outfits.

"There are three sets of coats, shirts, and leggings, each different colors and styles. Let me know if they don't fit right, and I'll have the tailor visit. I'll be back in a moment with shoes and smallclothes."

"Thank you. Your name is Lydia, right?"

She turned, careful to keep her eyes locked onto mine. "Yes, sir. That's right."

"I'm Keelan. I don't know what ridiculous title they'll make up for people to call me, but please just call me Keelan." Without thinking, I stretched my hand out as if to shake hers. My towel unfurled, and it was only quick reflexes that prevented an awkward situation from becoming even more so.

Lydia curtsied and scurried out of the room without a glance back. She was so flustered that she forgot to close the door as she left.

"I'll be back with your shoes!" she shouted from several steps down the hallway, a nervous giggle in her voice. I rolled my eyes and shuffled to close the door, struggling to hold my towel in place lest the entire Palace see all I had to offer. Before I made it halfway across the room, I heard Lydia gasp and giggle even louder.

Then Jess beat me to the open doorway.

Her eyes widened. However, unlike Lydia, her gaze was unflinching, drinking in every inch of bare skin like a woman dying of thirst.

"Should I worry about leaving my staff alone with you, Guardsman?" Her tone was playfully serious.

I fumbled with my darn towel, trying to tie it around my waist once more.

"I, um, just need a minute," I said, color flooding back to my ears again.

Clearly amused, Jess took a step into the doorway.

The panic on my face must've been her greatest reward. With both brows raised, she grinned wolfishly and said, "Had I known Melucians were so well put together, I might have told Lydia to forgo the outfits and simply give you towels to wear."

She glanced below my waistline at the soaked, sagging towel, winked, then turned.

"Get dressed. Lydia will check back in a few minutes and show you the way to the family dining room." Jess paused a moment, then smirked. "I will see about getting you some longer towels."

She laughed as she vanished down the hallway.

I couldn't help the grin that parted my lips as I leaned against the now-closed door. This visit to the Palace was turning out very differently from anything Atikus and I had planned, but that wasn't a bad thing.

When I entered the dining room a few moments later, Jess was staring at a painting of what I assumed was a great-grandfather, perhaps several greats back. Her head turned as a page announced my entrance, yet another tradition I'd have to get used to on this visit. The formality of the Palace was almost as imposing as the idea of dining in the Queen's private chamber. I fidgeted with the stiff golden collar of the charcoal-gray doublet Lydia had provided.

When I looked up, Jess was staring.

"What?" I looked down at my clothes, then back to her. "Gray coat, black trousers. It's about as neutral between Melucian blue and Kingdom green as we could get. The stiff cut will take a little getting used to. Is it all right?"

"That is the style these days—the more uncomfortable, the more fashionable." She waved a hand and smiled, her voice turning subdued. "The clothes suit you well. Please, come and sit. We only have a short time before the Council assembles, and I need to prepare you."

Over lunch, Jess walked me through the key advisors who would be in attendance, the office each held, and what she had tasked each with prior to leaving to meet me in the cave. I appreciated her efficient, direct style, a reminder of my many briefings in Captain-Commander Albius's office. That man wouldn't know how to flower a word if his life depended on it.

"Keelan, you saved my life—*twice*. I will always be Jess to you in private, but when we stand before my subjects, you must remember to address me as Your Majesty. Anything more familiar will raise suspicion and fuel unwanted rumors, neither of which we can afford right now." She took a sip of tea, then set the delicate cup on its gold-rimmed saucer. "This is an unscheduled meeting, so there will be no formal agenda. The Council will want to hear your account and will question you on the condition of the Kingdom forces following their retreat. They will also want to know the attitude of Melucia's new leadership toward the Kingdom and our overtures of peace. To a man, those you will meet were opposed to the invasion, especially my Ministers of Trade and Foreign Affairs, but they are fiercely loyal to the Crown and will be cautious. I doubt they will report anything while you are in the room, so do not be disappointed if you learn nothing new.

"Oh, one more thing, under no circumstance should you reveal the nature of your Gift, the cave, or the mirror-portal. Even if I trusted the Ministers completely, I would hold those secrets between us."

I leaned back, surprised by her caution with her own Council, many of whom she'd known for years. "I understand the need to protect the cave and the mirror, but my Gift? Anyone who's read the papers in Melucia knows what my magic can do. Why hide it here?"

"Another lesson my father drilled into me was to be wary of who you trust—and question *those* people carefully. I wish no one knew of your Gift. I would keep you at court just to advise me on deception and lies, which are more common in court than frills and lace. That sort of insight would be invaluable to a monarch."

"You almost sound afraid of your own people," I said, immediately wishing I'd kept my mouth shut.

She didn't flinch. "I am seventeen, Keelan. If I rule for fifty years, a day will not pass when I do not question someone's honesty. I know it is part of the job—my father knew it, too—but I hate it, the scheming and wheedling for position and power. Everyone thinks the monarch is the big fish, but sometimes it feels like being a minnow in a pond of hungry sharks ready to devour you and everything you care for."

Her hand shook as she reached for her tea once more.

I regarded her in silence. When we met, she'd been battered and bruised, frightened, and mourning more loss than anyone should experience in a lifetime. She'd drawn into herself, only opening up when she wanted to lash out at someone. I saw her as a petty, immature teenager whose life was spiraling out of control. I didn't like that girl very much, but I'd sworn to protect her.

Now, sitting at the Queen's table, dressed in elegant silks with her head held aloft, she spoke with the dignity and grace of a queen. She was a woman reborn.

Jess spoke with purpose, measuring each word as though the whole world depended on what she said.

Perhaps it did.

This time she caught me staring.

"What?"

I smiled. "Her Majesty is *remarkable*."

Crimson flared across her cheeks, and she struggled to compose herself as a page interrupted.

"Your Majesty, Council is assembled in the Throne Room." The boy bowed and backed out.

Jess straightened in her chair and nodded to the page. In a blink, her confident, regal mask snapped back into place.

"Guardsman, follow me."

CHAPTER 20

JESS

T he first two hours of the Council meeting went as I had predicted.

The Ministers listened for the first hour but peppered Keelan with questions as the afternoon wore on. By the time he was allowed to sit, the mood at the table was more collaborative than interrogative.

"Your Majesty." Mage Ernest rose as the conversation lulled. "The memorial for the late King and Prince will take place in three days, and your coronation five days later. We have planned each event in great detail but require your approval to proceed."

My face fell at the mention of my father and Justin.

I had barely had a moment to grieve, unless one counts the time I'd spent with Keelan and Atikus running for our lives. The idea of laying them to rest weighed on my heart.

"Mage, you are new to me but have served me well thus far. My family has known the others on this Council for many years. I trust each of you to honor my father and brother as you know I would wish it. I will leave the details to you." A moment of silence stretched before I spoke again. "We will discuss the coronation tomorrow. One day will not spoil any plans you have made, and I could use some fresh air. Ambassador, come with me."

I rose and led Keelan back through the door to the royal chambers. When I reached the point where we normally went in opposite directions, I turned. "Come with me. I want to show you something."

We followed a series of hallways, then paused before a plain, unmarked door that could have been a storage closet. I pushed the door open, and chill winter air rushed to greet us. A few paces farther, we were surrounded by the beauty of the famed Royal Gardens.

I smiled at the wonder on Keelan's face. "This is one of my favorite places. I used to hide here when I did not want to do my lessons or whatever chore my mother insisted was important. There is nowhere in the world I feel more at home."

I caught Keelan watching as I trailed my fingers across a prickly bush with pink flowers.

"Jess, it's *winter*. How is this garden blooming?" The dumbfounded look on his face made me laugh.

"Do you not have gardeners with special Gifts back in Melucia?"

Recognition dawned in his eyes.

I stopped to watch him as he took in my garden. Without warning, he turned and bowled into me, nearly knocking me over. His quick, firm hands caught me from falling.

"I'm sorry. I wasn't paying attention."

I looked up.

Our bodies were only fingers apart.

A thrill of tension raced up my arms and into my chest.

I tried to speak, but only whispered, "It's okay. I . . ."

Keelan realized he was still holding me and stepped back quickly, raising his hands in the air as if surrendering to an angry archer.

We stood frozen a moment, staring into each other's eyes until—

"Jess! Are you out here? *JESS*!" a young boy's voice called.

I huffed out an annoyed sigh, then shrugged at Keelan.

"Time for you to meet the royal chatterbox," I said with a smirk.

Before we'd made it ten paces, Prince Kendall Vester wheeled around the corner and slammed into me, wrapping his wiry arms around my waist.

"Hey, little man. What is this all about?" I mussed his hair, then pulled him away by his shoulders.

"Kenna wants me to study the inside of frogs. She said we have to kill one and cut it open. I can't kill a frog, Jess! You remember Felix? How could I cut up Felix? Or one of his cousins. Any frog could be his family. Jess, this is terrible!" The towheaded boy was so upset he didn't notice Keelan looming a few paces away. When his eyes found the giant man, they widened, and his face lit like newborn flame.

"You're *the Melucian*! The famous Guardsman who's solved a hundred crimes and stopped a thousand more! I heard you can read minds! Is that true? Read my mind now. What am I thinking? Can you tell me stories about your investigations? What's the craziest thing you've seen? Are all criminals deranged? Are you ever scared? I bet you're never scared. Have you ever killed anyone?

Who's the most famous person you've captured? Is it true you can't be stabbed or shot with an arrow?"

Keelan opened his mouth, then closed it. His eyes darted to mine, then back to Kendall's.

The boy prattled on about the supernatural powers he believed the famous Constable possessed, barely taking a breath between wild claims and even wilder questions. He was so enthralled with his new idol-made-flesh that his fear of the frog dissection vanished, and he completely forgot his sister, *the Queen*, standing behind him.

Keelan kneeled so he didn't tower over Kendall. My brother didn't flinch.

It was odd watching the pair of them together. Kendall was enamored. Stories of Keelan made the rounds the moment we set foot in the capital, but the childish exaggerations that flew out of my brother's mouth were beyond anything I could have dreamed.

But what pulled at my chest even more than wild rumors of the invincible foreigner was how that strong man gave the small boy before him his complete attention. Once past the initial shock of Kendall's verbal assault, Keelan engaged with him, asked him questions, egged him on. He smiled at each new revelation, more insane than the last.

I began to think he would heft Kendall onto his shoulders and march him around the garden if the boy asked.

When Keelan's pleading gaze found mine, my face was covered in tears of laughter. The hulking investigator paralyzed by the prepubescent Prince was almost more than I could take.

I couldn't help but trace the lines of Keelan's jaw with my eyes. They were more square—and likely more firm, than the stone corners of the Palace walls. The stubble he refused to shave, despite my urging, made the burly man appear even more rugged.

Standing in the garden, surrounded by unmatched beauty and peace, watching my baby brother and Keelan, something deep within me warmed in a way I had not felt since—

A wave of nausea and terror *whooshed* through me like the billowing wind of an oncoming storm.

I forced myself to examine nearby flowers.

Moments later, I decided it was time to save Keelan. "Kendall . . . Kendall! Take a breath." The boy startled and turned to face me. "Go inside and find something you would like to show Keelan. Just *one* thing, okay? We will be there shortly."

Kendall darted away without another word.

"Wow," Keelan said, running a hand over his head. "He's . . . a lot."

I giggled.

Me. Queen of the Spires. Giggled.

I wanted to dive into the surrounding plants and never climb out.

"It is safe to say he likes you," found its way out of my mouth.

"How could you tell? I don't think he came up for air the whole time."

"That is pretty much how family dinners go."

I meant the comment to be lighthearted, but I was reminded of three empty chairs at the family dinner table. I turned away so Keelan wouldn't see my sudden sadness.

The warmth of his hand spread across my shoulder.

"I'm sorry," he said, his voice low. "Everyone expects you to move forward as if nothing happened, but so much of your world has changed. I don't understand how you do it, how you hold it all together. You may be the strongest person I know."

I turned and examined his eyes. There was such deep empathy and . . . *something*.

"I do not know, Keelan." I reached down and cupped a fist-sized bloom. "Some days, I fear the seams will tear and I will fall apart. I just . . . take it one day at a time."

A moment passed, then I turned, looked up at him, and placed a hand on his arm. "I do know one thing."

"What's that?"

"I feel better knowing you are here."

CHAPTER 21

DANAI

I sat in my high-backed throne on the dais of the ceremonial chamber of the Children's Temple. Braziers blazed throughout the chamber, their magical flame snapping soundlessly in the cavernous hall. The marble statue of Irina had been returned from its perch above the Temple's retracted roof and now rested in its original position, towering over the most sacred room in the building.

A dozen men in silky brown robes kneeled before me with their heads bowed.

Prophecies fell out of favor centuries ago when most religions were discarded in favor of loyalty to the earthly Crown, yet there were always pockets of people who yearned for communion within the unknowable, people who craved mystery and mysticism.

Neither truly answered their longing or questions.

Where men of learning saw veins in a leaf bearing water and nutrients, believers witnessed the flow of their deity's lifeforce. In those men and women, in their open minds yearning to receive unfathomable truths, I knew my seed would bear fruit.

The Priests now crouched before my throne had spent the past month poring over ancient texts I had supposedly found deep in the mountains on the eastern border—at least that's what I told the blind, robed fools.

At first, they had doubted the faded words on the yellowed parchment represented more than the writings—ravings, really—of a deranged mountain hermit, but I urged them to dig deeper, to discern every meaning. I ordered them to find whether these documents held valuable truths or would be kindling for my hearth.

Buried within that holy script—just deeply enough to require some effort to uncover it—a prophecy foretold of the return of the One. The Priest who discovered the foretelling thought it odd. The text predicted the return of a false prophet would precede the true One.

I openly mocked them.

I tested and pressed when one or more would assert some divine meaning. I forced them to defend their positions, and in doing so, to *commit* to their arguments.

Their resistance transformed views into tenets of a new faith.

The change in their work—and in their eyes as they watched me—was remarkable.

Their belief was palpable.

I could barely contain myself.

How was it possible for prophecy to be so clear, so direct?

Everything fit perfectly with the timeline of events occurring over the past year. It was almost as though I had written them myself—which, of course, I had.

It had taken weeks to mix ink in just the right proportions to saturate the page as was the custom centuries before. I struggled to perfect the spell that would age the parchment well enough to fool even the sharpest scholars, but I'd done it.

Now all I needed were followers willing to buy what I was selling.

I looked no further than Irina's Children, the group I helped establish nearly ten centuries earlier. Their sole purpose had been to unravel the mysteries of the golden text on her monolith and carry out those instructions to bring about her return.

After Irina's failure, the Children were lost and adrift.

They had labored a thousand years to return Irina, and she had failed them.

It was a simple thing to turn their blind adoration for her toward a new scion of faith.

But I couldn't proclaim myself.

Rather, I needed them to discover the prophecy and, through their faith, call me to serve as their master. It had to be *their* discovery and *their* divine providence.

In the end, the morsels I buried in my holy texts worked better than I ever imagined. I was prepared to send them on quests, force them into trials, induce them with intoxicants that would produce visions and prophecies of their own—all magically controlled, of course—but none of that had been necessary. These men and women were devoid of purpose and clung to the first life raft to drift by.

I couldn't have been more pleased.

"Rise, my Children," I said. "It is time the people learned the tenets of our faith. You, my most trusted disciples, will carry word of my return to every city, town, and village throughout the Kingdom.

You will feed and clothe those in need, teach those who cannot read, and minister to the sick and dying as if they were your own kin.

"But remember this, the return of the One is a foretelling. The time for the people to learn of my return will come, but it is *not* today. You must build anticipation and hope in the hearts of our people first. Fan the flames of faith and build their belief, stone by precious stone. Only then will the path be laid for my return."

"By your command, Excellency," the figures intoned in unison.

The one on the end dropped to a knee. "Excellency, what if the people resist your words? What if they refuse our call?"

I smiled down at the sheep before me.

"My Child, you will help them follow our path through benevolence and compassion. From this day forth, you are no longer Children, but *Priests* of the One. You are my voices on the wind, whispering of my return to our people. Do not trouble yourself with those who fail to believe. Others among our Order will follow to help those reluctant souls see our Light."

"And what of the new Queen, Excellency? How should we speak of her to the people?"

"Hear my words," I said in a formal tone, as if issuing an edict. "Today, there is the State, and the Faith. Soon, the State and the Faith will be one. We welcome the Queen into her new role as the leader of mortal men and invite her to hear our words and subjugate herself to our spiritual guidance."

"Yes, Excellency," the man replied.

"Now go. Our brother, the Voice, attends to the new Queen in the capital. Hold to the faith, and know you bring peace and prosperity to our people."

The ten Priests bowed one last time.

"By your command, Excellency."

When the last of my disciples vanished through the doors, a tall man strode out from behind one of the massive marble columns clutching a mask in his right hand, an odd mix of a bear with feathers in place of ears. I was striding down the steps of the dais when Bear approached and bowed.

"Excellency, I have chosen five. They await your command."

"Five will do nicely." I steepled my fingers and grinned at the man. "You have done well, *Priest*. Bring them to me."

CHAPTER 22

JESS

Weeks passed in rapid succession following our return to the Palace. Much of my time was consumed with the work of rebuilding the military and reassuring my people of the Kingdom's commitment to peace with their neighbor.

Rumors still ran throughout the country carrying wild tales of Melucian demons summoned to strike down our righteous King and Prince, and no manner of royal decree would stop them. The stories Thorn carefully crafted prior to the invasion, those of Melucian malevolence, hadn't simply taken root; they had grown and flowered through taverns and inns, bearing fruit in temples and shops throughout the land. Hatred of our eastern neighbor hadn't waned with the conclusion of hostilities as I had hoped. It had actually grown with each tale of soldierly valor or Melucian deceit.

I marveled at the willingness of the masses to believe such lies and innuendo.

Amid this atmosphere of misplaced loathing, my popularity soared.

Sympathy for the Princess who'd lost every-thing, combined with nationalistic fervor fueled by beleaguered troops returning from their bitter defeat, made me the single point of hope across the land. Miraculously, the people had forgotten the petulant teenager who tried to abandon her duty and outrun her birthright only months earli-er. All they saw now was a beautiful, fierce Queen giving her all to knit together a war-torn King-dom.

Conjecture surrounding my relationship with Keelan buzzed among nobles and servants alike. I counted on his counsel and willing shoulder in ways I could never trust my own people, but our friendship was far less sensational than rumors claimed.

Still, wildfires were hard to suppress once lit.

Keelan was well liked, but the idea of the Queen consorting with a commoner, and a *Melucian*, left a bitter taste on many tongues, though they rarely stopped wagging long enough to savor it.

He didn't accompany me as I rode among my people, even in the safety of the capital, but I was rarely without his company as I strode through the gardens or Palace proper. The Council had even become accustomed to the towering Guardsman attending sessions, with his perpetually stern features and humorless advice. They grew to appreciate his thoughtful, direct insights despite his often-gruff delivery.

I tried to ignore the idle chatter.

I watched my father spin many plates as King, but I never truly appreciated the ever-present burden that rested on his shoulders.

Being a sovereign wasn't like a commoner's vocation where the workday ended and family time began. I was *always* Queen, *always* on stage, *always* on call. Even when I managed a moment of blessed quiet, a maid or messenger often sought me out to deliver news or request my attention.

It was overwhelming—and I loved every minute of it.

I delayed my coronation twice, insisting my Council focus on the needs of families who lost fathers or sons, and those of returning soldiers who witnessed calamity that would change them forever. I argued that my people were more important than a ceremony to assuage my ego.

By the sixth week, sentiment among the Council had turned against further delay. My advisors argued the need to cement my rule, and, more importantly, the need to give my people something to celebrate.

I was settling into the rhythm of the Palace well, but the art of understanding my people and their needs was often bewildering.

Gazing into the eyes of a widow and her daughter, I could wrap them in my arms and provide for their needs, but it was impossible to look *my people* in their collective eyes and understand their needs, much less provide for them. There was no magic salve to soothe public fears or the irrational wave of emotions that wafted through crowds unseen and barely contained. Those unwieldy phantoms mystified me, though I knew I would need to master them if I was to rule well.

There is so much to learn. Sometimes, I feel so small and lost. How did Father do it for so many years?

I stared up at the golden blooms of starflowers in the garden. Their petals spanned twice the length of my palm and shimmered in the sunlight. Against the emerald of their thick, leafy vines and the white of freshly fallen snow, the tear-shaped golden fronds were ever more brilliant.

The subtle sound of footfalls turned my head.

Keelan, sporting his sharply cut Guard uniform for the first time since our return, strode toward me.

"Want to run away before they can put that golden shackle on your head?" he teased.

"Golden shackle? You make it sound like a criminal sentence. Besides, shackles go on your wrists. The crown is a holy relic they will place gently on my head."

He smiled and nodded. "Criminal sentence? That's probably a better description, although I might amend it to fit with the legal code and call it a *life sentence*."

I stood and shook my head. "Thanks for giving me confidence before I go to the executioner's block."

"Woah . . . I was *imprisoning* you. Nobody said anything about *execution*—yet."

I slapped his meaty chest with my palm, then laughed. "You are impossible. I think putting you back in that Guard uniform addled your brain."

I let my eyes follow the rows of golden buttons as they curved about his chest then tapered toward his nonexistent waist.

He stepped back a half step and avoided my gaze.

"What?" I looked down and self-consciously adjusted my pearls.

"Jess, you look like a queen . . . I mean . . . regal . . ." he breathed more than spoke, then met my eyes. "I mean, you *are* a queen . . . and you've always been beautiful, but now . . . um . . ."

I blushed but lifted my chin and smirked. "Your way with words is . . . *um* . . . impressive."

"Just let me get this out, all right?" His gaze fell, then rose to meet my eyes. "You are so much more than beautiful, so much more than just a queen. I mean . . . not *just* a queen . . . you are a queen, you know. Spirits!" He huffed, and his shoulders slumped like a teen boy struggling to kiss his first girl. "You *see* people, really see them, and not just who they are but who they can become. You see their goodness and their possibility. And when you set your mind to a problem, nothing will stand in your way until you've solved it. I've never met anyone so strong and sharp and determined. I guess what I'm trying to say is . . . I admire the woman standing before me and respect the Queen she is becoming."

I had a sharp retort waiting on the edge of my tongue, but his words made my breath catch. A wave of heat flooded through me, and I found myself struggling to focus.

So, I did the only thing I could think of in the moment; I winked and began walking up the path toward the Palace. "Come along, good sir. The golden shackle awaits."

We marched from the hallway that spanned the royal family's private residences into the public passages of the Palace. Green-and-gold-liveried servants raced about. No matter their task, each attendant we passed stepped aside and bowed or curtsied. Every twenty paces, a pike-wielding soldier stood rigidly against the wall. The soldiers smacked the butts of their spears against the marble floor in salute to their monarch as we passed.

I chuckled as we passed the first pair of guards and Keelan jumped at their salute. "Is the big, bad Guardsman scared of a little noise?"

"I didn't expect . . . whatever that was. Um, Your Majesty."

I spit out a laugh as he *finally* remembered to address me properly in front of the servants and guards. None dared look directly at us, but I thought I caught one maid's brow raise along with an amused corner of her mouth.

"Fear not, my brave Melucian friend, it is I, not you, who faces the gallows on this day."

We entered the Throne Room through the side door closest to the dais, and I was surprised to find my Council assembled, each dressed in traditional black robes with the heavy golden chains of their office. Their ceremonial black hats trimmed in glittering gold made me grin. As a young girl attending my first state function, I asked a little too loudly why the Council wore fancy cooking pots on their heads. My father, ever present in his role as monarch, lost all composure as my tiny voice filled the audience chamber and stricken looks spread throughout the assembled nobles. I never heard the King laugh so hard in the Throne Room.

And now they wore those same cooking pots for me.

I stifled a laugh and strode forward.

Each Minister bowed, far more reverently than I had experienced from the nation's leaders before. Each in turn grasped my outstretched hand and kissed it. I was so distracted by their display of respect that I missed the man standing by the massive chamber doors. With a start, I ignored the remaining Councilors, lifted my billowing gown, and raced into the stunned man's arms.

"Uncle Ethan!" I squealed in a most un-queenly manner.

General Ethan Marks had returned to the capital after the Kingdom's crushing defeat in Melucia. The wintery journey covering hundreds of leagues and two mountain ranges had taken months. I had given up on him making it back for my coronation, yet here he stood, shoulders draped with the ridiculous hunter's fur he always insisted on wearing.

I didn't care about any of that now.

With my father, mother, and brother gone, Ethan represented one of the last vestiges of family I had left.

"I would have moved the Spires to be here for you today." He held my shoulders at arm's length and smiled. "I am so proud of you, and I know your father is proud of you, too."

At the invocation of my father, my smile drifted from jubilant to wistful, yet it did not fall. "When the ceremony is complete, we should talk. There is something I need to ask you."

He released my shoulders and bowed. "My life is yours, Majesty."

A moment later, I turned to face the Council, each of whom watched the exchange with Marks. "I suppose I cannot run away again, can I?"

The stricken looks on the Ministers' faces caught me by surprise. I meant the question as a lighthearted jest, but it appeared to strike too close to some unseen mark.

Ethan whispered from behind, "They fear *exactly* that, Majesty, after your most recent . . . adventure."

I straightened my back and made eye contact with each Minister. "You are our Privy Council, the heart of our government and our most cherished advisors. Each of you has pledged your life to my Kingdom and our reign. Today, we pledge ours in return. Hear the oath we speak from the dais, and know we willingly offer ourselves in service to this Kingdom until we draw our last breath."

The Ministers dropped to aged knees and bowed their heads.

Ethan followed their lead.

I was startled but noticed Keelan standing quietly in the corner by the door we had entered. He nodded through an unreadable expression.

Dozens of butterflies fluttered within my chest as I turned and, alone, passed through the chamber's entrance toward my waiting carriage.

Festive crowds lined thoroughfares and cheered along the entire length of road from Palace to Temple. My gilded and heavily armored box-on-wheels was sandwiched between a hundred men on horseback. The streets had been cleared of the prior day's dusting of snow to ensure easy passage and clear viewing for the anticipated throng.

The park that sat across from the ancient Temple was overflowing with well-wishing commoners, while nobles in their ceremonial finery and outlandish jewelry stood quietly behind rows of sharply uniformed guards who lined the walk that led into the marbled building.

As I emerged from the carriage and took my first few steps, the crowd erupted.

Men and women on either side bowed and curtsied in a continuous wave that preceded me by several paces. I had to remind myself not to look to either side, rather to hold my head erect and proceed in a slow, dignified manner befitting an incoming monarch. Everything was scripted and rehearsed, but nothing could have prepared me for my racing heart.

I approached the gilded doors of the Temple and was greeted by the High Priest, a kindly old man with unruly wisps of winter wafting in the breeze. He wore simple white robes trimmed in faded gold that spoke more of a humble servant than the exalted leader of the country's dominant faith.

I had always liked our High Priest.

The vicar bowed, adjusted his ceremonial cap, and said in a familiar, fatherly tone, "Welcome, child. Forgive me while I set my cook pot to rights."

Upon later reflection, resisting a laugh at his unwitting use of my private childhood joke might have been the most challenging thing I did that day. Only a small snort escaped before we were moving again.

Two towering guards smacked their pikes to marble, then opened the Temple's doors in a painfully slow motion. The High Priest rose, took my proffered hand, and led me inside like a father ready to offer his daughter to a new husband. The light, sweet scent of incense greeted us as tightly knit harmonies of a choir rose and fell in melodic beauty.

The Temple's interior consisted of one massive aisle lined on either side by five ascending rows of padded benches that faced each other. I always thought it looked like two opposing armies waiting for a bugle to charge forward. My father insisted this was a house of worship, though my innocent analogy held more truth regarding schisms in the faith than any child could ever understand.

Nobles stood before benches in ascending rank, those highest in the order of succession standing nearest the dais. Most of the men wore powdered wigs, another tradition I had never understood or appreciated. Women wore gowns, outlandish hats, and jewelry designed to match every other woman in sight.

Rows of soldiers formed ranks along the aisle facing inward.

As the procession reached the far end where the throne had been installed for this day, I noticed foreign representatives standing before pews to my right. Tribal leaders from the islands of Vint wore brightly colored blouses with wicker hats adorned by even brighter plumes. Clan leaders from Baz were covered in dark fur from head to toe. The continent's easternmost nations of Amnel, Pantrel, Orn, and Drea had also sent delegations.

The ancient isle of Rea Utu sent only one representative, a bent old crone who leaned on a gnarled staff and smiled at me through gapped teeth. I couldn't turn to view the woman with the procession moving forward but felt a keen intelligence in her ancient gaze.

Last among the foreign dignitaries stood a lone Melucian.

At least a head taller than any of the other representatives, Keelan was a beacon in the night. The Palace staff had worked miracles with his uniform, and the golden Lieutenant's chevron on his shoulder glittered nearly as brightly as my own trim. Conscious of the hundreds of eyes anticipating his reaction to the young Queen, he did not turn his head, but I caught a slight widening of his eyes as I passed.

My lips rebelled and curled a bit.

Before the final seat in the final row, the seat traditionally reserved for the Crown Prince or Princess, stood a terrified-looking Kendall. I shattered protocol of the tightly scripted ceremony and stopped to face my brother. His wide eyes rose to meet mine, and the loneliness I saw in his gaze pierced my heart.

I bent and cupped his cheek, then whispered, "I love you, baby brother. I'm *so* proud of you."

Kendall gripped my hand with his own, kissed it, and eyed the impatient High Priest, who struggled to get my attention. I squeezed the boy's hand one last time, then turned toward my duty.

We stopped before the first step of the dais, staring eye level at the Throne of Spires: a gaudy, gilded monstrosity that bruised the bums of kings and queens for generations. It was an impressive piece of furniture, but no monarch had ever admired it for its comfort. My father certainly hadn't.

I groaned.

The back is padded, why not the seat?

The randomness of my thoughts kept some of the nerves at bay but nearly caused me to laugh aloud as the chamber reached a moment of utter stillness.

That moment passed with the rap of the High Priest's staff, a whip-crack that brought me back to the present. I bent to rest my knees on the pleasantly *cushioned* faldstool and continued gazing at the throne.

Minister of Justice Willa Parto, the first woman to ever serve on the Privy Council, appeared from behind the throne. Unlike the High Priest's simple garb, Minister Parto's robes billowed with splendor. Seven hues of green representing the seven forested regions of the Kingdom ebbed and flowed throughout her gold-trimmed gown, while three ancient chains of office dangled from her neck. A saucer-sized silver pendent depicting the scales of justice beneath a crown consumed the center of her chest.

Minister Parto looked down and offered a comforting smile.

"Your Majesty," she bellowed for all to hear. "Your Royal Highness, Lords and Ladies, Honored Dignitaries, and guests, the King is dead. Now comes your Queen. Rise and face her."

As one, the assembled nobles and dignitaries turned from facing the opposite benches toward the throne. I rose and, with a guiding hand from the High Priest, ascended the four steps, turned to face the crowd, and sat.

In that moment, looking out at the nobles, *my* nobles, the entire world settled onto my shoulders. I suddenly felt its weight pressing against my chest. I placed a calming hand to my stomach and sat up straight, just as my mother had taught me, breathing slowly and deeply.

The High Priest rose, stepped around the throne, and lifted the crown from its velvet pillow with both hands. He turned toward the east and bowed with the crown raised above his head. "I present to you Queen Jessia, your undoubted

Queen. All you who come this day to do your homage and service, are you willing to do the same?"

Those now facing the vicar cried aloud with one voice, "Aye, we will serve. HAIL, QUEEN JESSIA!"

He turned toward the south and repeated his call, then the west, and finally the north, each time receiving an even louder reply, as if each set of nobles sought to outdo the others in their public pledge to their new sovereign.

The High Priest bowed to Minister Parto and stepped back to allow her to step forward. Parto faced me from the side, bowed, then spoke.

"Madam, is Your Majesty willing to take the Oath?"

"I am willing."

"Will you solemnly promise and swear to govern the Peoples of the Spires according to our laws and ancient customs?"

"I will."

"By the Spirits, and before these witnesses, I beg Your Majesty, rise and make your pledge."

I stood and drew one final breath of freedom, then spoke in a clear, unwavering voice.

"I, Jessia of House Vester, do pledge to lead, serve, and defend the Crown and its people from all threats within and without, without fear or favor, affection or ill will. I pledge to do right to all manner of people after the laws and usages of the Kingdom. To the people and the Spires, be it long or short, my whole life is yours. By the Spirits and the Spires, this is my pledge."

Minister Parto bowed low and stepped back into her spot behind the throne.

The High Priest stepped forward, raised the crown, and bowed once more.

"The crown of the Spires! Come all and look upon its majestic favor. Spirits, we beg your blessings on this crown and the brow beneath it. Sanctify this symbol and our servant, Jessia, upon whose head we place this sacred relic, that she may be filled with royal majesty, abundant grace, and princely virtue."

He moved to stand facing me, bowed once more, then carefully placed the crown on my head. As soon as his hands lifted, brilliant Light swelled from both the crown and the ring I now wore as sovereign. The High Priest shuffled to the lowest step and fell to one knee as the magic swirled around me, bathing me in an otherworldly glow. The crowd's collective intake of breath echoed through the chamber just before the magic flared one final time and exploded outward in a sea of sparkling shards above the heads of the awestruck nobility.

The High Priest dared not rise, but bellowed, "HAIL, QUEEN JESSIA."

The crowd rushed to mirror the priest's pose, falling to their knees with heads bowed, and echoed again and again, "HAIL, QUEEN JESSIA!"

For the first time since entering the Temple, I allowed my eyes to roam about the chamber.

Kendall beamed up at me, calling out in his squeaky, preteen voice.

I gazed across the visiting dignitaries and nobles, and my heart both raced and swelled with pride. My father had raised me for this moment, for the day I would succeed him. I always knew he would miss my coronation, as it was rare to succeed a living ruler, but I still smarted at his absence in my moment of glory. The vacant seats beside Kendall underscored other absences I felt.

I found Keelan again, kneeling along with the others. Even on his knees, he towered over those around him, and I caught him stealing a glance. He winked before returning his head to the correct position.

He winked *at me! Right after I received the crown!*

I tried to ignore the beginning of a mental debate over whether to be amused or annoyed with the Guardsman. What remained of my Privy Council was to my right behind the Royal Pew. A sea of nobles spread beyond. All were bowed low, only plumed bonnets and backs visible from my vantage on the dais.

Then my eye was drawn to a singular figure in the back of the Temple nave. Brown robes glinted in the light just enough to make me notice.

Why isn't that man kneeling like everyone else? And those robes . . .

There was something familiar about the man. I knew but couldn't place it.

His posture? The set of his jaw? His shoulder-length hair?

Something was *so* familiar.

And then I *knew*—and my breath caught.

CHAPTER 23

JESS

I blinked a few times and peered at the end of the Temple as the assembled mass rose. The back wall now stood empty, though I was sure a man had been there only a moment earlier.

I allowed myself to breathe again.

It wasn't him. You're just overwhelmed. Relax.

An hour later, my gilded carriage pulled up to the front entrance of the Palace. Dozens of guards lined the circular drive. On either side of the grand entrance, rows of neatly dressed servants stood to greet their new sovereign. They all knew me. Many had helped raise me.

But today I emerged a new woman, the Queen.

They beamed with pride and dared to look me in the eye as I passed. Some wept openly. When I came to the first row, I stunned them all by greeting each person by name and thanking them for their service to the Crown. This act took another thirty minutes but endeared me to my staff in ways I didn't immediately realize. I couldn't explain why I had done it; it just *felt* right in the moment.

I made my way into the Throne Room.

Miraculously, the staff had moved my throne from the Temple to its usual resting place while I returned by carriage. Before I sat, I turned to a young page and asked for a cushion. When he gaped but didn't move, I smirked and whispered conspiratorially, "If I have to sit here and listen to lords drone on for the next two hours on this hard chair, my bum will fall asleep. Your Queen *needs* your help. Get me that cushion."

The page, now more shocked by my familiarity than my request, couldn't contain his smile and bowed. "At once, Majesty."

Once seated, I nodded to the Royal Master, who then nodded to the guards standing by each of the gilded doors. As the doors opened, my eyes widened at the endless queue of dukes and barons—and every other flavor of nobility lined up and waiting. Each came to offer the Oath of Fealty to their new Queen.

The Warden of the East, the portly Duke Kinsley Parna who'd become familiar with the sharp end of my shrimp fork in a previous encounter, waddled before me. "Majesty," he said, then bowed as low as his stomach would allow. An awkward moment passed before he rose and whispered, as though we had some private, personal relationship I was unaware of, "This one is pleased to see you safe and enthroned."

I lifted a brow but said nothing.

For once, Parna took the hint and lowered himself to one knee, removed his sword from its scabbard and raised it in both hands above his head. "I promise to be faithful to the Queen of the Spires, never to cause her harm, and will observe my homage to her completely, against all persons, in good faith and without deceit. Long live the Queen."

I waited a bit longer than ceremony dictated, enjoying seeing my least favorite duke submit, then offered the ceremonial reply. "The Crown accepts, and pledges our justice and protection, now and for all time."

The next few hours passed exactly as expected.

Lords, ladies, and visiting dignitaries flowed in to pledge, in many cases bearing gifts of gold, silver, perfumes, or silks. One of the islanders presented me with an odd bird with colorful feathers in a gilded cage. I nearly lost my stately composure when the creature looked me in the eye and said, "Hail, Queen Jessia!"

Nobles in line burst into delighted applause while the islander smiled and bowed.

By late afternoon, the Royal Presence was fading.

My neck and back were sore from sitting under the weight of the Imperial Crown, and the rush of being coronated had worn off, leaving me physically and mentally exhausted. When the end of the line appeared, I made another mental note to award my young page a kingdom of his own for bringing me a cushion, though my bum had *still* fallen asleep.

Keelan approached the throne, last of the dignitaries, the traditional position of highest honor afforded to Melucia, the Kingdom's largest neighbor and trading partner. I hadn't noticed him until he stood before me. I had to school myself to stop a broad smile.

Keelan wore the annoying smirk of a man who knew what I was thinking. Again, I schooled myself, this time to stop from throwing the royal cushion at my honored guest.

He bowed and offered his respects on behalf of the Melucian people, then gave the scripted speech Atikus had prepared, proclaiming the

Melucian Empire's deepest desire to again walk hand in hand with their Kingdom neighbors.

"Guardsman Rea," I said once the formalities had been completed. "Please remain a moment while the Throne Room is cleared. There are matters of relations between our peoples I would like to discuss."

Keelan nodded and stepped aside to wait for the guards to clear lingering nobles from the hall. When the doors slammed shut, I reached up, removed the crown, and placed it on the smaller throne beside me.

"That thing is *so* heavy."

Keelan stepped forward and chuckled. "I'm sure you'll get used to it, Majesty."

"Oh, you had better not start bending and scraping, at least not while we are in private. I need someone other than my little brother I can talk to."

"Whatever you command, Majesty. I am at your service." He bowed dramatically. When he rose, the infuriating man's mouth was all smirk.

This time I *did* throw the pillow and nailed him in the chest.

"Royal abuse! The Crown is assaulting its guests! Help!" he cried to one of the guards standing against the wall.

That moment reminded me how rare it would be to truly be alone again. I had to be more careful with guards and servants always about. Even innocent comments said without thought—overheard—could find their way out of the Palace.

I snorted and stepped down, yanked the pillow out of his hands, and tossed it back onto my throne. "Enough, Guardsman. Please escort me back to my chamber. I need to change and freshen up before the banquet."

"It would be my pleasure, Majesty." He smiled and offered his arm.

We had made it nearly to my chambers when a horrified maid scurried from somewhere down the hall and blocked our path.

"Majesty, this room is no longer appropriate for you. We moved you into the King's . . . I mean, the Queen's chamber."

Keelan started to say something, some jibe or joke, but stilled his tongue when my brows knitted.

He leaned toward me and whispered. "What is it?"

"The royal chamber is . . . it's *my parents'* chamber," was all I could say before my voice broke.

The maid stopped at the door and turned. Keelan caught the hint and stepped back, untangling himself from my grip.

"Thank you for your time, Your Majesty. I'll see you at tonight's banquet," he said with a deep bow before disappearing down the hallway.

I spared a glance over my shoulder before allowing the maid to shuffle me into the suite where an army of dressing ladies assaulted me the moment I entered. I never had a moment to catch my breath or take in the regal bedroom I now inhabited. Oddly, I was thankful for the distraction of my clucking hens.

CHAPTER 24

KEELAN

I tugged at the tight, scratchy collar of my coat as the page announced my entry into the banquet hall. Most of the guests were already seated, and the chatter of hundreds echoed throughout the chamber. The chatter died to hushed tones at many tables as I passed on my way to my seat.

My collar might have itched, but the scrutiny of so many nobles made my skin crawl.

I was seated with several nobles and ambassadors from the smaller countries. Jess had been quite thoughtful in seating me with those whose interests most aligned with that of Melucia.

Our table's conversation began with pleasantries surrounding the coronation and banquet but quickly turned to the Siege of Saltstone. Each of our eastern neighbors had heard varying accounts of the battle and the months that followed. Their representatives were eager to glean any new information they could from one of the capital's top lawmen. When the dinner concluded and Jess left the hall, the men and women huddled closer around me, and the conversation turned as they asked more direct, inflammatory questions regarding our hosts in the Kingdom.

Thankfully, it only took an hour for the ambassadors from Pantrel and Amnel to decide the wine had gone to their heads. I relished the thought of escaping the festivities, but, as they rose to retire for the evening, a man in elegant brown robes appeared to stand behind the empty chairs at the table.

"Mind if I join you?"

I thought I sensed the others tense as the young man pulled a chair back and sat without waiting for their reply.

"You're dressed like a holy man. We don't see many of your lot around these days. What are you doing here on the Queen's Day of Celebration?" the ambassador from Orn asked with a bit of a sneer.

The newcomer's pleasant smile never faltered. "I am a Priest of the One, come to inform Her Majesty of my appointment as representative of the Order to the Crown."

"The Order? I thought you said you were a Priest of the Temple," a man to my left asked.

"Forgive me. The Order is what we call the movement behind the Temple's teachings. Think of it as the new name given to the Children."

I detected no falsehood in the man or his words, though my non-magical intuition vibrated with something uneasy I couldn't identify. The man's robes were consistent with what I remembered of the Children, though he wore no mask and did nothing else to hide his identity or intentions.

Something in his bearing felt so familiar.

I was sure I had never seen him before, but I *knew* him. Somehow, I knew this man. He played a role in some broader scheme I could scarcely fathom.

But still, I knew him.

"Please forgive our rudeness, especially at a royal banquet, but the Children's recent history gives many of us pause when we see brown robes." I paused a moment. "Where is your mask?"

The Priest cocked his head. "Ah, you know of our Order. The day comes when the One will walk among us, spreading his word and good deeds. We have shed our masks so everyone may know us. Our recent . . . history . . . no longer defines us."

When greeted by questioning glares, the Priest continued. "We seek to care for the sick and poor, teach children their letters, feed the hungry. Through these humble acts, we hope to build bridges of Light in the hearts of the people we touch. Ours is a message of mercy and compassion with the goal of a brighter future for the Kingdom and our people."

The Ambassador from Amnel snorted. "That sounds like wine and a song, very different from the Children's aims only a few months ago. For centuries, your cult fed on the people's ignorance and laid groundwork to return *evil* to this land. Why should you now be greeted as benevolent holy men instead of the murderers you are? The Queen's justice couldn't be too harsh for your lot, from what I've seen."

"Gentlemen, you must let forgiveness enter your hearts."

"Forgiveness?" I spat a laugh.

The Priest continued to stare at me, his face a mask of its own, so I decided to take a different approach. "Perhaps introductions would be in order."

The Priest stood and bowed to the table. "I am a humble servant of the Temple of the One and will serve as the One's Voice and ambassador here in the capital."

I offered the ambassador a shallow nod and watched as the others at the table made their introductions to the Priest. None appeared to have warmed to the man or his tale of his Order's new direction.

"Holiness? Father? Ambassador? I'm not sure how to address you. I am Guardsman Lieutenant Keelan Rea of Melucia."

"Lieutenant, there is no need for titles or honorifics. Please call me Danym."

CHAPTER 25

KEELAN

I could hardly believe what I just heard.

I was a seasoned investigator, used to strange situations and even stranger characters, but the Priest smiling across the table had stunned me into silence.

"Lieutenant, are you all right?" the Ornish ambassador asked, gripping my forearm.

"Fine . . . I'm fine," I stammered.

I nodded in thanks and returned my gaze to the Priest.

It had been months since Jess cowered in our fleeing boat and described her secret boyfriend's betrayal. I strained, trying to remember if she had described what he looked like. The Priest before me was tall, which matched my recollection, but streaks of silver peered through the sandy blond of his hair, which was now tied tightly behind his neck with a black ribbon. Fine wrinkles webbed the tender skin around his eyes.

Surely, the gray marked him a man in his thirties, more than a decade older than the High Sheriff's son. The bemused smile on the man's face might've triggered my alarms had the Priest not worn that annoying smile the entire time he sat at our table.

I couldn't very well ask if this Priest was the same man who kidnapped the Queen and participated in the deaths of her father and brother. Nothing in the man's words triggered my Gift's warning. Not only did the man believe what he said, his words rang true.

On top of everything, Danym was a common enough name.

This had to be a coincidence.

I dismissed the idea this was *that* Danym and pressed forward.

"What brings a Priest of the One to the capital? I don't recall seeing you in the receiving line earlier today when the nobles pledged their loyalty to the Crown."

"My loyalty is to the Faith," Danym said.

"Surely, the Faith serves Her Majesty?" the Ornish ambassador asked.

Danym inclined his head toward the man. "We recognize the Queen's place as a leader in *worldly matters*, but the Faith answers to a master far above any ruler. If you would come to know the One . . ."

"I thank you for the invitation but will pass. We Ornish have our own ideas of divinity, and they do not include murderous cults."

The balding representative stood, bowed to everyone save Danym, and strode from the table, shaking his head and muttering to himself. On cue, the other ambassadors excused themselves and scurried after their Ornish counterpart.

As I scrutinized the Priest, I realized the massive hall was now quiet. Most of the royal guests had departed. Servants, still in their finest royal livery, cleared plates and platters while others scrubbed tables and floors, returning the hall to its usual pristine state.

I rose. "I believe it's time I also took my leave. Good evening, Priest Danym."

"A good night to you, Guardsman." Danym's oily smile almost made me shiver.

As I made my way back to my chamber, one of the Queen's maids brushed into me as we passed in the hallway. I was so lost in thought that I barely noticed the woman walking toward me—until she was pressed against my chest.

Did she do that on purpose? I thought as I watched her disappear down the hall, giggling.

I shook my head and continued down the passage, only to encounter another maid.

"Excuse me," I said, causing the maid to freeze, bow, and stare at her shoes. "I need to speak to the Queen. Would you let her know, please?"

The maid bobbed a curtsy but didn't make eye contact. "I'm sorry, Ambassador, Her Majesty has retired for the evening."

I nodded and smiled. "Fine. It can wait until morning. I'm sure she needs her sleep after today's events."

The maid vanished down the hallway, and I found my way to my chamber, disrobed, and threw myself onto the bed. I hadn't realized how tired I was.

Comforting darkness closed around me, but my sleep was troubled. Images of the lanky Priest and his smarmy smile unsettled my dreams.

PART III

CHAPTER 26

LIAM

The sun had just peeked over the horizon when I groaned, stretched my arms as far as they would reach, and tossed back my thick woolen blankets. I shivered at the cold and frowned at the darkened coals in my bedchamber's hearth, then blew out a sigh, stretched one last time, and set about my morning routine.

First, I had to do something with my bushy tangle of sandy hair. It had somehow found ways to tie itself into knots that would make any sailor proud. The first few pulls of my brush tugged at my scalp, and then—the successive pulls hurt, too.

My hair was a mess. Had I wrestled a bear in my sleep?

Once satisfied I was presentable for my father's guests, I rinsed my face in the frigid water of my washbasin and donned my uniform, dove gray trousers covered by a pale blue smock embroidered with a sparkly silver crown. I traced a finger across the stylized symbol of the Kingdom's royal household.

Years earlier, King Alfred and Queen Isabel visited our town and stayed at our inn. That week transformed the town of Oliver's sleepy but reputable inn into a palace away from home for the couple. At least, that's what my father told anyone who would listen. To hear him tell it, he laid marble in every room, polished the cherry wood (though the walls were oak) to a mirror-sheen, and sold his soul for a chef straight from the Isle of Vint.

In truth, we dusted and cleaned as best a family of common innkeepers could, but the boarding house was the same as before the royals arrived, if a tad less dusty. The King's household provided the chef and foodstuffs for their visit. All Hershel, my father, had to do was help haul it into his storeroom and kitchen. The royal seneschal explained that only royal servants could attend their Majesties, which included serving food or wine, cleaning their chambers, or anything else that involved direct interaction with our vaunted rulers. Hershel and his household would be introduced to the royals upon their arrival, but there would be no further interaction once the King and Queen were settled into their chambers.

The day after the royals departed, I woke to a series of loud bangs outside the door of the inn—*on* the door of the inn, actually. My father had commissioned an artisan to create a new masthead for the business, one bearing our new name, *The Crown's Glory*, in sparkling silver, complete with a stylized replica of the royal household's symbol. He changed the crown just enough to comply with laws forbidding use of official marks but kept enough to make it clear to all that the royal couple had blessed his establishment with their presence.

The Glory, as the townsfolk called it, became the center of culture and entertainment in Oliver, such that it was in a small town. Traveling minstrels and players were present most nights, and the ale was never watered as it was in the lesser establishments down by the docks.

Most respectable nineteen-year-old men in Oliver were still snuggled in their beds.

But not me.

I was not a common commoner.

I loved to work.

I loved interacting with the minstrels and players, the cooks and washer folk, the farriers and stable hands. They gave the inn life, and I loved each of them.

Above all, I loved our guests.

Whether weary workmen, couriers traveling to some faraway destination, or wealthy nobles spending their time and fortune on leisure, I reveled in their tales, learning what made them laugh, and living vicariously through their journeys I longed to enjoy for myself.

Oddly, the other men of the town held no grudge for my passion, certainly not the way many women flung petty jealousies toward each other. Perhaps others accepted the royal blessing on our household. More likely, they were infected by my self-deprecating wit and ever-present smile.

Of course, that *had* to be it.

When I entered a room, even when laden with a tray of food and drink for a raucous table, heads turned. My bright brown eyes sparkled when I smiled, making most women—and even a few men—mirror my warmth. My laugh sounded like the rumbled gurgling of some ancient creature risen from the depths of the sea.

It was heartfelt.

It was infectious.

It was me in sonorous beauty.

I might not have been the handsomest man in Oliver, but I was surely the one folk enjoyed the most.

I splashed my face one last time with the wintry water and wiped my eyes, then padded downstairs toward the kitchen where vegetables waited to be chopped and eggs demanded cracking for the guests' morning meals.

The common room was dark and chilly, though a small fire still danced in the hearth thanks to the night clerk. As I wove my way through the tables toward the kitchen door, I felt a tingle, that unsettling feeling I always felt when I was being watched.

I froze and scanned the room.

The stage was clear.

The bar, with its hefty marble top, stood silent.

The tables near the hearth were empty.

Maybe my mind was playing tricks and I had yet to wake.

I shrugged off the feeling and resumed my trek—only to be arrested by a cough from a darkened corner of the room directly behind me. The *one* corner, I now realized, I hadn't checked.

"Hello? Is someone there? Breakfast isn't for another two hours."

A second later, a man stepped out of the darkness.

Raven hair fell to his shoulders with slight curls at the tips; shadowed eyes bore into me. The chiseled features of his face marked him handsome, and the tautness of the fabric across his chest hinted at muscled strength beneath his shimmering robe.

I wanted to smile, to offer my traditional welcome, but something in the man's bearing made me take an involuntary step backward.

"Child, do not be afraid. I am a Priest of the One, here to offer help and comfort to those most in need. I arrived late in the evening. There were no rooms. Your clerk allowed me the warmth of your common room. I will take my leave, but only if you will accept my thanks for such kindness."

The man's smile was easy, and he possessed a confidence that made me *want* to chat—and stare. Now that he stood in the dim light of the room, I saw deep brown eyes matched mine. They weren't the pits of swirling black my overactive imagination had conjured when he first appeared from the shadows.

The Priest bowed as if he were a commoner attending a royal. Then he rose and grinned, winked once, and turned to exit. As he gripped the door's handle, he turned back and smiled once more. "You really are handsome. Your wife is a most fortunate woman."

My jaw nearly smacked my chest.

Me? Handsome?

My wife?

Before I could protest that I wasn't married, the strange, striking man disappeared, leaving me dumbstruck with my brow furrowed.

Hours passed.

I cracked and whipped a hundred eggs, diced dozens of potatoes, and sliced more tomatoes than I cared to count. My smock remained spotless, though I still brushed and picked at it as if crumbs clung to its surface.

Why did I want to tell that man I'm not married?

He's a Priest, for Spirits' sake.

And . . . can a Priest even be with another man? Most folk are okay with our sort, but a religious man? Is that even allowed?

What difference does it make if he's handsome, or if his eyes made my legs wobble, or a smile—

"Hon, you all right? What's got into you today?" my mother asked as she tossed a fresh towel in my direction. "Help me wipe down the kitchen. We've a full house for dinner tonight. Your da thinks the duke might show up, though I can't see why. It's the normal troupe on stage playin' the same old tunes."

I woke from my daydream and tossed a devilish grin back at my mother. "You love those players, and I seem to recall you staring at a certain lead man last time they were here. You know, the blond with the tight pants that show off his—"

"Liam!" Ma swatted me with the towel still clutched in her meaty palm. "I'm a respectable, *married* woman of society. I would never—"

I barked a laugh. "Never? Oh Ma, you *did*, and I expect you'll do so again—tonight!"

She swatted again, but I leaped out of the way, leaving nothing but air and another round of amused giggles in my wake. Ma couldn't suppress her own chuckle and began whistling as we cleaned.

"See. You only whistle—"

"Not another word if you want to see another name day!"

My laughter rose again.

The rest of the day passed with the practiced routine of the simple life of commoners running a business in a small village. Cook for the guests, clean for the guests, cook for the guests again, shop for the guests, clean the stalls for the guests' horses, cook for the guests, clean the guests' rooms, cook for the guests, do the guests' laundry, cook for the guests again.

Someone was always appearing in the common room asking for a bite to eat. We posted times for meals, but Ma wouldn't hear of a guest being turned away. "The King wouldn't have it," she always said, as if she and the royal family remained in close touch after their decades-old visit. Most guests humored her, thankful she accommodated their stomach's every desire.

As we prepared dinner, I heard the familiar swell of conversation and laughter in the common room as folk, both guests of the inn and families from town, streamed in to claim their tables. It seemed the usual players were even more beloved than I thought.

Maybe Ma wasn't the only one to notice Blondie with the Bootie.

I chuckled as I chopped.

I'd lost myself in my thoughts when a strange feeling crept up my arms. It took a moment to realize that the raucous banter had quieted and only one voice rang out, loud and clear.

I recognized that voice.

The Priest?

For reasons I didn't understand, my heart raced. I strained to hear the man's words.

"... from the war. We believe every life is sacred and come to serve those in need with love and peace in our hearts. Each of us in this room is blessed by the Spirits with wealth and comfort, else we would not *be* in this room. I ask for your help, for the people of this beautiful town, for the—"

Whatever he said next was drowned out by the sound of Ma's cleaver slamming through the evening's meat. "Gonna stare at that door all night or help me get these meals out?"

"Sorry. It's just—"

"Chop now. Talk later."

"Yes, ma'am." I resumed my work but reserved part of my effort for more strained listening, though the stranger's tone had vanished in favor of the guests' raucous chorus once more.

Hours later, the last guest finally retired to their room, allowing us to remove tankards and wipe down tables. The evening had been a success, with the players and Mr. Pretty Bum stealing the stage and more than a few hearts.

Ma chattered away, but I heard none of it.

I couldn't stop thinking about the Priest.

I saw his eyes, his rounded lips, the curve of his chest beneath his clinging, silky robe.

Stop that, I chided, wiping my now-sweaty brow with a shirtsleeve. *He probably lives by some code of celibacy or reclusiveness or self-loathing. Who knows? Just stop thinking about him.*

I glanced down and realized I'd been cleaning the same spot for several minutes and laughed at my own silliness.

"Do you always laugh when you clean?"

I nearly jumped out of my smock.

"Forgive me," the amused Priest said from the doorway. "I did not mean to startle you."

"Well, you did!" I said sharply, immediately regretting my tone. "Can I help you?"

He smiled and gave me a deep bow.

What is it with him and his bowing?

"I did not see you earlier. Were you able to hear my words?"

I eyed him with a mix of suspicion and curiosity, unable to resist his gaze. "I heard a little from the kitchen. It's noisy back there, so I didn't get all of it."

"The players were kind enough to allow me their stage before the show. I used it to introduce myself to the town, and to ask for their support in caring for those affected by the war. Their needs are great, and the Crown can only do so much."

I stiffened. "I'm sure the Queen is doing all she can. She only took the throne a short time ago."

"I meant no offense to Her Majesty. I am sure you are right."

"I assume you didn't come here to talk about the royal family. Is there something I can do for you, Father? What do I even call you?"

"Seth, please just call me Seth. I may wear the frock, but I am just a man trying to do his best in a dark world."

I couldn't decide if my suspicion rose or fell at that.

"All right, Seth, what can I do for you? We're trying to wrap up for the night."

He smiled and ducked his head—*again*. "I came to see you."

A flush of heat ran through my arms and into my chest.

"Me?"

He smiled innocently.

I shivered.

"Yes, you. I understand you are *not* married, as I had . . . hoped. It seems no one in this town has managed to win your hand."

Another flush.

I dabbed my cheeks with the towel, then tossed it on the table. "I . . . well, no, I'm not married. What would that matter to a Priest?"

He took a step forward, and my heart raced faster.

"It has nothing to do with the Priest, but has much to do with the nervous man standing humbly before you."

I coughed a laugh. "Nervous? You? That's not a word I've thought to describe you all day."

His brow raised. "So, you thought about me all day?"

My eyes widened at the net tightening about me.

"Well, no. I mean, yes, I may have. Oh, bother, what do you want with me?"

"I would very much like to have a glass of wine with you and to learn more about the most en- chanting man I have seen in all my travels. Would that be all right?"

"Enchanting?" I snorted, though something kept my eyes glued to his. "Well, uh, I have to finish—"

"Two wines, coming right up." Ma's voice cut through the tension in the room. "He needs a drink 'bout now, I can tell."

Seth grinned as Ma chortled from behind the bar. I hadn't heard my portly mother enter, nor did I realize she'd heard the whole conversation.

"Ma!"

"Hush. I'll finish up. We wouldn't want a man of the cloth—whatever cloth that is—to stand around waitin', would we?"

I rolled my eyes. "I suppose I could have *one* glass."

The thunk of a newly opened bottle slammed onto the wooden table before I had finished speaking. Two glasses appeared a second later.

"Take yer time. He's off t'morrow, whether or not he tells ya that."

And with a flourish, Ma vanished back into the kitchen, leaving me staring at the bottle and Seth shifting nervously from one foot to the other.

Later that night, as I lay in bed staring out the tiny window in my room above the kitchen, I thought the stars shone a bit brighter than they had all winter. I leaned forward and squinted at the pin-pricks of light as they danced in the darkness, then shook my head at the boy who'd apparently had a little too much wine.

Still, thinking back to the hour or so with Seth, I couldn't help but smile.

He wasn't anything like I expected.

When we first met, he was cloaked in darkness and shadow, giving the impression his life would likewise be veiled in secrets, but that hadn't been the case. A few sips of courage had him recounting a childhood in the countryside with his older brother and two younger sisters. He laughed as he described antics that must've driven his mother mad.

As we talked, I realized his life—at least his life before donning his robe—had been similar to mine. He talked of tending his family's land and herds. I didn't have brothers and sisters to terrorize, nor did I tend livestock or till soil, but I did have routine and duty to my family and our business. I understood his upbringing and admired his openness and quiet strength.

My mind wandered to his square jaw.

Enough of that, I told myself. *You barely know the man.*

But a flush flared through me again as I saw his eyes in my mind.

I pulled the covers over my head and laughed before rolling over and drifting off to sleep.

CHAPTER 27

LIAM

The morning began as the previous one had, with annoyingly chipper sunlight streaming through the window. I lay awake, staring out the window, not really seeing anything. When it was clear sleep would not return, I released an annoyed huff, wiped my eyes, and rose.

I was supposed to work today.

In a family-run inn, there were no days off.

Ma had made that up last night when she saw a glimmer of hope that I might finally have an attraction to someone other than a cleaning rag or chopping block. She'd been nagging me for years to "find a good man," though I never could understand her rush. I was happy working with my parents and the inn, happy seeing guests every day and making them laugh, happy being part of something special.

Besides, most men wanted to find a good *woman*. Those who might lean in my direction too often acted like scared rabbits or stuffed-up braggarts. I was sure things were no different in larger towns, but in a tiny speck like Oliver, the menu held even fewer options.

But the night before, when Seth's persistent smile made my heart flutter, thoughts of the inn and cooking and guests were replaced by deep pools of brown and locks of ebony, with the cutest tiny curls at their ends.

I giggled when I realized I was twisting my own locks with my fingers as I daydreamed.

Despite my mother's unfathomable grace, I knew my day off would include a trip to the market to purchase essentials for the evening meal. There could be no respite from our guests' stomachs. I donned my dress, fumbling as I put one arm in the wrong sleeve.

After a quick visit to the kitchen to grab a steaming biscuit and affectionate kiss from Ma, I ambled out of the inn. It was too early for the stalls to be open, but I had nowhere else to be and enjoyed the thought of an aimless stroll on a chilly day.

I'd made it halfway to the docks when the cheerful squeal of children grabbed my attention.

Someone had worked a pack of little monsters
into a frenzy. They were screaming and laughing
with reckless abandon. The merry sound made me
smile, so I turned to follow it, curious to see what
had the little rascals so energized.

I rounded the corner of the apothecary and
stopped mid-stride. My grin widened at the scene
before me. A tall man facing away from me had a
toddler attached to each of his legs while a third
had her tiny arms and legs firmly wrapped around
his waist. Two more ran in circles around the man,
poking him playfully with their "swords," which
were little more than willow branches that bent as
the boys waved them.

A slender woman, her silver mane blowing
wildly in the winter breeze, sat some distance
away. Her laughter rose above even the children's
shouts.

The man let out a roar and raised his hands,
fingers crooked like claws, as he lifted one leg in
a dramatic stomp. The attached toddler squealed
with delight and screamed, "Get him! He's trying
to flee!"

The two swordsmen renewed their assault.

My own laughter joined the chorus.

The sillier the man acted, the grander his
gestures, the louder the children's giggles and

screams became. At the sound of a newcomer's amusement, the man turned, and our eyes met. The monster's mock snarl morphed into a warm, broad smile as Seth straightened, then bowed, a gesture made even more comical by his dangling darlings.

"M'lord, save me! I am but an innocent beast attacked by these ruffians. Please, have mercy, fine sir!" Seth's plea caused the thin woman to double over with laughter and sent the children into a frenzy.

High-pitched cries of, "No! He's mine. He's a monster," rang through the yard.

I raised both hands in surrender. "Poor monster, you're on your own in this fight."

I stepped around the fray and sat beside the older woman. We laughed until tears streamed down both our cheeks. When the swordsmen finally found their opening, the monster stumbled to his knees while the squealing barnacles still clung to his legs. He released cries and moans of pain, then dramatically uttered, "Oh, if I only had more time to live."

I laughed so hard that my side hurt as the children cheered in victory.

Seth lay still on the paving stones, his limbs strewn in mock-death, as the children danced around him with swords held high, cheering their heroic victory.

Seth peeked up from the stones with one eye, winked, then closed his eye again.

I turned to my new companion and tried desperately to avoid looking at him.

Before I realized it, Seth stood before me, one child attached to his back with her head poking over his shoulder, tongue extended toward me. "M'lord, might a humble monster accompany you on your errands this fine day?"

The older woman flushed at the handsome Priest. Clearly, she'd fallen under his spell. I straightened my back and looked imperiously up at the man.

"Monsters are not welcome in the market," I said. "But perhaps they may allow a Priest to visit—if accompanied by a lord of respect and renown, of course."

Seth lowered his head and shook it in mock disappointment. "Alas, I have found no such lord. I suppose I must go hungry."

I punched his arm, then rose. "Come on, you ridiculous monster, I would be glad of the company."

I glanced back to catch the older woman grinning from ear to ear.

It took a few moments to extricate Seth from his tiny pursuers, but we made our escape.

"There's a story for the bards: the Priest and the Innkeeper's Son Fleeing the Pack of Ravenous Children," Seth teased.

I laughed and shook my head. Seth's open warmth contrasted so deeply with my initial impression of the man. He caught me staring at him and raised a brow.

"What? Is there something still clinging to my neck?"

"No. You're free of knee-high knights." I grinned. "I guess . . . I just never imagined seeing you roughhousing with a pack of wild children."

"You envision every religious man hunkered over ancient scrolls in his stone Temple, on his knees, forever praying to his gods or the Spirits, right?"

I gave him a sheepish shrug and nodded.

"That's okay. It is what most people think, but the Order is different. We are here to help those in need, to be part of the community, rather than simply take from it. Everything we receive, we return. It is a vital tenet of our faith."

I wasn't sure I enjoyed the religious turn of our conversation, but I did admire what Seth had to say, and even more the commitment with which he said it. I could see in his eyes, feel in his words, that he *meant* it—all of it. I'd encountered priests and monks of other orders, and most of them struck me as hollow, self-serving men who cloaked themselves in beliefs that never transformed into deeds.

This Priest walking beside me seemed so different.

Seeing him with the children, hearing their laughter and witnessing his obvious pleasure in their play, made me wonder if there wasn't a ring of truth in his words.

"You are doing it again."

I looked up. "Doing what?"

"Losing yourself in your thoughts. Care to share?"

His gaze was so intense, so *beautiful*.

I looked away. "I was just walking through what we needed at the market in my head. That's all."

I thought I saw a grin out of the corner of my eye before his head turned to look ahead. "Taming that pack of wild pups was my only appointment today, so consider me at your service, m'lord."

CHAPTER 28

LIAM

D ays turned into weeks, each mirroring the last, with me going about my routine, and Seth finding excuses to accompany me. Ma had taken to saving the Priest a table each dinner and beamed every time he darkened our doorway, racing forward to grip him by the arm and usher him to his seat. She chittered about how happy I seemed these days, and how she credited the Priest for my buoyant mood.

For my sake, I thought my mood was always cheerful and harrumphed at the thought some man made me more so—until Seth appeared in the doorway and my smile widened ever so slightly. The flutter of my heart and flush of warmth throughout my limbs stirred with his gaze, more so now than before.

After our third week of market strolling, I allowed him to take my hand.

I'd never understood the magic in that simple touch. Sparks prickled my arms, and my chest swelled. Seth squeezed my hand, and the world stilled.

In our fifth week, Seth invited me to hear him address the people in the town square. Neatly printed flyers had been strewn about town, calling all to hear the *man of the Order* speak.

By then, everyone knew him.

He would have no trouble drawing a crowd.

I dreaded facing the tittering biddies and smirking boys who already spoke of me with jealous or derisive barbs, but I wouldn't dare miss supporting Seth as he spread his warmth and works among my neighbors. No one spoke of whatever grew between us, but looks told stories of their own. I struggled within but held my chin high and tried to ignore any who might frown on seeing us together.

Seth never faltered.

If he noticed the glances or heard the rumors, he strode above them like the stars soaring in the heavens. His eyes only ever found mine. His hand gripped my own. His fingers laced and squeezed, leaving no doubt about his heart's true intent.

". . . the weak, those who cannot do so well for themselves."

I stifled a yawn. I'd heard this speech from Seth so many times I could recite it from memory.

The whole town was gathered.

Spring was poking its shy head above the surface, and heavy cloaks were no longer needed. Farmers in coveralls and fishermen in rough leggings stood beside women and girls in their finest gowns and dresses. I couldn't stop my eyes from rolling at the obvious contrast and the townswomen's desire to impress at the largest public gathering of the year.

Seth's voice drew my attention once more.

". . . the Queen." Murmurs trickled through the crowd at whatever he'd just said. I couldn't tell if the crowd agreed with him, but Seth's words had drawn a reaction.

He held his arms out, asking the crowd to calm. "We respect the Crown and its role in keeping order among our people. They maintain laws and keep us safe, preserve our roads, and encourage trade with our neighbors."

The murmurs turned to nods and grunts of assent.

"And yet, who declared war on our neighbor?" Seth paused and looked from face to face. "Who spread the false tale of then-Princess Jessia's kidnapping at the hands of our Melucian brothers?

They were innocent of this charge, yet this vile accusation was the bedrock on which our righteous anger was built. Who laid that foundation?"

He paused again, and I felt the mood of the crowd shift.

The bitterness was palpable.

He'd struck a nerve.

A man's voice several rows back from Seth called out, "The one who wore the crown, that's who!"

Seth held up a hand again to quell the rising tide.

"That's right. It was the Crown itself who led our husbands and brothers to defeat and death. The Crown discarded a thousand years of peace in exchange for personal power. The King himself, Spirits rest his soul, was fooled into ordering our boys east. Is there a family present who hasn't lost a son or brother or husband? How many widows and orphans must the Crown create before we challenge their right to absolute power?"

I glanced around.

Even society's finest had forgotten their silk and lace in favor of brewing anger and resentment.

Every family knew loss from the war.

Every mother knew the ultimate grief and pain, the agony no parent should ever know.

He was striking the flint, lighting the flame, and drawing it skillfully into his palm.

Seth, what are you doing?

The Priest allowed the flame to catch before begging for calm once more.

"Good people of Oliver, you know me now. Your children know me most of all." This brought a few nervous nods and tentative smiles from knowing parents. "I came here to serve, to minister to each of you in your own time and need. I did not come to fan the flames of rebellion."

Brows knit in confusion.

"Of course the one who wears the crown is human, like each of us. They are bound to err, some more disastrously than others, as we've learned recently. Yet our faith does not teach revolution. Our mortal masters fulfill an ancient and worthy purpose when they serve and lead, rather than conquer. We praise the efforts of our new Queen. Tragedy tested her will and strength beyond what most could fathom, yet she endured to rise and don the vestments of power."

More nods spread among the crowd.

Queen Jessia had indeed become a popular figure, a beacon of hope following the disastrous war of her mother and father.

"What we believe is that faith and order must coexist, must rule the mind and body and spirit *together*. The Crown and the Order should stand side by side in service to the people of this land. The will of mortal men must always be balanced by the temperance of spiritual guidance. Only through faith and good works can we hope to reclaim the mantle of righteousness our Kingdom once possessed."

An impatient woman in the front row raised her hand and shouted, "I don't get it. You hate the Crown, then you respect it. You don't want rebellion, now you preach the faith should rule with the Queen. What are you saying?"

Seth smiled and nodded toward the woman.

"Thank you, madam. We Priests do love the sound of our own voices."

This drew chuckles and more than a few nods.

"We all know the ancient prophecy that foretells the return of the One. There is no child among us who cannot recite tales of Irina and her return by heart. Yet we now know Irina was a false prophet, a false goddess. She was never the One spoken of with reverence in the ancient texts. She was a usurper who used magic and power to further her own evil designs and drive our nation into the ground."

The ever-shifting mood flared toward anger once more at the mention of Irina.

"I come before you today, not with a message of anger and despair, but of hope. I come to proclaim the return of the true heir of prophecy, the true bearer of faith. The One returns—"

Gasps spread through the crowd.

The woman who'd spoken earlier crossed her arms and shouted, "What does the new One *want* now? We've got nothing left to give. The old Queen took my sons and husband!"

"My friends, the One comes to us with arms spread wide, inviting us into a warm embrace of love, kindness, and beauty. He comes to *heal* and usher in a new age of peace and prosperity for our people. He seeks neither land nor riches, nor does he care for conquest." Seth paused, tapped a finger to his lips thoughtfully, then corrected himself, drawing the crowd further to his words. "No, that is not right. He *does* seek conquest. He would conquer *every heart* and bring every loyal subject the *joy* and *peace* only found in righteous works and passionate, sincere faith.

"Tonight is a beginning. I am but a humble servant sent ahead of his master to prepare for his return. You are *my* family now. I ask only for your open minds and hearts. Go in peace, and think on my words."

No one moved for a long moment.

They looked unsure if they should.

Then Seth stepped down from the makeshift stage and made his way through the parting crowd to where I stood.

I gaped as he stood before me.

My mind raced. Barely a family in town remained untouched by the Taker during the war. Brothers, sons, and fathers left with pride in their hearts and songs on their lips. What they left behind were empty, quiet homes with husbandless wives and fatherless children.

Father tried to go, to join the King's army, but he'd been too old. They'd turned him back. Short of that mercy, Ma and I would be among those still mourning a loss.

Seth struck far more than a raw nerve. He pierced people directly in the heart.

"Was I *that* bad?"

I looked at my hands as my fingers fidgeted. "You spoke well, but . . . it's just so much, Seth."

My face held a stricken look, and I struggled to raise my eyes.

"It is a great deal to take in. I understand," he said. "May a humble Priest walk a handsome lord home?"

I looked around at the dispersing crowd, some casting glances our way, their expressions unreadable.

I nodded and let him hook my arm in his as we began our stroll toward the inn.

CHAPTER 29

LIAM

I returned to the inn to find my parents alone in the common room whispering angrily and trying not to disturb our guests, though my father's voice grew louder with every word.

"You can't tell me what that man was saying isn't treason!" Hershel slapped the table, then rubbed out his smarting palm.

I knew better than to jump into the middle but couldn't help myself. I strode into the common room and plopped down in front of my father. "Father, he never said the Crown should go or anything like that. All he said was that it should coexist with his faith."

My father fixed me with a sharp gaze and pointed one meaty finger my direction. "He *said* King Alfred led us to disaster and needs a leash. He *said* his prophet should be a check on the Crown.

Imagine that: a *check* on the Spirits-anointed sovereign! He *said*—"

I leaned forward and gently pushed his hand down, holding it once I felt it press against the table. "Father, I was there. He would never mean the Queen any harm. I *know* him. He just believes in the prophecy and wants this One, whoever that is, to be respected and listened to. That's all." I leaned back, releasing his hand. "Have you seen all the *good* he's doing around town? There isn't a widow or child who hasn't felt his positive influence, mostly in the form of food or clothes."

"Exactly!" he spat. "He shows up here in his shiny robe bearing pretty gifts. He's just pure and innocent, *I'm sure.*"

"Hershel . . ." Ma said in a warning tone.

"Don't *Hershel* me. I know what I heard, and there's *no place* for folk who talk against our Queen, especially this new One who hasn't even done anything yet! If I hear that nonsense again, you won't be seein' that boy anymore. You hear me, young man?"

I folded my arms and glared at my father. "I'm a grown man. I'll see who I want."

Hershel held my gaze a long moment, fire blazing between us, until his face softened. He sucked in a deep breath and looked down at his weathered hands. "Liam . . . I don't mean to talk down to you. Of course you're a grown man. I'm just worried you're gettin' mixed up with a bad sort, that's all."

My fire flickered out.

"I know, and I love you for it, but Seth is different. He's a good man. I know it."

Hershel grunted but didn't say anything.

"Liam, go on upstairs and get some sleep. It's been a long night." Ma shooed me away from the table with a look that said, *I need to talk to your father alone.* I caught her meaning, hugged my father around his neck, then headed up the stairs to my room.

Over the next two weeks, Seth stood in the town square each night to ever-growing crowds and spoke his prophecy and of the return of the One. Most of his hour-long message centered on spreading good works, helping the poor, and turning one's beliefs into actions. These ideas were met with universal approval, filling his donation bins to overflowing with each session.

And yet, woven within his messages of good faith and better works, he sowed seeds of loyalty to one's faith over worldly concerns—and worldly leaders. He apparently learned from his first sermon and never again used the Queen by name or title, but his meaning was clear. The faith should be the *first* place people looked to for guidance, not the Crown.

Hershel and several men and women of the town met each night around a large table in the back of the inn. Hushed tones contrasted with loud music from the stage and the cheering that accompanied it. As the players' tunes swelled, anger festered in the back of the room. Ma begged him to focus on the inn and mind his own business, but his anger wouldn't be pacified. The King himself had graced our inn, beginning a long span of prosperity for the town and our family. He wouldn't repay that kindness with betrayal.

No, the King—and his daughter—deserved better.

So, what began as disgruntled griping evolved into plots and plans.

Some favored speaking in opposition to the Priest, offering a counterpoint for the people to consider. Hershel argued Seth's carefully planted seeds had taken root far more quickly than anyone could've imagined, and, while talk might pluck a few leaves, it would do nothing to the roots as they twined ever deeper.

It was too late for talk.

It was time for action.

The evening was unseasonably warm, nearing pleasant springtime temperatures. Clouds dotted the sky, occasionally blotting out the sliver of moon and her chorus of stars. Seth's evening presentation was well attended, drawing folk from surrounding communities and throughout the countryside. Warm smiles mirrored the warmth in the air as the people stood and listened to the Priest and his good words.

Seth paused once when a pack of children raced through the crowd, a wide smile parting his lips. A mother began scolding her son, but Seth called out, "Please, let them play so the sounds of their laughter may lift our spirits. Would that each of us had the heart of a child once again."

The mother seemed unsure, but chuckles rang through the crowd as we watched the boy dart after his friends.

Seth didn't mention the Crown, nor did he speak of mortal leaders and their failings. He spoke of green sprouts he saw everywhere he looked, tiny glimmers of hope rising above the field of win-

ter white. He extolled the virtues he saw demon-
strated by townspeople, from simple dockhands to
wealthy landowners. He described how blessed he
felt to be a part of our family.

I stood, transfixed, in the front row.

How had this man crept into town and stolen my
heart?

I looked around and realized Seth had stolen
more than just mine.

Smiles, once rare in the post-war Kingdom
town, now spread like leaves on the breeze. I
couldn't remember ever seeing the poor standing
shoulder to shoulder with their betters, yet here
they were, listening and nodding, raising their
own voices each time Seth lowered his.

I had struggled to understand what I felt from
people as we strolled through the market, but now
I knew for certain.

It was pride.

Not the haughty assertion of one's dominance
over another, but the humble satisfaction of a job
well done. Even those of the lowest station seemed
to walk a little taller than before.

And, perhaps, I felt something more from our
strolls, from our clasped hands, from his lingering
gaze. I tried not to dwell. Such hopes were for
others, or so I had always thought.

When Seth's last words echoed through the yard and the final rambunctious youth was rounded up, I hooked my arm in his. We strolled from the square, headed nowhere in particular, returning cheerful nods and "good evenings" to others headed home.

As we rounded the corner and our inn came into view at the far end of the road, Seth stopped walking.

"Seth?"

He looked into my eyes, then away. If whatever shook his confidence hadn't sent a jolt of fear up my arm, his bashful lashes would have been adorable.

"I need to do something, and . . . I think it will be all right, but . . ."

"Seth, talk to me. What do you need—"

Strong hands shoved me against the side of the shop next to our inn where shadows hid us from the moonlight. Warm lips pressed into mine, and I thought the world might float away into the sky.

I'd never known happiness could fill a person's chest so fully until that moment.

CHAPTER 30

HERSHEL

T wo other men and I stood at the edge of the square and watched the crowd disperse. We painted on smiles and nodded, but beneath our masks, we brooded.

"We can't wait much longer," I whispered. "If he keeps this up, the whole town'd defend him even if he tried to stab the Queen in front of them."

"They'd say he was spreading his good works using a dagger," an embittered butcher grunted in agreement.

"Tomorrow night. We finish this *tomorrow night*," I said.

The other men's eyes locked on mine, then each man nodded once.

The butcher and wainwright turned and vanished into the night, leaving me glaring where Seth once stood. My stare could've burned the place down, if only I had the Gift of Fire.

The Order and its band of slicksters wanted
the same things most men standing in the square
wanted, attention and power. If I was any judge, I
guessed the latter was far more important to the
Priests and their prophet.

Their prophet.

The One.

What did *he* want?

Seth was laying the groundwork for his grand
entrance to the Kingdom's stage, but to what end?

I thought through everything that had happened over the past year as I wandered home,
oblivious to the falling temperatures and deepening darkness. When I looked up to see thickening
clouds obscuring the moon and stars, thoughts of
winter's last gasp pushed to the fore, and I knew
the coming days would spread a blanket of snow
over the town's spring-filled dreams.

Nothing to do about it but dig out, I thought as
I kicked a rock further down the path, thankful
for the momentary distraction from the town's
troubles.

I loved this place.

I met Anabelle here, raised my son here, and
planned to see my last sunset painted across the
ocean's shores here. There was no way some out-

sider would show up and tell me these people, *my* people, weren't decent and good.

I couldn't let that happen.

A chill gusted by and pimpled the skin on my arms. I laughed at myself when I realized, in my aimless wandering, I'd walked nearly a half league past the edge of town.

Time to go home. Anabelle's waitin' and'll be madder than a hornet if I'm any later.

I kicked another rock and turned back to head home.

A couple strides later, something rumbled and roared from behind.

I turned and blinked a few times, unable to move.

A massive bear, fur dark as the night, towered over me. It roared and bared its teeth as a head-sized paw flew out of the darkness. Dagger-sharp claws ripped into my chest.

I staggered backward, eyes wide from shock and pain.

I tried to breathe, but fire bloomed and spread throughout my body.

The bear lumbered forward, its eyes never leaving its prey.

As another swipe descended, the one that could sever the arteries in my throat and snuff out my dreams of another sunset, a flicker passed through the bear's eyes.

A recognition.

An almost *human* understanding.

Then the light of the moon and stars fled my eyes.

CHAPTER 31

JESS

"Your Majesty." Ethan bowed. "The last of our troops has returned. Of the eighty thousand we assembled, ten thousand bogged down in the mountains and never made it into the theater. Their units were composed of newer recruits and archers. I have posted them at Huntcliff to guard the border and continue their training."

I strummed my fingers against the arm of my throne, waiting for the bad news.

"Of the remaining seventy thousand, only twenty-two thousand have been accounted for. Of those, six thousand are wounded. We believe others will report over the coming months but expect no more than a few hundred. The rest either died, remained in Melucia, or returned to their homes upon crossing back into the Kingdom."

"What about machinery? Siege equipment and transports?"

Ethan's brow rose.

Had he not expected me to ask thoughtful questions? To understand the basic math and mechanics of warfare?

I tried not to be insulted. There was pride in his eyes.

Still, that surprise was his *first* reaction made my fingers strum harder against the armrest.

"Carts and carriages accompanying the ten thousand at Huntcliff survived with only minor, weather-related damage. Roughly one-fifth of our carts and other transports returned with surviving troops. All our siege engines, heavy ladders, rams, and other machinery were lost."

"All of them?"

He nodded.

"What about the navy?"

"Our fleet is intact. Few Melucian port towns possessed ballistae, and their ships were a collection of merchant vessels, so we encountered no resistance. I have recalled our ships to their home ports."

"Well, that is a rose amid the thorns, I suppose." I sat back and pressed fingers into the bridge of my nose. "General, by my math, we now have a functioning navy with a dozen well-armed ships and twenty-five thousand able-bodied men in our army, ten thousand of whom are green recruits stationed at the far end of the Kingdom with another six thousand injured. We have no heavy equipment, and only a small fraction of our land transports used to feed and supply our troops remain. Does that about sum it up?"

"Yes, Majesty, give or take a thousand men."

I turned my gaze to the man standing to Ethan's right. The golden badge of the High Sheriff's office glittered on his breast. I had only pinned it on the man an hour earlier.

"High Sheriff, what of our Constables? Surely, many joined the army and were lost. Are our cities secure? Is the capital?"

Bryan Cribbs, the new High Sheriff, bowed.

His unruly brown hair flopped as his head lowered, forcing him to flick it back into place as he rose. Curls flew in every direction. If the topic hadn't been so serious, I would have laughed at the spectacle. Despite the man's unkempt mane, his dozen years of service to the Crown had proved him an effective and loyal lawman. Of the eternal list of appointments pending my attention, High Sheriff had been the easiest. Cribbs was a good man and would make an even better Sheriff.

"Majesty, our ranks are thin but holding. Most of the losses to the army came from smaller towns and villages, so the capital and larger cities remain secure." Cribbs's eyes fell.

"What is it, Sheriff? What are you not telling me?"

"Well, Your Majesty, it's just—"

"Spit it out. It is just the three of us."

Cribbs looked back up. "I've received reports of . . . disturbances in a couple of our port cities."

"Disturbances?" I leaned forward.

"Nothing violent, Majesty." He fidgeted with his badge of office like some child standing before his teacher. "Priests of a new faith are entering the towns. They're ministering to the poor, feeding the hungry, that sort of thing."

"I am sorry, Sheriff, I do not follow. What is bad about any of that?"

"It's not their good works that bother me. It's what they're preaching." He locked eyes with me for the first time. "They are openly prophesying the return of the One. *The One* traditionally refers to Empress Irina, or some fictionalized version of her, but these clerics speak of the earthly return of some prophet or mystic god who will unite the continent's people under one faith—and *one banner*."

Ethan's head snapped up. "*One banner*? Are they talking about their god replacing the Throne?

Or the Queen being subservient to their faith's leader?"

"That is what we fear, but they talk in circles. When pressed, they go back to discussing good works and encouraging the people to take care of their brothers and sisters, that sort of thing. I am not even sure the people know what they mean by their veiled political references, but they are gaining followers through their ministry. Our agents fear they are building toward something; we just don't know what."

I thought a moment. "What are they calling themselves?"

"The men and women are called Priests, and their faith is referred to as the Order. It is similar to old tales of Irina's return and the insanity preached by the Children, but their Priests actually call Irina a 'false prophet' and blame her—along with King Alfred and Queen Isabel—for the disaster in Melucia."

"They blame *my father*? He never wanted war. That was all my mother's doing. Her and Thorn."

He nodded and cast an uneasy glance toward Ethan. "The reports are confusing and still a bit new, but I thought you should know everything as we learn it."

"Thank you, Sheriff. Keep an eye on this group and update me regularly."

"Yes, Majesty," Cribbs said. He bowed again, took two steps backward, then wheeled and exited.

Ethan relaxed as soon as the doors closed. "I think he's a fine appointment. You did well."

"We will see." I stood and stretched. "What do you make of that Order talk? With all of the wounded returning, the people need a little extra help these days. It all sounds harmless to me, save the part where they throw my parents in front of the cart."

"Theology was never my strong suit, though many soldiers turn to the Spirits in the heat of battle. I suppose any group offering food to our hungry in the dead of winter is welcome, but the whole part about 'the One' and putting their religious leader above monarchs and rulers walks a dangerous path. We need to learn more about their true purpose."

"And that is why I asked you to join these meetings today." I turned and strode to the Council table, then seated myself at its head in the High Chancellor's chair. Ethan took the hint and followed, taking the seat closest to me.

"So, Uncle Ethan—"

"You know, *little Jess*, you only call me that when you want something." The corners of his mouth quirked into an easy grin.

"You think you know me," I said with mock offense, then turned serious. "It seems I have several openings at this table."

"I wondered when we'd have this conversation. With the loss of Bril, War makes sense. What were you thinking?"

"There are others who can do a fine job at War. I need a *High Chancellor* I trust completely. Unless you know someone more qualified, someone who earned my family's trust over the years, I would like you to fill this chair."

Ethan's eyes popped wide.

He looked away and stared at some distant point in the corner of the chamber. After several moments, he still remained silent.

"Well?"

"Jess—*Your Majesty*—I have very little experience in diplomacy or dealing with nobles. You need someone polished in the art of kissing backsides. I'd be more likely to incite a revolt than quell one if I had to listen to those howling jackals all day."

I leaned forward and placed a hand on his arm. "I can deal with the nobles. I need someone to watch my back, to question everything *and every-one*, to be my eyes and ears throughout the King-dom. I need someone I can count on when every-one else turns away. You are the only one I trust completely." My voice faltered. "With my father and brother gone—Spirits, with my *mother* gone, too—there is no one left."

Ethan opened his mouth to speak, then closed it.

His hand reached up and tugged at his collar.

"If my Queen commands—"

"No," I interrupted sternly, then softened. "Un-cle Ethan, this is *Jess* asking, not your Queen. You have given your life to this nation. I will not com-mand you to serve more than you already have."

He stared into my eyes, then lowered his head and whispered. "I would do anything for you, Jess. Of course I will protect you and your throne in whatever way you need me."

I schooled my expression, straightened my back, and extended my hand toward him. "Thank you, High Chancellor."

Ever the dutiful soldier, Ethan dropped from his chair to one knee, bowed his head, and kissed the proffered signet.

"Thank *you*, Your Majesty."

A few days later, as I was setting my crown onto its velvet cushion beside the throne, ready to change out of my formal audience attire before dinner with Kendall, a page's head poked between the cracked double doors.

"Your Majesty, the High Sheriff is asking to speak with you."

Ethan and I shared a look.

Sheriff Cribbs had not returned to the Palace since accepting his office.

"Send him in," I said, adjusting the crown on its pillow, then turning to stand before my throne. Ethan stepped to the bottom stair on my right and faced the doors.

A harried-looking High Sheriff scurried across the long chamber and bowed before his Queen, his unruly curls as winsome as ever.

He eyed the crown. "Majesty, thank you for seeing me. I will not take long, as I am sure your day was long."

I waved a hand as I had seen my father do a thousand times. "Sheriff, our duty never rests. What brings you to the Palace?"

Cribbs locked eyes with Ethan for a moment, then looked toward me. I raised a brow at the interaction but said nothing.

"Majesty, there was a murder in the eastern quarter last night. The victim was a shopkeeper who sells pottery near the Temple. No one of prominence."

When Cribbs didn't continue, Ethan spoke. "And? Murders are rare, but they do happen, even in the capital."

"Yes, Chancellor, that is true, but two things concern me. First, the man was killed behind his shop in a densely populated area of town where he could only have been alone for a few moments. And . . . his body was mutilated."

"What do you mean? How so?" Ethan asked.

"It looks as though some wild animal attacked him. Massive rends across his chest and stomach appear to have been made by claws of some kind, and his face—it is barely recognizable."

I covered my mouth with a hand.

"The eastern quarter abuts the Spires. Is it unusual for wild beasts to wander down in winter, seeking food?" Ethan asked.

"No, of course not. We see bears and wolves on occasion, but they are rarely bold enough to attack. There are so many people packed into the capital these days that most wildlife is too afraid to venture close."

"You said there were two things that bothered you. What is the second?" I asked, impatient to be done with the day.

Cribbs looked to Ethan. "This is the *third* killing in three weeks that appeared to have been committed by wildlife. The other two occurred in Oliver and Featherstone."

"Oliver? I could understand Spoke. It sits on the eastern base of the Spires, but Oliver is a port town with nothing but fields at its back," Ethan said, scratching his stubbly chin.

"It gets stranger." Cribbs nodded. "The victim in Spoke appeared to be mauled by a wolf or some other smaller predator. In Oliver—I hardly know how to believe the description. Constables there report the man appeared to have wounds consistent with a *bear*. There were wide gashes across his chest and arms. Worse, whatever attacked him did not stop when he was down. It continued tearing at his flesh, his face in particular, until he was barely recognizable. Equally odd—and forgive this, Majesty—in neither attack was the victim . . . well . . . eaten."

"Eaten? Right." The color drained from my face as images flashed in my mind. I stepped backward and sat on the throne, my mind reeling. "Three attacks, all completely different. Spread out across the country. Coincidence?"

"If there were two, I suppose they could be. But three? That is a pattern, even though there is no obvious connection between the attacks."

"What about the victims? Were there any similarities?" Ethan asked.

Cribbs shook his head. "None that I've put together—a shopkeeper, a weaver, and an innkeeper—none were prominent or wealthy, ordinary in every way."

"All right, thank you, Sheriff. Is there anything else?" I asked.

"That is everything we have so far. I will keep you informed as we piece the details together. This may be nothing more than morbid coincidence, but I thought you would want to know about it before the papers piece things together."

"Thank you. Please keep us informed." I rose.

"Sheriff, wait a moment." Ethan stopped the man mid-bow. "Your Majesty, you have one of the most prominent investigators on the continent as a guest in the Palace. Do you think he might like something to do with his time?"

I tilted my head. "There is an interesting idea. I think he would love a new challenge. He has tired of the noble ladies nipping at his heels around every turn."

Ethan chuckled.

"Majesty? I'm not following," the Sheriff said.

"Forgive me, Sheriff. I would like a fresh set of eyes on this situation. Unless you object, I will ask Guardsman-Lieutenant Rea to assist with your investigation."

The Sheriff was quiet a moment, then nodded. "I think that's a fine idea, Majesty. We can use all the help we can get."

"Excellent. I will speak with him this evening. Thank you, Sheriff."

Cribbs bowed again, then backed out of the room.

"What do you make of all that?" I asked as we strode to the side door toward the residence wing.

"Hopefully, it's nothing more than an overcautious lawman with three coincidental deaths. But we'll see." Ethan bobbed his head. "Rest well, Your Majesty."

"Good night, High Chancellor."

CHAPTER 32

DANAI

Danym kneeled before my throne, his head bowed in perfect submission as he spoke. "Our Priests report great success in the towns and villages throughout the Kingdom, Excellency. Far better than we originally anticipated. Your approach of offering necessities before attempting conversion is working brilliantly."

I steepled my fingers and stared down. My liaison to the capital was proving a most effective leader among the clerics, allowing me to spend more time on overall strategy.

"And the detractors? Were they able to chip away at our support before the Five handled things?"

"There will always be those wary of our faith, but the Priests have not reported any more *vocal* opposition. Local Constables are chalking their deaths up to animal attacks, just as you predicted.

Each was handled well out of the view of anyone who might raise suspicion," Danym said.

"How many are we up to now?"

"Four have been eliminated, though that number may have increased since I received my last report. In some of the larger towns, that still leaves vocal detractors, but we followed your instructions to limit the Five to one incident per town . . . for the moment."

"Make sure our people remain true to the plan. The Constables are likely comparing notes and searching for a pattern. As long as we keep things limited, their trail will run cold."

"Yes, Excellency."

"Good." I stood. "What of the capital?"

Danym's brow furrowed. "Fontaine is . . . a challenge. The coronation was well received, and the new Queen rides a wave of popularity. This will change as her reign ages, but for the moment, the people flock to her whenever she leaves the Palace. They hang on her every word and gesture."

"What else? I can tell you hold back."

"It is the Temple, Excellency. Despite Irina going up in flames, adherents to the old religion remain strident in their beliefs. Our Priests have been welcomed with wary eyes, even when carrying blankets and food for the poorest in the city.

It will take some time for the people to accept our presence and good intentions."

"Press the Priests. I want Temples built in every city and town. Spring will be here in four or five weeks, and I want a toehold in each location by summer's end. If we had more Gifted, this would go much faster, but use what we have." I paused and thought a moment, then looked at Danym. "You have done well. Get some rest. I want you back in Fontaine as soon as possible. Our brothers in that city need your guidance, now more than ever—and I believe you have a date planned, do you not?"

Danym grinned as he nodded. "Oh, I do, Excellency. Your most generous offer should make for an interesting first audience with our young Queen."

CHAPTER 33

JESS

I adjusted the cushion, shifting from one tingling cheek to the other, wishing I had even more padding.

When a new monarch was crowned, every vassal and village presented letters offering their service to the new ruler. It was as if the Crown had been reinvented, and everyone was required to bend the knee all over again. I understood the significance of the tradition, as it forced even the most upturned of noble noses to lower themselves and pledge their fealty once more. They weren't exactly making a new promise, more renewing the lifelong one they made when accepting whatever appointment or office they held.

I sighed.

It was an important step, if a long and boring one.

"Guildmaster Devon Weaver, head of the Merchants' Guild of Featherstone," the page called out as the doors swung open once again. I straightened and tried to rub the weariness from my eyes. I hoped the man entering the audience chamber hadn't seen me rolling my neck to ease the stiffness, but I really didn't care at this point.

The stork of a man in his pale blue doublet and brown breeches stopped when he reached a mark on the floor some twenty paces from the base of the dais. He bowed, then continued forward to the final mark, lowering his eyes beneath his new Queen's gaze.

"Guildmaster Weaver. It is a pleasure to see you again. It has been, what, four years?"

The man's head snapped up. "Majesty? You remember?"

I smiled. "Of course I remember. It was a wonderful visit. I recall your kindness most fondly, though you might not say the same of my own . . . unfortunate behavior."

Weaver's eyes lowered once more, but I saw a grin pull at one corner of his mouth. "You were . . . young, Majesty. A little precociousness is to be expected of a child, royal or common, would you not say?"

"Precociousness?" I chuckled. "Yes, well, you are again generous with that description. Nonetheless, it is good to see you again. For what purpose do you seek audience with us?"

The shift in formality snapped him back into form, and Weaver dropped to one knee. "I come to congratulate Her Majesty and give my Oath, such that this humble servant of the Crown may offer."

"Your humility is refreshing in a chamber so often filled with blustery wind." Another grin tugged at the man's mouth. "Guildmaster Weaver, what is your pledge?"

"I, Devon Weaver, do swear that I will well and truly serve our Sovereign Lady Queen Jessia Vester and her heirs and successors. I will do right to all manner of people after the laws and usages of this Kingdom, without fear or favor, affection or ill will. By the Spirits and the Spires, I do swear."

I rose and placed a palm on Weaver's shoulder.

This was the only ceremony in which tradition required the monarch to touch one of her subjects, but doing so carried significant symbolism. I also knew the magic of the crown flowed through me and into my new vasal, binding their promises in a virtually unbreakable pact. My father never told me if the nobles comprehended this Gift, but he attributed much of his reign's longevity on the protections it afforded him.

As my hand contacted Weaver, a faint glow flared from my crown, and the familiar tingle of magic trickled down until it vanished from my palm into Weaver. He looked up, and his eyes widened as I spoke.

"Guildmaster Devon Weaver, the Crown accepts your fealty. In return, we offer you and yours our hearth and home, protection and provision, justice and righteous vengeance, without fear or favor, affection or ill will. By the Spirits and the Spires, we do swear."

A tear fell from Weaver's eye as he watched me step back. "Thank you, Your Majesty. Thank you." He bowed, then backed out of the chamber.

"This might be the longest day ever, but that part never gets old," I whispered to Ethan, who stood one step below the throne to my right.

He grinned. "You royals are all alike. Your father once said exactly the same."

"Really?"

Ethan nodded, his eyes twinkling with mischief. "All alike, I say."

"Oh, hush. Just because you—"

"High Priest Danym Wilfred, Ambassador of the Order to the Crown, Bearer of the Keys to the Faith, and Voice of the One."

Ethan blinked several times. "*Voice of the One?* He sounds full of himself. This should be good."

"Ethan," I whispered. "He said Danym *Wilfred*. Is that *my* Danym? I mean, the Sheriff's son?"

The one who betrayed me?

Before he could respond, the doors swung open, and Danym strode into the room, his dirty-blond hair now draped against the shoulders of his silky brown robe. His annoyingly bemused grin looked as though he'd played some devilish prank that was now being revealed.

I stood before my throne, fists balled at my sides, my chest heaving with barely contained rage. I was sure I'd seen him in the back of the hall at my coronation, but he'd vanished so quickly I wondered if my mind had wandered into moonlit woods.

Now, staring at the man I once craved more than breath, fire flowed in my veins. His eyes remained deep green with flecks of gold, yet all I saw were swirling pools of darkness. This man—this devious, hateful, wretched man—hadn't just cast me aside. He'd handed me over to those who sought to slaughter me.

And for what?

Surely, he gained no power in the bargain. My mother loathed Danym, and Irina . . . I could scarcely see that evil witch keeping him around past his usefulness. I could not fathom what led him to don that vile robe.

As much as I wanted to have Danym's wrists clamped in irons and his body hung from the highest tower of the Palace, the weight on my brow ruled my every desire. He was a representative of a faction, a cult, of some odd collection of misfits who claimed to no longer seek power or vengeance.

Was it duty or curiosity that compelled me to listen to him?

I was unsure.

I relaxed my fingers, then balled them again.

My guards noticed the change in their charge's posture and stepped forward to assume not-so-ceremonial positions on either side of the dais.

Danym stopped *exactly* on the first mark, bowed *exactly* the minimum depth required to not be rude, then marched to the second mark.

His petulant gaze never left my eyes.

He did not bow or kneel again.

"It is customary to take a knee before the throne, Ambassador," Ethan said, his tone darker than I'd heard since he returned from war.

"Forgive me, Your Majesty. The Faith *appreciates* the Crown for its, how should I say, worldly duties, but we do not recognize the monarch as sovereign over spiritual matters. I will show respect to you and your office, but the Order compels me not to kneel in submission or subservience."

Ethan's brow rose.

"Danym?" was all I could get out.

"Hello, Jess."

"You may not kneel, but you *will* address her as Your Majesty, *Priest*," Ethan snapped. The guards took another step forward, pikes at the ready.

Danym peered out the side of his eyes at Ethan as if viewing an irritating bug on his shoulder. "And you may address me as *Holy Voice*."

The room began to spin, and my breath became shallow, so I sat back on my throne. Danym took a step forward, his hand outstretched.

The guards crossed their pikes before him.

"No need for violence. I was merely offering *Her Majesty* a hand. She looks as if she has seen a ghost." Danym stepped back.

"I am fine," I said, waving my guards back. "Let us get this over with. *Holy Voice*, why do you seek an audience before the throne?"

"After all we went through, this is how you greet me. I was hoping for a happier reunion."

I clutched the arms of the throne and leaned forward. "You are lucky *my greeting* does not include the sharp end of a pike. You deceived me, betrayed me, and watched me nearly murdered. Now you come into *my* house and expect a warm embrace?"

"I was talking about a welcome, but if you're offering an embrace—"

"Enough!" I shot off the throne and descended one step to stand eye level with him. The guards were at Danym's sides before I had stopped moving. When I spoke, an angry, hissing whisper escaped my lips. "If you ever cared for me, you will get this farce over and leave. If I never see your face again, it will be too soon."

Danym's smirk vanished, and I thought I caught a hint of the boy I'd once loved emerge.

He whispered, "Jess, of course I loved you—*still* love you. It's not what it looked like. Give me a chance to explain."

My throat seized.

I couldn't think.

The room spun again, and I had to brace myself against Ethan's proffered arm to keep from falling.

Nothing made sense.

Danym *had* betrayed me, given me over to the Children to be slaughtered on the altar of sacrifice.

And for what?

What was in it for him?

He was a teenage boy who didn't want to live with his father anymore. He didn't care about power or religion. He barely cared about his place in Fontaine's society. I had had to coach him through everything.

Or was that all an act, too?

Was the quiet, brooding boy who seemed to stumble over his own feet feigning all that? Did I ever really know the man I fled the safety of the Palace with, only to travel halfway across the Kingdom to be kidnapped by murderous madmen?

No, not kidnapped by—*delivered to.*

Was that his plan all along?

Now he stood before me.

He was so cocky, strutting down the aisle and barely showing any respect due the Crown. How dare he? Who did he think he was? Who did he think *I* was? Some foolhardy, doe-eyed girl whom he could manipulate again—or worse?

He was about to learn exactly who this Queen was, and just how mighty her commands could be, no matter what his fledgling faith might think.

I stepped back, straightened my spine, and spoke formally. "Voice Wilfred, the Crown will hear your words. Speak."

The boy in his eyes vanished, and the annoying smirk returned.

"I come with an offer of friendship. The Order wishes the Crown no ill will. In fact, we offer to unite our strength with yours. The One returns with a message of hope, and we believe the time is right for the Crown and the Order to stand as one."

"Unite the Crown and the Order? What are you saying?" Ethan spoke the words I couldn't voice.

Danym locked eyes with me again. "The One offers a hand in marriage, to join through matrimony the spiritual guidance of our faith and the worldly governance of the throne."

I leaned forward, confusion replaced by a hawk's piercing gaze. "You said *a* hand in marriage, not *his* hand."

Danym actually laughed. "Oh, no, Your Majesty. The One could not marry, though I am sure he would be honored by your offer. He seeks to give *my* hand to Her Majesty, in the furtherance of peace and prosperity for the land we share."

I slumped into the cushion of the throne, stunned. "You want me to marry *you*?"

Danym offered a tilt of his foppish head. "I do."

I seethed as I glared at the man before me.

"Get out." The world froze for but a moment. "GET OUT!"

The guards rushed forward and grabbed Danym roughly by each arm, practically lifting him off the ground as they hauled him out of the hall.

As he vanished through the doors, he called out, "So you'll think about it?"

The doors slammed shut.

CHAPTER 34

KEELAN

I ran my fingers along the stem of my wine glass and stared into the pattern of interlocking gold and silver woven into the tablecloth. Servants stood stiffly along the walls behind each chair, ready to fulfill any wish or desire. All I wanted was a few moments alone with Jess, a chance to talk and laugh as we had on that first stroll through the garden.

I had only seen Jess a few times since her coronation. There were always servants or messengers or the occasional soldier scurrying about. I understood. She was Queen now, with more demands on her time and attention than any other person alive, but I couldn't ignore the tugging at my heart—or the boredom.

Over the past month, I explored every inch of the Palace, taking in both the extravagance of its interior and the natural beauty of the grounds surrounding the royal residence. Dittler hadn't seen any more of Jess than I had, and the stubborn stallion refused to let any of the stable hands near him. At their entreaty, I spent a few hours each day exercising, grooming, and tending my equine friend. For his part, Dittler had stopped nipping me every time I approached—unless I forgot the beast's daily apple. Without a bribe, I earned a crisp snap of the horse's teeth in reprimand.

My other hours were far less productive.

I wasn't a subject of the Crown and, therefore, wasn't allowed to take part in anything meaningful. Jess included me in some Council meetings, but it was inappropriate for a foreigner to become a regular attendee at meetings involving Kingdom security.

Honestly, I was grateful to be excused from those meetings.

The Council Jess assembled was made of fine men and women, but they still loved to hear themselves talk. Jess hadn't yet secured her Crown enough to stop the constant preening and strutting displayed by visiting nobles. I doubted any amount of royal security could ebb that tide, and I wasn't sure I could endure her hours of platitudes without offending some pompous official with my fist, or at least my yawns.

I tried talking the Sheriff into letting me help with some of his case load. The man, still new in his role, had thanked me politely but suggested internal matters were best handled by Kingdom officers.

The Royal Guard allowed me to train with some of their guards, and I was more thankful for the physical activity than they would ever know. My mind might have wandered, but my body, at least, had some measure of focus and routine. When asked if I could help with some duty or other work, the Guard offered the same polite, yet firm, refusal.

I couldn't remember a time when I felt more useless or adrift.

In those quiet moments, thoughts of Tiana troubled me. I saw her smiling in her infirmary, smoothing her spotless blue smock, tending some errant child who'd broken a bone. I saw her laughing at Ridley or slapping my arm, as she often did when I tried to make a jest.

And I saw her folding into the bottom of a cart.

Striding down the massive aisle in the Children's ceremonial chamber.

Gaping with wide eyes as the dagger sank into her chest.

Guilt warred with longing each time I relived that day. I was there to protect her, to save her—to bring her home.

And I failed.

I would never forgive myself for that.

How could I?

Which only made my feelings for Jess more complicated.

That same guilt, the pang that swelled each time I recalled Tiana's final moments, haunted the warmth I felt each time Jess entered a room. All I wanted was to be happy, to enjoy the moment with a woman who made me feel . . . whatever Jess made me feel.

Why couldn't life be simple?

If it weren't for my inexplicable, ever-present desire simply to be with Jess, I would've already headed home. I wasn't sure what existed between us, that feeling of togetherness, that longing, but I felt it every time she was near.

I felt it even more strongly when she left.

It pulled me, or pushed me—I wasn't sure.

The logical Constable's brain couldn't comprehend the utter illogic of me mooning over a woman I barely knew; but here I was, staring at her chair, willing to wait until the world stopped turning for her to arrive and smile.

Just as I was about to chide myself for being sappy, the doors flew open, and Jess stormed into the dining room. The servants, already stiff in their uniforms, snapped to absolute rigidity at the presence of their fuming sovereign.

A man in his mid-thirties with only a few strands of pulled-over hair scurried behind her, his eyes downcast and expression wan.

"Explain this to me, Lord Chamberlain. Did *no one* in this Palace know *the Sheriff's son* had returned? The one who sold me to be slaughtered?" Her voice rose with each word, and the man somehow bowed lower in her wake.

"I do not know, Your Majesty. No one reported this to me."

She wheeled to face him. "Stand up straight and face me."

He did, reluctantly, though his gaze remained fixed on her chin.

"Unless you want to be the *former* Lord Chamberlain, you will look me in the eye. Now." She waited as the man struggled to lift both of his chins. "Find the High Chancellor and get me a report from our eyes and ears. I want to know our numbers, strengths, gaps, and how the best network on the continent could miss something so obvious. Then I want to hear the plan to never miss so much as a whisper on the wind again. Am I clear, *Lord Chamberlain*?"

The man bowed several times nervously. "Yes, Majesty. Perfectly clear. I will find the High Chancellor at once."

"Now get out." Her voice had fallen to an indistinct murmur, which was somehow more intimidating than her raised pitch from before.

The man practically ran from the room.

Servants began their choreographed dance, pouring wine and water, removing chargers, and retrieving platters of rolled meats and cheeses from the kitchen.

I sat back as Jess turned and noticed me.

She sucked in a deep breath, then released it, then reached over her chair to grip her glass, drained half of its contents, and set it down.

"I am sorry you had to see that. You are not going to believe who showed up in court today."

I raised one brow but didn't speak.

"*Danym*. Can you believe it?"

"You mean Ambassador Danym? The Priest?"

Her jaw dropped. "You *knew*?"

I threw my hands up to fend off her rising anger. "I knew *a* Priest named Danym was appointed Ambassador. He was at the coronation banquet and paid me a visit at my table. Are you saying he's *that* Danym?"

"Yes, *that* Danym," she spat. "The one who tricked me into falling in love and running away with him, then gave me away to be killed. The one who laughed at me as those robed monsters dragged me into their Temple. *That* Danym!"

She grabbed her glass and finished the wine, slamming the crystal on the table so hard I wondered that it didn't shatter.

A servant materialized and refilled it as soon as she'd set it on the table.

I switched into investigator mode, insulating my newly found, highly confusing emotions from her wrath. I watched but held my tongue.

She gulped more wine.

"Well? No advice? Everyone else around here seems to have plenty. All day, every day. Nothing but 'You should do this, Your Majesty,' or 'Oh, no, don't do that, Majesty.' They never stop. Surely you have some counsel, too?"

I didn't budge.

She took another sip, eyeing me.

"I'm sorry, Jess. I didn't know."

She looked up, and her icy glare thawed.

I turned to the servant standing watch behind my chair and asked, "Would you ask the staff to give us a moment?"

The woman bobbed, looking relieved. Within seconds, Jess and I were alone. I stood and kneeled beside her chair.

"Do you want to talk about it?"

A tear threatened to flee the corner of her eye, and her lip quivered.

She didn't turn to look at me, but one hand reached down and gripped mine.

I felt her anger and pain through that simple touch. Warmth also flooded up my arm and into my chest at the feeling of her skin pressed against my own. I didn't know what to make of all the emotions competing for my attention.

I'd never felt comfortable dealing with one feeling at a time. A swirling host of emotions was overwhelming—and confusing.

"I loved him," she said in a small voice I strained to hear. "I *really* loved him. I never thought I'd see him again after . . . everything happened. And today, I was so happy, and then he appeared. He just showed up."

I had seen the glassy-eyed stare of survivors before, heard the monotone of their recollections, watched as they relived their terror again and again. Usually, their memories and emotions came in waves. Shock, pain, anger, grief, disbelief, belief, acceptance. Sometimes the waves respected the order, but mostly they came when wounded hearts and minds allowed, disjointed and unpredictable. I saw how Jess's mind and soul were under assault by more than a few of those feelings, and ached to help her cope, but I knew her own strength was required to survive such a journey.

I stood, lifting my hand, suggesting she stand, and held her in my arms for so long that the servants began returning before I released her to sit again. By then her tears were dry, though the redness of her eyes told of their passing.

The servants spoke with a gentle kindness I hadn't heard in the Palace before. It was the sharing of a burden only found within a special bond, within a family. I realized, in that moment, how unique those who served the royal household must be, and how critical they would be to her future success. I made a mental note to learn more about each servant and guard, especially those who worked within the private residence.

As plates from the main course were cleared, Jess broke the silence that dominated the meal. "Are you tired of me yet?"

I wasn't often surprised, but the look of utter shock that flooded my face made her smile for the first time that evening.

"*Never*. Jess, I—"

"Good. Me either." She reached across the table and gripped my hand again. "I need to ask you to do something for me."

Her tone had changed, and her back had stiffened just enough for me to notice.

"Is this Jess or the Queen asking?"

Her eyes widened. "Am I that obvious? Sometimes I forget you are a trained investigator."

When I didn't reply, she continued. "There have been a series of deaths scattered in towns and villages across the country, seemingly at random. They appear to be the work of wild animals."

"But you don't believe that, do you?"

"No. They are *too* random, if that makes any sense."

I nodded. "All right, what do you want me to do? Your Sheriff made it clear he didn't want me involved in Kingdom matters."

"Not to worry. I spoke with him, and he agreed." She took a sip. "I would like you to go to Oliver and see what you can learn. Our investigators have done their best but failed to uncover anything beyond the obvious."

"The obvious may be the truth."

"I would still like your eyes on this. Something *feels* wrong. It is . . . hard to explain."

"Of course, I'd do anything you asked, Your Majesty." I offered her a teasing bob of my head.

She snorted. "Not you, too! Stop that."

"As you wish, Your Most Serene and Majestic Majesty."

Another snort. Then a slap on my arm.

I didn't say anything, just stared.

"What? Have I got something in my teeth?"

"No. It's just . . . I missed your smile."

She beamed, and a flush raced up her neck. "Ooh, is it warm in here? I need some fresh air. Would you mind accompanying me on a stroll through the gardens after dinner? We can walk off some of this meal."

"I thought you would never ask."

We finished dessert, tossed back the last of our wine, and left the dining room to her army of servants. Jess raced fingertips across every plant and flower we passed while I fiddled with my fingers and timidly avoided eye contact. We'd strode halfway across the sprawling gardens before either of us spoke.

"Jess—"

"Keelan—" she said at the same time.

We both cut off our words.

"You go first," she said.

I returned my gaze to my rapidly twiddling digits.

"It's nice out here," I said.

She snorted. "That is what you were nervous saying to me?"

"I'm not—" I didn't look up. "I guess I'm just nervous about the trip."

Jess looked up sharply. "What? You mean going to Oliver? Keelan, you are one of the most storied investigators alive. Why would taking on a case make you nervous?"

"Because it's not just another case. It's a case *for you*."

"You have taken cases from the Triad. Why is one from the Queen of Spires so different?"

I met her eyes. "I don't care about 'the Queen.' I'm worried I'll disappoint *you*."

She missed a step.

I caught her arm. She gripped my hand and didn't let go. Both of us stared at our hands. After a moment of silence, she looked up.

"Keelan, you are an amazing Constable, one of the best, and you have magic that helps you serve people in need—but your skills and your Gift are not why I fell in love with you."

My head snapped up, and my eyes widened.

For some reason, my heart felt like it wanted to leap out of my chest and run through the flowers. Every last hair on my arms jolted upright, and my tongue was suddenly sandpaper.

She reached up and stroked my cheek. "Yeah, I said it. You will owe me for that." She winked. "You are a good, decent man, Keelan. You are smart and strong, and you would die before letting anything happen to someone you love. You act tough, but I have seen the real boy inside the hardened shell. He is scared sometimes, but mostly he wants to be happy, to be accepted, and to help others. I love that boy, Keelan, with all my heart."

I stared down at her with wonder in my eyes.

"Jess . . . I . . . you . . . what?"

"Keelan Rea, for such an intelligent, Gifted Constable, you are incredibly dense if you have not seen this."

The sound of her laughter was sunlight blazing through clouds.

Never in a million years would I dare to dream she might feel the same way I did.

I wanted to take the assignment in Oliver to get away from the Palace before I said something we both might regret, something she'd send me packing for.

But she loved me.

Me?

I couldn't believe it.

Beads of sweat formed on my forehead. I reached up and tugged at my itchy collar, and the darn gardens suddenly felt like the business end of a furnace.

Jess grinned as only a woman who knows she's flummoxed a man can.

Then she gripped my face in both of her hands and pulled me toward her.

I *tasted* her breath.

A magic all its own sent lightning up my spine.

As our lips met, warmth exploded in my chest, and all thoughts of animal attacks or Jess's resurrected ex-boyfriends faded from my mind. I was startled at first, eyes wide in panic, and tried to pull back, but she held me in place until I kissed her back. Our eyes closed, and the world drifted away.

She melted into me, and I knew I was at home in her embrace.

CHAPTER 35

KEELAN

By the time the outskirts of Oliver came into view, my backside and legs were achy and stiff. As much as I trusted Jess, my Gift told me she wasn't laying all the cards on the table. I had worked for the Triad long enough to be used to knowing only what they deemed necessary, but it still bothered me that *Jess* hadn't trusted me with the entire picture.

It made me question the feelings she professed in the garden.

Were we truly as deeply in love as she claimed, or were hers merely the words of a lonely girl clinging to a man who made her feel safe?

It made me wonder why I stayed in Fontaine so long.

Atikus and the Guard could certainly use my leadership and strong hands to rebuild.

My *home* needed me.

Yet here I was riding to some distant ocean town to investigate animal attacks that didn't smell right to a foreign ruler.

But she's so much more than just some foreign ruler now, isn't she?

Dittler snorted.

I reached down and stroked the stallion's neck. "I know. It sounds ridiculous when I think it. Please don't make me say any of it out loud."

Dittler looked back and whinnied.

I slowed our trot as we entered town. Oliver was larger than I'd pictured in my mind. While scattered farmhouses dotted the landscape for leagues around, the town itself was composed of a variety of tightly packed wooden and stone structures. Well-maintained cobbled roads wove between them with little apparent pattern for traffic flow.

It was an hour or two past midday.

The sun was beginning his lazy descent over the ocean. Men and women in simple clothing moved about with purpose, most carrying goods or children in their heavily laden arms. As they passed, most smiled or nodded in greeting to their neighbors, and the sound of chatter and laughter echoed off building walls.

At first glance, Oliver was a bustling, thriving town with warm and friendly citizens; but as I watched life unfold before me, I sensed an undertone of something—a feeling of loss and sadness—that drifted on the ocean breeze as it wafted by. It was as clear as the salty tang on my tongue. Whether this undercurrent of grief was born from the mysterious death that had occurred two weeks earlier or from the war that had torn many families asunder, I couldn't be sure. It was probably some measure of each.

A man in a silky brown robe stopped as I strode past, looking up at the massive horse I rode. "He's a beauty. I have not seen a Cretian in years. I almost forgot how tall they are."

The man whistled as his eyes traveled up Dittler's neck and met the horse's eyes. Dittler peered down, then snapped at the man's foolishly outstretched hand.

The man snatched his hand back, clutching it against his chest.

I chuckled. "He's a beauty but not the friendliest beast you'll meet, not without a bribe in your hand."

The man smiled weakly and nodded. "If it's all the same, I'll leave the bribing to you."

Dittler snorted, drawing the man's now-wide eyes.

"Yeah, he thinks he knows what we're saying, too. He's far too smart for his own good," I joked.

Dittler's head craned back as he snapped at his impudent rider, who simply stroked his neck and grinned.

The robed man stopped gaping and cleared his throat. "I am Seth. You look like you could use a break from riding. Been traveling long?"

"Keelan," I said while inclining my head. "Just arrived from Fontaine."

When I didn't offer more, Seth asked, "I do not recall ever seeing a blue uniform like yours."

I looked down at my dusty navy jacket. I'd forgotten I wore my Melucian uniform, a clear oversight I'd correct as quickly as possible. "I'm a Constable in the Saltstone Guard."

"Saltstone? Melucia's capital?"

"Yes. I came on behalf of our government to help repair the ties that were recently broken." The scripted and well-rehearsed line sailed off my tongue with barely a thought. Jess had insisted I offer only this explanation when asked why I was so far from home in what many still called *enemy territory*.

Seth remained silent a moment, then smiled and looked up. "Welcome. We are a friendly town, especially to those in need. I am the local Priest. If this humble servant can help with anything, please ask."

This man was unlike most vicars I'd encountered.

I didn't sense anything false in his words but knew from painful experience not to trust men wearing silky brown robes. I decided to keep a wary eye on the man while in town.

"I *could* use some directions. The roads around here seem to follow their own whims. Can you point me to the local inn?"

Seth brightened. "There are two inns in town, but you will prefer the Glory. The other inn is by the docks and tends to attract sailors and more troublesome folk. I was headed there now. You are welcome to join me."

I nodded. "Thank you, Priest Seth."

"Please, just call me Seth."

Moments later, we stood before the entrance to the inn. I eyed the two-story stone building with its stylized golden crown glittering above the door.

"The local legend says the King stayed here and loved the place so much he allowed the owner to use the royal crest. People still talk about the court's visit, but nobody knows if the owner made up the last part or not. Either way, the Glory is nice and run by good people. You will be comfortable here."

A boy in his early teens startled me, appearing from around the corner. "You checking in, mister? I'll stable your horse."

Dittler nipped at the boy's hand as his thin fingers reached for the bridle.

"If you'll lead the way, I'll take him back. He doesn't like most people. Some days, I'm not sure he likes me," I said as I dismounted.

On cue, Dittler turned and snapped at my arm, earning a playful swat from his temporary master. "Enough of that. You behave."

Once Dittler was settled, Seth and I entered the inn to find an empty common room filled with the sounds and smells of an active kitchen. My stomach made its presence known.

"Didn't eat much on the road?" Seth said with a smirk.

I didn't want to like the Priest but couldn't help warming to his easy smile. "Just some dried meat in my pack."

Before Seth could respond, a rotund older woman burst through the door, an empty pitcher in one hand and four beer mugs gripped by their handles in the other. Her head snapped up when she saw her guests, round eyes roaming to my face.

"Oh, Seth. You're early today. I can't let our boy go for another few hours." The woman gaped at me, the overly tall uniformed man standing by the Priest. "Who did you bring with you? I can't remember having a giant in our inn before."

Seth laughed. I shuffled my feet.

"It's all right, Ma. I'm just bringing you another guest: a Constable from across the mountains who just arrived in town."

She set the pitcher down and gave me her full attention, failing to hide her sudden unease. "Across the mountains, eh? What brings ya here?"

I offered a shallow bow. "I am here on a personal matter and need a room for a few nights."

Ma brightened. "Of course. We can fix ya right up. You'll be wanting to wash the road off first thing. I'll have our boy bring you hot bath water. We just cleaned up the noon meal, but I can have some cuts and cheese brought up if you're hungry to tide ya over till dinner."

"You're right on both counts. I'm starving and"—I looked down at my dusty coat— "definitely need to wash the road off. Is there someone who could clean my uniform?"

Ma nodded. "Just leave it outside your door. Boy'll take it and bring it back clean before the day's out."

I bowed again. "Thank you, ma'am."

"You hear that? He called me ma'am—and bowed *twice*!" Ma giggled and swatted at Seth. Through her laughter, she called over her shoulder as she left the room, "Wait one minute. I'll show you to your room."

Seth turned to me. "I will leave you to it, then. I hope your stay is peaceful and pleasant."

"Thank you." I set my pack on the floor and nodded. "Before you leave, can I ask you about something?"

"Of course. How can I help?" Seth asked.

"How long have you lived here?"

"Oh, it's been a few months now. It feels like I've been here forever, though. The place really grows on you fast."

"Did you know a man named Hershel?"

Seth's face fell, and his eyes hardened. "Yes. I knew him."

I held up a palm. "Forgive me. I know his passing was a tragedy. I am here to learn what I can of how he died. The local Constables' report was vague, and the High Sheriff in Fontaine asked for another pair of eyes. He couldn't spare his own

men, and I was about to climb the walls with boredom. So here I am."

Seth relaxed a bit, but his guard remained in
place. "They say it was a bear attack. What a terrible thing. I did not see his body afterward, but
folks who did said you might not know it was
Hershel. His face—most of it had been ripped
apart. Had we not known an animal was to blame,
I would say someone who hated the man killed
him with spite in their heart."

I listened carefully.

My Gift remained quiet, undisturbed.

The Priest believed what he was saying and held
nothing back.

"Thank you. I know it can be hard to relive
events such as this, but it is important we know
what happened to protect others from the same
fate."

The stable boy appeared through the kitchen
door and looked between me and Seth, as if sensing tension he hadn't felt before. Seth looked up
slowly and nodded. "I'll leave you now, Guardsman. Good day."

A couple of hours later, I returned to the common room cleaned, fed, and somewhat rested. I
had changed out of my uniform, in favor of more
comfortable civilian clothing, a muted-green tu-

nic and dark tan trousers—something Jess had provided. The thought made me smile as I donned the shirt.

I'd been away for only a few days and already missed her.

I hardly knew what to do with that foreign feeling.

I settled into a chair at a table near the hearth, letting the warmth of the newly stoked fire soak into my tired muscles. A few other guests had arrived and talked quietly at tables throughout the room.

A boy of seventeen or eighteen winters with curly, sandy-colored hair darted from one table to another. When he approached my table, he paused to catch his breath before speaking.

"Sorry for the wait. I'm Liam. I'm the only one here for now, so they've got me running. What can I get you to drink? Ale? Wine?"

"How about an ale and some water?"

He nodded and vanished as quickly as he'd appeared.

A moment later, Liam returned with a mug in each hand, set them down with a heavy thud, and scurried to the table two rows away without even looking up.

The ale was sweet with a touch of a citrus, unlike the tart beers back home—and there wasn't a hint of the water I expected from most inns or alehouses.

This might be a good trip after all, I thought, stretching my legs before the fire.

The front doors clacked open, and I looked up to find a man with broad shoulders and a square jaw entering. A stripe on the collar on his forest-green cloak glittered, a common enough sight in Melucia but a growing rarity in the Kingdom. The man stopped in the doorway and surveyed the room, taking in each table's occupants before moving on to the next. When his eyes fell to me, his scanning ceased, and he strode to stand before my table.

"Mind some company?"

My eyes fell to a piece of metal pinned to the man's inner coat, a crown over two small ships, their sails unfurled. I'd know a lawman's badge anywhere in the world. The symbols were different, but they *felt* the same.

To me, they felt like brotherhood.

I nodded and gestured with my mug. "Please, make yourself comfortable. Always happy to meet another Constable."

The man smiled, removed his cloak, and sat. "That obvious? Guess it is to another lawman. It's the eyes, isn't it?"

I shrugged and pointed. "I saw your badge."

The man's hand reached up and felt the pin. "Right. That'll do it, too." He chuckled. "I'm Chief Aengus Kerr, head Constable in town. It's a pleasure to meet the famous Keelan Rea."

My eyes widened. "Got all that from my eyes?"

"No, a bird. Received word from Fontaine to expect you around this time. They told me to give you whatever assistance you needed and to not ask too many questions."

I relaxed and took another sip.

"So, what's this all about?" the Chief asked.

Now it was my turn to laugh. "So much for no questions."

"Ever met a Constable who could let a good mystery go? You're just about the best mystery this sleepy little town's seen in a decade, and I've always been a curious lad."

The kinship I felt with the fellow lawman deepened as the man spoke. His words were clear, his laugh deep, and everything he said rang true to my Gift.

This was a brother in uniform.

"I'm not sure what all the secrecy's about. I've been sent to see if there's more to the killing from a couple weeks ago than was in your report."

Aengus's brows rose. "You mean the mauling? Why would they send someone to look into that? Poor man was torn to shreds just outside of town. His whole body was covered in claw marks, at least what was left of it. I can't see anything other than a bear causing that kind of damage."

"I was planning to come see you first thing in the morning, but since you're here, mind if I ask a few questions?"

"If I can have an ale while we do it, you can ask anything you want. Like I said, I'm under orders to help you however you need it," Aengus said as he motioned the serving boy over to the table. "The fella coming over here is Liam, Hershel's son. The round woman who'll bring out your meal is Ma, his wife. Best we not let either of them hear what we're talking about."

I nodded and held my mug to my lips as Aengus chatted briefly with Liam before the boy hustled back to the bar.

Over the next few hours, Aengus and I reviewed every aspect of the investigation into Hershel's death. From the start, the locals had seen it as a clear-cut case of an animal attack, though none could understand why a beast large enough to maul a man like Hershel would be so far from any forested area. Aengus couldn't recall a single bear sighting within fifty leagues of Oliver during his lifetime.

The next largest animals to routinely wander nearby were wolves. While wolves were dangerous enough in a pack, they ate what they killed, instead of tearing it to shreds and vanishing.

That part made little sense.

I sat quietly as Aengus launched into his dinner of pot roast, a well-known winter special of the inn. Virtually every table held the same hearty chunks of meat, dark sauce, and bowls of roasted potatoes.

I shoved my own roast around my plate as I thought.

Hershel's murder, I thought as I sipped. *Nothing in the facts* suggests *a murder, merely a killing, as the locals believe. It all seems so obvious, yet my instincts are screaming there's something hidden behind the mask.*

"What are you thinking?" Aengus asked between bites.

I sighed and set my mug down. "I don't know. Everything you said makes sense."

"But your gut's churning, and you don't know why?"

I glanced up and nodded.

"Tell me about Hershel," I asked.

Aengus set his fork down and looked around the room until he located Liam and Ma. When he spoke, I had to lean forward to hear him.

"Hershel was a good man. Stubborn and strong-minded, but loyal through and through. He and Ma bought this place twenty or so years ago. It wasn't anything until the royals blew into town. To hear Hershel tell it, the King kissed the floorboards and shat gold on the bar."

Aengus chuckled, but there was a sadness in his laughter.

"Was he well liked in town?"

"Liked? More loved than liked. Hersh could be a surly bastard when something didn't go his way, but everyone knew to just let him cool down and peace would be restored—usually at the business end of one of Ma's cooking spoons."

Aengus sipped his wine and stared into the fire. To my eye, the man saw memories more than flames. It was clear Hershel was more than just another citizen to the Chief; he was a dearly missed friend.

"Chief, I am sorry. I know this is hard for everyone, especially those who were close with him."

Aengus glanced up. "You don't have to do that, play the empathetic Constable to get me to talk."

"I didn't mean—"

"Yes, you did—and you were right to—but it's unnecessary. I want the truth as much as anyone, but I'm afraid it is a simple one that won't give any of us satisfaction."

Liam swung by and replaced our empty mugs with a pair filled to the brim. He seemed to sense the tenor of our conversation and slipped away without a word.

"Did Hershel have any enemies in town?"

"Not that I know of. He really was well liked." Aengus shook his head. "Oh, there's always one or two who don't like anybody, but they're that way with the lot of us, not just Hersh. I've been over this a thousand times in my head since he died, and I can't come up with one person who would've wished him harm, much less dead."

We focused on our ale as the stable boy, who seemed to do far more than manage the stables, stoked the fire, and a player took the stage. The room was now packed, every table filled, and two rows of standing patrons milled about the bar. With the first few notes of the gleeman's fiddle, the low murmur of the crowd swelled to a clamor in anticipation of the entertainment to come.

"Well, Chief, I thank you for your time—and company. Despite the topic, you've made a traveler feel at home tonight. If it's all right with you, I'll leave you here and start again in the morning." I finished my ale and set my mug on the table.

Aengus stood and gripped my arm. "The company was welcome. Get some rest. You look like you could use a good night's sleep."

CHAPTER 36

KEELAN

The day began with Chief Kerr, reviewing the written account made by officers who were first to arrive at the scene of Hershel's death. They were cursory and about what I expected. Aengus explained that unnatural deaths were rare, murders even more so. His Constables might face one murder in a dozen years. With that lack of experience, I thought it was a wonder the report contained more than "He was dead when we arrived."

The rest of the day was spent interviewing townsfolk.

Each was friendly, respectful, and visibly despondent at the mention of Hershel's death. As Aengus had told me, the man was well known and loved. No one could fathom a reason for foul play, and most expressed ongoing fear of a ravenous animal roaming free near their town. The people spoke of early nights, shuttering their businesses before sunset for the first time in a generation, and few willing to walk alone, even in broad daylight.

The normally peaceful seaside town was now firmly in fear's grip.

But there was no talk of murder.

No one even gave that serious consideration.

It was unthinkable, especially with a man like Hershel.

It could not have happened.

Something in their universal certitude made my neck itch. I knew it was an irrational reaction, but years of investigation had taught me to trust my instincts. I didn't know what it was, but I was missing something important.

I ran into Seth as I made my way back to the inn around sunset. As he'd done the day before, the Priest offered a warm smile and gripped my arm in greeting.

"It is good to see you again, Guardsman. Headed back to the inn?"

I nodded. "It's been a long day, and I hear tonight's dinner is roasted boar. I haven't had boar in years."

Seth grunted. "And Ma knows her way around that kitchen. I was headed there myself, though the boar is welcome news."

Something tickled my senses, and I eyed the Priest. "You visit the inn often?"

"Most days. It's a popular place around town, especially this time of year as Ma starts to run out of winter fare and move into the spring menu." His expression turned sheepish. "And Liam is always there."

"Liam?"

"The serving boy, Ma's son. He's . . . well . . . we've taken a few long walks together and . . . I don't know . . ."

"I didn't know holy men could have crushes, much less court." Seth's explanation rang true, and I released the tension I hadn't realized I'd held in my shoulders. Images of Declan's curly locks floated to mind, then Ayden and his fiery curls. Men coupling wasn't rare, but it was uncommon. The joy in Seth's eyes at the mention of Liam brought my brother's own happiness to mind.

I wondered where Declan was, how he was doing. I missed my baby brother and his smile and infectious laugh.

Seth's voice brought me back to the present. "The Order doesn't teach celibacy like some faiths, thank the Spirits. I could even marry one day, should someone be foolish enough to accept my offer."

I mirrored Seth's smile as we reached the door to the inn.

As promised, the common room was packed to the gills with townsfolk and thick with the aroma of well-seasoned meat. Festive music from a colorfully dressed pair on stage set the mood, as Liam and two serving girls raced from one table to the next.

"Join me for dinner?" Seth asked, noticing me scanning the room for an open table. "Ma and Liam have a table for me by the hearth. I'd be glad for your company. I doubt I'll see Liam much tonight."

We waded through the sea of tables and settled in for the evening. As I took my first sip of the evening's spicy ale, I was glad for the Priest's invitation and the fire's warmth that again reminded me of my dandelion-headed little brother.

CHAPTER 37

DECLAN

Atikus braced himself against the rim of the Well as I pushed him up and out of its opening. The Mage sprawled across the floor and lay there as I jumped up beside him.

"Atikus, are you all right?"

"Fine." His muffled voice bounced off the glassy surface of the cave's floor. "Can we not do that again—*ever*?"

A chuckle replaced concern as I gripped his arm to help him stand.

"We may need to make one more trip to get you back home, unless you'd prefer to take the gate and walk all the way from the mountains to Saltstone."

Atikus wobbled and sat on the crystalline bench across from the Well. "I might prefer a few decades of walking to riding that river of death again. How is your head not—?"

His last word trailed off as his eyes took in the cavern for the first time.

"What's wrong? Are you all right?" I asked.

Atikus spoke in awed tones. "For hundreds of years, I kept the secret of the Well. Velius and I spent countless hours guessing what the hallowed mountain might look like, how magic in the air might feel, at what wonders that were hidden and would never be revealed to anyone beyond its Keeper." He sighed at the mention of his old friend. "When you returned from your first journey here, describing the cave with a boyish gleam in your eyes, I never dreamed *I* would gaze at the majesty of the Well. You have helped me live a dream, son."

Atikus stood on shaky legs and braced himself against my shoulder with one hand. His head turned slowly—so slowly—as he took in every crystal and crevice, every shade and shadow, with widened eyes.

I gripped the old man's arm and watched as he surveyed the cavern.

"I was pretty stunned the first time, too. Look down."

Atikus took a reflexive step back as azure mist curled upward beneath its glassy ceiling, winding toward Atikus's feet. Once he realized it was harmless, he kneeled and placed a hand on the floor. The mist responded, hungrily racing to mirror his bony fingers and palm.

Atikus erupted in a childlike laugh that echoed off the crystalline walls.

"Oh, that's not even the big show. Come over here," I said, hooking the Mage under my elbow to help him stand. I walked him to the opening that was the Well of Magic, where mist wafted upward, unabated by stone or crystal or glass. It seemed to sense Atikus's approach and greeted him, enveloping his entire body in glowing, writhing fog.

Tears of pure joy trailed down Atikus's cheeks.

My heart soared.

I couldn't wipe the goofy grin from my face, so I swatted rebellious curls out of my eyes—an old childhood tick.

"Declan, I am rarely speechless, but this—" Atikus choked on a happy sob that racked his chest.

I beamed at the small boy in Mages' robes before me. "I know. I get chills every time I come in here, especially when the currents greet me."

Atikus kneeled and extended a hand toward the opening, toward the gently rushing magic that flowed beneath.

I caught his hand and pulled it away. "Oh, no. That's one thing you cannot do. Kelså says the currents will overwhelm and consume you."

"Then how . . . how did *you* travel in them? How did you bring me here?"

"I honestly don't know. It's an Heir of Magic thing, I guess." I shrugged. "The first time, I felt like I'd been dragged behind a horse for hours, then run over by a dozen carts. Though, I never felt any pain. Órla said I would always be safe in the currents."

"Órla?" Atikus's head snapped up. "Didn't she—"

"Yes, she sacrificed herself, but her Spirit returned to the Well as it always does." A confused look crossed Atikus's face. "Atikus, she isn't what we thought. She *is* magic's essence. She cannot die. She will be reborn in a new form."

"Sweet Spirits . . ."

"For now, she speaks through the currents. You couldn't hear us talking?"

"I was more focused on staying in one piece than listening to you babbling into the void. Yours was the only voice I heard."

I leaned closer. "Your eyes didn't change like mine did. That's odd."

"I may be the most knowledgeable Mage alive, but I feel like a new acolyte around you—and *all this*."

"Second most knowledgeable," a warm voice said from behind.

Atikus wheeled around.

His eyes widened and smile broadened as Kelså strode toward us.

"Kelså?" The astonished Mage struggled forward on unsteady legs. "It has been decades—no, *centuries*. You have not aged a day!"

"And you still remember how to flatter a woman, you silver-tongued Mage." Kelså reached us and wrapped her arms around her old friend, then peered over his shoulder and winked at me.

Then she noticed my eyes.

"Declan, *your eyes*—"

"I know, but it's all right. Órla warned there would be changes when I entered the currents. She doesn't know if this is permanent or not, or if there will be other side effects later on. Nothing else changed—at least that I can tell—other than people's reactions back home."

She released Atikus and stepped past him toward me, concern creasing her brow. "What do you mean, *people's reactions*? Last I heard you were being hailed as a hero everywhere you walked."

I shrugged as my eyes fell. "They're scared of me, like I'm going to attack them with my eyes or something. I don't know. Even the kids wouldn't come close. They run or hide behind their parents." My gaze strayed to meet hers, then shied away. I muttered, "Guess I'm alone again—"

Kelså closed the gap between us faster than an adder could strike. Her palms cupped my cheeks and forced me to look into her eyes. "Declan Rea, you are *never* alone. You hear me? *Never.*"

I stared and lost myself in my mother's ideal reflected through her vision.

She saw something I couldn't fathom, someone I didn't recognize. How could anyone believe in another person with such reckless abandon? I wished some measure of her confidence in me would take root in my own heart and grow—but I knew it was likely too late for that, especially with magic literally seeping out of my eyes every time I blinked.

Self-conscious under her maternal gaze, I said, "For whatever reason, Atikus was unaffected by his trip along the currents."

Kelså gave me a look I couldn't interpret but said nothing, turning back as Atikus coughed.

"Unaffected? I can barely walk after bouncing from the continent to this island!"

I snorted, relieved the spotlight shone else-where. "I meant magically. We can't help that you're old and frail."

"Hey!" Atikus smacked me on the arm. "I am *distinguished*. And hungry, now that we are talking about our feelings."

"Of course you are." I rolled my eyes.

"You boys come with me. I can take care of your stomachs while we talk about fixing Atikus's magic. As much as I would love to catch up, Órla's warning has me thinking there is little time to waste."

Nothing worked to restore Atikus's magic.

We tried Healing, then Healing combined with air, hoping I could somehow *breathe* life back into his Gift. It had seemed a silly idea at the time, but Kelså swore she remembered something akin to it working to Heal another Mage many years before. We were growing desperate, and Kelså's wild-guess theory failed as all previous attempts had.

On our fifth morning together, Atikus, Kelså, and I sat around the table on the landing overlooking the standing stone circles. Our bellies were nearly as full as our wine glasses.

As we transitioned from lunch to wine on the ridge, our conversation also shifted from Atikus's perpetual questioning of all things magic toward possible treatments to restore Atikus's connection. Kelså was disappointed the trip within the currents had done nothing to aid him and was surprised when Atikus described feeling none of the tingling sensation that assaulted me as I traveled. His lack of sensation, along with his inability to sense Órla's presence or hear her voice, underscored how complete his separation from magic truly was.

"I was afraid to let go of him while we traveled," I explained. "Maybe he needs to be exposed to the currents without me protecting him with my touch."

Kelså shook her head. "No, we should *not* try that. Putting him into the currents without you would likely kill him—or sear his consciousness so he would lose all sense of identity or self. You are the only person in my thousand years of life who has touched the currents and lived. We will save that for a last resort."

"What if I Called to his spirit, like a summoning, but inside?"

"Now that is just plain creepy, and I have lived long enough to see many things that would make your skin crawl," Atikus said.

"You might be onto something, as *creepy* as it may sound." Kelså chuckled at Atikus, then grew serious. "But you would have to be very careful. Interaction with a living being's spirit is dangerous, and not just to them. The will of a spirit is a fickle thing, and Atikus might not be able to control what it does."

"What are you talking about? It is *my* spirit. Why would I not be able to control it?"

"Yes, it is *your* spirit, as long as it is within you, but if Declan connected with it, there would be a path it could take through his consciousness to escape the bonds of your mortal body. In essence, Declan could be a conduit to allow your spirit to become sentient *in itself* and then be loosed on the world to do who knows what. Freed spirits are incredibly dangerous. That is why we must be cautious when constructing summoning circles. Think of it as a conscience-free Atikus in spirit form roaming the land."

"Sounds like another spirit I met recently, except without my sparkling personality," Atikus said sourly.

Kelså ignored his attempt at humor. "Exactly. Irina's spirit maintains her personality and some of her will but now lusts for vengeance of its own. The woman I knew would never kill innocents."

"The woman you knew was entombed for a very long time. I expect that dark prison changed her, even in spirit form," Atikus said.

I cleared my throat. "We're wandering. Back to helping Atikus. I don't like the spirit interaction idea anymore. Let's shelve that for now. What else?"

And so the afternoon and evening went, each idea more audacious than the last, and each being added to a very large and growing scroll of unpopular suggestions. When night's darkness fell and the stars' light guided our vision, we were nowhere closer to an actionable plan than before.

Kelså stood and downed the last of the wine in her glass. "We should get some sleep and start fresh in the morning. My mind cannot take any more tonight."

The next day, we sat eating a hearty breakfast and chatting about recent events on the continent. Kelså soaked in every bit of news about Keelan and the goings-on in her homeland. As Atikus reached across to fill his plate for the third time, a voice, clear and commanding, boomed throughout the mountain. It sounded—no, *felt*—like the mountain itself was speaking.

Órla's voice was an eruption of urgency. "KEL-SÅ! Someone has made it past the hut, past the wards. Hatred and anger burn in her wake. She is almost at the Well!"

"What in the void—" I started but cut off as my tunic flared to life, the Phoenix practically leaping from my chest.

Kelså shot to her feet. "Declan, come with me. If someone is powerful enough to pass the wards, I may need your strength to protect the Well."

I shot to my feet as well. Atikus moved to follow, but Kelså stilled him with a glare. "Atikus, stay here. If we get into trouble, you are the only one left who can go for help."

I charged after my mother through the winding corridors of the mountain. The crystals embedded in the walls, normally glowing with gentle light, now pulsed brightly, as if angered by the intruder.

As I skidded to a stop in the entrance to the Well's chamber, I was shocked to see its crystalline walls and ceiling pulsing even more brightly than the hallways had. The lazy river beneath its glassy surface roiled and raged, white caps pluming atop cerulean waves. It felt as though the currents begged for escape, for the opportunity to join the fight to come.

Kelså ran toward the platform containing the Well's opening and panted as she stood a few paces from the billowing mist that gushed forth.

I stood beside her a few heartbeats later.

The hairs on my arms and neck snapped to attention, and my skin pimpled at magic's touch.

My tunic's glow became insistent, almost painful to look upon.

Then the intruder entered the chamber.

"Larinda?" Kelså asked, dumbfounded. "How did you get in here?"

The old woman strode forward without a hint of the ailing joints I knew plagued her. She held her chin high and stared through bright, keen eyes.

But it was her smile I noticed above all else.

"It's not Larinda," I whispered.

Larinda waved a hand in the air while continuing her trek forward. "Listen to the boy, Kelså; he is brighter than he appears." She cackled at her own jest.

Kelså called to her Light, and the mist surrounding the Well poured into her mouth and nose. Her skin began to glow, and her eyes blazed with the light of the sun. With a wave of one hand, she erected a shell of swirling air around the Well.

I gaped, having never seen the strength of my mother's magic.

Larinda cackled again, more amused than concerned by the Keeper's display of power. She raised a finger and shattered Kelså's shield without so much as a grimace. Sparks of spent magical energy exploded throughout the room, forcing Kelså and me to throw up shields of air to protect from the blast.

When we lowered our arms, the woman who was no longer Larinda stood only a few paces away, raging fire blazing in each palm.

"Boy, I was using magic long before you were born. Do not waste my time. I have waited many lifetimes to *deal* with your mother."

Without further warning, Larinda flung both palms forward, and fire flew forth, one blaze aimed at each of us. I threw out my arms and pulled moisture from the air. Discs of water the size of my head appeared before my outstretched hands, flew forward, and doused the balls of flame.

Kelså threw her head back and cried out, "Eveth erna fertu!"

A dozen glowing crystals broke free from the wall and hurtled toward Larinda.

The ancient woman ducked and threw up a bony hand. A shock wave of air and energy pulsed from her raised fist, blasting Kelså's missiles away to shatter against the walls of the cavern.

Again, Kelså didn't hesitate.

With Larinda distracted by deflecting the crystals, she drew more mist into her chest and formed balls of pure azure magic in each palm, similar to the fire Larinda had thrown before. She hurled one ball, arcing it high in the air toward Larinda, while sending the second in a blazing streak toward the woman's chest.

Larinda managed a quick shield, absorbing the missile headed for her torso, but the second attack struck a half pace from where she stood. The soundless eruption lit the cavern with a kaleidoscope of brilliance, forcing me to shield my eyes with my arm. Sparks of shimmering magic flew in every direction.

Larinda screamed as the force battered her body and mind.

The attack bore no heat, but its strength assaulted Larinda's magical core.

Sensing an opening, I reformed my shield, this time drawing both air and water. I stepped forward, shield wall extended two paces before me.

Another step, then another.

Larinda's eyes widened, and she took a step backward.

Quicker than she could react, I threw my arms forward, hurling my shield into her.

The impact of hardened water and air slammed into the aged, frail body she now inhabited, sending Larinda's form flying backward and into the crystalline wall. Blood streamed from a gash on her forehead, and more flowed from another wound on the back of her skull. The inhabiting spirit didn't feel disorientation as Larinda would have felt from such a blow, but the body of her servant was slow to rise.

With moisture and heat nearly exhausted within the cavern, the temperature plummeted, and thick clouds billowed each time we breathed.

Kelså shivered as she screamed a warning.

I fell back on my Ranger training instead of using more magic, lunging forward, driving a fist into Larinda's sternum and doubling the old woman over.

I gripped her by her hair and pulled her head upward, readying another blow, but Larinda was faster. Her bony fingers bent, and hardened knuckles thrust upward into my neck.

I gagged and gripped my throat, straining for air as I staggered backward.

"Irina?" Realization dawned on Kelså as her teeth began to chatter.

"Took you long enough, *witch*. How dull you have grown over the years." The woman's head snapped unnaturally toward her, then cocked to one side. It has only been a millennium since you stripped me of my power and cast me aside—you and your *family of Mages*."

"Irina, I was not even there when the last battle occurred—or when your parents—"

"Enough!" Irina screamed. "I will reclaim my power and send you straight where you belong: into the void."

A wave of Compulsion blasted into Kelså, knocking her backward. My tunic resisted the spell, but Kelså's eyes glazed, and her body relaxed.

"Cast him into the Well," Irina commanded.

Without hesitation, Kelså stepped forward and gripped me by both shoulders.

Startled, I turned, but she pulled with all her strength.

My feet had been well set at shoulder width apart in anticipation of Irina's next attack, but I hadn't expected an assault to come from behind—*from my mother.*

I staggered into her embrace.

"Mother!"

Her eyes were wild orbs of glass that stared, yet saw nothing.

She yanked backward and dragged me toward the Well's opening.

I threw an arm behind me but couldn't dislodge her grip.

Irina, seizing the moment, flew onto the platform and punched my chest with her Enhanced Strength. My tunic raged at her touch, and her hands came away scorched.

She screamed in agony and staggered back.

But her shove had been enough.

Kelså tripped over her own feet and, still gripping my shoulders, tumbled backward.

I cried out but was helpless to stop our momentum.

The cavern spun above.

Larinda's bloodied face grinned down with maniacal hatred.

Kelså's grip vanished as she reached the current.

I threw my arms out, reaching for the edge of the Well, but its glassy surface slipped from my fingers. A thunderous clap rang through the chamber as the Keeper and Heir vanished beneath the raging river of magic.

CHAPTER 38

JESS

I strode into the throne room with Ethan trailing a couple paces behind. He'd interrupted my breakfast with several urgent missives and news of one important, unexpected visitor seeking an audience.

As I squirmed my way into a *somewhat* comfortable position on the throne, Ethan unfurled a scroll the size of his thumb and began reading.

"Constables in Cooper are reporting a strange death that appears to be a wild animal attack. This time it was a dock foreman. I will get this to the High Sheriff as soon as we finish this audience."

He rolled the scroll back up and shoved it in a pocket, then took the next scroll, then the next, and so on. Five messages later, he unfurled the final one and glanced up.

I'd been at the golden doors, lost in thought, and barely heard him.

"Majesty, it appears *Guardsman Rea* left Oliver yesterday."

The mention of Keelan brought my gaze to his.

"That puts him back in the capital tomorrow or the next day. The scroll doesn't say anything about his investigation."

"Did he say anything else?" I asked.

Ethan couldn't hide the smile that curled the corners of his mouth. "No, Majesty, only that he would be here soon. The scroll was written by the Chief Constable, not Guardsman Rea."

"Of course it was," I huffed under my breath, just loud enough for Ethan to hear. When he stifled a laugh, I shot daggers his direction.

"Sorry, Majesty. How *very* inconsiderate of him." His smirk widened to a grin.

"Are you not needed elsewhere, *High Chancellor*? A message to deliver? A cliff to jump off?"

"I will find a cliff straightway, Majesty." A laugh escaped as he offered an exaggerated bow. When he rose, his smile vanished, and his voice lowered. "Jess, please be wary of your next audience. The Order is growing in influence across the Kingdom, faster than I ever could have imagined. You have worked too hard building a solid reputation and good will to see a battle with the clergy do you harm. Most of their Priests are doing good work for people who need it. We may have ears in every corner, but they have wagging tongues and powerful voices."

I considered his words and nodded.

Ethan disappeared through the massive double doors, and the royal page entered.

"Ambassador Wilfred, Majesty." The page bowed toward the throne and waited for my reply.

"Great," I muttered. "Send him in."

Danym strode slowly down the center aisle, his eyes locking onto mine and never wavering. I thought he looked a little too proud of himself and regretted holding this audience without Ethan by my side to offer calming words or wisdom—or simply to hold me back. I wanted nothing more than to strangle the life out of my guest.

Danym stopped a few paces from the dais and bowed. "Majesty, thank you for seeing me."

Ethan's words echoed in my head, and I resisted the urge to spit curses at the man. Instead, I stood and stepped down from the dais toward the Council table.

"Please, join me for tea. It has been a long morning already, and my back cannot take sitting on the throne one moment longer."

If he was surprised by my cordial offer, Danym didn't show it. He nodded once and stepped toward the table.

The same guards who *ushered* Danym out following his last audience stepped forward, taking up positions on either side of the seat I indicated Danym should occupy. Rather than sitting at the table's head where we would be close, I took a seat on the opposite side, keeping the heavy oak table between us.

A servant materialized from the darkness and filled two cups. I raised mine and took a long sip.

Danym's brow rose, but he remained silent.

"What does the Order seek of the Crown today?" I asked.

He lowered his gaze and spoke in softened tones. "I am only pleased to be in Her Majesty's presence once again. I have missed our chats, especially those in the forest at night."

My grip on the cup tightened, and I had to set it down to keep from spilling my tea.

Of all things Danym could discuss, our evening rendezvous were the least welcome topic. Those had been the happiest moments of my life, filled with wine, fruit, cheese, and the most beautiful man I'd ever met . . . until our nights found me bound, drugged, and facing certain death at the hands of that same handsome man. My heart ached at the loss of a beautiful innocence, almost as much as it blazed with righteous anger over his betrayal.

When I looked up, the intensity of my gaze made him flinch.

"Just tell me why you are here so we can be done with this."

He had the good grace to look hurt. "Jess—"

"Never use my name again. Address me as *Your Majesty* or not at all," I snapped, immediately regretting the venom in my tone.

Ethan was right. I had to control myself.

"I am sorry. It has been a long day," I said.

His eyes fixed on a knot in the table's rich wood. "No, I'm the one who is sorry, Your Majesty. It won't happen again."

Silence loomed as we each stared at something, anything, that wasn't the other person. We might have been sitting across the whole country, not the table, in that moment. When one of the guards reached down to scratch an itch, the squeal of his armor scraping against itself turned my gaze back to Danym.

"Where did you go? After—"

"The Temple," he replied.

"You mean you were there? When Justin—"

Danym's head snapped up. "No. I was in the Temple, but not the chamber. I didn't know your brother was there, or what they had planned. You have to believe me, Je—Your Majesty. I didn't know."

"And when I was there? When they dragged me down that aisle?"

His head lowered again. "Yes."

"Yes, what?" My voice was now hardened ice. "Yes, you were in the chamber when they were going to kill me? Is that what you are saying 'yes' to?"

He didn't speak or look up for a long moment.

Then he said, "I was under *her* Compulsion."

"When you wooed me? When you asked me to trust you? When you promised to start a life together? Or when you stood by and watched my own mother drug me and try to take my life? When were you being Compelled? Please enlighten me."

He looked up.

His eyes pleaded in a way I hadn't seen since the night we fled the capital. "I felt her Call after that night in the inn, the one with the old couple by the fire. Not before. *Never* before."

His eyes glistened in the light of the table's candles. His lips quivered.

My mind raced almost as quickly as my heart.

This was the man I'd loved more than any other, the one I'd pledged to abdicate my throne for. I would have given up the whole Kingdom for him.

Now, I was ready to have him executed the moment he stepped one foot wrong.

Yet he claimed his actions had not been his own.

That made sense.

He'd loved me.

I knew it.

And I wanted desperately to believe him, to believe he would never intentionally betray me. I *wanted* to believe.

He reached a hand across the table toward mine, but I jerked back as his fingers brushed my skin. I clutched my hand to my chest as though it'd been burned.

"No," I whispered. "We can *never* go back to what we had. Even if your actions were not your own, I will always be haunted by the betrayal in your eyes. I still dream about that mask you wore, that mask you looked through as you *laughed* at my terror. How could I ever see beyond that? How could anyone?"

A tear trickled down his cheek.

He reclaimed his hand and slowly nodded.

"I understand," was all his voice could muster.

I took another sip of tea, desperate for strength and courage.

"Why do you still wear those robes? If Irina's Compulsion died with her, why stay with those awful people?"

His eyes became distant, his voice again a whisper. "Where else could I go? At least in these robes I can try to help people, do some good with whatever life I have left. I lost the only thing that mattered. What do I have left?"

I couldn't listen anymore. "I am tired. Return to the Palace tomorrow, and we will discuss whatever it is your Order seeks us to consider." I stood, wheeled from the table flanked by the two guards, and vanished out the side door, leaving Danym alone in the massive chamber.

I barely slept that night.

Memories of Danym flooded my mind, and I couldn't find the magic to banish them. In my dreams, he smiled up at me as I rode Dittler through town and splattered mud all over his cloak and hair.

The dreams would shift to the forest where he lifted a pastry to my lips, his eyes twinkling in the midnight moonlight. He gripped my hand from across a rough wooden table, adoration flowing beside sparks of flame that went through his skin into mine.

And then he wore a mask.

That mask.

His eyes held amused loathing, no longer twinkling with anything but cruelty and spite.

Unable to bear the dreams any longer, I rose and strode, bleary-eyed and grumpy, into the family dining room two hours earlier than normal. Steaming platters of eggs and bacon waited. The servants always knew *exactly* when I would appear and ensured everything was in order. If I'd been more awake, it would've amazed me, made me smile. I might even have said something to one of the invisible, uniformed purveyors of domestic magic.

One of my maids entered as I finished my meal.

A quick gasp was followed by whispered words near my ear. "Majesty, please, come back to your chamber so I can do something with your hair before the Council arrives."

It must be bad, I thought.

An hour later, I sat erect on my throne and greeted each member of the Privy Council as they entered the chamber. The domestic magicians had struck again, as my hair was as silky as my gown.

By noon, the Council had beaten every dead horse from Fontaine to the mountains. They'd reviewed troop levels following the latest round of recruitment, discussed talks of renewed trade with partner nations, including Melucia, and even debated opening talks with the more primitive island nations to the south, hoping to increase the flow of goods.

I never spoke.

Councilors looked to me for opinions or guidance, but I nodded and shifted my gaze to Ethan, a look he understood was his cue to make a decision and move the agenda forward.

Ethan was about to call the session to a halt when a royal page rapped twice on the door, indicating the Queen had a high-ranking visitor outside. The page entered and called out, "Holy Voice Danym Wilfred of the Order."

I cringed.

Every member of the Council turned to me with astonished eyes.

They had, no doubt, heard rumor of the dead High Sheriff's son making a surprise appearance, but none had the temerity to believe the rumor held any truth.

Yet here he was, begging audience with their Queen.

I looked to Ethan and nodded once. "Let the Council hear his words. We may need their wisdom upon receiving the Order's request."

He turned to the page. "Show him in, please."

No one stood as Danym entered. It violated protocol and custom, even simple good manners, but the Queen remained seated, so her Council followed suit.

For his part, Danym looked as unkempt as I felt.

His normally well-brushed hair tangled rather than hung to his shoulders. Its shine was somehow dull. His eyes carried bags I'd never noticed before, and his shoulders slumped in contrast to the proud posture he regularly displayed.

Good. At least I wasn't the only one to lose sleep.

A twinge of *something* passed through me as I watched him enter. Despite everything, part of me wanted to comfort him, to rush forward, grip his arm, and help him into the room. I shook off that silliness and turned my expression to steel.

He stopped on the golden mark, bowed toward the throne, and waited.

Ethan spoke coldly. "Voice, to what purpose do you interrupt a session of the Privy Council with Her Majesty?"

Danym rose.

The ice in Ethan's voice somehow granted him strength, and his eyes hardened. He ignored Ethan and looked directly at me.

"I came hoping you had considered the One's offer. It has been nearly a week, and he grows impatient for your reply. I fear, without this marriage, the Kingdom may experience . . . *difficulties* . . . that could otherwise be avoided."

My brows rose, as did the heat coursing through my veins. Chairs groaned as a few of my Ministers shifted in their seats.

"Are you *threatening* the Queen?" Ethan asked.

Danym shook his head. "Only advising, as is my duty to the Crown."

Others began to speak, to ask questions and raise their voices. I silenced them with a raised palm, then stood and walked a pace from the table.

"What sort of *difficulties*? Please, *advise* us."

"Your Majesty's people suffered great loss following the folly beyond the mountains. Husbands, sons, fathers—so many were lost. Our Priests minister to the needs of *our* people. We understand the value of faith in a time of sadness and grief. *Our* people seek shelter in our arms when the Crown's own embrace is . . . lacking. The One fears *our* people's reaction should the Crown reject the Faith's honest offer of alliance and friendship."

I balled my fists and forced myself to breathe slowly and deeply. Not only had he threatened the Crown with possible unrest, but his continual use of *our* people claimed *my* subjects were shared by his One. Everything he said was an affront to me, my family, my crown, and my Kingdom. I knew Ethan had been right to advise caution and a level head, but I could not let this weasel spew such filth, not in *my* Palace, before *my* Council.

"You think we *considered* marrying you? Or marrying your Faith? Or whatever insanity you were proposing? Does your One think we have completely lost our mind?"

As I marched forward, guards reacted, encircling Danym with pikes at the ready. I pointed an accusing finger at him and spoke with the wrath of a royal.

"Tell your *master* the answer is *no* and will *always* be no. I will not marry a dog on a leash, even if that leash glitters with gold." I sucked in a breath and glanced apologetically toward Ethan before returning my eyes to Danym's. "And do not bother returning to the Palace—*ever*. I, Jessia Vester, First of her Name and Queen of the Spires, hereby sever all relations with the Order, and therefore expel the Order's representative to the Crown from the capital. Your Priests may continue ministering to *my* people, but enter the capital again at your own peril."

I turned and nodded to Ethan. "We are done here. We shall resume tomorrow. Guards, get *that man* out of my Palace. Escort him to the city's border once he has gathered whatever belongings he might need. If he resists, send his head to the One as a token of our love and affection."

I marched from the chamber without so much as a glance back.

CHAPTER 39

IRINA

The mist flowed faster, glowed brighter.

I stepped toward the Well, then froze, my head tilted to the side.

The chamber fell silent as the world paused.

Then the mountain trembled.

The pulsing of light inside the crystalline cavern seethed as crystals began falling from the ceiling. A scraping sound wailed from somewhere deep beneath the Well.

Tremors grew as the mountain woke.

I stood before the Well and stared into its angry waters, ignoring the chaos erupting around me. I muttered rapidly, a whisper that grew into a cacophonous shout, my head bent backward as I screamed the final words of my incantation.

My spell complete, the rending sound grew to a roar so loud I had to cover my ears. It sounded as if the whole world were being broken apart. I stared down in wonder and fear as a fracture appeared in the floor, a tiny crack at first that grew and splintered and spread.

Mist seeped through the rend.

Starting at the base of the Well, it clawed its way across to the far entrance of the cavern, dividing the room in two and allowing the river of power to swell and spill onto its unmarred surface.

Everywhere the currents touched, mist sizzled and snapped, a poisonous acid devouring everything it touched.

In its wake, plumes of dark vapor clawed against the pure blue fog, infecting it with malice, turning glowing life into something dark and foul.

Near panic gripped me as I watched the brilliant cavern descend into darkness, yet I managed to calm myself enough to picture *home* in my mind: my small house in the Kingdom where my father and mother had raised me, had loved me—*and where they had died.*

The last I saw before Traveling was an aged man in blue Mages' robes appearing in the entrance to the cavern.

CHAPTER 40

DANAI

D anym kneeled before me.

    I forced the idiot to remain cowed for over an hour, only allowing him to look up when answering a question.

I couldn't recall the last time anger boiled within me so fiercely.

"Do you honestly believe you had *any* other use to me? Or had you deluded yourself into thinking your brilliant wit could serve some purpose in my cause?" My words dripped with contempt as I stared down from my ivory throne.

"Master—"

"Shut up! That was *not* a question. Even *you* should understand sarcasm when you hear it." I stood. "You had only one mission, and you failed. What more might be said?"

"Excellency, forgive me. Jess—I mean, the Queen—she would not be moved. I managed to get a private audience with her, to get her thinking about our time together before—"

"Do you think I care?" I shouted, punctuating each word. "You *failed* me, and now you—and any other representative I might wish to install—are banished from the capital. I cannot begin to calculate the harm you have caused. I should get my staff and Turn you here and now. At least then you *might* be of some use."

"Master, no—"

"Stop it, Danym. Just stop groveling. You have destroyed months of work. I cannot allow your incompetence to threaten our mission any longer."

"But, Excellency—"

Danym's words cut off as I waved a hand and bright flame enveloped him. He writhed and screamed until the fire's hunger stilled his voice, leaving little more than the charred ruins of a Priest and his robe.

I stared at the smoldering mess as I sat and sorted through what the reckless child's folly had cost.

Moments later, a lanky Priest entered. His loose-fitting robes flowed behind him as he strode the length of the chamber, only slowing as he passed Danym's remains. The man wriggled his nose and covered it with a sleeve, then kneeled and remained cowed until I bade him rise.

"Efrem, our plans for the Queen have failed. *Danym* failed. If I cannot have her join us willingly, I need her out of the way. Unless I miss my mark, that brother of hers should be much easier to handle. He is simple and gullible and has no ill memories of the man I was at court, unlike our current monarch."

Efrem's expression never wavered. His eyes never blinked. He stared and listened.

The perfect Priest, I thought.

"Do you have a preference as to method, Excellency?"

I steepled my fingers and thought a moment. "No, do what you must—but whatever you do *must not* be traced back to the Order. Understood?"

"Yes, Excellency. Your will be done."

As Efrem vanished through the golden doors, I removed the crown and cradled it in my hands. I traced a finger along its interwoven gold and silver, landing on one of the diamonds inlaid in its base. The bloodred pulse echoed through every facet of the stone, drawing me into its fearsome beauty. I wondered what the imprisoned spirit must think. Could it see or hear what went on before it? Could it even still think? Its power pulsed through the relic and into me whenever I called, yet I knew nothing of the individuals trapped within.

And I really didn't care to.

It was more curiosity than anything.

Like my Priests, those trapped souls were merely tools, weapons to be wielded for my greater cause. And like Danym, when they failed or served no further purpose, they were dead to me.

I sat staring into the stone for long moments, lost in thoughts and plans for a world beneath my banner. For the briefest moment, as Jess's face passed through my mind, a twinge of regret pricked my soul. We were never close. Still, she had been a child, and there were times . . .

I shrugged those thoughts off as quickly as they had arisen and chuckled at my own foolish sentimentality.

PART IV

CHAPTER 41

ATIKUS

I stared into the darkness.

What had once been the most beautiful, vibrant sight I had ever seen was now devoid of light or life. Even the residual glow of the crystals along the hallway through which I'd run as the mountain shook had begun to dim.

My head swiveled, searching for any speck of light.

"Declan? Kelså?" I cried over and over, stumbling through the darkened cavern.

The only answer was my own voice echoing through the mountain's heart.

As I nudged my way forward, my foot caught on something jagged that shouldn't exist where I knew smooth, transparent flooring should have lay.

I kneeled and felt with my fingers.

Sharp edges scored a line across one bony digit. Unseen blood trickled into the chamber's gaping wound.

"Damned darkness," I muttered, wishing for light to see how deeply I'd cut my finger.

I stumbled back as a ball of swirling, pulsing light bloomed before me. The chamber was suddenly bathed in a dim, flickering glow.

"Sweet Spirits, how—"

I looked down at the massive crack in the floor, and horror hammered in my chest.

The currents of magic I recalled drifting beneath, with their gentle mist stretching upward, now oozed like sludge, bubbling and hissing as they passed beneath the crack. It looked more like syrup or oil than a mystical spring.

A foul scent of *wrongness* prickled my nose, and I had to smother a cough in the crook of my elbow.

The glowing orb waited a few paces before me. When I moved to inspect the Well's platform, it led the way, casting its eerie light some twenty paces in every direction. I wished for brighter light, and the ball blazed.

"How—"

The rational scholar seized control and began testing every insane theory that flooded my mind.

First, I held out my palm and thought of ice. An instant later, the air around me *warmed*, and a ball of pure, frozen water formed in my palm. I'd just pulled the heat from the surrounding air, combined it with moisture, and frozen it, all with barely a thought.

That is not possible. I have no Gift for . . . any of this.

I tossed the ice aside and held out my palm again, this time thinking of fire. The surrounding air cooled, and sapphire flame erupted and hovered above my hand.

My stomach growled, so I pictured the platter of bacon still sitting on the kitchen table. Barely an eye blink later, the blaze was replaced by a platter of fried pork. I gasped and stumbled backward, dropping the platter to scatter across the floor.

"I wish Pel could see this," I breathed, closing my eyes and pinching the bridge of my nose with gnarled fingertips.

"Atikus?"

My eyes flew open, and I found myself standing above Mage Pel's bed, the bleary-eyed, startled man staring up.

I drew a sharp breath and bowed my head.

"The Gift has been shattered."

CHAPTER 42

DECLAN

Kelså opened her mouth, as if to scream, but the mist, now thick with a dark residue, raced into her lungs.

Her head spun about, finding my eyes wide with fear.

I wasn't afraid for myself.

I knew the currents. I was of the currents. They were part of me.

But magic was a fickle mistress. What would she make of Kelså? It might not matter that my mother had guarded the Well, protected the currents, given her life to keep them secret and safe for generations.

Magic was a force of nature, and nature would never be denied her due.

Our hands remained clasped.

The currents churned, tossing us feet over head again and again, threatening to break us loose.

I felt my mother squeeze tighter.

Waves of heat and power buffeted my body. I could only image how they battered my mother's mind. Her Light, normally a peaceful core, looked like a dagger's tip digging deeper and deeper.

"Don't let go of my hand, no matter what!" I screamed in her mind. *"We just have to hang on until we reach the opening at the guild. Hold on!"*

Angry waves tossed us like children's playthings.

The Light in the flow dimmed as darkness gained strength.

My tunic still beamed, a beacon in the swelling darkness. I willed it brighter, an anchor in Kelså's mind that seemed to strengthen her grip.

"We're almost there. I can feel the Silver Mountains."

The currents twisted and turned, bouncing us off unseen walls of the river's course.

Kelså was battered. Blood leaked from gashes across her arm and forehead.

I felt her grip loosening.

She squeezed even harder.

A finger came loose, and I began to panic.

Another finger slipped.

"Mother! Hold on! Grab me with your other hand! We're almost there!"

My tunic was nearly invisible in the inky dark, and I felt her connection to magic failing as her fingers slipped away.

Then I was thrust upward, expelled from the river, and spat onto the shores of the Silver Mountains. The world of light and sounds overloaded my senses as the froth of the river fell away. I gasped at the coolness of the cavern's air against my skin.

I thrust my free hand back into the currents and reached for my mother's arm.

It was almost impossible to see, but I felt her shoulder.

I pulled her up by two fingers and tried to grip her blouse, but a wave of power slammed into her body as her face neared the surface. My hand slipped from her shirt as her final finger slipped from my grasp.

Through the film of murky magic, I watched in horror as my mother's form dissolved into specks of dim light, then faded and dispersed within the blackened flow.

"NO!" I cried as I dug into the current with both hands, desperate to feel my mother's touch once again.

But Kelså Rea, the Keeper of the Well and Protector of Magic, was gone.

CHAPTER 43

AYDEN

A fter what felt like an eternity of sulking before the endless wine of the cavern, I finally stepped through the sliver of an opening and onto home soil. The forest canopy, thinned by winter's wrath, failed to keep snow from covering everything in sight. Moments after abandoning the warmth of the cave, my breeches were soaked to my knees, and chills raced up my spine to spread to every fiber of my being.

I should have shivered and complained, felt demoralized or dejected; but oddly, my spirit soared as crisp air flowed into my lungs and fresh thoughts of a brighter future filled my mind.

For the first time since Kingdom soldiers poured across the border and ravaged our land, I had a purpose: I would rebuild the Ranger corps.

Hours became days of trudging through frosty muck. There were no Kingdom soldiers in the woods. The only snapping branches came from animals skittering from my path. I knew there must be some soldiers making their way home following a bitter defeat. While I hoped to avoid them, given their likely animosity, I chose to step confidently rather than creep back home like some burglar approaching a house at night.

Soldiers would not stop me.

Winter held no sway.

Neither the cold nor the damp could douse the hope flowering in my chest.

I felt important again. I felt *needed*.

The Rangers were vital to protect the Empire. Our failure in stopping the Kingdom forces underscored this as much as any success of the past. The people—the nation—needed us. I would see our force rebuilt such that any foe would think twice before challenging our swords and bows.

None would ever cross the mountains in anger again.

Determination drove me forward.

Then an owl hooted in the distance, and my mind whirled. Thinking of Órla made me think of Declan. I couldn't help it. I didn't want to.

Spirits, I missed him already.

How long had we known one another?

How had that man become so entwined in my mind and heart in such a short time? How had he wormed his way inside and taken over my every dream? When had I surrendered to him?

I chuckled and shrugged off each question.

None of them mattered.

I loved Declan Rea more than life itself. I loved him with the force of a storm crossing the sea, with the swell of the rising tide, with the dawning of every new day that ever brightened the sky.

Seeing Declan smile, watching him flick his unruly curls or run fingers through his tangled mess, filled me with warmth more powerful than any flame.

It made no sense.

It felt like I had leaped off a towering cliff and fell . . . and continued to fall . . . and would forever fall.

My entire life revolved around my family name, our wealth, our power and position. My entire future was designed to become Lord Byrne, to fulfill all of the duties and expectations that came with that title: I would grow strong, learn well, marry, sire heirs, and rule.

That was the plan. It was what my father had taught me since the day I could understand his words. It was the banner on which my mother stitched all her hopes.

And then I met Declan.

Fucking Declan Rea.

The moment our eyes met that first time, I knew my life had changed forever. I might not have understood how, but I knew it would never again be the same.

I knew he would be part of my life until I had no more life to live.

And my heart swelled with that knowledge.

Now, separated by a continent and a sea—and divided by magic's whim—my duty included him. More aptly, my duty was bound to him as much as any person or city or nation.

I was his.

And he was mine.

How had the Spirits shone so brightly on me? Why had they favored me thus?

My cheeks pinched as I smiled too broadly for my face.

When Declan returned and could finally be himself again, I would make sure his family of green-cloaked men and women were there to welcome him home. He might now be an immensely powerful hero, something that still confounded and terrified me in equal measure, but he remained Declan, the boy who craved acceptance and love as much as any man, perhaps more so.

I would see him embraced if it stole my last breath.

He deserved that much.

He deserved so much more.

Ideas swirled like fish in a frenzy. I hoped I could remember each thought when I finally returned to begin the work. Still, it felt good to lean into something useful, something that mattered. It felt important.

Of the thousands of Rangers who served prior to the invasion, only a handful, perhaps fewer than a hundred, remained. Most of those would still be posted in coastal towns or standing guard on our eastern border, the border where Melucia abutted neighbors who barely owned weapons, much less armies. Their presence served to quell the occasional smuggler or bandit more than guard against an enemy force.

We would need to rethink that strategy. Perhaps the Guard could take over the eastern watch. Constables might serve better for those duties, freeing up dozens or more to join the western rebuilding effort.

Rebuilding.

I stepped through the tree line and froze.

Grove's Pass—or the shell of where Grove's Pass once stood—spread before me.

My heart fell into my shoes.

Only a few buildings still stood. Most were skeletons of their former selves, haunted specters of wood smeared with char and ash.

The palisade, once strong with waist-thick logs and tall as any man, now lay in shambles. At the center, the tavern rose, though much of its roof had caved beneath the weight of winter's many snows. Beyond, the rubble of the Ranger headquarters lay buried beneath a blanket of white.

No Rangers practices in the yard.

No villagers milled about.

No one stirred.

"How am I supposed to rebuild all of this?" My billowing breath spoke more loudly than my words.

The unmistakable *thwack* of an axe against wood nearly made me soil my breeches. I scanned the barren town, desperate to spot some movement—any movement.

There . . . on the southern edge . . .

"Ho, the Ranger!" an aged man's voice echoed against the mountains.

I covered my brow with a hand and squinted against the sun. A withered form a few hundred yards away waved with one hand. The axe in his other hand hung limply toward the ground.

I raised a hand, then chided myself for waving back at the only other human I'd seen in days. Clearly, the man was chopping firewood or logs to build something.

Someone was doing *something*.

I was no longer alone.

The hope that had dimmed when I first stepped out from the forest flickered back to life as I secured my cloak about my frozen shoulders and strode toward the solitary figure.

CHAPTER 44

JESS

"Majesty, we are now investigating *nine* mysterious deaths. Each appears to have been a vicious attack by a wild beast that occurred in a different location and against a random member of their community."

"Have you discovered any pattern to the deaths?" I asked.

The High Sheriff shook his head. "We have looked at this from every conceivable angle and found no commonality regarding sex of the victim, station, occupation, or any other measure we use. In some cases, the victims were torn apart by massive claws, like those of an enormous bear. In others, the attacker was a raptor or other bird of prey."

Sheriff Cribbs folded his hands and stared across the table. His eyes were lined with dark circles, and his normally well-kept uniform was as disheveled as his ragamuffin hair.

I strummed my fingers against the wood of the Council table as I mulled over his report. "Chancellor Marks, any word from your ravens? Or our network of ears?"

"Actually, Majesty, something interesting arrived by raven just before the Council assembled. I have not had time to route it to my people for further review, but it may provide us another avenue of inquiry." He reached into the leather folio containing sheaves of parchment, removed a tiny scroll, and read,

"The dead innkeeper in Oliver was angry at the Order's local Priest and his speeches about the Crown. Rumor has it, he was stirring up a small group to chase the Priest out of town before he was killed, though none of that group will speak of him or their plans. This was overheard in the dockside tavern by a barman." - V

Treasurer Dask scoffed. "Are you suggesting a wild bear was angered by the man's hatred for a Priest? That may be the most ridiculous thing ever spoken at this table."

Cribbs chuckled, but his smile didn't reach his weary eyes. "It does sound far-fetched. Is that all we have?"

Ethan held my gaze, despite the others' reactions. "On the surface, Treasurer Dask is right. This sounds ridiculous, but we have little else to go on. I suggest the High Sheriff have his men in each town revisit their interviews and ask about the Priests and their speeches. Local Constables may already know of royalist passions but failed to link them to the killings."

Cribbs leaned forward. "Majesty, I can have my men ask quietly in their respective towns, but this whole thing sounds like a child's fever dream."

"It sounds like dreams *I* had as a child, thanks to stories our dear High Chancellor told me before I was sent to bed." I looked from Cribbs to Ethan. "But the Chancellor is right—we have little else to go on, and asking a few questions seems simple enough."

Cribbs nodded once. "Yes, Majesty. I'll send birds when we finish here."

"Good," I said, squinting at the upside-down writing on the parchment stretched before Ethan that detailed our lengthy agenda. "What is next, Chancellor?"

"Trade with Melucia and Vint. Our representatives—"

The audience chamber doors flew open and banged against the stone of the walls as Mage

Ernest raced into the hall with a royal page a step behind.

"Majesty! Mage Dane Ernest," the flustered page called belatedly.

Everyone at the Council table startled at the sudden interruption.

"Majesty! They're gone! They're just *gone*!" Ernest cried out, a strange mix of terror, anguish, and helplessness suffusing itself into his words.

His expression was even sadder than his voice. His eyes were wild, and his arms flailed as he ran. Halfway down the aisle, he seemed to remember where he was and slowed to a not-so-stately trot until he stood, huffing, before his Queen.

"Mage Ernest? Are you all right?" I stood, my own eyes rising at the man's unusual agitation.

"No, Majesty. *None* of us are." The Mage remembered to bow, then rose and met my eyes. "Gifts are gone."

"What are you babbling about? Whose Gifts?" Ethan asked in annoyance.

"Majesty." Ernest sucked in a few breaths. "*All* of our Gifts have vanished. I can no longer sense the flow of magic. None of our Mages can cast even the simplest spell."

I shot a glance at Ethan, then turned to Dask. "I cannot tell if my Gift works without an animal nearby. Treasurer Dask, please try yours?"

Dask shot me a glare.

"Barnabus, do it. You are the only one present who still believes your Gift is a secret."

Amused eyes turned to Dask as he looked from Ethan to Cribbs.

A heartbeat later, panic flooded his eyes.

"Majesty, I cannot—"

"Dear Spirits," I muttered.

"Majesty, people all over the city are pouring into the Guild Hall, seeking a remedy for what they believe to be an ailment. This is not limited to Mages. Our Gifts, *all of them*, are gone."

Chaos erupted as every Councilor stood and began talking at once. It was impossible to hear what any one person was saying as they shouted over each other.

Mage Ernest sank to the floor and pulled his knees to his chest, like some child whose parents had just taken away his favorite toy.

I drew a deep, calming breath, then another, as my father taught me. He'd warned of many things, but his lessons on crises were his most frequent—and most forceful.

"Jess." He'd stabbed his forefinger for emphasis. *"Every crisis will be different, but two things will always remain beneath the noise. First, everyone will look to you for leadership, even if you have no knowledge, background, or training on the matter at hand. You will be Queen, the one wearing the crown. As such, people will expect—no, they will demand—you to make the impossible decisions.*

"Second, you will want to run out of the room. Your heart will race, and sweat will pour from places you never knew could sweat. Those same people demanding leadership will see it all. They will watch your every movement, hang on every word. They will seek meaning where none was offered, all in some desperate attempt to feel secure in a time of uncertainty. You must gird yourself, especially in those times. Find strength within yourself. Widen your stance, breathe slowly and deeply. Speak deliberately and with purpose, if for no other reason than to buy yourself time to think."

In that moment, with Mage Ernest in a near meltdown, my Councilors chattering like temple gossips, and word beginning to spread through the city like summer flames, I knew the wisdom of his words.

And I breathed again.

"Everyone, sit." My voice pierced through the cacophony, and every head turned. "Do not stand there staring at me. I said sit!"

Slowly, the leaders of the Kingdom gathered themselves and took their seats. Ethan helped Mage Ernest to his feet and ushered him to his chair at the foot of the table. All eyes turned toward me as I stood before my own chair.

"I want each of you to listen to me right now. I need you. The people need you. *This Kingdom* needs each of you." I looked around the table with a stern gaze. "The people look to us for strength, and *they will see strength* when they look at each of you. Do you hear me?"

Mutters of "Yes, Majesty" scattered around the table.

"Good." I took my seat, back straight, head high. "Sheriff, send your birds. Find me answers regarding the killings. Chancellor Marks, I want other birds sent to every guild in every nation, starting with Melucia. Find out if their Gifts are also affected."

General Sento, my new Minister of War, began to protest.

I silenced her with a raised palm and a withering glare.

"I understand we are tipping our hand by asking the question. They will know we are wounded without our Gifts. Your objection is noted. Chancellor, send the birds. Everyone else, assess how to move forward with your respective areas assuming there are no Gifts to assist with your work. I want outlines of your worst-case scenarios by tomorrow. Mage Ernest, stay with me a moment. Everyone else, get to work. This session is adjourned."

The Councilors rose and scurried out of the chamber.

While some of the men had witnessed my youthful tantrums, none had ever seen me command a room as I just had. I was sure a few left the chamber with memories of my mother's famous wrath.

When the last advisor vanished and the doors slammed shut, I walked the length of the table and sat in the chair closest to my Mage. His head was bowed, and he didn't look up.

"Mage, look at me," I ordered.

His eyes rose to meet mine.

"Do you know of any time in our history when the Gifts failed?" I asked.

He shook his head. "No, Majesty. I have had our historians scouring the Royal Library since the first report. Since the time of Irina, the Gifts have flowed through the bloodlines without interruption."

I thought a moment. "Is there a spell . . . or some artifact . . . that could block someone's Gift? Mute it?"

"I know of one man who could Silence those within a certain radius, but he died many years ago. If such existed, even in the other nations, the Mages would have shared that information. It would have frightened every serious magician to their core. To have someone able to steal—"

"Stay with me. Focus." I rested a hand on his arm to try to calm him, but the Queen's touch nearly made him jump out of his robe.

"Majesty, forgive me. I was startled. You *touched* me."

I let out a sigh. "My skin isn't poisoned."

"No, but you are *Queen*."

"Fine." I sat back, lifting my hand a tad too dramatically from his arm. "Just focus. I know your people are working on this already, but the Mages are our best hope of finding a solution. Do whatever you must. Ask for whatever you need. There is no price too high for the return of our magic. Understand?"

"Yes, Majesty."

"And, Mage, please try to *remain calm.*"

He nodded frantically. "Yes, ma'am—I mean, Majesty."

CHAPTER 45

KEELAN

I t had taken four days of steady riding for me to make it back to the capital. I was tired, hungry, and covered in sweat and dust from the road. The last thing I wanted was to deal with the mass of people clogging the streets. I didn't think it was a festival or market day, but who knew what days were special in the Kingdom? I reined in Dittler and picked my way carefully through the crowd.

As I passed the first handful of people, I thought an odd fear painted their eyes.

This definitely isn't a festival crowd.

An old woman and her daughter scooted out of my way following an angry snort from Dittler. When the woman looked up, I nodded my head respectfully and asked, "What's going on? Is there a market day today?"

The woman's daughter tugged at her arm, urging her to ignore the large man in his dusty blue uniform—his *foreign* uniform—but the old woman stepped closer and stroked Dittler's neck. The stallion allowed her touch without so much as a whinny.

"Everybody's gathering at the Temple. The Gifted are asking the Priests for help."

"Help? Why do the Gifted need help? Especially from the Priests?"

The woman shushed him, looking over her shoulder nervously. "Who else are they going to turn to when their Gifts are gone? The Queen can't do nothin' about magic. They need the Spirits now," she whispered loudly so I could hear her atop my horse. Her daughter gave me a dark look and pulled the woman away.

I sat up straight and scanned the crowd. I had paid little attention before, but every good sense I possessed screamed for me to be on alert.

I passed another small group who were clustered around a small child who wore the Gifted gold. The girl was crying hysterically. I stopped and dismounted, then carefully made my way to the group. When they spotted my own golden collar, they parted to allow me to kneel before the girl.

"Are you all right? Don't be afraid. I want to help if I can," I said in as gentle a tone as I could muster.

She eyed me through wary, reddened eyes and wiped her tears with balled fists.

"I can't hear Gretta anymore," she managed before her sobs returned.

I waited, then gave a questioning look to the woman who held the girl.

"Gretta's her cat. Her Gift lets her hear animal thoughts, or see their images, however it works. She's the only one with a Gift in our family, so we don't really understand it all." Then she noticed my collar. "How are you being so strong without yours? All the others wearing gold are a wreck."

I fingered my collar. I hadn't even thought to test my own Gift.

"I am a Constable from far away, and my Gift is telling whether or not someone is being honest with me. Unlike your girl, I can't make my Gift work; someone has to lie to me for it to trigger." Then an idea struck. "Can you tell me something about yourself that is true, but throw in some false things? Just so I know if it's working or not."

The woman scrunched her nose as if smelling something rotten, then nodded. "My name is Macey Brie. I work as a weaver around the corner." She paused, thinking. "Um . . . my girl here, Bess, takes that darn cat with her everywhere. At least she did before all this."

I waited, but the woman remained silent.

"Well, anything?"

I cocked my head. "Are you done? I was waiting for you to tell me something false."

She patted my arm with her weathered hand. "Son, this is my granddaughter. Her name is Jemma, and she hates that raggedy cat, even if its thoughts keep her company sometimes. Just about everything I told you was a lie, except for my name and where I work. Looks like your gold is just as tarnished as the rest of the Gifted."

I stared at Macey.

My pulse quickened, and my breathing become shallow. I couldn't believe what she was saying. My Gift had been my constant companion since its first manifestation. It wasn't just some talent or learned skill—it was part of me. How could something woven into the fabric of my being simply vanish?

My legs grew numb from squatting so long, and I nearly toppled backward into Dittler.

Macey gripped my arm and helped me up.

"You might want to join those folks heading to the Temple. Maybe the Priests can help you, too."

I shook my dazed head. "No, I need to get to the Palace."

Without another word, I stood, mounted Dittler, and continued threading my way through the crowd.

CHAPTER 46

JESS

I watched the Mage vanish through the doors and slumped back into my chair.

First mysterious killings—by animals, no less—now magic failed.

What is next? I thought. *Is this really what my reign will be? Chasing one disaster after another?*

A moment later, I rose and turned to head to my chambers. I needed a long soak in a hot bath like a dying man needed redemption.

"Your Majesty," a page's voice called from the entrance before I could escape.

I tilted my head back and sucked in a breath.

"Yes? What is it?" I asked, turning toward the page.

The liveried boy scooted out of the way, and a tall, broad-shouldered man in a dusty blue uniform entered. Our eyes met, and my exhaustion evaporated.

"Keelan!"

He dropped his pack just inside the chamber. When the doors closed behind him, he barely blinked.

I took a few steps forward, my brow creased with concern. "Keelan, what is it? What is wrong?"

"Jess, I—" His voice broke.

I raced to him, and despite his road-worn state, wrapped my arms around him and held him. I felt the warmth of his breath on my neck, then the pressure of his hands against my back. His powerful arms encircled me—and his chest heaved.

"Oh, Keelan. What happened?" I couldn't imagine what could reduce such a strong, steady man to tears.

I lost track of how long we held each other.

He finally spoke in a hushed voice. "I can't feel my Gift anymore. Jess, I tried over and over. I can't feel the nagging sensation when something isn't right. I can't tell when someone is lying. I can't protect you—or Atikus or Declan—or *anybody* anymore."

I pulled back and gripped his face with my hands. "Keelan, look at me."

I waited until he gathered himself enough to hold my eyes. "*Everyone's* Gifts are gone. Everyone's. Even the Mages'. It is not just yours. Something has happened to magic that we have yet to understand, but we are working on it."

He tried to look away, but I held his face.

"We *are* going to fix this somehow. We will make it right, but your Gift is not what makes you special. It is not how you protect people. Your Gift is just a tool. Yes, it is powerful, and yes, it is part of you, but it does not define who you are, and it certainly *does not* take away your ability to help those you care about."

He nodded, but I wasn't convinced he believed me. The small boy looming over me looked more frightened than I had ever seen him, and I had no idea how to reassure him with more than hollow words. My heart ached as I stared into the anguish of his eyes.

Hours later, when I entered the family dining room, Keelan was already standing politely behind his chair. He'd shed his dusty uniform, bathed, shaved, and donned a sharp, tightly fitting charcoal-gray coat piped with golden thread.

His eyes were so brilliant against the darkness of his coat I nearly missed a step, wobbling on one foot before righting myself. Keelan was there in a flash, offering a hand to steady me, never looking amused at my predicament.

That simple act made my heart flutter even more.

Dinner was served exactly one half hour from the time I asked my maids to alert the kitchens. Being Queen carried unfathomable weight and responsibility, but the food and service were to die for. The staff brought platters of roasted turkey and vegetables lathered in garlic and butter.

The fresh, steaming bread appeared to be Keelan's favorite.

He hadn't eaten that day and was clearly starving.

He dove into the turkey with ravenous abandon and savored rich sauces that drenched the vegetables. Midway through, a frightening thought struck—would the stink of the herbs and garlic prevent a repeat performance of our kiss in the gardens?

Conversation was awkward at first, until I caught one of the older serving women grinning, her eyes glittering. The Queen emerged and sent that woman to the kitchen for more . . . *whatever*.

The maid curtsied and giggled as she scurried out of the room to bring her moonstruck Queen a giant platter of *something*.

At that point, we were able to pull ourselves together enough to start a proper conversation.

Keelan asked how things were going with Council appointments, knowing that particular duty still nagged at me daily.

I asked about his journey, avoiding the gruesome parts. He obliged with small talk of the people and village of Oliver.

I asked how Dittler was treating him, grinning as I remembered how the stallion nipped at the giant man every time he came near.

His fork froze halfway to his mouth. "Jess, I'm so sorry. I completely forgot. You haven't seen Dittler in over a week. I'm sure he would love a visit. Care for a walk by the stables, then through the gardens?"

I beamed. "I cannot believe I had not thought to visit him either. I would love that."

I set my fork down, having licked it clean of the blueberry dessert we'd just devoured, as he rose and extended a hand. "May a humble Constable take the Queen for an evening stroll?"

I giggled like some love-maddened girl and stood.

Taking his hand, I lifted my chin and said in her most imperious voice, "We are pleased with your offer. Lead on, good sir."

A few moments later, we stood outside the stables. I still wore my garnet gown and pearl necklace. The plan was to pay Dittler a quick visit, then stroll through the gardens. I would come back in the morning in my riding leathers and give my stallion a bit of proper exercise.

Keelan appeared in the opening to the stables, reins in hand, with Dittler nipping at his shoulder and whinnying each time Keelan tried to shoo his bites away.

I grinned at the pair.

"Looks like you two learned to get along."

"If you count me getting nipped every five seconds as getting along, then sure." He chuckled and pushed the horse's toothy snout away again.

At the sound of my voice, Dittler's ears shot forward, and his head snapped up. He began dancing on his front legs and surprised Keelan by yanking the lead out of his hand with a quick tug. Within seconds, the massive stallion had kneeled on his front knees before me, his snout nuzzling against my chest.

I laughed and stroked the horse's ears in exactly the spot I knew could make him weak.

He let out a gruff snort—something akin to what a thousand-pound cat might do when given a good scratch.

"My baby boy," I said, pressing my cheek against his forelock.

The powerful-beast-turned-helpless-puppy dared not move; he breathed and snorted as his mistress praised and stroked him. After a few peaceful moments, he pulled back and eyed me.

"What is it, boy?"

He snorted and stamped once, then resumed staring at me.

"My Gift is not working. I cannot see your thoughts in my mind."

He snorted and stamped again.

Keelan stepped up beside me, careful not to startle the stallion. "I think he senses something's off but doesn't know what it is or why you're not understanding him."

Dittler leaned toward Keelan and nudged his arm with his muzzle, then nickered and bobbed his head.

"Did he just agree with you?" I asked in amazement.

Keelan laughed. "Jealous? I'm pretty sure we bonded on this trip."

On cue, Dittler lunged forward and nipped Keelan's coat.

"I see how you boys bonded." I laughed. "And I think you are right. He has always been more perceptive than people think. Part of it is being a Cretian—everyone knows they are the smartest of horse breeds—but there is magic at work here, too. It might not be a Gift exactly, but he has shown me many times over how much he understands."

That earned me another nuzzle.

"Traitor!" Keelan quipped. "Nip me but nuzzle her."

Dittler turned and nipped Keelan again.

Both of us laughed, and I thought I heard Dittler snorting a little too merrily himself.

Then Dittler let out a deep-throated roar of alarm.

All at once, the peaceful night turned into a blur of motion.

The sound of another horse's hooves on the cobbles clanked through the yard, and a mottled gray steed broke through the darkness from around the stables, headed straight for me.

I screamed as Keelan pulled me to the side as the horse reared and missed, nearly striking my head with its front hooves.

"Get back inside!" Keelan yelled as he ducked away from the horse's angry teeth.

I turned to run, but my gown and shoes were made for dinners, not sprints, and I sprawled face-first across the cobbles a few paces away.

At the sound of my cry, the gray horse turned from Keelan and charged for my prone body.

Dittler, enraged, snapped at the horse's neck, gripping a mouthful of its mane in his mighty teeth. He yanked backward, twisting the smaller animal's head around. The gray pulled himself free and, in the same motion, turned his hindquarters toward Dittler, landing a painful blow with both of his rear hooves straight into Dittler's side. The Cretian snorted in pain, stumbling sideways a pace, then he charged forward again, teeth bared. The two reared on hindquarters and exchanged vicious blows on the other's neck and head.

In battles for dominance, such fights were common.

To an outsider, it would appear the challengers were trying to kill one another, but this wasn't usually the case. Horses generally fought until one submitted, then the order of supremacy in the herd was restored or remade.

But the gray horse wasn't trying to dominate. He wanted to *kill*.

And though he fought Dittler, his eyes kept returning to me.

Keelan darted out of the way of the dueling beasts and helped me to my feet. I threw off my heels and turned to run for help. The gray broke free of Dittler and charged again, this time slamming into Keelan, knocking him several paces away and onto his back.

My protector out of the way, the gray locked eyes with me and reared.

His enraged whinny tore through the night, and sharp hooves glared down at me, their helpless target.

As its hooves were inches from crashing into my face, Dittler charged and rammed his entire weight into my attacker's side.

The gray, still on just his hind legs, was knocked off balance and flew into the side wall of the stone stables. His head smacked into the hard surface, and blood oozed from a massive gash the impact had created. The horse's eyes lost focus, and he struggled to rise on wobbly legs, but Dittler was there before he could stand, battering him with forehooves and biting into his throat and withers.

Keelan shook off the last blow he'd taken.

He darted into the stables, returning with a manure fork he found hanging on the wall. It wasn't perfect, but it would have to do.

He raced back to where Dittler continued to stamp the wounded gray.

The gray continued to bite and struggle.

In one lucky thrust, it managed to rake Dittler with a hoof, scoring a bloody line across the stallion's chest.

Dittler staggered back a few paces, leaving an opening for the gray to try to rise.

Keelan was there before he could stand.

He raged and roared like a man driven by the lust of battle, stabbing the fork into the gray's head and side again and again until the horse lay motionless on the bloody stones.

Keelan's chest heaved.

Dittler wheezed and panted as sweat foamed over his sides.

His eyes were frenzied, so Keelan staggered away slowly, giving him space to calm.

I ran to Keelan and threw my arms around him.

He winced as I gripped his likely broken ribs but still pulled me into him. A moment later, silver-plated guards poured out of the Palace.

"The Queen! To the Queen!" they yelled.

Before Keelan could speak, we were safely surrounded by a protective ring of iron.

"I am all right," I said in a small voice as I pulled away from the safety of Keelan's embrace.

A man with a bright-green plume on his shiny helm stepped into the circle. He bowed curtly. "Your Majesty, are you hurt? What happened?"

I drew in a few breaths, then looked up at the man. "I am fine. Keelan may need a Healer, and Dittler definitely will, but I am unharmed. That horse came out of nowhere and . . . I do not know . . . *attacked* me. It all sounds insane now, but that is what happened."

The guard's brows knitted in confusion as he looked from me to where the gray horse lay, then back to me. "A horse attacked you, Majesty?"

I nodded. "That is right. He is right over—"

My words caught in my throat as I turned and pointed to where the horse had lain only moments before.

There was no horse.

There, lying in a pool of his own blood that still poured from his head and chest, was the body of a man in silky brown robes. Pieces of a shattered mask depicting a snarling gray horse with stubby antlers lay a pace away.

CHAPTER 47

DECLAN

T ears flowed as I searched the inky darkness with both hands.

I cast a swirling ball of light beneath the swells and thrust my hands into the river's surface. Each time they rose from the current, they held nothing, simply dripped with oozing blackness.

My mother was gone.

She was truly gone.

I sat back against a stone and stared at nothing.

I looked down and scrubbed my hands against my trousers, angry at the poisoned substance that had just made me an orphan, desperate to remove its stain from my skin.

How long I sat in that grotto, revisiting every moment I'd had with my mother, I would never know.

Minutes?

Hours?

It felt like a lifetime—but a lifetime wasn't enough.

There could never be enough time.

I wept again.

When weariness of heart and body ebbed, I rose and made my way to the cavern's entrance. Darkness had fallen on the early spring night, and stars shone in the cloudless sky. I could just make out the lights of the guild and trudged slowly toward them.

Why were so many burdens laid on my shoulders?

"Declan, can you hear me?" a familiar voice called in my mind, startling me out of my pondering.

"Atikus?" I asked, unsure if returning the mental missive would even work. *"How—"*

I *felt* the Mage's rumbling laughter in my mind. *"I have no idea, but you are not going to believe what else I can do now."*

"Atikus, where are you? I need to tell you something, and I'd rather—"

"Wait! You are responding Telepathically! Does this mean your Gifts still work?"

I'd had no reason to test my Telepathy before that moment. It had worked a few times, speaking in Ayden's mind, but this felt different somehow . . . *more.* Though more of what, I couldn't fathom.

A thousand questions flooded my mind.

How far away was Atikus?

How far could we communicate?

How far could I—?

"Yes, my magic works . . . just differently. It's hard to believe, and even harder to explain. Where are you? We need to talk."

"I have returned to the guild. I just thought about home, and the next moment, I was here. It is incredible!" Excitement flooded our mental channel.

Emotions. I could *feel* his emotions through our communication.

Sweet Spirits, what next?

"All right, I'm almost there. I need a bath and a meal, but we should talk first. This is really important."

Atikus sobered. *"Son, are you all right? What's wrong? I can feel it through this bond, whatever this is."*

"I'm fine. Meet me in the dining hall in fifteen minutes. I should be there by then."

"Okay. I'll head down and ask cook to whip up something to eat. See you then."

I sat across the table from my adopted father.

We'd eaten our fill of cold cuts and dried fruits, and Atikus had recounted the events in the mountain as he'd experienced them, letting me finish my meal before delivering my news.

"I didn't just get my Gifts back; I got *all* of magic!" Atikus vibrated like a boy who'd just tasted his first ale.

I looked up from my plate, said, "Me, too," then took another bite as if I hadn't spoken anything of import.

Atikus cocked his head.

He opened his mouth, then closed it.

He blinked beneath bushy brows.

For once, the man was speechless.

"Maybe I should tell you what happened," I said as I washed the last bite of my dinner down.

"Yes," Atikus said, his enthusiasm quelled. "Perhaps you should."

I struggled to begin. Where does one begin with a tale that ends in his mother's death? My heart ached to be done, to never begin, to have just one more day . . .

The Spirits ignored my prayers.

So, I wove my way through the events in the Well's cavern, the battle with Irina, and my harrowing journey with Kelså in the currents. When I got to the last part, I lost the last measure of composure and wept.

Atikus stood, stepped around the table, and pulled me into a tight embrace.

He held me until the tears ebbed, never uttering a word.

"I couldn't save her, Atikus. I tried, but the currents were raging, and the poison was killing magic all around us. I could barely see, much less hold on." I peered up with reddened eyes. "She vanished while . . . *while I watched.* I saw her break apart in the currents."

When Atikus remained quiet, I pulled back, anger blazing in my eyes. "Irina did this. We need to banish her once and for all, Atikus. I don't care if I die fighting; that witch is going to the void where she belongs."

Atikus pinched his eyes shut, then nodded. "Yes, yes. Of course, you are right. We cannot let her spirit continue wreaking havoc, but . . . I don't even know where to begin looking for her, much less how to banish her." He sat back and gripped my arm with his bony fingers. "You look like you could use a bath and a good night's sleep. I know I need the rest. We'll both think better in the morning. I can get some of the Mages I trust to help us plan."

I nodded weakly, then locked eyes with Atikus. "I never said *thank you*."

The Mage cocked his head. "For what, son?"

"For being the only family Keelan and I ever had. For taking us in and always believing in us, even when we—I—didn't believe in myself."

Atikus's face softened, and his eyes moistened. "Declan, son, you two filled my life with laughter and my heart with joy in ways I never knew was even possible. I should be thanking you."

We embraced once more, then left the dining hall to find rest.

The next morning, someone had slid a note beneath my door instructing me to meet Atikus and several other Mages in the study for a private breakfast. I grinned as I entered the paneled room and found the rotund, ever-jovial Mage Pel piling his plate with eggs and bacon. Pel fumbled for a place to set his breakfast down, then waddled toward the entrance to greet me.

Reunion complete, I loaded my plate and sank into one of the large leather chairs, which normally faced the hearth but had been turned to form a circle.

Atikus set his steaming tea down and cleared his throat. "Keep eating, everyone, but we should get started. What we have to discuss is too important to wait. I will ask you to forgive my caution in advance. What Declan and I are about to reveal must never leave this room, and I will bind each of your minds with magic to ensure no one could ever pry these memories from you, something I wish had been done for me before Irina could rummage through my head." He looked each Mage in the eyes, waited for their nod of assent, then cast the binding spell that would wipe any trace of their conversation from their minds within a few days.

He then summarized the events that had occurred over the past days, which translated into weeks in non-island time. I interjected at points, but Atikus's perfect memory hadreturned, and his details were impeccable.

I marveled at Atikus's perfect recall as the Mage recapped the plans we'd devised.

"The top priority is locating Irina," Atikus said, as if reading from a list. "She is powerful; we assume she has regained *all* her previous powers, just as we have. We need one Mage to scry for her. I will power his efforts with my magic. With her new powers, she should light up like a star in any scrying bowl.

"Next, we have to find a way to banish her—for good this time. Unfortunately, we have far more questions than answers. Is banishment even possible with a Mage of her power? Is her spirit separate from Larinda's body, or do we need to kill the woman formerly known as Larinda and *then* banish Irina's spirit? If so, will a summoning circle be needed to contain her spirit until it can be banished?"

As happened far too often when a group of Mages sat in the study, the conversation meandered on and off topic, and I found my mind drifting. I snapped back to the present when they moved on.

"Finally, we have to cleanse the currents and restore Gifts to the world," Atikus said.

A tiny voice inside me wondered if I would lose many of my newly acquired powers if Gifts were restored. I was just getting to know these new powers, and we were already talking about stripping them away, returning me to only what I, as Heir, possessed.

I would be reduced to, what, six or seven Gifts? Then I chided myself for such selfish thoughts.

My charge was to protect the people and magic itself, not hoard it like a dragon with a pile of golden coins. I realized in that moment how bitterly Irina was likely to resist having her powers taken from her once again, especially after a thousand years of imprisonment.

This was going to be a lot harder than any of us thought.

Atikus turned to the historian in the group. "We need you to dig through the stacks of historical scrolls maintained in the guild's vault for any reference to the spell used to splinter magic and create Gifts. It *has* to be there. Mages were the original pack rats. We never destroy anything, especially if it was written on parchment."

The Mages chuckled at their own penchant for hoarding.

The group disbanded shortly after lunch, each Mage hurrying off to research his or her assigned task. We would reconvene for dinner and review each other's progress.

Atikus and I headed to the Guild Hall with the scrying Mage, hoping the circle embedded in that building would be powerful enough to locate our quarry. It would have been a simple matter from atop the Mages' tower, but that option crumbled when its stones fell.

I had never seen the gold-and-silver inlaid circle in the casting chamber of the Guild Hall—there'd been no reason, as I'd grown up believing magic had shunned me. Now, upon entering the well-lit room, my eyes widened as I took in the crafts-manship of the perfectly inlaid circle. One golden circle in the center surrounded by a silver square wrapped in a final golden circle.

The whole thing flared when Atikus and I entered.

"Well, that's new," the scrying Mage said.

Atikus shook his head. "We are seeing all sorts of new things these days. It appears anything invested with magic responds to our presence."

"Interesting. That might be helpful when we get to the fighting stage of the plan," I said.

A white marble pillar stood waist high in the center of the circle. The scrying Mage poured water from a pitcher into a shiny brass bowl and placed it on the pedestal, careful not to spill anything inside the circle.

"Is it too much to hope that you have something personal to Irina?" he asked.

I barked a laugh. "I don't know that anything matters to her anymore. She's the purest kind of evil."

"Declan's right that we don't have an item of hers, but he's wrong in painting her with one solid color. While I agree she's turned dark, no one is *entirely* evil—or good, for that matter. We are all shades and hues."

"Maybe she's shades of *black*," I mused.

"Let's focus on locating her, shall we?" Atikus steered us back to our purpose.

The scrying Mage stepped up to the bowl and looked at me. "It's a simple process. Whichever of you is performing the scrying, place both hands on the outside of the bowl, but don't touch the water. Call your Light. When your magic responds, focus your thoughts on Irina, what she looks like, every detail you can remember. If she wore a certain scent, try to recreate that memory. Everything helps. We wouldn't normally need to be this de-tailed, but without an artifact, your mind will have to be the bridge. If you do everything correctly and maintain steady focus, the water will ripple and show images of where Irina is currently."

Atikus raised a brow. "Would you like to do the honors?"

"I'm not sure this counts as *honors*, but sure. I have never done a scrying before. You may have to guide me," I said, stepping up and gripping the sides of the bowl.

I closed my eyes, and my Light flared at my call.

I heard a gasp and opened my eyes, disrupting the process.

"What happened? Is everything okay?"

Atikus chuckled and looked to the scrying Mage, whose eyes couldn't have grown any wider.

"I don't think he's seen your tunic light up before," Atikus said with a flourish of bushy brows and a chuckle.

"Sorry," the Mage said. "It's . . . incredible. I'll stay quiet this time."

I allowed myself a grin, then closed my eyes to focus again.

As before, my Light responded quickly.

I replayed the scene from the Well in my mind, first with Kelså and me running into the chamber in response to Órla's alarm.

Then Irina appeared wearing the mask of Larinda.

I focused on the details as the Mage had instructed, recreating every wrinkle and weathered spot on the old woman's face and bare arms, her stringy snow-white hair, and her colorful island dress. I could hear Larinda's voice, the warmth and depth in her laugh, taste the salt in the air as I breathed deeply.

I held that image, those sensations, for five minutes, then ten.

Finally, I felt a hand pat my shoulder, and the image fell away.

I opened my eyes to find the other two men staring at the bowl in frustration.

"Were you able to remember details?" the scrying Mage asked.

"Of course. I spent a lot of time with Larinda. That wasn't hard."

"Well, the water didn't so much as ripple, much less show us anything," Atikus said. "I could feel waves of power wafting off as you focused. Having strong enough magic is *not* our problem here."

"Wait," the Mage said excitedly. "You said *Larinda*."

I nodded, confused. "That's right. That's the face Irina wore when I saw her."

"True, but we're not looking for Larinda, we're looking for *Irina*. Her spirit could have left Larinda's body to inhabit another. Regardless of what body she wore, it's *Irina's spirit* we are trying to locate. Try again, this time focused on Irina."

"This just got a lot harder. I've never seen Irina. No one has, at least not in a thousand years."

Atikus raised a hand like a schoolboy.

"You've got to be kidding," I said.

"Perfect memory, remember? I have studied the Kingdom War, read much of what still exists detailing Irina's rise. There are no busts or sketches of her, but her appearance is described in vivid detail in Matias's Histories."

"Of course, he even remembers the name of the boring book he read," I grumbled.

"Yes, my boy, I do. Stand aside and watch your Arch Mage work."

I rolled my eyes, more for the scrying Mage's amusement than for Atikus's sake, then backed away from the bowl and watched as Atikus took over the process. Within a few heartbeats, the old Mage had closed his eyes, called his Light, and caused the water to ripple violently, then settle into images of a building none of us recognized.

"It looks like an old warehouse. There are candles hanging everywhere; there must be a hundred of them hanging from lines stretched across the ceiling. I've never seen so many in one place. Does that mean anything to either of you?" Atikus asked.

The Mage shrugged, but I stared into the water.

"When I was on border patrol, there were a few traders who would come through from the Kingdom with carts laden with candles. We are the producer in the trading relationship with the Spires, but there are a few items where they do most of the production and selling. Candles are one of those items."

"Do you know where they're made? Where the Merchant sells them?"

"No, but Keelan's over there, right? Why don't we pay him a visit with our shiny new powers? He may know someone who can help—*like the Queen.*"

"My boy, you may become the smartest of us all." Atikus grinned. "I have been to the Palace several times, so Traveling there should not be a problem. Let's go see your brother."

CHAPTER 48

JESS

The next day's duties began far too early.

By the time I strode into my audience chamber shortly before sunrise, the entire Council was already seated and devouring pastries and spiced tea. As I approached my seat with Keelan following closely behind, everyone stood.

My portly—and horribly clumsy—Trade Minister, Destin Carver, was startled and fumbled his pastry. Confectioner's sugar plumed in every direction. A cloud of white powder lingered above the table near his seat a moment after he recovered the rogue pastry. I stifled a laugh.

"Good morning, everyone. Please sit," I said with a voice that brooked no discussion. "I assume each of you received a briefing on the attack that took place last night. Were it not for the heroic efforts of our guest from Melucia, Guardsman

Rea, your morning might have been consumed by another succession crisis."

Heads bobbed.

"This was planned and orchestrated by the Order. Their Priests have been infiltrating our towns and cities, winning over the hearts of *my* people, preaching against the Crown. They pose a clear threat that must be dealt with. Does anyone disagree?"

I looked from one Councilor to the next.

Some wore bewildered looks, having missed the aforementioned briefing. Others masked their expressions, either unsure how to respond or afraid to challenge me when my mind appeared set.

Ethan was first to wade into the deep waters. "Majesty, while I agree we must deal with those behind the assassination attempt swiftly and without mercy, the Order and its Priests have established themselves across the nation as peaceful caretakers of the poor and destitute. Whether true or not, our crisis with Gifts has cemented their role as intercessors for the Spirits in the minds of many."

"You have to be joking. They are *Irina's Children* without the masks. They are the people who kidnapped and tried to kill me—*twice*."

Ethan raised his palms in surrender. "I know that, and you know that, but the people have bought their story. What we thought were a handful of Priests scattered through the countryside turned out to be one or more Priests in *every* town, village, and hamlet in the Kingdom. There isn't a place with more than three families without a Priest ministering to their needs, preaching goodwill and the call to care for a neighbor."

"And the need to supplant the Crown!" I shouted, then tried to calm myself. "I get it. They have taken a huge lead in the propaganda war, but we did not even know we were in a battle, much less put up a fight. That changes today."

The men and woman at the table were speechless.

They worked shoulder to shoulder with the people—well, with the *rich* people of the nation—and the nobles had bought the Priests' message just as the commoners had, likely more so since they wore most of the golden collars and were desperate to recover their magic. That the Queen would go to war with the Priests was unthinkable.

"No one? Not *one* of you will speak up?" I straightened my spine. "When I see you again, I want options to take down the Order. If we need to leave the Priests in place with a narrow mission of good will, fine—but I want their leaders dealt with so they can never threaten the Crown again. Am I clear?"

A muffled chorus of "Yes, Majesty" made its disorderly way around the table.

I turned and stalked out of the room.

CHAPTER 49

LIAM

I was beyond exhausted.

My day began, as it always did, long before the sun bothered to show its lazy face to the world. I helped my mother prep, cook, and serve breakfast to our guests, then rushed through a cursory cleaning so I could make it to the market before other Merchants gobbled up all the fresh produce.

The air was blessedly cool, almost crisp, with a light breeze blowing in from the ocean. I still returned to the inn sweaty and stinking from my day's effort. Ma sent me upstairs with orders to make a quick bath so I could help cut vegetables and roll dough for pie crusts for dinner.

Such was the life of an innkeeper—and an innkeeper's son.

That night, the common room overflowed.

Every major city in the Kingdom was holding qualifying rounds of the annual Tournament of

Spires, the chief event of the year where men tried to poke other men with pointy things.

At least, that's how I saw the games.

There was sword fighting, jousting, marksmanship . . . yeah, I was right—men and sharp, pointy things.

Whatever one thought of the games, the trials drew crowds from all over, and that was good for business.

I raced from table to table taking orders, delivering food, and slinging more mugs of ale than I thought possible. Three separate times, I was called to the kitchen for an emergency cleaning of piled-up tankards, only to immediately fill them for delivery to new patrons. The seasonal nature of the inn's business could be maddening in slow times, but when things were good, they were *very* good.

The musicians started slower songs, the part of their set designed to calm the rambunctious, highly intoxicated guests before the staff shuffled them off to bed or on to other adventures around town. I shared an appreciative smile with the fiddle player as his bow caressed the strings with a sad, almost melancholy rapture. The guests quieted and sank into the emotional ballad. More than a few eyes were moist by the time the players struck their last chord. With that final note, the players began packing up their instruments and passing their very deep hat one last time to squeeze every drop of juice they could.

I began clearing and wiping tables as most of the patrons took the hint.

One pair of men remained at a table in the corner.

Something in their posture, the way they leaned a little too far and whispered a touch too low, made me uneasy.

I knew both men.

They were among the more successful business owners in town.

What are they scheming about? I wondered.

Unable to overhear any of their conversation, I continued about my work.

When the last of my tables was cleaned and the dishes in the kitchen were put away, I gave the common room one last scan. The two men were still there, still whispering, their eyes still darting around the room. They were *definitely* up to something.

I couldn't resist and walked over to their table.

"Can I get you gentlemen anything else tonight? We're about to close up."

"Oh, no, Liam. We're just finishing up. We'll be out of your hair in a few minutes," one of the men said. The other stared at his hands and avoided looking up at me.

"In that case, mind if I wipe down your table real quick? I can leave you to your conversation once the table's clean. Stay as long as you like."

The talkative man smiled. "Go right ahead, and thank you."

As I walked away, taking as much time as I could without looking obvious, I caught a tiny snippet of their conversation.

". . . has to end. Tomorrow's our best chance to take care of him. Are you with me?"

The other man, the hand starer, spoke. "Aye. Tomorrow."

And with that, the pair stood, bade me goodnight, and left.

I blew out a long breath.

Nothing in what I heard made any sense, but it caused my stomach to do flips all the same. I didn't like it one bit.

"Liam," Ma's voice called from the kitchen, snapping me out of my thoughts.

"Yes, Ma. I'm wiping down the last table. Be there in a minute."

The kitchen door swung wide, and Ma appeared in the doorway, her lips quirked to one side.

I knew that look. I was about to run yet another errand.

Amazing.

"Dear, I completely forgot Mrs. B. We were supposed to drop a dinner off at her place an hour ago. She's been laid up with a terrible cold all week, and I told her we'd handle her cooking tonight. If she's not miserable, she'll be madder than . . . well, that doesn't matter. Would you mind running this over to her place? I'll finish up here."

I knew both the common room and kitchen were finished but smiled at my mother as if she'd saved me days' worth of cleaning. "Yes, ma'am. 'Course I will."

I walked to Ma and exchanged my apron for the wrapped box in her hands, then gave her a peck on the cheek.

Mrs. Betner, known as Mrs. B. to anyone who'd ever set foot in Oliver, lived in a tiny wooden hut on the outskirts of town. At a leisurely pace, it took me forty minutes to make the trek. The widow was asleep and hadn't even realized dinnertime had come and gone. She was one of Ma's more talkative friends, but I got off easy. She called out for me to leave the box on her porch so I didn't risk catching a fever.

If one could even catch a fever, I thought.

I was more relieved to have avoided what surely would've been an hour-long chat than any ailment. I could cope with the sniffles, but diarrhea of the mouth was incurable.

The night was chilly as winter battled spring for supremacy.

Clouds blanketed the sky.

I folded my arms and rubbed them for warmth.

I'd only made it a quarter mile from Mrs. B.'s house when I heard a muffled cry. I thought I recognized the voice but couldn't quite place where I knew it from. I slowed my pace and crept toward the sound, stopping cold as I rounded the apothecary's dull brick façade.

My mind struggled to process what I was seeing.

A man lay bleeding on the ground, his arms raised as if to ward off an attack and blood pooling beneath his head and chest. Towering above him with paws poised to strike was a massive brown bear.

I'd never seen a bear in person, but I was sure the sketches I'd seen didn't mark bears at ten feet tall with claws as long as soldiers' daggers. As I watched in horror, the bear flung its full weight down on the man, ramming its razor-sharp claws into his head and chest until only the meat of its paws was visible.

The man didn't twitch or moan.

He didn't spasm.

He just died.

But the bear wasn't finished.

As if it held some personal grudge against the poor man, the bear lunged again and again, digging and clawing until there was little recognizable left on the bloody street. I covered my mouth with a palm and told myself to breathe quietly. The bear's back had been to me, but I didn't want to give it any reason to turn.

Then, as strange as the mauling had been, something else happened.

The bear dropped to all fours and lumbered a few paces away. It reached down and picked something up off the ground and held it up to its muzzle.

Then the gigantic form shrank to average human proportions.

Its fur vanished, and a silky brown robe flowed with the breeze in its place. I ducked behind the building as *the man* turned toward where I stood.

If I was afraid before, I was terrified then.

I waited a long moment until I heard footfalls fading, then peered around the corner.

The man was gone.

I took a few tentative steps from my hiding place and strained to see the dead man in the darkness. I couldn't recognize his face through all the blood and gore, but a piece of his shredded shirt caught my eye, and I realized where I'd known his voice.

He was the quiet man at the table in the corner.

The one who wouldn't stop staring at his hands.

CHAPTER 50

DECLAN

C ooks raced between boiling pots and siz-
zling pans as they prepared the royal household's noon meal. Heavenly aromas of herbs and
fresh-baked bread hung in the air. The Royal Chef,
leader of the brigade, kept a watchful eye each
time a cook added ingredients or seasoning. He
wore a perpetual scowl as he dipped one of the
dozen clean tasting spoons from the pocket on his
sleeve, then thrust a taste into his mouth. Most of
the time, his scowl turned into a relieved grin, and
he would nod appreciatively to the cook.

So absorbed in his work was the man that he had
failed to notice Atikus and me suddenly appear
where one of his white-coated cooks had stood
only seconds before.

The Chef nearly jumped out of his puffy hat.

The smallest cook, who looked more than fourteen years old, ran out of the room screaming, "Guards!" at the top of her lungs.

"You *would* have to land in the kitchen of all places." I turned to Atikus with a smirk and an eye roll.

Atikus wiggled brows above twinkling eyes. "It is lunchtime. If I remember correctly—and you *know* I do—the Palace has the best chefs on the continent. Just smell that bread! *Of course* I landed us in here."

The Chef ventured a nervous step forward, baffled by our banter almost as much as our sudden appearance. "Uh . . . hello?"

Atikus smiled broadly and offered a shallow bow. "Please forgive our rude arrival. We did not mean to startle you. I am Arch Mage Atikus Dani, and this is Declan Rea. I am not quite sure what title he has now. We are here to see your Queen and her guest, Guardsman Keelan Rea, but . . . would you mind if we tasted a bite of that hot bread before we bother Her Majesty?"

I couldn't cover my mouth fast enough to stifle the laugh that tumbled out.

Silver-plated guards arrived as Atikus finished his first roll.

He was still licking the butter off his fingers when sword points appeared at his collar. We were ushered into a small room that looked strikingly similar to the study back at the Saltstone Guild. Atikus flopped into a leather chair, kicked off his shoes, and poured a glass of liquor from a nearby decanter.

I shook my head. "Really? Make yourself at home. Think I should ask one of the guards outside to bring us a pillow for your feet?"

"That would be wonderful," Atikus said, wriggling his toes through stockings that showed more bare skin than fabric. He held up the decanter. "They wouldn't put this here if they didn't want us to enjoy, now would they?"

I chuckled and shook my head, then tossed myself into a chair across from my insufferable traveling companion.

A moment later, the door flew open, and Keelan barged in.

When he saw Atikus, his entire face lit up—and then he saw me.

He stumbled into a side table.

My big brother's discomfort made me flinch. "I know. They're weird, and everybody's scared of me now."

My head drooped.

Keelan closed the gap between us in two strides and lifted me out of the chair, wrapping me in a tight hug and lifting me off the ground so my feet dangled like I was seven years old again.

"You'll have to do better than swirling eyes of death to scare me away, you puffy-headed idiot. You should know better."

I didn't fight the embrace the way I had when we were children. Instead, I wrapped my arms around Keelan and buried my head in his shoulder.

"It's so good to see you, Kee. You've got no idea how much." The beginning of a sob shuddered through my chest. Keelan started to release me, but I clung to him as a desperate man clings to a life raft in the ocean.

That's what Keelan had always been for me: a beacon in every storm. I'd just been too wrapped up in my own insecurities to see it.

I knew he would be there for me no matter what.

Keelan's arms were the safest place in the world. They always were.

Even now, as a twenty-year-old with immensely powerful magic, I found comfort in my brother's embrace.

Keelan pulled back to find my face streaked. "Dec, what's wrong? What happened?"

Atikus stepped forward and placed a hand on my shoulder.

"Our mother is dead," I blurted out. "I mean . . . I lost her. Kee, I tried so hard . . . but her fingers . . . I couldn't . . ." I began sobbing uncontrollably.

Atikus guided me to one of the chairs, while he took the other. Keelan kneeled beside me and gripped my arm.

For what felt like an eternity, no one spoke.

Keelan watched me as I mourned. It wasn't until that moment that I realized how few tears I'd shed over my mother's loss—over all of our losses, really. Everyone expected me to be strong, to use my magic to fix all of their problems and set the world to rights.

Who was supposed to do that for me?

I might've turned into a powerful Mage, but the small boy who smarted at the slights of others and never grasped his own worth still battled within my soul.

Atikus, racked with his own sudden grief, stared with pooled eyes into the dwindling fire in the hearth.

After what felt like forever, I spoke, sounding very much like that small boy Atikus had first met seventeen years ago. "I know you never got to know her, Kee, but she was so strong. And Spirits, she was beautiful, inside and out. There were so many times I thought about just staying on the island with her and never coming back, but she knew what was at stake. She gave me strength and taught me to believe in myself for the first time. Imagine that. The mother we never knew did the most motherly thing possible just before—"

Another wave of sobs overcame whatever I was going to say.

Atikus pulled himself out of his own thoughts and leaned forward. "Declan, she was proud of you—of both of you. I cannot imagine a greater gift a son could give his mother than the time you spent with her. On the island, it was, what, a year?"

I tried to steady myself. "More like a year and a half, the way we counted it. It wasn't enough. Dammit, it wasn't enough."

Atikus reached over and patted my hand. "If it had been a hundred years, it wouldn't have been enough. Take that from someone who's lived a *very* long time."

Keelan released my arm and leaned back against Atikus's chair. "What happened? Are you okay talking about it?"

I let out a humorless laugh. "Guess we'll see."

I walked Keelan through everything, starting with Órla's first warning about Atikus being attacked through my own arrival in the cavern at the base of the Silver Mountains earlier that day. Somehow, I managed to get through the whole thing without breaking down again.

"I still don't understand." Keelan turned to Atikus. "Don't get me wrong, I'm happy to see you, but *how* did you get here? Everyone else's Gifts fell silent weeks ago."

"The Gifts are part of the reason we are here, but first we need to find Irina's spirit and send her where she belongs—to the void. If she is allowed to continue roaming free, there is no telling what kind of havoc she will cause. We fear she may also have the same unrestricted use of magic Declan and I now share."

"Unlimited magic? What are you talking about?" Keelan looked between us with wide eyes.

I tried to smile, but a grimace was all I could manage. "Let's just say we don't have Gifts; we have magic. It isn't unlimited, but it's . . . a lot. Remember the old stories of the original Mages and how they could do almost anything? Back before Irina?"

Keelan nodded. "Yeah, I remember tales about that. Never believed any of it."

"Well, it was all true. Turns out, several of those Mages sacrificed themselves to cast a spell that stripped the others of their magic and gave it as a Gift to normal people around the world. The spell had to be performed at the Well, the same Well *our mother* was the Keeper of."

"Holy Spirits," Keelan whispered.

"Literally." Atikus chuckled despite the somber mood in the room.

"Anyway"—I shot the old man a scowl—"when Irina took over Larinda's body and did whatever she did to the Well, she shattered the spell. Gifts ceased to exist. We believe we received our magical abilities because we happened to be the only people in the room at the time of Irina's attack. If she hadn't fallen into the Well, Kelså might've had the same powers, too."

"But that still doesn't explain why you popped up out of nowhere to scare the schnitzel out of my kitchen staff."

Our three heads whirled.

The Queen stood in the doorway.

It seemed none of us had heard her enter.

I scrambled to my feet. Atikus followed suit as quickly as his old knees allowed. Unsure how to greet a monarch, I fumbled an awkward bow, then extended a hand as if to shake hers.

Keelan reached up and gently lowered my hand with his own.

"A bow is fine." He exchanged an amused smirk with Jess. "Gentlemen, may I preset Her Royal Majesty, Jessia Vester, Queen of the Spires."

"Oh, stop that." She stepped forward and waved a hand like she was swatting a fly. "It is just us here. There is no need for bowing and scraping, though I do rather enjoy it when Keelan shows deference to me, *as he should*."

Keelan reddened.

Jess chuckled.

Atikus looked from Keelan to Jess, then back to Keelan. His eyes widened, and he turned and poured another glass of amber liquid. This time, he handed it to me. "Here, you're going to need this."

Befuddled, I took the glass, shrugged at Keelan, and downed the liquor in one shot.

Jess cleared her throat. "Declan, it is nice to meet you. Keelan can be tough to pry conversation out of, but when he opens up, it is usually with some story about you."

"Really?" I was genuinely surprised.

Jess nodded. "Declan the Terrible, I believe was one of your first nicknames?"

"Jess . . ." Keelan tried to cut in.

"Do not interrupt a Queen in her Palace," she snapped, then tossed him a wink.

"Great, thanks a lot." I jabbed Keelan with an elbow.

Atikus stepped forward. "Your Majesty, it is good to see you again, too. You look much better than the road-worn girl I recall."

She smiled. "That was . . . a very different time. I will never be able to thank you for rescuing me and helping me return home."

No one quite knew what to say after that, so everyone stood and stared at the floor or their hands.

"So," Jess leaped into the conversation void. "We are all glad you are here, but you still have not answered why you scared the life out of my cooks."

I barked a laugh. "Because Atikus's first thought would be of food if the continent were sinking into the sea."

"Well, now that you mention it, I am a tad hungry," the Mage said seriously.

"I think we're more curious what drove you to visit." Keelan chuckled and saved Jess from pressing her question a third time.

"Ah, right. I suppose lunch can wait a few moments longer," Atikus said. "We did a scrying in search of Irina's spirit. We know from the vision that she is here in your capital, but neither Declan nor any of our Mages recognized the building. We thought one of the Queen's Constables or staff might be able to help. Declan and I have a plan to banish her, but we have to locate her first."

Jess nodded. "Of course my people will help. I will summon the High Sheriff and Mage Ernest to join us for lunch. They know this city as well as anyone and will be able to coordinate assistance, should you need it."

Atikus offered a shallow bow. "Lunch would be most welcome—oh, and the assistance, too."

As we were finishing the last of our meal, Sheriff Cribbs, Mage Ernest, and High Chancellor Marks entered. Each paid their respects with deep bows and quick introductions.

"Gentlemen, come join us. We need your help on a critical matter," Jess said. "Are you hungry? We were just finishing, but the staff can bring you whatever you like."

They thanked her but declined more than water and tea as they took their seats. Marks studied me intently, his eyes returning several times to the golden tunic poking up from beneath my cloak. When his gaze traveled to my eyes, I could hardly tell curiosity from terror.

"There is a *person of interest* hiding in a building here in the capital," Jess threw pleasantries aside and aimed straight for the point. "Mage Dani and Ranger Rea need your help to identify the location they saw in a scrying. Once determined, I need you to provide them whatever assistance they may need to deal with the culprit."

"My Constables will help any way we can, Majesty, but may we know more about this person? What they've done? Who they are?" Cribbs asked. "Why two Melucians appeared in our capital in pursuit of this person?"

Jess looked to Atikus and me and lifted a questioning brow.

Atikus thought a moment, then nodded. "Of course. We are looking for Irina's spirit. She is currently inhabiting an elderly woman from the island of Rea Utu, a mystic of great value to their people. We saw her walking around a darkened shop or warehouse filled with candles. That is all the information we have."

Cribbs whistled as Marks sat back, his eyes wide.

"Irina's spirit? Really?" Marks asked. "And you're sure she's here?"

Jess nodded once.

"We are certain she *was* here roughly two hours before we arrived. Whether she is still in that building, or even in the capital, we do not know," Atikus said.

Marks leaned forward again. "Speaking of your arrival, I've heard some fantastic rumors today. Care to share how you made it from Saltstone to Fontaine so quickly?"

"Later, Chancellor," Jess said.

"There are only a couple places that could be," Cribbs said. "We supply most of the candles for both the Kingdom, Melucia, and some of your neighbors to the east, too. There's a large factory on the southern edge of town that handles most of the manufacturing, but there's also a large shop that makes and sells sticks only a few blocks from the Palace. Do you have any idea why she would want to go to a candle factory?"

Atikus shrugged. "No clue."

"All right, it will take a little time to gather the men and get them there. I can have teams in both locations in an hour or so. Would that work?"

Atikus looked to me.

"I think so. But Sheriff, tell your men *not* to enter either building. We believe she has an overwhelming arsenal of magic at her disposal. If we're right, she could kill your men with barely a thought," I said.

Cribbs nodded. "Meet me at the constabulary in thirty minutes. We can go over the plan and ride to the buildings together."

"Excellent. I have other meetings this afternoon. Declan, Atikus, please let Chancellor Marks know if you need anything else. The Kingdom is at your disposal." Jess stood.

Marks and Cribbs rose, bowed, and left.

Jess gave Keelan a peck on the cheek and left to begin receiving her afternoon audiences.

Atikus and I stared openmouthed at Keelan.

"The Queen just *kissed* you!" I blurted.

Keelan chuckled. "She does that a lot these days. You'll get used to it."

Then he winked at Atikus.

"This just gets stranger by the moment," I said.

Atikus grunted.

PART V

CHAPTER 51

ATIKUS

D eclan and I decided to split up so one of us could accompany each team.

If Irina really was in Fontaine, we were the only ones who could do anything about it. We also decided not to enter a building if Irina was present at either location but wait and call for the other to Travel to that location so we could fight her together. Uncertainty around just how powerful she really was, as well as fear we might only get one shot at banishing her, drove us to extra caution.

My team approached the southern warehouse, a sprawling one-story building that spanned the length of three or four moderately sized homes. The walls were stone, while the roof was an odd mix of wooden planks and thatch. Smoke filtered through the thatch and rose into the cloudless sky.

We were far enough from the center of town that there was very little traffic—foot or carriage—nearby.

A dozen Constables, shields at the ready and swords unsheathed, fanned out and surrounded the building. The men were well coordinated, their movements practiced and sure. Each remained a perfect distance from those to his left and right, encircling the building in a wide net before gradually approaching to tighten the noose.

The clanking and whooshing sounds of a working factory drifted out open windows but weren't as overpowering as the mixture of melting wax and the dozen aromatic oils used to create the candles' scents. I buried my nose in my arm and wondered how workers survived the malodorous assault each day.

A few quiet moments passed before one of the Constables appeared from the back of the building and walked unhurriedly toward Sheriff Cribbs and me.

"Sir, we looked through several windows. It's only workers inside going about their routine. Nobody matching the description."

Cribbs nodded. "All right, Sergeant. Have one of your men go inside and interview the foreman, see if anything seems amiss."

The man snapped a nod and turned to carry out the Sheriff's orders.

"These are some of my best men. If there was anything out of place, they would've noticed it. My guess is that Declan is at the right place," Cribbs said.

"I need to warn him. Give me a moment."

I closed my eyes.

It wasn't necessary, but it helped me concentrate, especially with all the sounds and odors pouring out of the factory's windows. I'd also learned over my centuries of life how a little stagecraft helped those without magic understand it better, regardless of its utility in the casting.

"Declan, she's not here. We are on our way to you."

Declan's reply was immediate. *"Understood. We're outside the shop. There are civilians everywhere. This is a busy market district and a terrible place for a magical showdown. I'm not sure we can do more than observe."*

"Keep watching. I'm coming."

I opened my eyes.

"Sheriff, we need to get over there. Declan said there are quite a few civilians around, so we might not be able to go in and confront her."

Cribbs gripped the pommel of his sword, then released it, a nervous tick I'd noticed when we first arrived at the factory. "It would be a lot better to do this at night. We can reassess after you learn whatever is there."

"I will Travel to him. Have your men follow as quickly as possible." Without any additional stagecraft, I vanished.

CHAPTER 52

DECLAN

I stood by a fruit vendor's stall across the road from the candle shop.

The shop's wooden façade was painted dusty blue. A bright yellow sign squeaked as it swung above the door. Several artistic candles of various colors proclaimed what was sold inside.

Dozens of well-dressed men and women strolled by. Some carried shopping bags or boxes, others clasped hands or wrestled children. The road lived in a state of perpetual motion, and the mood among passersby was light. On any other day, I might've enjoyed sitting and watching the people pass by, but not today.

Most who strolled by glanced at one officer, then another. Smiles fell, as curiosity over the sudden concentration of Her Majesty's Constables grew.

Atikus appeared directly behind me.

"Anything?" the Mage asked.

"Freakin' Spirits!" I exclaimed a little too loudly, drawing a few glances from Constables and citizens alike. "Can you ring a bell or warn me with a mental whisper next time? I nearly soiled my breeches."

Atikus chuckled, then lowered his voice. "Sorry, I thought you heard me pop up behind you. I guess Traveling makes no noise. You know, in all my years, I never thought about that."

"Atikus, focus." I shook my head, then looked back toward the building. "We have Constables all over the place, but there's too much foot traffic here to do anything. They can't even get close enough to look inside."

"Why not? It's a shop, isn't it? Just go inside like you're looking for some candles."

I turned and stared at the Mage. "Well, I feel stupid."

Atikus grinned and shrugged his bushy brows. "See how focused I am?"

Unable to ignore his jab, I said, "I would send you in there. Who'd suspect a frail old man?"

He poked my arm with a bony finger.

"You scream Mage walking around in that robe anyway," I said. "My riding leathers aren't as high-brow as most of these shoppers, but they're better than a Constable's uniform or your robe for remaining undetected."

Atikus grunted. "Just be careful. Try not to use any magic while you're in there. She might be able to sense it. I know it makes the hairs on my arms stand up whenever you do anything powerful."

I nodded, then turned, wove my way through the passing throng, and approached the shop.

Bells tinkled merrily as I entered.

The door clicked shut behind me.

CHAPTER 53

IRINA

Two hours earlier (island time)

In a moment of sheer terror, as the Well began to blacken, its cavern darkened, and the mountain shook with anger, I closed my eyes and focused on the safety of home. The magic coursing through me responded, understanding my need, and I Traveled instantly. I was bewildered when I appeared in the storeroom of a candle shop. Several sticks dangling from lines strung across the ceiling clattered and smacked me in the head as I fought to gather my bearings.

A stream of questions flowed through my mind.

I was thinking of *home* when I Traveled; but that home, where I was born and raised by loving parents, and where those same parents were murdered, couldn't still stand. That home had not existed for ten centuries.

So where had magic delivered me?

The room spun, and nausea threatened from the depths of my stomach.

I forced myself to calm.

There was no mountain about to crash down on me, so this was an improvement. I needed time to think and sort everything out.

I started by surveying the musty room.

A sliver of light trickled in from the partially covered window.

I ran a hand across the candles that assaulted me when I first arrived. The ancient, weathered look of the back of my own hand gave me a moment's pause. I used to be so young and beautiful. Now, I wore the skin of an aged woman who would have passed through Death's Door years ago had she not been protected by her island's magic.

I longed for a day when men would turn as I entered a room, would stumble over themselves if I glanced their way, a day when I was wanted and desired. I closed my eyes and recalled my silky-smooth skin and lustrous black hair, my brilliant green eyes.

Then I sighed.

I had lost so much from my imprisonment.

When my attention returned to the candles above, and my fingers continued their journey, I was astonished for the second time in an hour.

Smooth, supple skin replaced the wrinkles.

My hand flew to my face, and I felt the same smoothness of youth I saw on my hands.

Had my magic answered my call again?

How was this . . . ?

On a whim, I held my palm before me and called moisture from the air, forming a swirling, wobbling ball of water. I gasped, and the ball fell apart, spilling on the dusty wooden floor.

That is not one of my Gifts. I have never been able to call or manipulate water.

My head spun at the implications.

Something had happened to me at the Well.

Far beyond taking revenge and breaking that wretched place apart, *my true magic*, the magic of my youth, had returned. I was powerful again, invincible so long as that blasted Phoenix stayed dead.

The boy who fought me—the one with Kelså—was powerful, too; but I saw him fall into the Well, dragged under the sickened waves with that witch.

Now, I was the last living Mage, the only *true* Mage left.

A wave of euphoria washed away the prior moment's nausea as I realized I could do anything, *be* anything.

I could *rule* the Kingdom.

Spirits, I could rule them all.

That had been my goal all those years ago, and now I could accomplish it.

The only question was, did I want it? Destroying my enemies was so much more satisfying than ruling feckless, needy people. As Empress, I had to pretend to listen, pretend to care what people thought.

How tedious.

I would have to think on that.

I shook myself out of those thoughts and returned to cataloguing my present situation.

I stood in a storeroom.

By the combative wax sticks dangling above, I guessed it belonged to a candle maker's shop. On the wall with a window, several barrels stood stacked on one another, likely ingredients for the maker's craft. On the opposite wall sat a small writing desk littered with parchment.

I crossed the room and scanned a few sheets. Most were invoices or inventory tallies, even a few personal letters. I set the last of the letters down, careful to place it exactly as I found it.

Satisfied there was nothing of interest in the room, I crept to the door and peered onto the large sales floor.

The shop was still.

The counter stood empty.

I thought it odd for the owner to be absent in the middle of the day, but customs of this time might differ from my day.

Or maybe the maker had gone out for lunch or to run errands.

I really didn't care.

I stepped into the sea of tables and candles and surveyed the room.

Nothing jumped out until I stepped toward the front door. Pinned to the wall where exiting patrons would see it was a flyer. I reached up and plucked it off the wall. Local Priests were holding a meeting to support their efforts in the city later that week. A hand-drawn sketch of a man in long robes was pictured to the side of the lettering.

The flyer proclaimed, "The day is coming soon. The One shall return, and the faithful shall take their rightful place by his side."

I stopped reading as realization crashed into me.

The room shrank.

Anger bubbled and boiled inside me.

Danai, that bastard! He stole my *prophecy.*

That conniving, thieving snake.

In that moment, I knew my goal was not to rule.

I needed no crown.
I wanted one thing, and only one thing.
I wanted *vengeance*.

CHAPTER 54

DECLAN

The door clicked shut, and I looked around.

A tall woman with silky black hair trailing down to her waist stood glaring at a parchment in her hand. Despite the tinkling of the bells, she hadn't seemed to notice me.

And then she looked up.

Our eyes met.

I had forgotten about my eyes and their swirling magic.

She *knew* me.

I saw it in her gaze, the recognition, the flash of anger and hatred.

Before I could think, a wall of air blasted me into the back of the heavy wooden door.

I lost my footing and landed on my rear.

Dazed, I looked up at the woman. Venom and hatred glared back.

Then she vanished, and the crinkled parchment she held drifted to the floor.

I climbed to my feet and stared at where the woman had stood a moment before. I threw up a shield of air in case she returned, then took a couple of tentative steps forward, scanning the area.

My head swam a moment before settling.

The door squealed as it flew open, and two uniformed Constables entered with swords drawn. "Are you alright, sir? We heard the crash and thought you might be in trouble."

I released my shield and turned to the men. "I'm fine. The shop is empty. The woman got away."

"How?" The men glanced at each other. "We have the place surrounded. There's nowhere for her to go."

"Officers, would you get the High Sheriff, please. We will explain everything once he arrives," Atikus, stepping into the shop, answered before I could say a word.

I kneeled and retrieved the parchment Irina dropped as she vanished. I held it up and turned to say something, but Atikus silenced me with a mental note. *"Not until we're alone."*

The moment the door closed behind the Constables, I stepped forward and handed the flyer to

Atikus. "I'm not sure if this is relevant to finding her, but she was reading this when I walked in. I caught her crumpling it up. She looked angry . . . well, angrier than her usual pissedoffness."

"Pissedoffness?" Atikus harrumphed, then skimmed the flyer. "The Order again. Seems like they are in the middle of everything these days. When we see the Sheriff, I will ask him to assign some men to sniff around."

He rolled up the flyer and shoved it into his robe. "Now, tell me what happened."

I recounted the brief encounter with the woman I presumed was Irina. When I described her hair and eyes, Atikus nodded. "That's her. She used her magic to change her appearance back to how she looked before. If I understand the mechanics, that is akin to Illusion, and not a true transformation. She should still be inhabiting Larinda's body, which means the physical limitations of an old woman still work to our advantage."

"Maybe. She's a magically enhanced old woman. She tossed me back like I was nothing."

"Her magic is powerful, but she caught you by surprise. In a fight you knew was coming, I doubt she could do that without you having time to shield yourself." He smoothed his beard as he thought. "Using magic takes a physical and mental toll. That is its price. Larinda's constitution is robust, but she is still ancient. Without the magic of Rea Utu to restore her health, her body will fail."

"You're already planning our confrontation, aren't you?"

Atikus nodded. "We will need to get this right when the time comes. If we can keep her contained and throwing her magic around long enough, she will wear her body out. It should be like watching a flame flutter and go out. We should then be able to banish her without her power resisting us."

"We just have to survive her attacks long enough while keeping her contained somehow. Sounds easy enough." I tried not to roll my eyes again. And failed.

"This was never going to be easy, but that is the best idea I have at the moment. You are welcome to come up with a better plan."

"Oh, no. I'm a Ranger, not a tactician. I'll be the hammer; you be the brains."

Atikus laughed. "Finally, you recognize my mental prowess and your . . . well . . . *other* abilities."

"Thanks a lot, I think." I smirked. "Let's go see the Sheriff."

We made it a dozen paces out of the candle shop before a uniformed officer approached with a message from Sheriff Cribbs asking us to join him at the Palace. There were developments, and the Queen wanted us to be part of his briefing. After a short walk, we passed through the golden doors of the audience chamber and were greeted by Jess, Keelan, Cribbs, and Marks, who were all seated around the Council table.

Heavily armed guards stood everywhere.

One towered quietly along the wall behind the throne, ten paces from the next.

Four additional guards stood near the Council table, two on either side of Jess's chair.

Keelan noticed my eyes widen as I scanned the room.

"There was an incident here at the Palace. Security has increased," he said without explanation. His eyes were hard, and his mouth was set in a grim line.

Jess stood and greeted us, then motioned to empty seats.

"Sheriff, we should hear from Declan and Atikus. You can brief everyone on the Oliver situation after," Jess said.

Atikus took the lead, bringing everyone up to speed on our actions at the two candle shops. I remained silent until he cocked a bushy brow, his not-so-subtle indication for me to help to fill in details. As we concluded, Atikus withdrew the flyer from his robe and handed it to Cribbs.

"This is all we have to go on at the moment. We are not even sure it is connected to anything," Atikus said.

Cribbs glanced at the parchment and handed it to Jess.

"These are all over town, Majesty. Nothing unusual there," Marks said, leaning over the table before settling back into his seat.

Jess set the flyer down and turned to Cribbs. "If there is nothing else there, Sheriff, it is your turn."

"We received a bird from the constabulary in Oliver. Unfortunately, the scrolls are tiny, so our information is limited. I'll just read it to you."

Another murder. Witness saw large brown bear maul victim. Witness watched bear don mask and change into man following killing. Man wore brown robes. – FL

Cribbs tossed the scroll onto the table. "Majesty, without speaking with my officer or the witness, I have no way of affirming the veracity of the claim. This could be a drunk who saw nothing, or something far more troublesome."

"He's right. The message doesn't give us enough to go on," Keelan said, clearly in his element discussing a criminal investigation.

"We have—" I started.

Keelan cut me off. "What we *do* have is a pattern. First, the Order shows up trying to strong-arm the Queen. Then murders begin, but only one in each city or town, each committed by an animal.

"Has anyone here ever heard of such a wave of murderous beasts within such a brief window?"

I watched as everyone considered his words.

"Then the Queen is attacked by a horse who shifted into a man after he was killed—a man wearing brown robes," he continued. "Now, another animal attack, this time with a witness who saw the live assailant shift back into his human form and walk away from the scene—again, wearing brown robes.

"Your Majesty," he said, turning to Jess. "We cannot act on supposition, but it should guide the next steps in our investigation."

She stared at him for a long moment. "Go on. What are you proposing?"

He looked toward Cribbs. "I need to go back to Oliver to interview this witness and the officers, confirm whether or not the story is credible. While

I'm there, Atikus and the Sheriff should continue working toward locating Irina."

Jess leaned back and crossed her arms.

"It's a three- or four-day ride. By the time you get there, do the interviews, and get back, who knows where Irina will be or what she'll have been up to." Cribbs mirrored his Queen, crossing his arms.

I leaned forward and cleared my throat. "I can help with that. Using my magic, I'll take Keelan to Oliver, then bring him back. Your four days will be a blink if we Travel, and Atikus and I can coordinate using Telepathy. Now that we both have that ability, we can conduct a two-way conversation."

"I like it," Atikus said. "Jess—I mean, Your Majesty, do you think your Mages would be willing to help? I could use some extra minds thinking this through."

"Chancellor, summon Mage Ernest to the Palace," she said to Marks before turning back to me. "Ernest is sharp and a good man. You will like him. He can get whoever you need involved." She leaned forward and placed her palms on the table as if to rise. "Are we agreed? Anything else?"

Everyone looked around at each other, but no one spoke.

"Fine." She stood and turned, then looked back at me. "Ranger Rea, please keep Keelan out of trouble."

I shot Keelan a startled glance.

Keelan returned a lopsided, boyish grin.

Jess rolled her eyes and strode out.

I gripped Keelan's arm. "You may be a little dizzy when we get there. It'll pass in ten or fifteen minutes. Now, picture the area just outside the inn's front door in your mind—as detailed as you can."

Keelan nodded and closed his eyes. When he opened them, he looked at me.

And then he threw up all over my trousers.

"Aw, really? You couldn't hold on for just a minute?" I groaned. "Are those chunks of apple? Ugh."

"Sorry, but if you'd just stand still—" And he threw up again.

I walked my pale brother to the front of the inn and sat him on the ground.

"As big as you are, I thought you might be able to handle that better. Just sit there until the nausea passes. I'm going to find somewhere to clean up."

Keelan didn't look up. He just raised a hand in acknowledgement and let his head loll forward. I disappeared into the inn, returning several minutes later with somewhat cleaner trousers and a serving boy named Liam in tow.

"Lieutenant?" Liam said from behind me. "Didn't you just leave us?"

Liam kneeled down and helped Keelan drink some water from the mug he'd brought out.

"It's a long story," I said. "We need to see your Sheriff, or whatever you call the head Constable in the town."

"That would be Chief Kerr. He's a few streets over. When the Lieutenant is back on his feet, I'll take you there. It's right on my way to the market."

Keelan looked up, focus slowly returning to his eyes. "Thank you. I should be all right in a minute."

It took another twenty minutes for Keelan to stand without wobbling, then another ten to reach the Constabulary, but we made it. We thanked Liam and entered the building.

"Ah, Keelan, come in." Chief Kerr rose from behind a heavy wooden desk in the back of the one-room space to greet us. Four other desks faced the door from various points in the room. Two were occupied by green-uniformed officers.

We settled into a pair of simple wooden chairs opposite the Chief's desk and were handed mugs of steaming tea.

"Chief, this is my brother, Declan. When we get into what we have to tell you, you'll understand why he's here. Would it be possible for us to have some privacy as we talk?"

Kerr quirked a brow, but before he could ask his officers to leave, I held up a hand. "No need to send your men out, Chief. I'll silence the room so only the three of us can hear our conversation. There, done."

Kerr's eyes widened. "How—"

He looked up at one of his men working at a desk across the room. "Edward. Hey, Edward!"

The man didn't flinch, just kept scribbling on a parchment.

"No one's Gifts are working. They haven't for a bit. How did you do that?"

Keelan leaned forward and whispered, despite my magic barrier guarding our words, "There's a lot going on, and we're neck deep in it. We can't talk about parts of the investigation, but what brought us here may be the key to securing the new Queen's throne from danger."

The lawman leaned back and whistled. "The Queen? Really?"

Keelan nodded, then launched into his prepared explanation detailing what we knew about the attacks in the other cities and the one on the Queen. He left out the whole Irina-has-returned side of the investigation.

"And now you want to know more about the bird we sent, about that last killing?"

Keelan nodded again. "That's right. As crazy as it sounds, your witness's story fills in a lot of holes for us."

"Crazy is right, but explain something to me. Why would the Order and their Priests do something like this? Most of the people have come to love the Priests. Those who don't at least respect the work they're doing. Why go after the Queen—or any of these people, for that matter?"

"We're hoping your witness, or someone in town who knew the victim, can help us with that. We might also want to talk again with anyone who knew your first victim, Hershel."

"That's right. Town was torn up over his death, now one of his best friends gets killed. It's just too much."

Keelan's eyes narrowed. "One of his best friends? The victims knew each other?"

"That's right." Kerr nodded. "You think there's a connection?"

"I don't know, but it's another piece, and there's been too many pieces showing up for them not to paint a picture at some point."

"All right, where do you want to start?"

Keelan thought a moment. "Right here. I'd like to talk with your officers who dealt with the latest killing first. Then we can move on to witnesses and acquaintances."

Kerr gave a smile that didn't reach his eyes. "Solid plan. I'm starting to see why you're Melucia's famous top cop now."

"Not sure I deserve all that." Keelan shrugged. "I'm just trying to protect people best I can. Who should we start with?"

Kerr pointed to several uniformed men. "Take your pick."

The Constables were friendly and helpful, offering detailed accounts of their investigations and interviews, all of which resulted in more questions than answers. Keelan thanked them, and we moved on to a witness list the Chief provided us, complete with locations and directions.

"Wait," Keelan said as he read through the list. "Liam? Is that the same Liam who works at the inn?"

"And the same Liam who's Hershel's son. That's right," Kerr confirmed.

"Huh," was all Keelan said.

Kerr offered to accompany us as we left the constabulary, but Keelan waved him off, and we made our way to the first name on the list.

Four hours later, Keelan and I were down to the last name: Liam.

As we strode toward the inn, Keelan turned toward me. "Did you sense anything from those people we just talked to?"

I cocked a brow. "Sense anything? What do you mean?"

"You know, feel anything strange? Get a tingling sensation, say, between your shoulder blades?"

"Are you feeling woozy again? That's the strangest thing I've heard all day—and we're arse deep in strange already."

Keelan grunted a chuckle. "I'm talking about sensing truth, like I could do before the Gifts vanished. You remember my bees? How they'd sting just below my neck? You teased me *for years* about calling it that. That only happened when somebody was hiding something or lying."

"Oh, that?" I paused and thought through the conversations we'd just completed. "No, nothing jumps out. That one guy, the butcher, wasn't very talkative, but I didn't get any tingly magic alarm or anything. I'm pretty sure I would've noticed a hive attacking me."

"Nice. Keep rubbing it in." Keelan smirked. "I thought the same about that guy. Maybe we should pay him another visit before we leave. For now, just pay attention when we talk to Liam. I've got a feeling—"

"All right, I'll keep an eye—or a neck—out for the bees," I quipped, earning a brotherly punch in the arm.

A short time later, we sat at one of the round wooden tables in the common room of the inn. Liam stared across, fingers fidgeting.

"I know it sounds crazy, but I swear that's what I saw. The bear reached down to the ground, grabbed a mask, put it on, and turned into a man, then walked away into the night. I was hiding behind the apothecary not twenty paces away."

Keelan looked to me, then nudged me with his foot.

"Uh, okay. It does sound crazy, but I believe you're telling us what you think you saw."

"I *saw* it. It's not what I think. Don't you call me nuts, too. I deal with that enough around here already. The whole thing was supposed to be kept secret, but it's all anybody's talking about." He put his head in his hands as if to cry.

"I know this is hard, but what you're telling us is important," Keelan tried to reassure him. "The bear put on a mask and turned into a man. What did that man look like?"

Liam looked up slowly, his lips pursed as he tried to remember. "It was dark, but I could see he wore robes. The moonlight reflected or shimmered off them as he walked away. I never saw his face, but he had short hair. I think it was brown or black."

"Was he tall or short? What was his build like?"

"It was hard to tell. He was so big as the bear, then he shrunk down. I guess he was average height, maybe a little taller. His robes were flowy, so I couldn't really tell anything about his body."

Keelan watched him fidget, then asked, "Liam, what aren't you telling us? I can see you're holding something back."

He looked up. "I've told you everything I know, everything I saw."

"But not something you suspect?" Keelan guessed.

"How—?" His eyes widened, then he looked back to his hands.

Keelan decided to go in a different direction. "How well do you know the local Priest?"

Liam's head snapped up. "Seth? Pretty well, I guess."

I leaned forward and gave Keelan a meaningful look.

"What's he like?"

Liam sat up straight and crossed his arms. "He's a *good* man who helps people. What more do you want to know?"

"Easy." Keelan raised a palm. "We're not accusing him of anything, just trying to get to know the people in town. I've been an investigator for years, and you never know what tiny clue might help crack a case."

Liam's arms unfurled, and his hands dropped back to his lap, clutched tightly. A far-away look came over his eyes as he remembered and spoke. "Seth and I started seeing each other a few months after he came to town. He visits in the morning as we're getting ready for the breakfast crowd. We have dinner a few times each week and take long walks around town. He's even helped me with my market runs a few times. Like I said, he's a wonderful man."

"What can you tell us about his work with his faith?"

He beamed at this. "He helps more people than anyone I've ever known. He says it's why the Spirits called him to the Order, to help those who can't help themselves. Poor, lame, sick, old, it doesn't matter to him. He does whatever they need, whatever he can."

"How does he spread the word about his faith? Does he hold meetings in a Temple, or speak somewhere?" Keelan asked.

"Oh, yes, he holds meetings a couple times each week in the town square. There isn't a Temple here, so he stands on the steps of the courtyard and folks gather around. Most folks make at least one of his meetings each week."

"I assume you attend these meetings?"

Laim nodded. "I don't miss many. I like seeing him talk, watching how the people react to his message of kindness and generosity."

Keelan sat back in his chair and tapped his forefinger on the table as he thought.

I leaned in. "Liam, I'm not a Constable, just a Ranger. We take care of animals and trees mostly. Keelan and I haven't seen each other in a while, and I thought traveling together might give us time to reconnect."

He smiled tentatively, clearly unsure where I was headed. "That sounds . . . nice."

"It has been, except for him throwing up on me, of course." I smiled innocently. "But I've listened to most of his conversations today, and something you said tickled my neck. Can you go back to before you left on your walk that night, the one where you saw the bear? You said you saw the man who was killed lingering at a table, chatting with some other man. Could you hear anything? See anything?"

He scrunched his mouth in concentration. "I tried to listen in. They seemed so secretive. It made me curious, but they were whispering most of the time. It didn't make any sense, but I think they said something like, 'This has to end,' like they were planning something. I'm sorry, I really couldn't hear them."

Silence lingered before Keelan leaned forward. "I only have a couple more questions."

Liam nodded.

"What does Seth wear? Does he have a uniform or some symbol of office? As a Priest, I mean."

"He wears his robe," he said.

"Long, brown, shimmers in the light?"

He sucked in a breath and nodded, then looked down.

Keelan waited.

"I . . . It can't . . . He wouldn't hurt *anyone*. I know Seth."

Keelan tapped his finger on the table. Even I shifted in my seat before the silence was broken.

Liam whispered without raising his head. "I don't know. I can't believe Seth would do anything—would *be* that."

"It might not be him, but we need to find out. No one in town will be safe until we do." Keelan rose. "Thank you, Liam. I know this was difficult, but you've been very helpful."

He shot to his feet. "What are you going to do? Please don't hurt him."

Keelan put up his palms again. "We're just investigating. Hopefully, the facts rule him out, but we have to follow them, not decide what we want them to be."

Liam's head drooped again. "I know you're right. This is all so terrible."

I stepped forward. "It is, but we're here to help."

He nodded in thanks and gave me a weak smile.

"We need you to keep this conversation between us for now, okay. Whoever killed that man—*and your father*—wouldn't take well to a witness walking around."

Liam nodded and walked us to the door.

"We'll check on you later tonight, all right?" Keelan said as we exited.

We stepped outside, and Keelan asked me to shield our conversation like I'd done in the constabulary.

I nodded once, then Keelan asked, "What do you think of his story?"

"Something was nagging at me about the victim's conversation that night, but everything else lines up with what we already knew. I couldn't feel anything false from Liam. He's dating the Priest, but he didn't rule out him being the bear-shifter-thing, whatever you call it."

"Let's go with *bear* for now. If we're overheard somewhere, it'll raise less suspicion in the community," Keelan said. "I agree with you on him being honest. He didn't want to make his suspicions real by talking about them but opened up when pressed. I believe him. Now we need a way to rule Seth out."

"We could just ask him," I said.

Keelan laughed, then looked up. "You're not joking, are you?"

I shook my head. "No joke. Remember, I have your Truthreading Gift now. If we ask him and he lies, I'll know. Bam! Bear trap."

Keelan groaned. "Now he jokes."

I laughed and gave my brother a playful shove. "You missed me. Admit it."

Keelan chuckled and shook his head. "Let's go *bear hunting*, little brother."

We found Seth playing with a group of children at the edge of the market square. I had a hard time picturing the man as a menacing bear as he ran in circles with three-year-olds dangling from his legs and laughing hysterically.

After a moment, the Priest noticed us watching and forced the children to set him free so he could greet the newcomers.

"Hello, gentlemen. Were you hoping to be the hunter or the prey today?" Seth asked with a broad smile.

Keelan stiffened, but I laughed.

"He means with the children, dummy," I whispered in Keelan's mind.

Keelan shook off the odd sensation of having me inside his head and nodded toward the Priest. "Forgive us for interrupting, Seth. Looks like you had a real fight on your hands. This is my brother, Declan. Mind if we ask you a few questions?"

"Of course not. How can I help?"

Keelan motioned for us to step out of earshot of the children and the woman tending them. I nodded, indicating the silencing shield had been erected once more. Seth looked at Keelan.

"Have you ever heard of a man who could turn into an animal?" Keelan asked without preamble.

Seth rocked back and barked a laugh. When we continued glaring, he sobered. "You're serious?"

Keelan waited, his eyes never leaving Seth's.

"Only in children's tales."

"What about within your Order? Are there *tales* of men with this ability?"

Seth's brow furrowed. "I've never heard of such. Where is this coming from, Keelan? Why are you asking *me* these questions? And what would the Order have to do with something so horrific?"

Keelan watched him a moment, then sighed. "I'm sorry, Seth. We're following leads found at the scene of the mauling. Some are disturbing and make little sense, but they're all we have."

I spoke. "I think we have everything we need. Thank you for your time."

Keelan gave me a questioning look, but I motioned for us to leave.

"We may have more questions later, if that's all right," Keelan said.

"Of course," Seth said. "You don't think the people here are in any danger, do you?"

"We think the bear fled after the attack and hope that's the last we see of him," Keelan answered.

We had made it around the block when I turned to Keelan. "He's telling the truth. He had no idea what you were talking about when you mentioned a man turning into an animal. The shock on his face was real."

"I could tell that *without* magic. He would've been the best liar I'd ever met otherwise."

"What now? That really was the best lead we had."

Keelan rubbed his chin. "I guess we let Liam know his man is innocent, then head back to Fontaine."

CHAPTER 55

KEELAN

I staggered forward as we Traveled back to the Palace.

I took two steadying steps, then threw up all over the audience chamber floor.

"Well, that is a first during my reign." Jess raised a brow from her seat at the Council table.

Chancellor Marks, Sheriff Cribbs, and Atikus turned.

Declan grinned back at our audience and bowed. "My carriage rides are a tad bumpy for the uninitiated."

I retched again.

A servant standing in the shadows rushed forward, curtsied, and vanished, returning a moment later with two others, a bucket, and a mop.

I stumbled to the bottom step leading to the throne and sat with my head in my hands. I was certain my face glowed a putrid shade of green.

Declan stepped up and placed a palm to my forehead. Light exploded from his hand, then winked out.

I looked up with wide eyes. "The nausea's . . . gone," I exclaimed. I scrunched up my face at my brother. "You could've done that all along, couldn't you?"

Declan grinned and shrugged. "Honestly, I didn't think of it until now. That's the first time I've used Healing since gaining all these new powers, but I did owe you for ruining my breeches."

I gave Declan one last annoyed glance before attempting to stand, surprised how solid the ground now felt under my feet. Declan and I took our seats and joined the Queen's meeting.

"Atikus was just about to tell us of the scrying he did with our Mages, but I think we should hear from you two first." Jess turned to me and gave me a hint of a smile. It felt like my insides were jelly again, this time nothing—and everything—like my nausea from before.

My return smile was far more than a hint.

Declan grinned.

The others shifted in their seats.

"Your Majesty," I began. "Most of the interviews were fruitless. However, we spent a good amount of time with the witness to the latest killing. He is familiar with the robes of the Priests and is convinced the killer wore those same robes when he resumed his human form."

"The Order again." Jess strummed her fingers so hard her knuckles whitened.

I cleared my throat and continued. "We also questioned the local Priest. By all accounts, he is well respected throughout the town. We found no evidence he knew anything of the killer or anyone else in the Order with the ability to shift. Among Declan's new abilities, he can Truthread."

I looked to my brother and tried to keep the bitterness from my voice. The idea of turning to someone else, someone who wielded my Gift, was almost more than I could bear.

Declan eyed me a moment before responding. "I sensed no lies, nor did I find either of them to be hiding information. They were both forthright and credible."

Cribbs leaned forward and shook his head. "Incredible. I was certain this was a talk of a drunk or mad woman."

"I was, too, until we met him and the Priest," Declan said.

"Did you find anything else, a motive, anything connecting the Order to the killings?" Marks asked.

I shook my head. "No, nothing. The witness recalled seeing the victim talking in hushed tones with another man at the local inn a few hours before he was killed, but he only overheard a few random phrases, nothing that made any sense."

"What did he hear?" Cribbs asked, quill in hand.

"Something like, 'This has to end,' he thought. He wasn't completely sure and had no idea of the context."

Cribbs scribbled a note. "What would they be plotting about that could cause one of them to be killed? Oliver is a small town, but they enjoy healthy trade from both the ocean and roads. There hasn't been a serious crime like murder or kidnapping there in years. What changed?"

Declan opened his mouth to speak, then stopped.

"What? No holding back at this table," Jess said.

"It's just ... the Priest. I know we're already wary of them, and I don't want to jump to conclusions because of that, but he showed up, what, five or six months ago?" Declan asked.

"Right, but you heard Liam. He's basically the town saint," I said.

"If they can shift into murderous animals, they can fool us into thinking they're good people."

"What about preaching against the Crown? Did you hear any more about that?" Marks asked.

I shook my head. "Not really. A few of the people we interviewed said they'd heard the Priest talk about unifying under the One, but they thought he meant as an addition or support to the Crown, nothing like rebellion."

Silence lingered a moment as our report sank in, then Jess spoke. "Thank you both for going down there so quickly. Atikus, would you tell us what you and the Mages found?"

The old Mage leaned forward. "Mage Ernest suggested we scry for Irina using the crumpled flyer she was holding before she vanished. It had only been a couple of hours since she possessed it, so he hoped we might get a reading. If we had waited another few hours, it would not have worked at all." He paused and took a sip of water. "We are now certain she Traveled to Irina's Seat. The image in the scrying bowl was the Children's stone Temple in that village."

I sat back and scratched at my scalp. "Irina's Seat? I hoped to never see that place again."

Jess muttered. "That makes two of us."

Declan cocked his head. "Atikus, what aren't you telling us? I can sense you're holding something back."

"Bees get ya?" I asked with a smirk.

"Shut it," Declan said with a grin of his own.

Atikus looked between us and shook his head. "I thought of something while you were talking about your trip to Oliver, but it may be too crazy, even for this situation."

"I doubt this could get any stranger. Let's hear it," Declan prodded.

"Well, the flyer referenced an upcoming meeting the local Priest was holding."

"Right," Declan said.

"It highlighted a message about the Return of the One. We always assumed that ancient prophecy referred to *Irina's* return. What if this One is using her prophecy for their own gain? How do you think she would react when she learned that her legacy was stolen?"

"She would want to rip their eyes out," Jess spat.

Atikus nodded. "She just Traveled to Irina's Seat, and Declan, the last person to see her before she went there, said she looked angry as she read the flyer."

"Holy Spirits. That makes sense," I exclaimed. "Dec, Atikus, we need to go there right now. We may not get a better shot at her."

"Woah. Hold on, big brother. Remind me what magic you have to fight an all-powerful, wildly angry sorceress."

I glared a moment, then deflated. "Fair point, I guess."

"Atikus and I are the only ones who stand any chance of banishing her once and for all. I hope she really is the only other person with magic. If she were to team up with this One and they both had power, it might be more than we could handle."

Atikus grunted. "That is true, but we have to try. Keelan might not be able to join us, but he was right about not missing this chance. We need to go quickly."

No one objected as all eyes shifted toward Jess.

She stared into table for a long moment, then nodded.

Everyone wished Declan and Atikus well, and the pair vanished.

The Councilors retired for the evening, offering bows to Jess and polite nods to me.

"I hope we did the right thing sending them," Jess said as she and I stood alone—save for her guards—in the Throne Room.

I wrapped my arms around her and held her close.

"Me too," I whispered into her neck. "They're the only family I have left."

CHAPTER 56

IRINA

D anai sat on *my* throne.

Two Priests kneeled before him.

None of them noticed my sudden appearance in a darkened corner of the hall.

"Excellency, there was no way to know the boy was watching. I checked the area before killing the man, and it was empty." The kneeling Priest sounded terrified, even from where I listened.

Danai leaned forward and sneered. "And yet he was there, watching you. He reported everything to the Crown, you idiot!"

The second figure, a woman with a high-pitched voice made shriller by Danai's wrath, spoke. "Excellency, if the four of us who remain approached the Palace at the same time—"

"Stop!" Danai raised a palm and glared down as the woman threw her head to the stone floor. "You want me to send you back to the Palace? After the Horse's failure with the Queen and your inexcusable negligence in Oliver? The Queen's guards will be more alert now than during the fucking war."

"But Excellency—"

"Silence!" he bellowed. "You will go nowhere near her. It is more likely you would be killed—and, as *displeased* as I am at the moment, you are far too useful to die—*yet*."

My blood boiled watching Danai act as though he ruled the world.

Then I realized he was wearing *my* crown.

I held my palms before me and called a ball of flame into one, while water mixed with air appeared above the other. With a thought, I froze the water solid, creating a spiked ball similar to those I recalled seeing on the end of mace's chain. I threw my palms forward and urged my missiles into the air, then drew more air and shoved it behind them, propelling them faster and faster.

The ball of ice struck first, slamming into the back of the Priest's head with a sickening crunch that echoed throughout the chamber and splattered blood and skull fragments all over the woman and the floor. The man's body lurched forward and splayed across the cold stone.

The fire didn't strike the woman as much as it engulfed her the moment it touched her skin, clawing until her entire form was covered in writhing flame. Her robe blazed as she screamed in agony. She managed to stand and run several paces before the flames overcame her. She toppled to the marble, a burning, billowing pile of unrecognizable flesh, dead before she hit the ground.

The stench made me want to flee—*nearly*.

Danai shot to his feet.

His eyes were wide, but he paused only a second.

His gaze followed the line traveled by my missiles, and he locked onto my stare with a hate-filled scowl of his own.

One of the bloody diamonds on the crown flared as he called Enhanced Strength and hurled a heavy silver pitcher across the hall.

I ducked behind a column.

That split second gave Danai time to prepare another attack.

He gripped the silver staff that leaned against the throne as another diamond flared. A column of flame taller than Danai erupted a few feet from where I stood. It inched toward me, expanding, curving at its ends as if to embrace my whole being.

In all my centuries, I had never seen a wall of flame.

My heart lurched as panic seized my chest and heat swelled around me.

The flames forced me into the corner of the chamber and began to nip at the edges of my dress.

I called as much moisture from the air as I could hold and hurled it outward.

The flame wall sizzled and dimmed but would not be stopped by mere water.

It pressed forward.

Then I remembered I had far more than my simple Gifts.

I Traveled the length of the room, away from the flame, and immediately in front of Danai.

He leaped back.

But he was so startled by my sudden appearance that he tripped over the bottom step of the dais.

I shot forward and drove my own Enhanced punch into his gut.

He crumpled and clutched his stomach, gasping for breath.

I called fire again and hurled it into the fetal form curled before me, engulfing him.

Danai writhed, but a third diamond flared, and he Healed himself as quickly as he burned. Shimmering light flared from the length of the staff, and the flames surrounding his body turned from hues of auburn, golden, and scarlet to a translucent azure.

He rose, a man still consumed in flames, yet unburned.

Now I staggered back, horror and shock streaking through me.

Danai gripped my arm.

Angry flames clawed at my skin.

They crawled up my shoulder and seared away the fabric on my back.

I screamed in pain and rage, cast my own Healing, then hurled a gust of wind at Danai's head.

The spear of air sailed wide.

Standing not two paces away, I missed.

Danai laughed.

But I used that split second to my advantage. At the clanking of metal on marble, and his mirth froze.

"Looking for something?" I asked from behind as I bent and retrieved the crown.

He whirled around to find me leaning casually against the throne.

He howled and tried to step forward, but the flames still raging across his body, once again the colors of the rising sun, were now free to burn and destroy.

The staff clanged loudly as it tumbled down the steps of the dais.

Me holding *his* crown was the last thing he saw before darkness took him.

CHAPTER 57

DECLAN

A tikus and I appeared on the balcony above the ceremonial chamber. It was just as Keelan had described: well above the central hall with a banister that obscured the view of those below. I was relieved we hadn't Traveled ourselves into one of the pillars or walls since neither of us had ever seen the inside of the place.

A man shouted below, sounding arrogant and angry.

I snuck a peek over the railing.

"There are three people down there. One on a throne wearing a crown and two kneeling in front of him. The two on the floor are wearing robes and masks," I whispered in Atikus's mind.

Before Atikus could respond, a bright flare lit up the far end of the hall. We watched as the echo of its light streaked the length of the aisle, then struck something.

Sounds erupted a heartbeat after the light blazed.

The sickening sound like a melon splattering against a wall.

A blood-chilling scream that lingered before dwindling to nothing.

The maddened screech of a woman in the throes of her own wrath.

Atikus and I braved another glance and stared, transfixed.

Blood and gore splattered across the polished marble before the dais.

Smoke curled from what must have been a body moments earlier.

A man in a black coat held a crown, his eyes fixed on a point at the far end of the chamber. I followed his gaze, and my throat clenched.

"Irina's down there. She just ducked behind a column," I said without turning.

"What the—" Atikus startled as he ducked behind the banister.

Another battle erupted below.

I was at once sickened and fascinated.

"Should we attack now while he's distracting her?" I asked.

"No, let him wear her down. Whoever survives will be weaker when they face us."

When the man fell and Irina stood with the crown in her hand, Atikus rose to a crouch. *"Now it's time. You go to the right side; I'll take the left. Hit her with everything you've got."*

CHAPTER 58

IRINA

Danai's carcass smoldered.

The ungrateful thorn had festered beneath my skin for a thousand years.

I was free.

I looked down at the crown in my hand, *my* crown.

The diamonds pulsed their steady rhythm, as if welcoming their mistress home. I grinned and placed the golden band carefully on my head.

A wave of white-hot power rippled through my body.

I turned to exit the chamber, eager to walk the halls of my former home once more, when the sound of leather slapping against marble snapped my head around.

The man *from the candle shop* stood twenty paces to the side of the dais, the *same* man who'd attacked me at the Well. While his appearance startled me, it wasn't the man himself or his strangely swirling eyes that drew my attention most; it was the solid-gold tunic emblazoned with the Phoenix on his chest that arrested my breath.

It glowed brighter than the fire I'd just thrown at Danai.

The man took a step forward and threw out a hand.

I threw up a shield of air.

The man's attack pressed me backward but couldn't penetrate my defenses.

Then I heard something behind me.

I chanced a glance over my shoulder as an old man raised his arms.

The massive throne rose from the dais and hurtled toward me. It cast a mighty shadow just as I Traveled to avoid its crushing blow. The chamber echoed with the roar of a mountain's rage as a thousand pounds of marble slammed into the ancient stone of the dais. Shrapnel burst in every direction.

I Traveled again and reappeared midway down the aisle.

The man in the tunic lunged behind a column as shards of shattered stone pelted everything in sight.

The old man wasn't so lucky.

So focused on launching the throne, he failed to shield himself when it fell. Pieces of rock sliced into his chest, arms, and face.

He tumbled to the ground and did not move.

"*Atikus!*" the other man screamed.

The old man lay still.

CHAPTER 59

DECLAN

"Everyone around you dies, Declan Rea."

My head snapped up.

"Yes, I know you, Pretender of Magic. Death is your shadow. It is your cloak," Irina needled. "First your mother was swallowed by the Well, now your old Mage fell by his own folly. Who is next? Who is left for you to lose?"

Her voice inched closer with every word.

My heart leaped into my throat as anger seared through my mind.

I wanted to squeeze the life out of this woman with my bare hands, watch her struggle for air and fall limp as Atikus just had.

Rage had never felt so intense, so powerful.

It consumed me.

The column behind which I hid shuddered. Stone rent against stone.

She's going to bring the Temple down!

In a blink, I was behind her, casting my own wave of fire and air, using magic as a bellows to nurture my ire.

Without turning, Irina raised a palm, and a massive wave of water fell from above, extinguishing my flame and dousing us both.

She yanked the column she'd cracked and hurled marble toward me.

Two columns, not one, thousands of pounds each, blasted where I had stood. A crater gouged into the floor where they struck, and a plume of dust and debris rose into the air.

Irina waited, and so did I, for what felt like forever.

There was no sound, no movement, beyond the clattering of falling stone and settling of debris.

Eventually, Irina breathed deeply and wiped her brow, adjusting the crown.

When the point of my dagger tore out the front of her chest, she looked down, confused, as though her laces were in disarray.

Then blood flowered across her dress.

I withdrew the dagger, then dragged it across her throat.

She gasped for air.

Her hand flew to her throat and came away slick with blood.

Life poured out of her weakening body.

I tore the crown from her head as she fell to her knees, then stood above her, crown in hand.

She looked up. Pain and fury flooded her eyes.

I closed my eyes, opened them, then nodded once.

Eyes wild, Irina looked about for what had changed—then screamed at the gold and silver lines emblazoned in the marble surrounding her.

Terror added its thrill to her bellows.

Then I did the unthinkable.

I placed the crown just inside the outer circle, and, using Enhanced Strength, I shattered one of the bloody diamonds.

Irina's eyes widened as the form of a man rose like mist from the shattered gem. He lunged at me, but the circle flared, and the man's hands slapped against an invisible barrier.

I stepped into the circle and crushed a second stone, releasing a woman in tanned leathers. Her form flitted about the circle, confused, pressing palms to the invisible wall, a prisoner trapped in yet another cell.

Again, I smashed.

Another spirit appeared.

Four, then five, six, and finally the seventh.

Prince Justin's innocent face glowed with ethereal light as he drifted to stare down at Irina's bleeding form. The other spirits joined him, forming a circle around the broken, bleeding woman.

The man, the first to emerge from his stone, turned a wretched gaze toward me.

"What do you want from us? Set us free!" His voice was metal against stone, a screech of pain and loathing.

In that moment, I knew this was no longer a man but a fiend bent on hatred and vengeance.

"I grant each of you rest," I said, my voice that of steel, folded and strengthened by fire and mallet. "But only if you help me banish this abomination. Until she is vanquished, no one will be free."

The spirit laughed. "Why would I care if you're free, boy?"

My tunic flared to life.

The Phoenix leaped from my chest, an apparition of the mighty bird swelling until it filled the chamber. It turned its beak toward the spirits and roared so loudly I fell to my knees and covered my ears.

"BECAUSE I COMMAND IT!" Órla's voice shook the already shattered hall.

Waves of Compulsion magnified a thousandfold by the Phoenix flowed from my core.

Seven spirits streaked toward me and crashed against the barrier of the circle. They clawed and scratched.

They wailed in anger and pain.

I lifted my chin, and Light burst from my chest. It felt as if my own spirit had joined the fray. Shimmering magic cloaked the spirits, transforming each into a beacon of white.

The rage fell from their faces.

Their heads lowered and stilled.

I drew my will into my Light and cast it into each of the seven, commanding them, Compelling them into action.

As one, they turned and encircled Irina.

Each spirit placed an ethereal hand on her body, and their energy flooded into her. The seven's images dimmed, and Irina's form grew brighter and brighter as they poured their essence into her.

When the spirits had faded to reflections of themselves, and Irina glowed so intensely it hurt to look upon her, each phantom released their touch and shattered before my eyes, sending specks of brilliant light in every direction.

Irina thrashed and screamed as her spirit was expelled from its mortal shell.

The body that fell to the floor transformed, its hair turned from black to silver, its skin wrinkling, until Larinda's kind eyes looked up. She smiled as her Light faded and her own soul drifted into night.

Irina's spirit, now ethereal, raged against its confinement, but the circle would not yield. Its lines blazed like the sun each time she tried to penetrate its borders.

I braced myself for the jolt I knew would come, then began the incantation my mother made me learn before I lost her in the Well. The words were foreign and meant nothing to me, but their invocation stirred ancient magic to life.

Irina's spirit writhed as she fought my commands.

She darted around the circle, thrashed against its shield. She screamed every curse a thousand years of life had taught her.

Yet nothing would stop the unshakable force of my will.

As I uttered the final words, Irina's spirit howled one final time and shattered into brilliant points of light.

When the chamber dimmed, nothing remained of the great Empress Irina.

I slumped to my knees and hung my head, exhausted.

One spirit, barely visible in her faded blue smock, floated to hover before me. I looked up, and we locked eyes.

As the wind whispers across a winter field, her voice drifted across my consciousness.

"Tell Keelan thank you for trying to save me. He is the best of us."

Tiana's form scattered, sparkled like shimmering snowflakes, then winked out.

I snatched up Irina's ruined crown and ran to the end of the chamber where Atikus lay unmoving. Blood no longer leaked from the cut on his forehead, but it pooled beneath his neck.

There were even more cuts on his hands and face.

A trickle dribbled from the corner of his mouth.

His eyes stared into nothing.

"Atikus, look at me! Please, if you can hear me, open your eyes," I begged.

Nothing.

"Atikus, don't you die on me. You hear me, old man. Don't you dare . . ." Tears streaked my dust-covered face, and a swell of panic threatened to overwhelm my senses.

But Atikus needed me.

This, I could do.

I steadied myself, then placed both palms above the Mage's chest. Brilliant Light flared from my palms and flowed into Atikus. I found internal damage—so much damage—and broken ribs, one now piercing the Mage's lung.

Hour after hour, I poured myself into the Mage. Stitch by stitch, his body mended.

The building trembled, and stones fell from above.

As badly as Atikus needed rest, we could not remain, lest we win one battle only to lose ourselves beneath its rubble.

I grabbed the staff, hooked my arm through the crown to carry them both, then returned to grip the Mage's arm and Traveled to the refuge of the Queen's Palace.

CHAPTER 60

ATIKUS

Weeks had passed since Thorn fell and Irina was banished.

The Palace Healers declared me recovered, though I still used my brush with the void to skip heavy lifting or enjoy special treatment at every turn, mostly in the form of extra meals.

Declan teased me relentlessly.

"I feel like I could eat for days," I said as I stuffed another corn muffin into my mouth.

Declan laughed. "And that's different from any other day how?"

"Son, you know better than anyone how grave my wounds were. It was a close thing, you saving me. Any Healer worth their blues would command a patient to eat solid food to recover their strength. I am only doing what is *medically* prudent. Now, pass me that bacon again, and maybe those eggs."

Declan shook his head . . . but passed the bacon.

Keelan and Jess strode into the room, their fingers interlocked.

"You two are in a good mood these days. I cannot remember the last time I saw Keelan smile this much—or show *any* emotion, for that matter," Declan teased.

"Yeah, yeah. Don't be jealous."

Jess had barely settled into her chair before the team of lurking servants leaped into action. Her charger vanished, her teacup was filled, and fresh plates of every breakfast food imaginable appeared on the table near her.

In the past few weeks, the absence of Gifts had made itself keenly felt.

For a millennium, magic was engrained in daily life. Simple tasks that previously only required one Gifted person with Enhanced Strength might now involve an engineer's mind and the muscle of twenty stout men.

Spring had yet to bloom in its fullness, but farmers dreaded the planting without Gifts of horticulture to speed up and enhance growth and ward away pests.

Royal advisors were sent to every corner of the Kingdom to gather information on the impact and assist with what everyone hoped were temporary solutions.

Midway through breakfast, Declan set his fork down and looked at me. He spoke in my mind. *"I don't know why I didn't think of this before. Mother talked about the spell used to create the Gifts. I think she referred to it as the Sundering Spell or Spell of Sundering, something like that."*

"Spell of Sundering. That is right." I looked back at my plate and kept eating, not wanting to alert anyone to our conversation. *"I have had the Mages here in Fontaine looking through the library and vault, but they came up empty. Our own Mages in Saltstone should also be looking for references to the spell, but they have no Telepath to report progress, so I do not know if they have found anything or not."*

"Mother said there's a copy of the spell in her library in . . . that cave."

The fork slipped from my hand, clanked against my plate, and fell to the floor. Jess and Keelan looked up.

"You all right?" Keelan asked.

"Fine, fine. My fork slipped. I must have had too many of those buttered rolls." I grinned.

Keelan grinned and turned back to Jess.

"You mean there is a copy of the spell in the cavern where Kelså lived? A whole copy?" I said, taking a

replacement fork from one of the ever-diligent servants and trying to contain my excitement.

"Yeah, that's what she said, though I never saw it. There really wasn't a need, and I was still so new to magic it wouldn't have meant anything to me. But there's a problem."

"What?" I asked, turning to look at Declan.

"She said it took five of the original Mages, using their combined power, to cast the spell—and it consumed all of them—except her. By design, she wasn't part of the casting—she was an object of it. That's how she became Keeper."

I nodded. *"I knew about her becoming Keeper through the spell but had not realized the other Mages were consumed by it. I assumed a couple may have died, while the others were lost to history after leaving the island. The bigger problem here is how much power was needed for the casting—and they were casting into a purified Well, not the muck we are dealing with today."*

"We need to go back to the island. The answers are there. I can feel it."

I held his eyes a moment. *"Can it wait until after I finish breakfast?"*

Declan laughed out loud, turning Jess's and Keelan's heads once more.

"Care to share?" Jess asked.

"No," Declan said through chuckles. "Just Grampy and his appetite."

Two hours after I tossed my napkin on my plate, Declan and I hugged Jess and Keelan goodbye. I told Jess we were headed to Saltstone to review scrolls my Mages had unearthed, a lie that deeply bothered Keelan. It pained me, lying to Jess, but the security of Rea Utu was paramount. The Compulsion cast on Keelan's mind to protect the island and its inhabitants would have allowed us to share our destination with him, but Declan argued against it. Jess and Keelan had grown close, and he did not want a secret to drive a wedge between them.

With a last wave and pair of tight smiles, Declan and I Traveled to the island.

On our third day on Rea Utu by island time, Declan's magic-enhanced voice bounced through every corridor of the cavern. "Atikus! Come quickly. I found it!"

A moment later, I shuffled into the library, wheezing from my brisk walk from the kitchen where I'd been making lunch. I passed a rectangular worktable that was now buried beneath dozens of unfurled scrolls to find Declan pacing between two stacks near the back of the grotto. A ball of undulating magic bobbed as he walked, somehow keeping up with his frantic movement.

His eyes never left the scroll he held.

I gripped his arm to stop his pacing, then peered around his shoulder to peek at the parchment.

"What language is this?" I asked. "I don't recognize it."

Declan grinned. "Keep looking."

I furrowed my brow at the strange symbols, then something astonishing happened.

They began *shifting*.

Symbols splintered apart and formed letters in Melucia's lilting dialect. Whole words vanished as others appeared.

The inky dance was mesmerizing.

"Sweet Spirits. I have never seen magic do that," I muttered.

When the spell settled and I could read each line, I released a long breath and allowed myself to relax. "My boy, you have done it. You found it!"

I slapped Declan on the back, then sobered. "There is just one problem."

"What now?"

"The Well is still poisoned, and I do not know how to cure it."

Declan looked back to the scroll. "Could casting this also purify the currents?"

"Hmm." I fiddled with my beard as I thought. "Maybe—or it won't. We could waste an immense amount of magical energy and destroy our only hope of fixing things."

"Immense amount of magical energy. I've heard you use that exact phrase before." Declan dove into his memories. "What about using the crown? The one we recovered from Thorn and Irina?"

I shook my head. "That will not work. The crown lost its magic when the diamonds were shattered. It magnified whatever Gifts the wearer possessed but also granted the Gifts of the spirits trapped within each diamond. Those were lost when the spirits were freed."

"Wait! I think—you weren't talking about the crown when you said that phrase; you were talking about *Irina's staff*, how it magnified her power." Declan paced. "What if we used the staff to magnify our power as we cast the spell?"

Both my brows raised. "I have never studied her staff, but in theory, I suppose it could work."

"If there's even a chance we can restore the Gifts, we have to try."

I sighed. "It is never this easy, Declan, but I suppose you are right. We do owe it to everyone back home to exhaust every avenue. It is why we came here, after all."

A few moments later, adopted son and father stood on the glassy dais of the Well of Magic, staring down at the blackened ooze that was once magic's untainted lifeblood.

"When you brought me here and I saw the current for the first time . . ." I swallowed hard. "Declan, when you think about the past, do you have one or two moments in time that seem frozen in your mind? If you close your eyes, you can see every detail, hear and feel and taste *everything*."

Declan's eyes grew distant as a smile curled his lips. "When I met Ayden."

"Yes, I suppose that would be one of yours." I returned his smile and patted his arm. "In all my life, I remember three or four *perfect moments*. Standing here with you, seeing the Well and its majestic flow that first time, was one."

"This place is beyond amazing."

"I am explaining this poorly. It felt like I was an excited, innocent child again, thrilled at magic's first touch, though I had no idea what it even meant. It filled me with wonder and a sense of possibility, with dreams so distant a moment earlier but suddenly within reach."

I let my hand fall from Declan's arm, then turned, sat on the stair, and stared down into the murk. It absorbed much of the light normally present in the cavern, and Declan had to cast several globes above us just to see a few paces around the Well.

"Now, all I see is darkness. This real poison here is the absence of hope. Son, we have to succeed, because my heart tells me the whole world will dim if we fail."

Declan sat and put an arm around me.

"You are the smartest, strongest, *kindest* man I've ever known. And I'm Keelan's brother, which means I have to protect everyone and be grumpy doing it."

I spit a laugh despite my mood.

"We'll make this work. One way or another, we'll find a way."

I looked up at Declan, and my lip quivered as I spoke in a strained whisper, "I am so proud of you, Declan. You have grown into quite the man."

Declan's face reddened, then a grin quirked the corner of his mouth as he ran a hand through his curly mess of hair.

"I know. It is such a burden being amazing sometimes."

I barked another laugh as the mood lightened.

"Enough of you! Let us cast a spell."

I stood and gripped the staff in both hands. Power thrummed through me—*my own magic*—reverberating through the cold metal. My heartbeat quickened.

Declan rose, and we approached the opening of the Well shoulder to shoulder, father and son. Declan uncoiled the scroll and held it so we could both see its contents.

We called our Light and poured it into the scroll.

Triggered by the touch of our magic, the scroll's lettering glittered to life, transforming from faded black to brilliant gold.

We read aloud.

With each spoken word, the symbols and letters brightened, and their strokes *flowed* on the page.

Declan's tunic flared to life, outshining the globes hovering overhead.

The incantation began.

Biotáille solais, glaoimid ort. Éist linn.

Pinpricks of iridescent light flickered amid the charred current.

De réir cumhachta táimid faoi cheangal. D'fhéadfaimis réimeas.

Flowers of light bloomed in darkness.

Mist rose from the mire and engulfed us.

Our voices rose, and wind began to swirl and howl about the cavern.

De réir cumhachta theipeann orainn. D'fhéadfaimis titim.

The air in the chamber grew cold and thick with power.

Declan's eyes blazed and leaked cerulean mist.

I strained to stay on my feet.

Ceangal ár n-uacht. Ceangal ár gcumhacht. Briseadh ár slabhraí agus sever dúinn. Briseadh sinn.

Light balanced darkness in the Well as the power of pure magic fought against the insidious poison leeching warmth from the world of life.

But the infection battled back.

It strained against the invocation now damning its existence.

Pain seared into my chest.

The staff scored livid burns across my palms.

Yet I held firm.

I continued to chant, more wail than prayer, as magic warred within my soul.

Declan fell to his knees as lances of agony pierced his eyes.

The Phoenix on his chest burst forth, now freed from the golden fabric, an ephemeral beast bent on serving its fallen master. The mighty bird grew to consume the space before us, then, with wings dripping power, dove headfirst into the embattled river below.

The blackness convulsed, coalescing around the Phoenix, clinging to wing and beak and claw. Yet when the mighty bird vanished, far more blue than black flowed in the ancient brook.

One line remained.

Sunder cad a tugadh agus Tabhair cad a bhí sundered.

We shouted.

Sunder cad a tugadh agus Tabhair cad a bhí sundered.

And a third time . . . louder.

Sunder cad a tugadh agus Tabhair cad a bhí sundered!

Power flooded from the current and out from our chests.

Declan screamed as magic was ripped from his core, his soul torn asunder.

He fell to the crystal floor.

Weakened and spent, I was lifted from the glassy stair as raw magic tore from my spirit. Higher and higher, the Light raised my body, until I hovered ten feet above the Well.

Unable to speak or move or scream, I gaped in terror at the raging river below.

The staff slipped from my weakened grasp and fell into the opening of the Well.

The river writhed, and a wave billowed forth.

There was nowhere to hide.

There was no spell or power to protect from the current's ire.

I fell from its grasp and plunged beneath its foaming waves.

I heard Declan cry out as he dove toward the Well.

He leaped above the opening and threw out his hands to pull me to safety, but magic would not be robbed of its price.

Declan's emerald eyes were the last things I saw as I slipped from his grip and vanished beneath the surface.

CHAPTER 61

KEELAN

L iam grabbed Seth by the shoulders, spun him around and straightened the clasp on his cloak. The silver buckle fashioned in the shape of a maple leaf nearly leaped off the deep emerald of his doublet.

"Will you two knock it off?" I said, biting back a laugh at how many times one or the other of the pair had fiddled with clothing or buttons or clasps. It made sense that Seth might feel a bit out of place in his courtly attire. He claimed it was the first time he'd worn anything other than his Children's robes in years. The fabric likely made the skin of his neck itch.

My hand moved to loosen my own annoying collar at the thought.

Liam peered over Seth's shoulder at me. "You might be bedding Her Majesty, but we lowly commoners are entering the royal presence for the first time. Just look at those doors. They shine brighter than the sunrise over the ocean."

I glanced at the doors I'd walked through a hundred times and realized they did, indeed, reflect almost as clearly as a mirror.

"Liam, relax," I said, more amused than annoyed.

"That's easy for you to say. You are a famous Guardsman used to swimming in deep ponds. We're just—"

The sudden appearance of a royal page stilled Liam's tongue. The boy offered a precise quarter bow, then locked eyes with me. "Lieutenant Rea, Her Majesty will receive your guests now."

I chuckled as Liam's sharp intake nearly cracked the page's perfect shell.

When the doors swung open, the page stepped in and announced, "Lieutenant of the Guard of the Melucian Empire, Keelan Rea, and his guests, Liam, son of Hershel, of Oliver, and Seth, a Priest of the Order of the One."

"Former Priest," Seth corrected.

"Former Priest," the page bellowed.

Members of the Privy Council and minor nobles lined either side of the grand aisle. Jess sat on her throne, her most elaborate crown gleaming in the sunlight that streamed through windows whose curtains had been tied back. Prisms danced from large diamonds, scattering their colorful hues throughout the chamber.

Her face was stone, her mouth a thin, unreadable line.

I had to suppress a grin as Liam swallowed hard behind me as I led us forward.

We stopped at the first inlaid mark, a golden diamond with rays radiating in every direction.

I bowed, then continued five strides to the second mark. No one gasped or cried out. I took that as a sign my companions properly offered their respects.

When the three of us stood lined up before the throne, Jess, her back perfectly straight and chin high, asked, "Guardsman Rea, for what purpose do you seek audience?"

I bowed again, as was the custom.

"Your Majesty, if it pleases the Queen, I should like to introduce her to citizens of Oliver who assisted with my investigation, one of which, I believe, will be of special interest to Her Majesty."

Jess's mouth twitched just enough for me to see. She'd spent most of the morning teasing me about taking on a more formal role in today's proceedings, accusing me of becoming a "proper gentleman" rather than a "rogue Melucian."

I failed to find the humor.

That only encouraged her.

"Proceed," she ordered.

I stepped aside and allowed the pair to take my place on the second diamond mark.

Seth bowed. Liam forgot and received an elbow in the ribs.

Again, Jess bit back a grin.

"Your Majesty," Liam squeaked. "Thank you for seeing us . . . I mean, receiving us."

"You are Liam, the innkeeper's son? You witnessed one of the attacks?" Jess asked.

"Yes, Majesty."

"And your father was killed in another attack?"

Liam's shoulders slumped. "Yes, Majesty."

"The Crown is saddened by your loss."

Liam looked up, his eyes wide. "Thank you . . . Majesty."

"And you"—Jess turned to Seth—"are the Priest?"

"I was, Your Majesty."

One of Jess's brows peaked. "We were unaware of the Children allowing their Priests to, how would you say it, leave the Order?"

Seth hesitated, his eyes darting toward me, before he replied, "When the One—the false One, I should say—fell, I felt no Compulsion to remain within the Order. Liam helped me see that I could continue my good works without donning a robe or bending a knee."

Jess leaned forward, her eyes narrowed.

"To the Order," Seth hurriedly explained. "I bend the knee to the Crown, Majesty. Very much."

Seth dropped to his knees and pressed his forehead to the stone floor.

"None of that," Jess snapped. "Rise, and receive your sentence."

Seth's head snapped up, and Liam stumbled backward.

"Sentence?" Seth croaked.

Jess stood and took a step forward, positioning herself on the top step so she loomed over us.

"Yes, your sentence. Did you think the Crown would allow your actions to go . . . unaddressed?"

"But . . . Majesty. . . I thought—"

"Silence!" Her voice was a lash.

Seth stood on shaky legs.

"We have heard of your preachings, your works, your guidance and offerings to the people of Oliver. Guardsman Rea returned with quite the tale of how you wore your robes and stood before our people in the name of your false prophet."

Sweat beaded across Seth's forehead as Liam struggled to stand still.

"We are well aware of who and what you are." Jess moved one step down, then another, until she stood eye level with Seth. "We also know what you are not."

Confusion mingled with frayed nerves as Seth's gaze rose to meet his Queen's.

"We believe your works in Oliver to be sincere, offered freely from a desire to help uplift our people. Our Constables, Councilors, and . . . others . . . reported as much."

"I . . . I do what I can, Majesty."

"And the Crown thanks you for that." Jess's tone softened. "The folly of my mother's war has left too many in our Kingdom wanting. We need men of conscience and good will to minister to them. We need those around us, leaders, for whom the greater good outweighs their own desires. We need good men, Seth."

Using his name staggered the former Priest as he gaped at the Queen.

"I am at Your Majesty's service," came out breathless.

Jess smiled, and her voice rose once more, taking on the regal tone I knew radiated from an iron backbone.

"Seth, no longer of the Order, for the service you have provided to our people, and for those words and deeds yet spoken and performed, the Crown names you Minister of Benevolence. From this day forth, your works shall be those of the Crown."

Seth's mouth opened, but no words flowed.

He blinked.

He stared.

After a pregnant moment, Jess took another step forward so she stood close enough to whisper. "Most people express gratitude or offer acceptance of a royal appointment. Some bow again or kiss our hand. You should choose one of those."

I spat a laugh, earning sharply narrowed eyes from Jess.

Seth dropped to one knee.

His voice was filled with awe as he spoke. "Your Majesty, I . . . I have no words. You honor me beyond any imagining."

Jess waited.

Seth remained kneeling, head cowed.

The silence stretched.

She glanced at me, then back to Seth.

I leaned over and whispered, "You still haven't given her an answer."

Seth's head snapped up. "It would be the honor of my life to serve Her Majesty."

On some unspoken cue, a page appeared with Jess's royal sword on a velvet pillow. She raised it

high, then set it on one of Seth's shoulders, then
the other, then back again.

"We create you Lord Caritas, Minister of Benevolence. Rise, Sir Caritas, Minister of Benevolence.
Greet your Queen."

As Seth stood on unsteady legs, Jess began to
applaud. The assembled nobles and Councilors
followed suit, each trying to outdo the others in
offering their support for the realm's newest Minister.

Liam beamed.

I'd almost forgotten him as he stood behind
Seth, so engrossed was I with the game Jess
played, teasing and taunting the poor man before
offering him a royal appointment.

Relief and bewilderment brightened Liam's
eyes, and my heart swelled as I watched Seth turn
and meet his gaze for the first time since Jess's
decree. What flowed between them was pure joy
and unbounded love I'd seen too rarely over the
past year.

It reminded me of how Declan and Ayden
looked at each other.

A swelled heart ached for my brother. I missed
him and his puffy-headed mischief.

Then Jess caught my eye. She smiled, and tiny
lines bunched about her eyes as she did.

It felt as though the sun had descended to brighten the chamber.

The Councilors and nobles faded away.

Liam and Seth vanished.

There was only Jess.

My mouth grew dry, my tongue thick.

She winked, then an expression . . . something sneaky—no, impish—crossed her face.

"Silence!" she commanded, and the room stilled once more. "How thoughtless of us. There is one final matter before the Crown, a matter of the gravest import."

Hushed tones echoed through the audience hall as nobles whispered speculation and rumor. The silly men and women had no idea how to read their Queen's mind.

She offered me the slightest smile, then turned to face Liam. We had discussed her plans for Seth, but she shared nothing of an edict for Liam.

"Master Liam, son of Hershel, approach."

Liam looked to Seth, then me. His gaze darted so quickly I thought he might try to bolt through the bronze doors.

Instead, the quaking boy took a step forward and lowered himself to one knee.

"Majesty?"

"Master Liam, the Crown has learned of your . . . relationship . . . with our Minister." Her stare hardened. "It is most unseemly for one of his new station."

I swallowed almost as hard as Seth in that moment.

Then Jess tossed protocol to the wind, reaching down to grip Liam by his shoulders and lift him up to face her.

"We offer our royal blessing on your marriage, should you and the Minister wish to unite."

For the hundredth time that morning, my heart seized as I looked at Jess. In that moment, I knew she was the most brilliant, kind, amazing woman the Spirits ever allowed to walk the land.

And I was jealous of the blessing she had just bestowed on others.

CHAPTER 62

DECLAN

I sat staring at the mountains across the island. My feet dangled off the edge of the cliff. I'd been out there for hours.

The sun had begun her graceful descent, and the sky was painted with more hues than I thought were possible. A gentle, salty breeze tickled my nose.

I relished the taste of the island air, inhaling deeply.

A week had passed since the spell was cast.

A week in island time.

Months or a year elsewhere?

I wore my tunic and still enjoyed the Gifts I'd studied with my mother, but my limitless grasp of magic no longer availed itself. Fire refused to bloom in my palm. I couldn't speak in another's mind at will. Healing's restrictive rules returned, as I learned the first time I tried to Heal myself and was punished with bouts of nausea that lasted hours.

Worst of all, I could no longer Travel.

That had become my favorite power.

Beyond its practical uses, Traveling would have allowed me to find Ayden, to be with him, even if I had to return quickly to help with one thing or another. If it worked as it once had, I could even take him with me.

Without the ability, we remained a world apart.

Months had passed since we'd last seen each other, since we last kissed.

I longed for his embrace.

Moreover, a part of me wondered if he still waited for my return.

How long would anyone wait without some glimmer of hope?

There was no use dwelling on dark thoughts. Ayden loved me. I knew it in my bones. I had faith he would love me still when we were reunited.

He would.

I prayed.

I released a wistful sigh, remembering how it felt to blink and instantly appear anywhere in the world. There was far more than power in that ability; there was *freedom*. I longed for that freedom again, yet it eluded me.

At least the pitcher of magical wine is still bottomless. I chuckled as I took another sip from my glass.

"You have been out here for hours. Are you not hungry?"

The deep warmth of the familiar voice soothed my angst.

The man's perpetual hunger made me laugh.

"Atikus, you old goat, will you ever stop eating?"

Bony hands dug into my shoulders, but in a playful, fatherly way—the way that hurt just a little more than intended.

"Never! Besides, after all that Healing you did on me, I could eat for days. Come on now, it is past time for supper."

I reluctantly peeled myself from nature's canvas and followed the Mage into the mountain.

When Atikus had vanished beneath the waters of the Well, my world ceased to spin. It was, as he had called it, one of those moments when the world froze. I stabbed my hands into the water but found nothing to grasp. So, I did the only foolish thing I could think of. I dove in.

Power, both Light and Dark, bolstered and battered my body and mind.

One moment, my spirit soared and I could move mountains; the next, I gasped for breath and fought to keep the night at bay. Only when I stilled my mind and opened myself to the Light did I see him, lifeless, floating, drifting with the surge and flow of the endless stream.

I may never know how I reached him and swam back to the opening within the cavern.

Each moment moved faster than the last.

I could barely think, could barely breathe.

Colors swirled in my vision.

Light flashed and flared.

Darkness cloaked.

And somehow, by the grace of the Spirits, we washed ashore.

Technically, we were spat onto the cold, glassy floor of the cavern—but that was the most exquisite shore I'd ever seen. Even the crystals of the cavern's walls, those not shattered by the battle with Irina's spirit, glowed in greeting. As I drew blessed air into my lungs, the beauty of the place struck me dumb, and I fell back and laughed.

It had taken several days of Healing for Atikus to regain consciousness—and another day for his strength to lift him from his bed. Whatever happened beneath the currents, he had escaped with his life.

Over a meal of roasted turkey, seasoned vegetables, and mango pie, we chatted and laughed as if we hadn't just saved the world of magic from a bitter end.

I think it was too much for either of us to face aloud.

We needed the comfort and safety of small things just now.

And yet . . .

"Atikus, I still don't understand how you survived the currents. Magic had been Sundered when you fell. You should have dissolved and your Light returned to the flow."

Atikus set his fork down, a sure sign things were about to get serious.

"Son . . ." He struggled. "I did not escape unscathed."

"What do you mean?"

"Magic always demands her due. There is a price to every Gift and every spell. When the staff fell into the waters, its power completed the cleansing, but no price had yet been paid for the Sundering. It would not be complete without one."

"But it didn't take you. Magic gave you back."

Atikus struggled to meet my eyes. "Not *exactly*."

I thought my heart might stop in that moment.

"Declan, there is no easy way for me to say this. Magic . . . did not give me back. It kept me. I suppose it is more accurate to say that I am keeping it now."

My puzzled expression turned to excitement. "Wait! Does that mean—"

"Yes, I am Keeper now. I will live, but only so long as I remain on this island."

I exploded from my chair and wrapped my arms around the old Mage. "Atikus, that's amazing!"

Atikus returned my smile, but his grin failed to reach his eyes, and his shoulders slumped.

"What? This is a good thing, isn't it?"

Atikus stared into his plate, unable to meet my eyes again. "You and Keelan have found someone to love, and I am forever grateful to have witnessed it all. Now, you will marry and raise a family. You will see the world and conquer it. And . . . I will miss it all."

"Atikus—"

"I know being Keeper should be a gracious, selfless act, but I cannot help thinking about all the things I will sacrifice in magic's bargain."

I blinked a few times, warding away the moisture that already leaked from my eyes. "Atikus, I know you'll miss Saltstone and the guild, but there couldn't be anyone better suited to protecting magic and the Gifts. Keelan and Ayden and I can come visit you. I love this place. Spirits, I'm a little jealous."

"Jealous of an old man trapped on an island far from those he loves?"

I knew the bitterness in his voice would fade. There was no one alive who cherished and respected magic more than Atikus. It would be the honor of his long life to serve as its Keeper.

Still, his reaction struck true.

There were always sacrifices. There were always demands.

"We'll find a way." I tried to smile. "Between you and me, we still hold more power in our hands than anyone alive. We understand magic and casting in ways most could never dream about. You will always be at the center of our family, no matter how small or big it might get. We will make this work. I promise."

CHAPTER 63

KEELAN

By the time Declan returned to Fontaine, six months had passed on the continent.

Spring turned to summer.

Summer surrendered to fall.

The Spires were ablaze with leaves of red, orange, and yellow, and a brisk wind blew, heralding the coming of colder months.

It was a beautiful time in the Kingdom.

I strode down the cobbles of the principal thoroughfare carrying a crisp new suit Jess had made for me. She would've had it delivered to my chamber at the Palace, but I waited so long for my fitting that she'd made me fetch it myself.

I knew she would skin me alive if I was late on *this* day, so my quick walk was nearly a jog.

Throngs of people lined the streets. Most wore green and gold to honor the royal house. Vendors selling everything from trinkets to funnel cakes barked out their pitch, luring festive citizens to their cart or door. Everywhere I looked, people smiled and laughed.

I couldn't remember the last time a city felt so good.

Guards in polished silver plate and shiny helmets plumed with golden feathers greeted me at the gate with a respectful nod.

Stepping past a page and through the golden doors of the Throne Room, I braced myself for a whirlwind of activity.

I was not prepared for a full-scale battle near the Council table.

The guards lining the walls glanced at me sideways, their eyes widening slightly as I entered. One shook his head, as if to warn me away from a dangerous trap. The others ignored eye contact.

Thankfully, no one else noticed me enter.

"Jess, please," Chancellor Marks said. "I am not asking you to do anything other than consider all sides, to think through all the consequences of every decision you make. It is what your father urged me to do for him. It is what my oath to you demands."

She paced before the throne, her gaze never leaving his.

Her voice was low, restrained—but only barely. "I appreciate your advice, Ethan. I really do, but I am certain we passed the time for this lecture months ago."

He crossed his arms and raised his voice. "If you would have allowed it, we would have had this *conversation* months ago. You shut it down every time I brought the topic up."

"Maybe you should have taken the hint," she snapped.

"Jess—"

"Ethan, there are three reasons today will move forward, and my High Chancellor *will* respect them."

She held up one finger.

"One, being Queen is lonely and hard and . . . *impossible*. It is particularly impossible when I am doing so by myself. I need someone who loves and supports me, someone I can trust."

Marks started to speak, but she held up a second finger and quirked an imperious brow.

"Two. The Kingdom has yet to heal the wounds *we* inflicted. I know we are doing a lot of good work on this front, but it is not enough. The people—including those in Melucia who lost their homes in our ridiculous invasion—need more than sacks of grain and carts of wood. They need hope. Today will give them some measure of that."

She held up a third finger.

"And three. I am Queen. I will marry *whoever I want.*" She stepped toward Marks, her shoulders squared, chin high, and eyes daring him to speak. "I am marrying Keelan Rea. Today. Do I make myself clear, High Chancellor?"

I gawked, unsure whether to speak or duck behind a pillar.

Marks held her gaze for a long moment, then something softened in his eyes. His head lowered, and he smiled.

"What? Why are you smiling?" she snarled.

"Because . . . you are your father's daughter." He swallowed hard, then struggled through words. "I see him in you, Jess. I always have, even when you were a babe. I was there when you were born. Did you know that?"

Jess's entire being relaxed as she nodded. "Father told me many times."

Marks placed a hand on her shoulder. His smile grew warmer. His eyes grew distant with memory. "You squalled and squealed, demanding attention and obedience. I remember the moment your mother put you in my arms. You were born to wear that crown."

"Uncle—"

"Please, let me finish," he urged gently. "Jess, you are my goddaughter. You are my friend. You are my Queen. I love and respect you more than I ever dreamed possible. I . . . Your father would want this for you. Today, I mean. Keelan. He liked him. In truth, we all do. You chose well."

He wiped his brow and looked away, then drew in a breath and looked back. "Jessia Vester, baby girl, I am so proud to stand in your father's stead and give you away."

She stared. Her mouth opened, then closed. She blinked several times, then pushed Marks back with both hands.

"High Chancellor Ethan Marks, if you make me cry and I ruin this face paint, I will exile you to the smallest island on the farthest corner—"

Marks's arms pulling her close silenced whatever edict she was about to issue, and a tiny girl's chin settled on his shoulder. "Thank you, Uncle Ethan."

CHAPTER 64

DECLAN

K eelan tugged at his collar for the hundredth
time.

"If you don't leave that thing alone, you'll pull
the stitching out," I scolded as I finished fastening
the last of his gilded buttons.

"Does the damned thing have to itch? And why
is it so tight? My skin feels like it wants to crawl
off and run away."

"Sure that isn't just you?" I patted his chest and
stepped back. "And stop sweating. You'll send the
whole staff into a tizzy if you—"

"Dec, I'm freakin' marrying the Queen."

I couldn't decide if there was more pleading,
nervous energy, adoration, or awe in his voice.
Whatever it was, the words were strained, reminding me of a small boy trying to pass a particularly
large turd.

A rough laugh slipped out, and I had to turn to cover my mouth.

"Laugh all you want, Dandelion, your day will come."

When we were boys, he tormented me with that nickname, feeding to all the others who studied with the Mages so they, too, could harass me about my unruly, utterly ungovernable hair. Keelan hadn't called me Dandelion in years.

He really was nervous.

I turned back to face him.

Keelan was the strongest man I knew—likely the strongest I would ever know—and not just because he towered over most people and had muscles on top of already bulging muscles. Keelan's true strength lay in his character, in the man he was, in his belief in the goodness of others and his willingness to fight to protect those he loved. He might have been the most steadfast person in all of Melucia.

He knew what was right, and he never wavered in its pursuit.

I worshiped him when we were children. Now, despite the blessings of the Spirits and the Phoenix, I looked up to him in ways that defied understanding. He was the man others looked up to, followed, and believed in.

He was the man I dreamed I might one day become.

But in that moment, his eyes held none of his usually unflappable confidence, the glare that told the world he could mount it and ride into the sunset if the mood struck. Now, only the unsure gaze of my nine-year-old big brother stared back.

My heart melted.

I pulled him into a fierce hug. Screw our fancy coats.

"Kee," I whispered as he bent to bury his face in my shoulder, something he had *never* done. "Jess may be Queen, but she is a woman who loves you with all her heart. I see that in how she looks at you, how she lights up whenever you walk into a room. I hear it in her voice when she speaks to someone else, then turns to you. It's in her touch and in her smile. Spirits, if she loved you any more, I think she'd combust."

Keelan snorted into my shoulder.

"If you get snot on my tunic—"

He snorted again, then pretended to wipe his nose on my golden fabric.

I shoved him back.

"Thanks, little brother," he said through a warm smile, then watched me strain to look at where his imaginary nasal drip had smeared.

I held his gaze. Doubt still swirled. I could *feel* it.

I glanced around the room to ensure we were still alone, then lowered my voice again.

"Do you love her?"

His whole face bunched up. "Of course I do. More than anything."

"All right, then. What's the problem?"

"Dec . . ." He started to tug at his collar, but I caught his hand and shook my head. "Sorry. It's just . . . she's *a Queen*, and I'm what? A local Constable from a foreign country? How is this going to work?"

I brushed my tunic out, then straightened my cloak. This was a ridiculous conversation.

"Fine time for you to ask those questions."

"Right?" He flopped into a nearby chair.

"What's the worst that can happen?"

He thought a moment. "I cause an international incident."

I spat a laugh.

"What?"

"We just survived a war, not a year ago. I think you're in the clear for international incidents."

"Fine. Still—"

I kneeled and gripped his shoulders. The fucker was almost as tall as I was—and he was sitting.

"Look at me, Kee." I waited until he didn't shy away. "Someone is going to knock on that door any minute now, and we are walking into the Throne Room where you are marrying the woman you love. There's no getting out of this, so stop squirming. Jess needs to see that arrogant, puffed-up peacock she fell in love with. Spirits know why."

"Hey! I'm not puffed up!"

"Fucking peacock."

He shot to his feet and shoved me like he was about to rumble with his baby bro.

I hopped back.

"There's the big brother I always looked up to."

He froze and cocked his head like some dog who'd just heard the word; "treat."

"You dumb ox." I rolled my eyes with all the drama of a troupe. "*Of course* I look up to you. I always have. I'm so damn proud to be your brother . . . Mother would be proud, too."

Keelan stared, then swallowed. "Thanks, Dec. I love you, too."

Before we could devolve into a pair of mushy, ugly crying men, three sharp raps sounded as the door swung open. High Chancellor Ethan Marks stepped in, wearing his gods-awful black trousers, black tunic, and black cloak lined with the fur of some unfortunate beast. He looked like a Ranger who'd gone into mourning.

Marks bowed toward Keelan. "It is time, Your Majesty."

Keelan's brows bunched. "Ethan, why—"

"You will be King. Perhaps King-Consort, though I suspect Jessia will simply name you King. She had not made up her mind when I spoke with her earlier today. Either way, you will need to get used to the bowing." Marks nodded in my direction. "Are we ready, Prince Declan?"

"Well, shit," Keelan said, running a hand over his stubbly head. "I was. I really hadn't thought about what marrying Jess might make me . . . and *him*."

Marks gaped. "You had not thought of becoming King? Seriously? You are a seasoned, decorated investigator, are you not?"

"In a country without a throne or a Queen, sure," Keelan said defensively, as color snuck up from his collar.

I turned to Marks with a mischievous grin. "Good thing there's no real power with his new title. He's not the sharpest axe, if you know what I mean."

Marks snorted.

I smirked.

Keelan scowled.

"Let's go before you soil your soon-to-be-royal breeches." I gave Keelan one last check before stepping aside and motioning for him to follow Marks.

Marks escorted us through the hallways that led to the Throne Room's side entrance, the one Jess used to move to and from the residence wing of the Palace. A page waited near that door to guide me to another door on the opposite side.

Nobles and guests of every station packed the massive hall, each wearing a small nation's worth of gold and precious jewels. The tiaras and circlets alone could have fed and clothed half the people of the Kingdom for years. Vines covered in white flowers encircled each column from base to as high as I could see, and globes of light cast cerulean auras, bathing the great hall in magical brilliance.

I didn't know many in attendance, but a few familiar heads nodded in greeting. The page led me to stand on a spot at the base of the first step that led to the thrones, the position of highest honor for the family of the groom. An empty place stood between Marks and me, a spot Keelan insisted remain open in honor of our adopted father.

It pained me to lie to everyone, concocting a tale of gallantry and sacrifice in which Atikus gave his life to save mine in the battle against Irina. None could know of his new role or home. I knew the old Mage would allow me to tell Keelan soon, possibly bring him to Rea Utu for a visit, but not this day.

And so, his space remained empty, his memory an ache in an otherwise joyous day.

I gazed up at the seats of power not ten paces away, massive gilded and bejeweled chairs from which rulers guided a nation and influenced the world.

My brother would sit on one of those in mere moments.

He would be the right hand of the Queen.

Spirits save us all.

The page bellowed from the open doorway, heralding the entrance of some duke or duchess. I missed the announcement. My gaze slipped from the thrones to the rows of guests standing uncomfortably on the opposite side of the hall. The new arrival, decked out in crimson, forest green, and gold, took her place among her peers.

I scanned the crowd.

About halfway down the row began the foreign dignitaries. Representatives of the Isle of Vint wore grass skirts and strange shirts made of shells.

Melucia's small eastern neighbors were each represented by one or two finely dressed men or women. Rea Utu stood tall with a giant, reed-thin man I recognized as the innkeeper in the village. He had been selected to take Larinda's place as the leader of their people. I found that a fine choice.

I was about to turn back to my study of the thrones' carvings as the page's clear voice again rang out, "The Right Honorable Lord Ronan Byrne, Ambassador to Her Majesty, the Queen, from the Empire of Melucia, and his retinue."

Ronan *Byrne*? Ambassador?

Everything had moved so quickly over the past months, and Atikus's situation had been so dire, that I hadn't kept up with politics back home. I'd never paid much attention to the machinations of the ruling class, at least not beyond those who governed the workings of the Ranger corps. The new Triad had appointed a new ambassador. That wasn't surprising. *Who* they appointed was.

I craned my neck, looking around members of the Privy Council, to watch as a middle-aged man with more silver than black poking out beneath his velvet navy cap strode forward.

A flash of red behind Lord Byrne caught my eye. And my heart leaped into my throat.

Ayden, striking in his perfect leathers and sharp verdant Ranger cloak clasped with its gleaming silver owl, smiled at me.

The chamber of nobles and thrones and pages and guards—all of it faded away.

There was only Ayden.

CHAPTER 65

AYDEN

The ceremony was a blur of liturgical formality, far more prescribed than anything we would see back home. Then again, this was the marriage of the Queen of an ancient kingdom. I supposed it warranted a degree of fanfare.

Every eye was glued to the Queen and her intended.

Every eye except mine . . . and Declan's.

I tried to focus, to do as my father had instructed and represent Melucia well. I wanted to hear what was said, how vows were given, how the Queen wed before her people. I had always been a romantic at heart, anticipating this occasion throughout the months-long trip from Saltstone.

This wedding would be the stuff of legends for generations to come.

But Declan's gaze was more powerful than any force I had ever encountered.

He caught me staring, and I looked away, narrowing my eyes to focus on some stitch on the Queen's dress I hardly cared about.

Then he caught me again.

Midway through the ceremony, I surrendered and stared across the massive aisle, longing to wrap him in my arms and never let go.

His eyes never averted. No matter how many times I tried to free myself, each time I snuck another peek, he still stared. His lips still quirked upward at the corners. His eyes still glittered in the magical light.

Had my father turned and seen me so distracted, there would have been hell to pay. He was a kind man, of a sort, but his office was a sacred duty. Therefore, mine was, too.

Some lordling I was.

I almost laughed out loud at that thought.

Declan's grin widened as though he heard my thoughts.

What had this man done to me?

When the newly married couple turned, and Jess stunned the assembled nobles by announcing Keelan as King, I nearly broke rank and ran across the hall.

Alas, there was a ceremony to entering and exiting.

An order.

A deliberate, painfully slow, agonizingly long process.

The King and Queen left first, followed by Declan and the Privy Council. I watched as a part of my soul vanished through the doorway, saddened to no longer bask in his gaze but giddy at the prospect of being near him soon.

". . . us out."

My father had been speaking to me.

"Uh, sorry, sir, what?"

He frowned as other guests stared, wondering at the delay.

"Lead us out, son, before the Vintners start shaking their shells."

A joke?

Had my father cracked a joke?

That might have stunned me more than seeing Declan.

"Right. Yes, sir. Sorry, sir."

When we reached the enormous room where the Queen held state dinners, I panicked. Declan was seated by Keelan at the head table. A page directed us to a side table midway across the chamber.

Declan's eyes darted from Keelan and the Queen to me, and I could tell his attention was divided between a royal conversation and keeping track of where I sat. Something in the simplicity of that act felt like a thousand caterpillars dancing a jig in my chest. I could not have scraped the smile off my face with a mason's tool.

Toasts were offered.

Dinner was served.

Glasses and mugs sloshed and were refilled more times than I could count.

After so many months of darkness and enmity between our nations, this might have been the most joyous occasion I could remember since the troubles began.

A serving girl startled me as she reached across to refill my goblet. By the time I looked back toward the head table, Declan's chair stood empty. I glanced around, but he was nowhere to be seen.

The King and Queen chatted as though nothing was amiss.

My heart began to race.

Where had he gone?

Was he all right?

Was—

"The Queen has given us leave, should you wish it." The voice I would know anywhere was low and raspy. His breath stirred heat. It tickled the skin of my ears and sent a surge up my spine.

Without turning my head, I lifted my freshly filled glass to my lips and whispered.

"Get me out of here, please."

I *felt* him smiling behind me.

Loud enough for anyone nearby to hear, Declan said, "Lord Ambassador, it is a pleasure to see you. Would you mind if I stole your son for a moment? The Queen asked that I give him a tour of the Palace."

Lord Byrne had just taken a healthy bite of roasted boar. He tried to swallow a bit too quickly and had to chase it with wine to keep from choking.

"Yes, yes. Thank you for taking him off my hands."

"Thank you, Lord Ambassador, and congratulations on your appointment. Ranger Byrne, please come with me."

It took every ounce of control I possessed to rise in a manner resembling anything stately, pay my respects to those about us, and turn to follow Declan.

It took even more control to resist grabbing his face and kissing him right there before the whole of the Spirits-damned Kingdom.

I felt a hundred eyes stare as we strode back toward the head table, then exited through a door flanked by two royal guards. The men, resplendent in their polished plate, gave Declan a quick bob as we passed.

"Did they just—"

"Yes," he growled. "You should address me as Prince or Your Highness now."

I snorted. "First, the Heir of Magic, now a royal of the Kingdom? Irina's tits, you skipped all of the Ranger ranks and went straight for world domination."

Declan ignored my jibe and continued walking, though I did catch his shoulders shake with soft laughter.

The hallways were brightly lit.

Servants scurried everywhere we walked. I had hoped we might find a moment's privacy before reaching whatever destination Declan had in mind, but that was not our fate.

Finally, he stopped before a large wooden door.

A girl of fifteen or sixteen curtsied. "Highness."

I stifled a laugh.

Declan's ears flushed.

He elbowed me without looking back.

"Please ensure we are not disturbed? Ranger Byrne and I need to discuss sensitive matters vital to the Crown."

"Of course, Highness." The girl curtsied again. When her head lifted, a tiny curl had formed at the corner of her mouth.

Declan entered. The moment the door shut behind me, I released the laugh I'd nearly choked on in the hallway.

"Sensitive matters?"

Delcan spun around, grabbed my wrists, and shoved me into the stone wall beside the door, pinning my arms above my head. His body pressed against mine, knocking the air from my lungs. The fire of a thousand suns burned in his eyes.

When our lips met, I thought he might devour me whole.

We were a blur of lips and tongues and teeth.

"Ayden *fucking* Byrne, I never want to be apart from you again," he moaned into my ear.

It had been over six months since we'd seen each other last. I feared his longing for me might have diminished.

What a foolish thought that had been.

He released my wrists.

My hands dove into his hair. I yanked his head back, exposing his neck, and sank my teeth into his tender skin.

He gasped, then groaned.

I licked up to his ear and nipped his lobe, teasing at first, then harder.

He winced but didn't pull back.

His fingers fumbled at the clasp that held my cloak. Before the heavy woolen wrap could hit the floor, he was already working the buttons of my jerkin. My undershirt flew over my head and off my arms, baring my chest and torso.

Declan's mouth attacked my nipple, as his fingers etched the lines of my stomach.

I braced myself against the wall, grateful for its support, and tried to keep stars from flooding my eyes.

"Someone is happy to see me," he teased as his hand brushed against my tented breeches.

"Open your present and see what I got you."

Declan grunted, then grabbed my pants with two hands and yanked them down. My cock flew free, slapping against my stomach and standing at full attention before his face.

"There's my baby. I missed you so much," he said before licking my head, then staring up at me with my cock in his mouth.

I could have come right there, looking into his eyes, seeing his tongue lapping up the slickness that leaked down my shaft.

Instead, I twitched, which made his grin widen.

"I want this inside me."

I twitched again, this time so hard I smacked his nose.

He grabbed my cock in one hand and took it halfway down his throat. I reached back, desperate to grip something, finding only cold stone.

His hand lowered, and he dove further, taking me to the base in a sloppy wetness that prickled the skin of my arms.

"Fuck, Dec."

He freed my cock long enough to say, "Yeah, you're doing that, too."

Then he took me again.

And again.

By the time we made it to the bed, I was naked and he still wore the ridiculous hose contraption nobles in the Kingdom donned on formal occasions. I tried to find where to pull at them but failed more than succeeded.

"Did you put these blasted things on yourself? Are they nailed to your legs?"

He laughed and raised my chin to kiss me again.

"Let me get those. They're kind of tricky."

"Promise me you will never wear those again. In fact, I would prefer it if you never wore pants—*or clothes*—ever again."

His smile was brighter than any of the globes in the audience chamber. I thought I might die right there.

"I fear the royal household might not share your enthusiasm for my nakedness."

I rolled my eyes. "They are a silly lot."

Declan stripped the hose and tossed them aside, allowing me to drop to my knees and return the favor. He tasted of salt and sweat and . . . lavender? I wanted to make a jest but decided his cock in my mouth was more than enough entertainment for the moment.

I shoved him onto the bed on his back, then spread his legs so I could continue worshiping him with my tongue and mouth.

By the time I lifted his legs to my shoulders and slid inside him, sweat coated our bodies, and the bedchamber smelled of musk and sex.

Out of practice from our time apart, we both came far too quickly.

"Can we do that again? I didn't mean to race you."

Declan chuckled through drained exhaustion. "Hold me for a while, then we can do it until they kick us out."

I stroked his hair and kissed his forehead as he nuzzled against my chest. "They can't kick us out. You're a royal pain in the ass now."

He grunted or laughed—I wasn't sure which—but it came out more of a groan followed by the heavy breathing of a man who'd fallen into a peaceful slumber.

CHAPTER 66

DECLAN

M y feet dangled over the ledge again as I leaned against a stone pillar. Ayden sat beside me, his feet flopping like a child kicking water in a pond. His hand lay atop mine—where it belonged.

We returned to Rea Utu as the last of the wedding festivals ended. Keelan and Jess made a striking couple. I even caught my big brother smiling and waving at the cheering crowds.

Magic was clearly alive in the world.

I knew we should go inside, to see what Atikus was destroying in the kitchen, but something in the night air held me in place. As much as I always said I craved freedom, I was coming to realize that the *peace* I felt in this place was far more important than the power to roam freely.

Here, I was alive.

Here, I was free.

The brine of the ocean tickled my nose.

"You are thinking. I can see steam curling out of your ears." Ayden's smirk was infectious.

I laughed and shook my head. "I do think from time to time."

"Care to share?"

I smiled, a fond sadness seizing my heart. "I was just thinking of my mother."

"I wish I could have met her."

I didn't have the heart to tell him that he had met her, that she had wrapped him in her arms and kissed his cheek, accepting him with the love only a mother can bestow. There would have been no harm in telling him. The magic of the place would steal that memory, too, when we again headed home.

It seemed somehow cruel, dangling that knowledge before him, knowing how it would frustrate him to not remember someone so special.

"Despite the swiftness of the outside world's turning, our time here was measured in years. I didn't just meet the mother I thought long dead; I came to know her. I came to love her."

"I'm sorry, Dec." He wrapped an arm around my shoulders and squeezed me tight against him.

"When I close my eyes, I can still see her bright eyes and mischievous grin. Keelan would probably say I inherited both of those traits."

"He would be right."

I chuckled and stared out into the forest below.

"I was so young, a boy of only three, when I was told my parents were gone. I think I understood, but who truly knows the mind of a child?"

My mother did.

That thought curled my lips again.

"I know it sounds crazy, but she came to mean so much in such a short time." I blinked away tears. One still managed to escape. "She taught me how to tap into my power. Spirits, she taught me that I *had* power. Her patience was as limitless as the sea. But she taught me so much more than magic."

Ayden's arm fell away, and I rested my head against the pillar.

"I was so lost when I arrived on Rea Utu." I couldn't look at him as I spoke my next words. "Life made no sense back then. I'd fled the capital and joined the Rangers, more to escape than to run toward anything. I spent so many nights alone in the woods atop the mountains that I wondered if being around people would ever feel natural or good."

And then I met Ayden.

That arrogant, irritating noble's son who refused to be ruffled by my bitterness. How I hated that man and his perfectly coiffed hair and glistening teeth. Who is drawn to men with red hair anyway? What madness possessed me?

I couldn't imagine life without him.

Without his smile . . . or playful winks . . . or infuriating positivity.

I shifted our hands so mine gripped his, and I held him as a drowning man clings to a raft.

"Mother accepted me. Without question or complaint. That was an act of magic and healing I doubted even she understood. She hadn't just given permission for me to love another. She showed me how to love myself."

Staring out at the waning sun casting rays of brilliance across the island, I missed her more than I could express.

Spirits, how I missed her.

"Tell me more about your Rangers," I said, desperate to change the subject to something—anything—that didn't make my heart ache.

"My Rangers?" He chuckled. "They named me a Captain, but I am not the Captain."

"It's only a matter of time. You lordlings always end up in charge. If it isn't some ridiculous birthright thing, it's all those coins you keep hidden beneath your bed."

He snorted and punched my arm. "I keep my coin buried in the ground, thank you very much."

I shook my head. "Sound plan. Now, back to the Rangers. You've been hard at work. I had to kidnap you and drag you to a faraway island just to get a little alone time."

"Is that jealousy in your voice? My, my, Mister High Holy of Magic."

Now it was my turn to punch his arm, but he snatched my fist before it could connect and raised it to his lips. I thought my heart might melt and dribble down the cliff.

Ayden released my hand and sobered. "We are recruiting as quickly as possible. Before we left the mainland, our count had just reached four hundred."

I whistled. "That many? In, what, eight months? Even with all the damage to the capital?"

He nodded. "We are vetting applicants carefully, ruling out those who have families who need them to help rebuild. Without those guardrails, we would be well over a thousand. Our goal is to ultimately build a force of five thousand green cloaks."

I blinked. Five thousand Rangers. Melucia had never fielded so large a corps.

"I know." He chuckled at the surprise in my eyes. "It is . . . overwhelming."

"Ayden, it's amazing. You're amazing."

The most beautiful crimson flared across his cheeks as his head ducked, though he couldn't hide the smile that curled his lips.

"How's Grove's Pass?"

His smile fled.

"The first Mages arrived a few weeks ago. The guild only has so many to spare. They lost . . . we all lost so much."

We sat in silence for a long moment, savoring the mountain air and waning sunlight, each lost in memories of days—and people—before the war.

"Dec, we are going to rebuild everything. The corps and headquarters—hell, all of Grove's Pass—will be stronger and better than before. One of the Mages is planning the whole thing out. You should see his models. They're marvels in themselves."

"I can't wait to see them."

"But . . ." He hesitated. "We are doing more than simply rebuilding. We want to remember. No, we want everyone to remember."

"What do you mean?"

"The first thing the Mages built was a monument to those we lost. It is . . . I hardly know how to describe it. It looks like glass, but it's not. The Mages . . . Dec . . ."

I cocked my head. Ayden was never at a loss for words.

"It's a sculpture as clear as ice but made of stone. It is a giant flame that towers far above the height of the old headquarters. And . . ." He squeezed his eyes shut, as if picturing the flame in his mind. "It never stops moving. Dec, it looks as if real flames churn within the glassy surface."

"That sounds . . . beautiful."

"And terrifying, if I am honest." He looked back at me. "The name of every Ranger lost flares in gold, a perpetual roll call of those who died. The Mages really outdid themselves."

"Sounds like it."

A faint scraping noise caused my head to turn. Ayden tensed.

I squinted and shielded my eyes but couldn't make out what had caused the sound.

I turned back to enjoy the last rays of the dying day.

Then the scraping came again.

Slowly, I peered out of the side of my eyes, careful not to make any sudden movement.

On the ledge, not ten paces away, skittered a tiny tuft of fur.

A rusty-colored tuft with a fluffy white tail.

Ever so slowly, I turned my head to face the intruder.

Giant eyes blinked.

The shadowed creature shuffled back.

I froze. Ayden's head turned, but he didn't speak. He barely breathed.

Curiosity drove the furry critter forward again. It stopped only a few paces away.

Now, within the light from the lantern on the table, I saw my guest clearly.

A baby fox, whose tail was larger and fluffier than its entire body, stared up at me. In my peripheral, I could make out Ayden's grin widening.

"Shy little fella, aren't ya? How did you get up here?" I glanced around at the sheerness of the cliff.

The fox cocked its head as if trying to figure out why the silly human was talking to a baby fox.

A childlike joy flooded my chest. I couldn't explain why, but a sense of hope blossomed within me.

I carefully reached to my other side where Ayden and I had been snacking, found a couple of macadamia nuts, and tossed them toward the fox.

I wished I had some of the dried meat I usually carried when traveling but figured the nuts would at least show good faith.

The fox cocked its head to the other side, scooted forward a couple of paces, then back.

I remained as still as possible.

After another few seconds, it repeated the dance until its prize was within reach.

What the fox did next stunned me speechless.

Ignoring the nuts, a paw tickled the back of my hand that was palm down on the ledge's stone. I chanced a glance just as the fox crawled over my hand and onto my left leg.

It froze.

And stared.

And blinked.

When I didn't respond, the creature released a yawn that stretched its mouth nearly the span of its tiny head, scratched at my breeches a few times, then curled up in my lap.

I glanced at Ayden.

He stared at the fox and smiled.

I looked back down to find our new friend fast asleep.

I had always had a way with animals, but this was beyond strange. I waited another minute before reaching a finger down to stroke the fox's head. At my touch, the furball emitted an oddly familiar sounding high-pitched whirr.

My heart flew into my throat, and tears filled my eyes.

I croaked out, "Órla?"

The fox's eyes flew wide.

She nuzzled my outstretched hand, cooing and purring the entire time.

Then she curled back into the safety of my lap and drifted off to sleep.

About your Author

Casey Morales is an LGBT storyteller and the author of multiple award-winning and bestselling MM romance novels. Born in the Southern United States, Casey is an avid tennis player, aspiring chef, dog lover, and ravenous consumer of gummy bears.

www.AuthorCaseyMorales.com

BOOKS BY CASEY MORALES

ROMANTIC FANTASY
Of Crowns & Quills

ROMANTIC SPY THRILLER
Of Shadows & Secrets

TEASER

CONTEMPORARY ROMANCE
Heartstrings of Honor

Nashville Spicy

Raised by Wolves

.

Made in the USA
Columbia, SC
30 June 2025